LONNIE GENTRY AND THE CURSE OF SKULL CANYON

LONNIE GENTRY AND THE CURSE OF SKULL CANYON

A LONNIE GENTRY DUO

PETER BRANDVOLD

WISE WOLF
BOOKS

WISE WOLF BOOKS
An Imprint of Wolfpack Publishing
wisewolfbooks.com
1707 E. Diana Street
Tampa, FL 33610

LONNIE GENTRY AND THE CURSE OF SKULL CANYON: A LONNIE GENTRY DUO.
Text copyright © 2025 (As Revised) Peter Brandvold

Paperback ISBN: 978-1-968733-26-1
eBook ISBN 978-1-965596-13-5

LONNIE GENTRY AND THE CURSE OF SKULL CANYON

LONNIE GENTRY

This book is for my friend
Jason Bruner—
Wild Man of Mount Milner!

ONE

SOMETHING SCREECHED through the air about six inches in front of Lonnie Gentry's face. Lonnie felt the warm curl of air against his nose.

The fast-moving object made a loud *whunk!* as it crashed into a tree ahead and left of the thirteen-year-old. The shrill crack of a rifle cut through the afternoon silence of this high mountain forest and flatted out over the valley below, chasing its echoes like a rabid dog trying to bite its own tail.

Lonnie shouted a curse as he leaped back along the cattle trail he'd been following on his search for calves that might have gotten bogged in mud or entangled in brush. He stumbled back so quickly, his heart turning somersaults in his chest, that he got his boots and spurs tangled up and went down hard on his butt.

His hat went flying.

He cursed again. The pain of the fall felt like an ax handle slammed against his rear end. This time the curse was drowned by another bullet screeching in from his right to ricochet loudly off a mossy, gray boulder on the upslope to his left.

"What the *hell?*" exclaimed the boy, who reserved his "barn talk", as his mother called it, for when he was in the company of only his horse...or when someone was trying to drill a tunnel between his ears with a bullet!

Lonnie grabbed his hat, scrambled off the trail's downslope side. The rifle crashed again on the heels of a dull thud, which was the bullet plowing into the pine-needle-carpeted slope on the other side of the trail.

That shot was well shy of Lonnie, which told the boy that the shooter had lost track of him. Holding his hat as he lay belly-down between two tall pines and staring along the slope in the direction he'd been heading, hot fury washed through Lonnie Gentry. His first thought had been some cork-headed fool had mistaken him for a deer or an elk, but the persistence with which they'd continued shooting had made him ponder other possibilities.

Now a man's voice yelled from the densely forested upslope, "You git him, Willie?"

And another man's voice answered, "Not sure! Seen him go down, but he might've hotfooted it!"

The rage in Lonnie turned to fear.

Nope, they hadn't mistaken him for game. They'd known he was two-legged, and they were either after money, which he didn't have, or his horse. Possibly the Winchester .44-40 repeating rifle riding in the scabbard attached to his saddle. Which, in turn, was attached to his horse, General Sherman, whom he'd left down trail a ways to forage for himself along Willow Run, a cold mountain stream cutting straight down out of the mountains.

"Let's move in slow-like and check it out," called the man on the upslope. "Take care—the rest are prob'ly close!"

The hair along the back of Lonnie's neck pricked. They were heading toward him, and he hadn't liked the sound of their voices. They were pinched voices. The voices of determined men. Likely, desperate men.

Probably outlaws on the run from some posse. Maybe in need of guns, ammo, and horses.

Lonnie lay frozen in fear, his mind and heart competing with each other like two horses running a Fourth of July race, for nearly a minute. Then he saw movement through the trees on the upslope. He heard the crunch of pine needles of someone moving along the trail he'd been on himself a few minutes ago. The trail angled down from a low ridge. Lonnie couldn't see over the ridge, but his bushwhacker must be coming from the other side of it.

Lonnie's mind continued to churn. His hands were sweating and his toes felt like mud inside his boots. If he continued to lie here, shivering, he'd be wolf bait. No one would ever see him or hear from him again. He'd be one of those legends that streak these Never Summer Mountains of northern Colorado Territory—mysterious legends of those who'd simply disappeared.

What happened to such lost souls, no one knew. But it sure was fun to speculate around lonely campfires on a cold mountain night during roundup, say, or on an elk-hunting trip. Lonnie had to admit he'd enjoyed such stories himself. They'd given him an odd thrill. This one, however, wouldn't be nearly as thrilling. At least, not to him. Not to his mother, either. She'd likely spend the next several years bawling her eyes out and sobbing herself to sleep at night.

Men were after him. Bad men. Men who'd likely kill him as soon as they saw him and turn his pockets inside out. They'd find nothing in there but lint, but they'd eventually find General Sherman and the rifle...

The rifle.

Lonnie scrambled to his feet, turned, stuffed his hat down tight on his head, and ran at a crouch downslope through the columnar pines. He ran hard, his pointed-toe stockmen's boots slipping and sliding on the thin, needle-strewn dirt. His spurs rang with every step. He leaped deadfalls and ducked under those that had fallen against other trees. He was angling down the slope, in the direction from which he'd come.

Behind him, a man's voice echoed eerily through the silent forest. "See him?"

The reply was a little louder: "No, but I can hear him. He's hotfooting it, all right! *Git him!*"

TWO

A RIFLE BARKED LOUDLY. Lonnie jumped with a start. He thought for a second he'd been shot, but then he realized that he'd just imagined the bullet.

The sudden punch of cold terror had caused him to lose his footing again. He fell on the downslope, and rolled. Again, he lost his hat as he continued rolling down the steep slope and into a snag of willows lining a rocky spring. The willows stopped him.

A weird, terrified energy was coursing through him. He had to get to his horse and his Winchester—his prized Winchester '66 Yellowboy repeater that his father had left him when he'd died. Between imagined images of the devilishly grinning men stalking him, all he could see was General Sherman and his rifle.

If he had the Winchester, he'd have a way to defend himself, possibly even discourage his stalkers.

In a blur, he gained his feet, retrieved his hat, stuffed it down on his head again, ran through the willows and the little trickle of water gurgling out of the rocks, and continued running toward the pulsating rush of what he knew was the stream tumbling out of the mountains ahead of him, farther on down the slope.

He scrambled up and over a low ridge. As he ran down the other side, he saw the rush of water tumbling down the slope from his right to his left. Willow Run was about thirty yards across, but even now in mid-summer the spring-fed stream was a rushing torrent as cold as hell was hot. It was sheathed in ferns and willows.

On the other side of the white roil of spraying water, near a low stone escarpment, Lonnie's buckskin stallion, General Sherman, stood tied to a root angling out of the scarp. The horse was staring toward Lonnie and twitching his ears curiously, probably wondering what the shooting had been about. Horses' ears were keen. He would have heard the shots even above the roar of the stream.

Lonnie glanced over his shoulder as he continued running toward a fir tree that had fallen across the stream, providing a natural bridge. He could see nothing behind him amidst the murky, dark-green forest, but when he was halfway across the stream, carefully negotiating the half-rotted pine, a bullet slammed off the escarpment near General Sherman. The rifle belched behind Lonnie. The horse whickered and backed away, his eyes growing large and round. He pulled at the reins that Lonnie had tied to the root.

"No, wait, General!" Lonnie yelled, holding his arms out as he set one slippery boot down in front of the other, on the pine's spongy trunk bristling with lance- and dagger-like broken branches.

The water roiling over and between the boulders littering the stream sent mare's tails of water splashing and spraying at Lonnie, filling the damp air with the wet smells of mud, stones, ferns, and cold mountain water.

Another bullet screeched off a rock to Lonnie's right, on the bank of the stream. The General whinnied and shook his head, gave the reins a hard tug, pulling them free of the root. Lonnie hadn't tied the reins very tightly; he'd just looped them over the root.

Lonnie had gentled and trained the stallion himself, and, like most western riders, he'd taught the General to remain with his bridle reins, even if they just hung to the ground. The looping over the root had only been a precaution. The General had not been trained to remain with his reins when he was being shot at, however, and now he began to turn away and to ready himself for a run to safety.

Lonnie leaped off the end of the fir and made a mad, scrambling dash toward the horse. The twin bridle reins were two snakes twisting and sliding along the ground in front of him. They slithered away faster...too fast. He wasn't going to catch them.

Then the General's hindquarters slid up hard and fast on Lonnie's right. Lonnie glimpsed the walnut stock of his Winchester protruding from the old leather scabbard strapped to the saddle. The gold plate at the end of the stock glistened in the sunlight filtering through the forest canopy.

Leaving the reins, Lonnie reached for the rifle. He wrapped his left hand around the stock and pulled. The rifle had just come free of the boot when the General's left hip slammed into Lonnie like two barrels tumbling from a beer wagon.

Lonnie left his feet and flew sideways. He saw the horse galloping down the slope, away from him. The General was shaking his head as though at a swarm of stinging yellow jackets. Lonnie momentarily had the wind knocked out of him, but when his senses returned, he found that he was holding his Winchester carbine across his sharply rising and falling belly with both his gloved hands.

At least, he'd gotten the rifle.

Dust and pine needles plumed in two places around him, blowing grit over his right boot. The rifles of his stalkers echoed softly above the thunder of the stream.

Lonnie lifted his head from the dirt. Two men were running down the slope on the stream's far side. They were both bearded and wearing Stetsons, bright neckerchiefs billowing down their chests. Leather chaps flapped against their denim-clad legs.

The man on the right, shorter than the other one, and with long, dark-brown hair, stopped suddenly to pump another cartridge into his rifle's chamber while the one on the left continued running toward the stream.

Lonnie cursed, heaved himself to his feet, and ran downslope as fast as he could, squeezing the carbine in his hands.

"There he is, Willie!" one of his pursuers shouted behind him. *"Git him!"*

Another bullet nicked Lonnie's right boot heel. It nudged his foot wide and sent him flying. He rolled toward the stream, felt the Winchester leave his hands. He heard the plop as the rifle hit the water.

Mindless of his aches and pains, fear a living, panting beast inside him, Lonnie made a mad dash for the stream. The Winchester lay in a side eddy that was about two feet deep. The brass butt plate flashed.

Glancing once upstream and seeing the two men running toward him, on the same side of the stream as Lonnie, he dipped his hands into the water, and pulled out the Winchester. His hands shaking from the hot blood of terror flowing inside him, he pumped a cartridge into the chamber, twisted around, and fired without aiming.

He'd just wanted to slow his pursuers' pursuit.

He slowed it, all right. He stopped one man altogether.

The one who'd stopped was a short hombre with longish brown hair and a thick mustache and goatee. His head snapped violently back on his shoulders as he continued running toward Lonnie. Then the man's arms dropped. He released his rifle, which clattered to the ground in front of him. He kicked it.

Then he fell to his knees. He had a funny, dull look on his face, which was pink with sunburn. His head wobbled until his dark-brown Stetson tumbled off his shoulder.

As he knelt on the thick, green grass about six feet away from the stream and on the other side of a deadfall pine from Lonnie, Lonnie saw a red spot in the dead center of the man's pale forehead, where his hat had shaded it from the sun. He also saw something bright and shiny on the man's brown leather vest, beneath the green neckerchief that hung down over his heart.

A badge. A five-pointed lawman's star.

As the man stared toward Lonnie, his eyes rolled back into his head, until all Lonnie could see was eggshell white. Then the man fell forward and hit the ground flat on his face.

THREE

"WILLIE!" the other man yelled, running toward his partner.

Lonnie looked at the smoking Winchester in his own hands. It was as though he were seeing the rifle for the first time. It was like suddenly realizing that what he'd been holding wasn't a rifle at all but a deadly diamondback rattlesnake. But he did not drop the weapon. That diamondback might very well have saved his life.

Lonnie rose stiffly, as though his joints had become fouled with mortar, and ran in a shambling gait on down the slope toward his horse. He didn't see much of anything before him.

All he really saw was the bearded face of the man with the red spot in the middle of his forehead.

Lonnie didn't know how far he'd run, for his head was swimming, when he dropped to his knees and the jerky and baking-powder biscuits that his mother had packed for his lunch came roaring up from his guts, and splattered onto the rocks before him.

He vomited once more, and ran the sweaty, dusty sleeve of his shirt across his mouth. As he did, he squeezed his eyes closed, trying to wipe from his brain the memory of the man he'd shot. Of course, it did not leave but became even more vivid for his wanting to forget, tightening his guts in a knot that would have driven more food out of his stomach if there had been more in there.

There was nothing left but bile, and, swallowing hard, he managed to keep it down.

His knees were weak and his hands were trembling.

Killer. He was a killer. And he hadn't killed just any man. He'd killed a lawman. He had not intended to, but he'd killed the man, just the same, and if he was caught he'd likely hang.

Lonnie looked behind at the forested ridge he'd run down from several minutes ago. Now he was in Wolf Creek Valley, which, running north to south in the shape of a dogleg, was carpeted in short blond grass, mountain sage, and willows, with Wolf Creek running down its middle. The creek lay another hundred yards beyond, sheathed in dense, green willows.

But Lonnie's attention was on the steep, forested slope he'd just left.

An ominous silence hung over the ridge. There was no movement amongst the trees that formed a gauzy, dark-green carpet shrouding that long hogback mountain. The only movement in the area was a bird of some kind, circling the ridge crest from high in the cobalt sky above, beneath a couple of thin, ragged-edged clouds that were as white as fresh linen against deep, dark blue.

The dead lawman was still up there in those trees. And so was his partner, who was most likely also a lawman. So far, the dead man's partner didn't appear to be following Lonnie, but Lonnie wasn't taking any chances. He didn't want to hang any more than he wanted to have his young hide perforated with lead.

He got up, holding his carbine with one hand, ran a grimy sleeve across his mouth once more, and continued running. He figured that General Sherman had headed for the creek, and he was right. He spotted the horse's back end sticking out of the willows, the buckskin's black tail switching at blackflies.

Lonnie slowed when he was fifty yards from the creek. The horse had heard Lonnie coming, and he turned his head sideways to look askance at his rider. Water dribbled from the horse's leathery, black snout. The General twitched one ear and then the other in dubious greeting.

Lonnie walked slowly forward so the horse wouldn't spook. The General wasn't normally the spooky type, but he didn't normally hear as much gunfire, either. Lonnie didn't want to chance the horse galloping off and leaving him out here on foot, with a crazed lawman dogging his heels.

Why the men had been after him, he had no idea. All he knew is they'd been shooting first, apparently content to ask questions later, and now that Lonnie had inadvertently shot one of them, he was probably more wanted now than he'd been before.

He wanted to get home—back to the relative safety and comfort of the ranch. Not that the law couldn't follow him there, but where else could he go?

He managed to walk up on General Sherman without unduly frightening the horse. When he had a hold of the reins that were dusty and cracked from being dragged and stepped on, he adjusted the saddle, which had slipped onto the horse's left side during the General's run out of the mountains.

"Thanks a bunch for leavin' me up there, General," Lonnie said, grunting as he pulled the latigo tight. He glanced toward the eerily quiet ridge bathed in golden, late-afternoon sunshine. "Really appreciate your loyalty in extreme circumstances, you ole hayburner."

The horse whickered and testily stomped its front left hoof down close to Lonnie's right boot. The horse had a jeering cast in the big, brown eye it was directing at Lonnie.

"You step on my foot, galldangit," Lonnie said, talking only because he was nervous, his blood still surging, "I'll bite one of your ears off. How would you like that, you old cayuse?"

The General gave another testy whicker.

Lonnie toed a stirrup and, grabbing the horn with his left hand, the cantle with his right, heaved himself up into the leather. He turned the horse and headed south along the willows lining the gurgling stream. The General bounced into a spine-jarring trot. Glancing once more toward the ridge, Lonnie touched his spurs to the horse's flanks, and the General shook his head again testily and lunged forward into a rocking lope.

He and the horse ate up the ground, making their way along Willow Creek for two miles before Lonnie turned the horse across the shallow stream and followed Wolf Creek, which fed Willow Creek from the north, toward a distant ridge. His ranch lay at the foot of that ridge. He considered it his since only he and his mother lived there now, his father having died so long ago that Lonnie couldn't even remember what Calvin Gentry had looked like.

Three years was a long time to a thirteen-year-old boy.

Lonnie couldn't see the cabin and barn until after he and the General had ridden hard another twenty minutes, rising and falling over a couple of low hills stippled in pines and aspens, following a two-track wagon trail. Dropping down off the shoulder of the last hill, he saw smoke lifting from the cabin's stone chimney and making a soft, gray wash against the pine- and fir-cloaked ridge behind it. The ridge was turning darker and fuzzier now as the sun fell behind the shadowed, western mountains.

The General followed the trail through the ranch portal, which was a stout birch log stretched between the tops of two peeled pine poles driven into the ground on each side of the trail. The birch plank had the Gentry Circle G brand burned into it. The name GENTRY had been painted in an arc over the brand, but the paint had long since faded so that you could only make out the name if you were right up on it and were looking for it.

Beyond the portal, the General shook his head and whickered disconcertingly. The horse stopped, and Lonnie tensed as he stared over the General's head and into the yard, which consisted of the one-and-a-half-story, shake-shingled log cabin, sitting with its back to the ridge, on Lonnie's left, and the barn and corrals on his right, across the yard from the cabin. There were a few outbuildings, including a keeper shed for meat and vegetables, as well as a small bunkhouse used by the two or three hands Lonnie's mother hired during the spring and fall roundups but which sat empty for most of the summer and all of the winter.

As Lonnie looked around, he saw that what had troubled the General were the three strange horses in the pole corral on the near side of the barn, standing separately from the half dozen horses in the Gentry remuda. The horses were eating the fresh hay that had been forked to them from the crib fronting the corral.

They were what bothered the General. What bothered Lonnie, however, were the men the horses obviously belonged to—the three men sitting on the cabin's long, brush-roofed front stoop.

FOUR

THE MAN on the porch who bothered Lonnie the most was the big, rangy, hawk-nosed, blond-headed man on whose knee Lonnie's mother was sitting, though, seeing Lonnie, she climbed awkwardly to her feet and cast sheepish glances toward her son, grinning with embarrassment and swatting at the blond gent's grabby hands.

Maybelline Gentry apparently hadn't seen her son ride up. She'd been too busy making time with Shannon Dupree, the big blond gent who was funning with Lonnie's mother, grabbing at her skirts and apron while casting his jeering, hawkish gaze into the yard at Lonnie.

The other men sat around Dupree—two dull-eyed tough nuts Lonnie recognized from previous visits. The short, stocky man with long, black hair and wearing a necklace of wolf teeth over his buckskin shirt, which was open halfway down his chest, was a man whom Lonnie knew only as Fuego. Fuego was half Indian, probably Arapaho. He rarely smiled or even spoke, and the few times Lonnie had seen him, he'd reminded the boy of a dangerous, wild beast who always smelled so strongly of sour sweat that it had made Lonnie's eyes water.

The other, younger man wearing a thin, sandy-colored mustache and sideburns and whose pale-blue eyes were set too close together, was Childress. Childress smiled a lot but in a mocking way, not in a friendly one. It was as though he were always thinking about a joke he could play on someone else. Lonnie thought his first name was Jake, or something like that. Dupree, Childress, and Fuego all rode together.

A Winchester rifle leaned against the front of the cabin, between Dupree and Fuego. The three were passing a bottle around and staring at Lonnie with expressions stretching the gamut from bland indifference to sneering condescension.

Those snakes formed knots again in Lonnie's gut. Everything was coming clear, and he was fighting not only fear of who might be following him, but fury at the men sitting so casually on the stoop of his own cabin. Yes, *his* cabin. He may have only been thirteen, but the cabin was half his, because he did the work of a full-grown man around the place, and without him, there would no longer *be* any ranch in the wake of his father's passing.

Without Lonnie, his mother would have headed back to Arapaho Creek. Shannon Dupree came by every once in a while. He'd play at being a rancher for a few days or weeks at a time, but mostly he'd play at being Lonnie's boss while he caused more work than he accomplished and spent most of the day drinking and eating or "taking naps" with Lonnie's mother.

Lonnie booted the General ahead, turning him toward the barn. He kept his eyes off the men on the cabin's porch, as though his not seeing them meant they were no longer there.

He knew they were still there, though. He also knew that their presence here at the Circle G meant trouble. Probably *had already meant* trouble. Everybody knew that Shannon Dupree and the men with him were outlaws. They'd likely robbed a stagecoach or a bank or something, and that's why the lawmen had been on the ridge earlier. The lawdogs had probably lost Dupree's trail and had been looking around for him when they'd run into Lonnie, and, not getting a good look at him, probably thought he was one of Dupree's bunch.

Because of Shannon Dupree, Lonnie Gentry was a killer.

Lonnie trembled as he swung down from the General's back. The barn doors were standing partway open. He swung them wide and led the General inside.

As he reached under the buckskin's belly for the latigo, footsteps sounded behind him. He glanced through the barn's open doors and out into the soft saffron light mixing with the deepening shadows and the cottony smoke from the cabin's chimney. The smoke was perfumed with the tang of burning piñon. Lonnie's mother, Maybelline Gentry, was walking toward the barn, holding her yellow skirt and the hem of her white petticoat above her black patent, side-button shoes.

Lonnie's mother was a pretty woman. She turned heads everywhere she went. Lonnie didn't like that about her. He didn't like the way men looked at her, the way Shannon and the other men on the porch were looking at her now as she strode toward the barn, her yellow-blonde hair hanging in a strategically messy braid down the right side of her head, with many vagrant strands sliding against her peach-colored cheeks. She'd gussied herself up for Dupree in a fresh yellow housedress, which hugged her a little too tightly, with white lace collar and sleeve cuffs. Lonnie thought she'd added a little blush to her face and red paint lips.

Lonnie often wished he had a fat, ugly mother like Oscar Lomax's mother on Dead Mormon Creek, so that men would leave her—*and Lonnie* —alone.

Lonnie turned back to his work as she entered the barn. He considered whether he should tell her about the trouble—about his having killed the lawman. He wanted to tell her. He wanted to get it off his chest in the worst way.

At the same time, it felt like too much of a confession right now, in light of the presence of Shannon Dupree. He didn't want Dupree to know. He thought his killing someone might cause Dupree to think that he, Lonnie, now had some sort of kinship with Dupree, a known outlaw. But nothing could be farther from the truth. Dupree had likely killed many men though Lonnie didn't know that for sure.

Lonnie had shot that lawman accidentally, and he just wanted to forget it had happened. It sure as hell didn't mean that Lonnie was anything like that cross-grained, bottom-feeding trash, Dupree.

"What's he doin' here?" Lonnie said, reaching up to slide the saddle off the General's back.

May Gentry stopped inside the barn door. "He rode in this morning, right after you rode out."

She had a light, free and easy tone, and Lonnie turned to see that her cheeks were flushed and that her blue eyes were fairly glowing, as though a lamp inside her head had been turned up bright. The sick, shaky feeling inside of Lonnie, the feeling that he'd been stabbed with a rusty knife and that the blade was still in there, twisting, got even worse.

It was the look on his mother's face that had made it worse.

"Oh, no," Lonnie thought, feeling his knees quake. "Oh...*no...!*"

His mother was smiling and fiddling with her hair. As she glanced back toward the cabin where the three outlaws were passing the bottle on the porch and laughing and talking in secret, jovial tones, she said in a quiet, delighted little voice that made Lonnie want to vomit again—"Lonnie, honey—I have most wonderful news. Shannon's asked for my hand!"

FIVE

A HARD KNOT formed in Lonnie's throat. His head was swimming. So much to take in: killing a lawman only hours earlier, Dupree here at the Circle G with Fuego and Childress. Now, on top of all that, Dupree had asked his mother to marry him.

A man Lonnie hated above any other he'd ever known—even more than he hated the Devil—had asked his mother to marry him.

Lonnie already knew the answer to his next question, but, hell, things really couldn't get any worse than they already were. So he drew a deep, calming breath, and asked, "What...what'd you say, Momma?"

May Gentry smiled down at Lonnie angelically. He could tell it was not only her love for Shannon Dupree that made her look that way. She'd probably taken a couple of nips from Dupree's bottle. But she blinked, and the angelic smile lost some of its luster. She wrinkled the skin above the bridge of her nose and stepped toward Lonnie, turning her mouth corners down and tilting her head to one side.

"It'll be all right, Lon. Really, it will."

"What'd you tell him, Momma?" Lonnie couldn't help the way that had come out. His nerves were jumping around beneath his skin like the baby snakes he'd once seen writhing around inside an old cabin wall, and he hadn't been able to keep himself from practically shouting the question.

His mother's face turned sunset red. She bunched her lips, then her arm swung up and forward, and *crack!* The palm of her right hand smacked Lonnie's left cheek. It felt as though she'd laid a hot iron against that side of his head.

Lonnie grunted and stepped back. Tears welled in his eyes and a sob was rising in his throat like a slow croak, but he fought back both the tears and the sob, blinking his eyes and swallowing hard. There was a toughness in Lonnie Gentry that sometimes surprised even him. He wasn't sure where it had come from. It was sort of like realizing your hands were no longer sore after a hard day's work, because they'd acquired a hard layer of calluses.

That's kind of what had happened to Lonnie's heart over the past three years, since his father had died and he'd had to take over responsibility for the bulk of the outdoor work around the Circle G, knowing that if he couldn't keep up, he and his mother would either starve or they'd have to head to Arapaho Creek and maybe live in a boarding house.

Lonnie wasn't sure which would have been worse. He just knew he wouldn't want to do either. So he worked twelve, sometimes sixteen hours a day during the busy seasons—during spring calving, the summer hay cutting, and the fall branding and roundup. And somehow, doing a man's work at thirteen had given the boy a working man's thick skin that only a few things could penetrate.

A slap wasn't one of them.

That seemed to puzzle his mother, who stared down at him, frowning, until she glanced toward the cabin, and said in a hard, accusing voice, "You never have liked Shannon." She turned back to Lonnie, lines of anger cut across her lightly tanned forehead. "No, he's not your father. But he could be, if you'd let him. You probably don't remember, since you were so young, but your father was no saint. No man is. There is no such thing, Lonnie. But we could use a man to take charge around here—you an' me."

"Leave me out of it." Lonnie knew he'd crossed a line there, but there was so much fear and anger surging inside him, he couldn't hold it all back. "We're doin' fine, Momma."

"We've done all right, but we need help."

"I don't need no help. All Dupree ever does when he's here is suck on a bottle the way the calves suck the heifers' teets. Besides..."

Lonnie glanced toward the cabin. One of Dupree's "boys"—he always called them "the boys" though they were as old as Dupree, well into their thirties—walked around the front of the cabin and headed toward the privy flanking the place. Jake Childress's feet looked a little light and unsteady. He had to reach out and grab the cabin wall to establish his balance.

Dupree and Fuego were still on the porch, smoking and taking turns with the bottle, as they stared toward the barn, their seedy eyes glued to Lonnie's mother, who was only twenty-seven. She'd had Lonnie when she was fourteen. Fuego had the Winchester across his knees now, and he was rubbing it down with a rag, a quirley smoldering between his lips.

"Besides what?" Lonnie's mother said.

Lonnie licked his lips and canted his head in the direction of the cabin. "Besides, you know what they been up to? Before they came here? You know where they were?"

"They were working over at the Fifty-Five Connected for Mort Bradley in the Mummy Range. Why?"

"Do you know that for sure?"

"What are you saying, Lonnie?"

"How do you know they didn't rob a bank or somethin'?"

"Because Shannon told me months back they were through with all of that. Shannon did his time. He's a changed man. I don't like how you're talking to me, Lonnie. I hate that tone. You know that." May Gentry glanced toward the cabin and lowered her voice. "And I will not have you talking Shannon down to me anymore."

"I saw some lawmen up Willow Run," Lonnie blurted out, his knees feeling weak again. He could not confess the killing. Not to his mother, not to anyone. It was just too awful. "I seen some lawmen...from a distance. They wore badges, and they were carryin' rifles and they were lookin' around at the ground like they were trackin' someone. Outlaws, maybe."

A dark cloud of apprehension scudded across May Gentry's face. She studied Lonnie pensively, then she said in a quiet, defensive tone, "There's plenty of outlaws in these mountains," she said. "You know the Never Summer range is their favorite place to hole up after they committed some robbery in Cheyenne or Julesburg. There aren't enough lawmen to cover all this country..."

Mrs. Gentry let her voice trail off and she glanced back at the cabin. Shannon Dupree lifted his head to peer over his boots resting on the porch rail, and called, "When's supper, May? Me an' the boys are so hungry our bellies are startin' to think our throats have been cut!"

Lonnie's mother forced a smile and waved. "Comin' hon," she yelled. To Lonnie, she said, "Supper's ready. Get washed up."

"I ain't hungry," Lonnie said, pulling a curry brush off a nail.

"Finish with the General and get washed up," his mother said firmly, and headed back to the cabin. "Scrub beneath your fingernails and comb your hair. Like it or not, this is a special night."

SIX

LONNIE TOOK his time with the General, first wiping him down with a scrap of burlap sacking and then slowly currying his coat. He checked all four hooves to make sure they hadn't picked up any sharp rocks or thorns, and cut burrs out of the General's tail. When he was sure the horse had cooled down enough, he brought him a bucket of water, and when the General was finished drawing water, Lonnie looped a feed sack of oats over the horse's ears.

When he'd turned the stallion into the corral with the other horses, he forked some hay from the crib and turned to the cabin. Lonnie gave a ragged sigh. It was nearly dark now, only a little green light left in the sky. The high, forested ridges that rimmed the ranch yard were black as ink. A lone wolf was howling somewhere on the mountain behind the cabin.

The cabin's lower story windows were all lit. Through the sashed window right of the door, Lonnie could see his mother sitting at the kitchen table with Shannon Dupree and "the boys". Lonnie glanced back along the trail that was a faint, butterscotch line in the darkness. No movement out there. Not yet. There was a chance the law would not come for him. There was a better chance that they would. Maybe not tonight or tomorrow. Maybe not for a few weeks. But eventually they would.

A posse, probably—five, maybe ten men.

If the dead lawman's partner came for him tonight, what would Lonnie do? Would he confess his sins, or run? He'd heard that when you killed a lawman, you were done for. Other lawmen took the killing of one of their own personally. So did judges. That it had been an accident wouldn't matter to anyone. Especially not to the partner of the lawman Lonnie had killed.

Besides, who would believe him? His mother was known by some in the Never Summers to "cavort with owl hoots". They'd see Lonnie as an owl hoot, too. A thirteen-year-old murderer.

Lonnie would drop through a trapdoor and hang by his neck, kicking and dancing in midair, until he was dead. He'd seen a man do that in Cheyenne once, in front of a crowd who'd gathered to watch, and the image haunted Lonnie to this day. The boy shuddered as he remembered how the hanged man had kicked so hard that he'd kicked off one of his boots.

Lonnie considered saddling a fresh horse, packing a cavvy sack and a war bag, and riding out. All hell had broken loose. But the cabin door opened, throwing a wedge of yellow light across the porch, and his mother called impatiently, "Lonnie? Supper's gettin' cold!"

Lonnie made a sour face. Oh, well, he was too tired to ride out tonight. He'd fill his belly, get a good night's sleep, and consider his options again in the morning.

He headed back to the cabin and washed up at the tub perched on a wooden stand on the porch, against the cabin's front wall, beneath a cracked mirror a little larger than Lonnie's hand. His father used to shave in that mirror. From the rain barrel standing in a corner of the porch, he dipped up tepid water and thirstily drank several dippers full, then raked his fingers through his close-cropped brown hair that wore the shape of his hat, and stepped to the cabin door.

Reluctantly, he drew it open and stepped tentatively inside.

"Hey, Squirrel!" intoned Shannon Dupree, who rose from the near end of the table, where Lonnie's mother usually sat. His wet, longish blond hair showed the lines of a comb, and he wore a checkered oilcloth bib tucked into the collar of his red-and-black-plaid work shirt. He also wore a pistol on his hip.

"How you doin', Squirrel?" Dupree said, turning to Lonnie and punching him twice lightly in the belly.

They were soft punches but in Lonnie's mood, and in light of his feelings toward the outlaw, they might as well have knocked the wind out of him.

"Come on, kid," the outlaw persisted, feinting like a boxer and wagging his big, red fists in Lonnie's face, swiping at his chin. "Come on! You got some sand, don't ya? Let's see what you got, Squirrel!"

Lonnie exploded, and though Shannon towered over him, over six feet tall, the boy lurched forward and drove both his fists into the big man's hard, flat belly. It was like hitting a side of beef hanging in the keeper shed.

The big man roared with glee, blowing his sour whiskey breath. "There ya go, Squirrel. Don't take nothin' off'n nobody. Hah!" He bent down, wrapped his arms around Lonnie's waist and picked him up as though the boy weighed no more than a bucket of water. Lonnie felt his boots rise up over his head until he was upside down and facing the open front door, punching only air.

Fury boiled even harder. Fury fueled by helplessness and humiliation. He heard himself sob and his fury doubled. Flailing with his fists and feet, Lonnie screamed above Dupree's loud guffaws, "You go to hell, you gutless, raggedy-heeled outlaw!"

Dupree stared down at Lonnie. Lonnie glared up at him and Dupree opened his arms, dropping Lonnie straight down to the floor.

Lonnie's mother screamed, "Oh, Shannon!"

Lonnie hit the floor on his shoulders, the back of his head taking a glancing blow. He was on his back, gasping, trying to force air into his lungs. He wasn't on the floor long, however, before Shannon Dupree, his long, slanted, gray demon's eyes looking flat and dead and mean as a rattlesnake's, reached down and picked Lonnie up and threw him up against the wall between the window and the door.

The eerie, menacing flatness in Dupree's eyes told Lonnie that he was about to die.

SEVEN

DUPREE HELD Lonnie against the wall with one hand wrapped around the boy's neck, digging his long, thick fingers into Lonnie's windpipe.

"Oh, Shannon, no!" Lonnie's mother beseeched, running around the table and throwing herself against Dupree.

Dupree stood like a brick wall. Lonnie flailed at the man's sunbrowned, muscle-corded arm, trying to work the iron grip free of his throat. He felt like a bug on a pin, at the big man's mercy. When the room started to grow dim around Lonnie, and his knees started to buckle, Dupree removed his hand from Lonnie's throat.

The boy dropped to his knees, sucking air down his aching throat and into his lungs. His head throbbed, ears burning. He felt as though his eyes would explode from their sockets.

"Shannon, that was mean!" May Gentry admonished Dupree as she knelt beside Lonnie and placed a hand on his back. "Lonnie, honey—are you all right, son?"

"Ah, hell," Dupree said, all fun and games again. "I was just funnin' with the boy!"

He wrapped a hand around Lonnie's arm. Lonnie fought against the man, but there was no use. Dupree was four or five times stronger than the thirteen-year-old. Dupree pulled Lonnie to his feet and patted his head, laughing. The other two men sat at the table, regarding their gang leader and the boy uncertainly. Childress chuckling, close-set eyes glowing from all the whiskey he'd been drinking.

The stocky half Indian, Fuego, kept shoveling food into his mouth.

"You all right, son?" Dupree said. "Sorry if I hurt ya. I was just funnin'. Oh, come on—you can take a joke, can't ya? Why, I got no respect for a man who can't take a joke. Sit down, and I'll buy ya a drink!"

"Shannon, let him go," Lonnie's mother implored as Lonnie jerked his arm free of Dupree's loosening grip, and stumbled out onto the porch. He was still trying to work the kinks out of his windpipe with his fingers as he stumbled down the porch steps and started dragging his boot toes across the yard toward the barn.

"Ah, come on, Squirrel!" Dupree yelled behind him. "Get in here and eat your supper." More quietly, he said, "Ah, hell, May—I was just havin' a little fun with the boy. I thought we were just horsin' around. You know—like a boy and his pa!"

Mrs. Gentry said something that Lonnie couldn't hear beneath his own choking as he continued toward the sanctuary of the barn. But her voice rose in the quiet night behind him, "Lonnie, come back. Shannon didn't mean it. Son, you have to eat!"

"Ah, that's too bad," Lonnie heard Dupree say inside the cabin. "I thought the boy had a thicker hide than that. I was just horsin' around, May!"

Lonnie fumbled one of the two big barn doors open, and slipped inside. It was almost dark outside, and it was even darker inside the barn. It smelled of hay and horses and moldy tack leather and of the milk cow that was out in the rear pasture. Lonnie knew the layout by heart, so he didn't bother to light a lamp.

He stumbled back into the rear shed addition, which served as a tack room and an extra sleeping area for a hostler. Lonnie slept in the tack room whenever his mother was "entertaining" Dupree. Fuego and Childress sacked out in the bunkhouse, and Lonnie didn't want to be around them, so he stayed in the side shed, where he had some gear including a bedroll.

His rifle was in there.

Lonnie fumbled around until he got an old hurricane lamp lit. The lamp's glow revealed the cramped quarters stuffed with shelves overflowing with tack of all kinds—harnesses, hames, bits, saddles of all ages and states of disrepair, and even some horseshoes. There were ropes, one wagon wheel, and odds and ends of Lonnie's father's gear from before the

Civil War, which he'd fought in. Cobwebs hung everywhere, and mouse droppings littered the place.

There were two old Civil War-model Confederate pistols that Lonnie kept clean and enjoyed shooting from time to time, when he was caught up on his work. Shooting the old pistols made him feel a little closer to his father, whom Lonnie had never really known and now, of course, never would.

If Shannon Dupree thought he was going to become Lonnie's father, Dupree had best think again…

Lonnie had set his Winchester '66 against the tack room wall. Now he picked it up, brushed his hand down the fore stock that still had some mud on it from its bath in the creek, and he racked a shell into the chamber. Lonnie's heart was racing. Bells of fury and humiliation continued to toll in his head.

"One shot," he seethed through gritted teeth. "One bullet to Dupree's black heart, and that would be the end of him."

Lonnie moved to the tack room door. He stopped suddenly. In his mind, he saw the lawman he'd shot earlier—the man's head snapping back with the red spot on his forehead.

Again, Lonnie's belly writhed as though he'd slugged a quart of sour milk.

A sneering voice inside his head said, "Two men in one day? Sure you got it in you, Killer?"

Dupree's cold, dead, menacing eyes flashed in Lonnie's mind. He could do it. At least, he thought he could now, with the rage coursing through him. He could burst into the cabin and shoot Dupree in the heart. But what, then, about Dupree's "boys"? Surely, they'd kill Lonnie.

And what about Lonnie's mother?

Could he put her through all that?

Lonnie felt his grip on the Winchester loosen. He slammed the tack room door, threw his back against it, and loosed a mewling wail of frustration. Tears streamed down his cheeks. He hastily leaned the rifle against the wall and threw himself belly-down on the cot. He mashed his face against the musty, cornhusk pillow covered with blue-striped ticking that smelled of old sweat. He felt the dam inside him break, loosing a veritable earthquake of pent-up emotion.

He hadn't cried in a long, long time. In fact, he couldn't remember the last time he'd cried. But now his body was racked with wails that the pillow muffled. He writhed on the cot, closing his hands over the wooden frame, kicking his booted feet against it, ramming the pointed toes into the bedroll covering it.

He was not crying about Shannon Dupree. He was not crying about the man he'd killed earlier that day. He was crying about all of it together and about his seeming powerlessness to do anything about this mountain of trouble that had suddenly grown up in front of him.

He had done so much to keep the ranch going, to make it possible for him and his mother to remain here on the range. He'd done the work of two men. Three, maybe four men. But now he'd hit a mountain wall. All his hard work and determination were like spent cartridges in a gun's cylinder.

The gun was empty.

And, to top it all off, he was lying here crying into his pillow as though he were still in rubber pants!

That thought sobered him. He gave one last, shuddering sob, and rolled onto his back. He drew a couple of deep breaths, kicked out of his boots, curled onto his side, and closed his eyes.

It took a while, but he managed to sweep all the shrieking, razor-clawed demons from his mind, and the gauzy sanctuary of sleep closed over him like a favorite quilt.

EIGHT

"LONNIE?"

His mother's voice came as though from the far end of a long tunnel. Lonnie groaned, smacked his lips. Then there was a light, wooden knock, and he recognized the creak of the tack room door's rusty hinges.

"Lonnie?"

He didn't want to reenter the horrific world he'd fled, but his mother's voice tugged at him as though it were the hondo of a lariat looped around his neck.

"Son, wake up. I have to talk to you."

Her hand was on his shoulder and he heard the cot creak as she sat on the edge of it. He smelled food. His stomach reacted to that, and he lifted his head from his pillow.

Mrs. Gentry had a steaming tin plate in her hand—slow-cooked steak smothered in onions and dark-brown gravy. The gravy also covered a helping of mashed potatoes and green beans from a can. A chunk of his mother's crusty, dark-brown bread teetered on the edge of the plate.

The fragrant steam bathed Lonnie's face. His stomach opened its mouth and roared. He hadn't realized how hungry he was. He sat up against the wall flanking the coat, drew up his knees, and took the plate from his mother.

He saw that there was a tray on the bench running along the wall opposite the cot. On the tray was a glass of milk. His mother fetched the glass, and set it on the backless chair beside the cot.

"I thought you might be hungry," she said softly. He could tell from the glitter in her eyes and the paleness of her drawn cheeks that she'd been crying.

"Obliged," Lonnie said, instantly forking a heap of gravy-drenched potatoes into his mouth, and chewing as he cut into the meat.

"I'm so sorry, honey," his mother said, running a hand through his short hair, and pressing her lips to his temple.

Lonnie canted his head away from her. He wasn't in the mood for apologies. In fact, he wasn't in the mood for *her*. Only the food she'd brought. He wished she'd leave, go back to the no-account scoundrel she was going to marry. Soon, she and the no-account scoundrel would ruin everything Lonnie had worked so hard for.

He had no doubt about that. None at all.

"Did you hear me, Lonnie?" she asked again, again running her hand back from his forehead.

"I heard."

"He'd been drinking," she said, as though that explained or excused Dupree's behavior.

"Yeah, I s'pect so," Lonnie said curtly, continuing to shovel food into his mouth. Shovel and chew, shovel and chew. God, he was hungry!

May Gentry removed her hand from her son's head with a sigh. She had a blanket over her shoulders. She sat on the edge of the cot, holding the blanket closed at her throat, staring down at the wooden floor beneath the deerskin slippers she was wearing. She seemed to be waiting for something, or maybe thinking intently.

When Lonnie was nearly done with the meal but still shoveling and chewing, she turned to him, and her eyes were large and grave.

"Lon?"

Lonnie stopped shoveling. Chewing, he looked at her, frowning. "What?" he said around a mouthful of food.

"I need a favor."

Lonnie swallowed and sat staring at his mother, puzzled. Apprehension raked the back of his neck. He rested the plate atop his upraised knees, and waited.

May Gentry rose from the cot and walked to the door, which was closed. On the floor beside the door was a pair of saddlebags that hadn't been there before. She picked up the saddlebags, slung them over her shoulder with a grunt, her blonde hair spilling across her shoulders, and sat down on the edge of the cot once more.

"What're those?" Lonnie asked.

His mother stared at him, her eyes still wide and grave, fearful, hesitant. She closed her upper teeth over her bottom lip and opened the flap of the pouch hanging down her right shoulder. She reached into the pouch, withdrew something, and showed Lonnie the two-inch wad of paper money resting in the palm of her open hand.

Lonnie's eyes snapped wide. "Holy cow!"

The smell of ink and paper mixed with the leather smell of the saddle-bags pushed against his face, nearly taking his breath away. It was an exhilarating smell. Even more rich and intoxicating than the food had been. Lonnie's heart hammered as he stared, his lower jaw hanging nearly to his chest, at the wad of what appeared to be ten-dollar greenbacks secured with a paper band in his mother's open hand.

He slid his gaze from the single wad of bills to the bulging pouch. "There's *more?*"

"Oh, yes," his mother said grimly. "Lots more."

Lonnie laughed and slid his hand toward the wad of bills, but before he could touch it, his mother returned the wad to the pouch hanging down her chest. And then, through the knee-jerk glee of seeing that much money and semiconsciously speculating on what could be bought with it —how easy a fellow's life could suddenly become!—Lonnie was assailed with what felt like the blow of an ax handle.

The money was not his and would never be his. Dupree had brought the money.

Speechless, Lonnie looked into his mother's dark eyes.

"Shannon's asleep in the cabin. Earlier, I saw him shove something under the bed. When I was sure he was dead asleep, I dragged it out." Lonnie's mother's voice broke. Tears rolled down her cheeks. "It's stolen money." She paused, swallowed. She swiped the back of a hand across her cheek as she stared down at the pouch in shame. "They robbed a bank. Or a payroll, maybe. I don't know."

Her lips quivered. She turned her face away and cleared her throat.

"Holy cow," Lonnie said numbly, without the delight with which he'd said it before. He'd suspected that Dupree was on the run from a robbery of some kind. But now, seeing the concrete proof of it...not to mention that much money... Lonnie felt like he'd been dropped on his head all over again.

"I knew it," he whispered, thinking back to the two lawmen.

"Yes, you did," his mother whispered, hanging her head in shame. She sniffed.

Lonnie felt sorry for her. "What're you gonna do, Ma?"

Mrs. Gentry turned to him again gravely. "Not me, Lonnie. *You.*"

NINE

LONNIE SAID, "ME?"

"Son, I want you to do your mother a big favor. I want you to saddle General Sherman before dawn and take this..." She let her voice trail off as she looked distastefully down at the bulging saddlebag pouch, as though she wasn't sure what to call it. "This *money*...this *loot*...to the town marshal in Arapaho Creek. Say you found it out on the range somewhere, maybe in the line shack."

Lonnie scowled, incredulous. "Why in hell should I do that?"

Under the circumstances, he thought he was due a curse or two. His mother seemed to agree, because she ignored it, saying, "Because I want you to."

"He's a bank robber, Momma," Lonnie said. "Why should I help him?"

"Because by helping Shannon, you'll be helping me."

Lonnie found his tongue tied for nearly a minute as he stared in bafflement at his mother. May Gentry couldn't hold his gaze for even half that long. She lowered her eyes in shame.

"Momma," Lonnie said gently, her miserable expression touching his heart. "You aren't really thinkin' you're still gonna marry him, are you?"

"Lonnie, we all make mistakes."

"You think robbin' whatever bank he and them other two men robbed was just a *mistake*?"

"He'd been drinking," Lonnie's mother said, her eyes desperate, pleading. "When Shannon drinks, he does things he wouldn't do otherwise. I think those other two men, Fuego, especially, got him drunk and then, once he was good and pie-eyed, talked him into stealing this money. I don't think Shannon would have done such a thing otherwise. He promised me he wouldn't!"

Lonnie didn't know what to say to that. What his mother was spewing was nonsense. But she was not usually a nonsensical woman. The fact was she was lonely. So desperately lonely that she was sitting here spewing nonsense in defense of the bank robber she'd fallen in love with.

Lonnie had known she was lonely. Until now, he hadn't realized how lonely and sad she really was. A hand reached into the boy's chest and twisted his heart counterclockwise, and he had to swallow the hard knot in his throat to keep from sobbing.

He set his plate on the floor and dropped his boots down to the floor, as well. He sat beside his mother, wrapped an arm around her waist. "Momma, I—"

He stopped when she turned her fear-bright eyes on him. "Lonnie, if lawmen come for Shannon, they'll take me, too."

"No, they won't."

"Lonnie, word has gotten around about me an' Shannon. Folks know he comes by here from time to time. The lawmen who come for him will think I provided a place to stay for him and the other two, knowing what they'd done. They'll think I'm part of it. They might even think you are, too."

Lonnie shook his head. "We'll tell them otherwise, Momma." But then he remembered the lawman he'd killed, and fear jolted him like a lightning bolt striking a lone pine on a high mountain ridge.

He looked toward the night-dark windows reflecting the wan lantern light, and he saw the twisted, thick-lipped, black-eyed faces of a thousand demons staring in at him, laughing. Silently teasing, jeering. A shudder racked him.

His mother wrapped an arm around him and gave him a squeeze as she said, "Please, Lonnie. Before first light, ride on out of here and deliver these saddlebags to the marshal in Arapaho Creek. Tell Marshal Stoveville you found them along the trail or in the line shack up on Eagle Ridge. It's not right to lie, but under the circumstances, I don't see any other way."

Lonnie brushed a tear from his cheek. His mother's desperation deeply pained him. "Are you sure you're not just doin' this for Dupree?"

"For him," she said, smiling thinly and giving a slight nod. She knew how lame it was to feel something for a worthless owl hoot, but because of her loneliness, she couldn't help herself. "But for us, too."

"He'll find it gone first thing in the mornin'."

"He won't stir till noon. None of them will. Not after all they drank. It'll be all right."

"No, it won't. He'll be mad. He'll hurt you."

Lonnie's mother gave a weak smile and placed a hand on her belly. "He won't hurt me, son. I'm carrying his child."

That was like a fist buried deep in Lonnie's gut. He gaped at his mother. He felt the blood rush to his face. He was at a total loss for words.

"I can handle Shannon, Lonnie," she said. "You worry about getting to Arapaho Creek. Once you've returned the money, don't come back to the ranch right away. Spend a night or two at the line shack."

"What are you gonna do, Momma?"

May Gentry sighed as she set the saddlebags on the floor and slid them under Lonnie's cot. On one knee, she squeezed her son's hand reassuringly. "Like I said, I know how to handle Shannon. When he gets all that poison out of his brain, he'll come around. He'll know he done wrong. He doesn't want to lose me. He doesn't want to lose our child."

"Momma," Lonnie said, slowly shaking his head, dead certain that she was wrong but knowing he couldn't convince her.

His mother picked up his plate and glanced at the untouched glass of milk on the chair. "Finish your milk, son. I'll fetch you out a bag of biscuits and jerky for the ride to Arapaho Creek. I'll throw in some food to tide you at the line shack. There won't be time for breakfast tomorrow."

And then she left. She returned a few minutes later with a small croaker sack of trail food, which she set on the counter. She kissed Lonnie's forehead, and left again, and Lonnie turned down the lamp and lay on the cot, staring at the dark ceiling, thinking.

When the maniacal thoughts in his head finally tired themselves out, he drifted off...only to be awakened by what felt like a blackfly stinging the underside of his chin.

Instantly awake, he swatted at the unseen insect.

The back of his hand hit something unyielding before him. The blackfly stung him a little harder, then he smelled the stench of sweat and whiskey. In the wash of pearl moonlight angling through the tack room windows, Lonnie saw the silhouetted face of Shannon Dupree hovering over him.

The moonlight winked off the wide, silver blade in Dupree's fist. That's what was stinging Lonnie. Not a blackfly. Dupree was holding the up-curved point of a Bowie knife against the underside of Lonnie's chin.

TEN

DUPREE'S EYES, framed by his blond hair, were as black as black marbles. He stretched his lips back from his teeth that appeared unusually large in the darkness, and he said quietly, "You call out, I'll cut you from ear to ear."

Lonnie lay stiff as a board, head tipped back and away from the razor-edged point of the massive blade. The blade looked as wide as Lonnie's thigh. The boy drew shallow breaths, felt sweat bead on his upper lip.

The money, he thought.

Dupree had seen Lonnie's mother remove the money from under the bed in the cabin. Lonnie saw no reason to be a hero. Dupree would find the money on his own if Lonnie didn't tell him, so Lonnie was about to tell him it was under the cot, when Dupree said, "Wanted to have a little chat with ya, Squirrel. About tomorrow."

Lonnie was puzzled. Mostly, though, he was horrified, and the point of the knife digging into his jaw wasn't helping matters.

He waited, drawing shallow breaths as he stared into the cold, black, dead eyes of Shannon Dupree.

Dupree said, "Tomorrow, me an' the boys are gonna ride on out of here...with your mother. She don't know it yet, but she will in the mornin'. I wanted you to know so you don't make no trouble, understand? You stay out here in the barn and keep your mouth shut."

"Why...why're you...takin'...M-Ma?"

"Insurance," Dupree said, spreading his mouth with self-satisfaction. "You make any trouble, I'm gonna take out this big ol' Bowie knife and cut your throat from ear to ear. Nice wide gash, understand?"

Lonnie stared at those dead eyes, speechless. His heart sputtered, hiccupped.

Dupree said, "And then I'll kill her, too. Same way. Hate to do that, her bein' such a fine-lookin' woman. But I'll do it. You know I will." That grin again. "So you just stay out here until me an' the boys an' your ma have rode away. All right?"

"All...all right," Lonnie said, wincing as Dupree pressed the point of the blade a little more snugly against the underside of Lonnie's chin. Lonnie felt the point pierce the skin. He felt a blood drop grow around the stinging point. The blood was cool and wet.

Dupree pulled the blade away, and straightened his legs. He was so tall that his head disappeared into the darkness above where the moonlight was angling through the tack room window behind him. He hiked a boot onto the chair beside the cot, and there was the soft screech and snick of the Bowie knife being returned to a sheath inside of the boot.

"Good boy, Squirrel. Play your cards right, you might make a man someday."

Dupree tussled Lonnie's hair with menace. Turning, he stumbled drunkenly, and for a second Lonnie thought the man was going to fall on top of him. There was a sharp, sickening stench of whiskey and sweat. Lonnie slid to one side and threw up his hands to shield himself from the big man's body. Then Dupree got his feet beneath him and, chuckling, stumbled on over to the door and went out without closing the door behind him.

Lonnie heard the outlaw chuckle once more, and his stumbling footsteps dwindled away until for a time there were no more sounds except for a slight breeze pushing against the barn and the frogs croaking down along the creek.

Lonnie lay frozen, bathed in cold sweat, staring up at the dark ceiling relieved in shadows cast by the pearl moonlight. When he heard the faint, muffled scrape of the cabin door closing, he scrambled up out of the cot, stepped into his boots, donned his hat, and grabbed the Winchester. Vaguely, he noted the sting on the underside of his chin, and brushed a couple of knuckles across it. They came away lightly blood-smeared. He'd live.

At least, the slight cut beneath his chin wouldn't kill him. If Dupree looked beneath Lonnie's mother's bed to reassure himself the loot was still there, and he was given no such reassurance, Lonnie and her mother were likely wolf bait.

That's why Lonnie rummaged around for a box of .44-40 cartridges, and loaded the carbine. When he had it fully loaded, he pumped a cartridge into the action and positioned the hammer to off-cock. All he had to do was pull the hammer back, aim, and fire...

He drew a light denim jacket on over his shirt, and left the barn. He closed the doors behind him and stood with his back to them, where the barn's shadow concealed him. He stared toward the cabin. No lamps were lit. All was dark and quiet.

So far...

Lonnie had to make sure his mother was safe.

To that end, he ran at a crouch across the yard, trying to stay out of the moonlight as much as he could. When he gained the foot of the porch, he moved around to the cabin's left side and hunkered down outside the window of his mother's bedroom. He was in the moonlight here, but Dupree's men were in the bunkhouse on the other side of the cabin, so there was no one out here to see him skulking around.

Lonnie pressed his right shoulder against the cabin's rough log wall. He held his breath and pricked his ears, listening. Inside, there was nothing but silence. Dupree must have gone back to bed as soon as he'd gotten back inside the cabin. Lonnie's mother was likely asleep. She was a sound sleeper, always had been.

But Lonnie wanted to make sure Dupree didn't check under the bed for the stolen money. If he did, things would go even farther south around the Circle G than they already had. If he did find the stolen money, Lonnie would enter the cabin and shoot the man before he could harm May Gentry. Then he'd likely have to deal with the other two men—Fuego and Childress.

Probably easier thought about than done...

Lonnie looked down at the rifle he held in his hands. It quivered slightly. Could he shoot straight if he had to? If he had to, by criminy, Lonnie would shoot Shannon Dupree like he was nothing more than a Thanksgiving turkey that Lonnie had come upon in the forest.

If he had to...

But it looked like he wouldn't have to shoot tonight. After he'd been outside the window no more than two minutes, Lonnie heard Dupree's long, raking snores. He listened for a time, making sure they continued, and then he hotfooted it back to the barn, and sat on a saddle tree, thinking through his options.

His main concern was for his mother. What would happen to her if Lonnie did her bidding and hightailed it with the stolen money? Dupree had threatened to kill her if Lonnie impeded the plans of Dupree and "the boys" in the morning.

What would stop him from killing Lonnie's mother when he found out she'd tricked him and sent Lonnie to Arapaho Creek with the money? Likely, the child she was carrying. Despite his threat earlier, no man could harm a woman carrying his child.

Still, to be sure, Lonnie's best option would be to go into the cabin and shoot Dupree as he slept. But what if he missed Dupree and shot his mother instead? And even if Lonnie was able to kill Dupree—which was a long shot, for he'd never intentionally shot another man before today and he wasn't sure he really had the nerve to do such a thing—what about Fuego and Childress?

Lonnie paced in front of the barn doors.

After he mulled the situation over for a good twenty agonized minutes, he decided to follow through with his mother's plan. He just had to hope Dupree didn't kill her when he discovered the ruse. Chances are he wouldn't because there would be no point except revenge. And, again, she was carrying his child. Besides, Dupree would want to come after Lonnie as fast as he could, and overtake the boy before he reached the marshal in Arapaho Creek.

There seemed no risk-free solution to the mountain of trouble before the boy. But heading to Arapaho Creek seemed his best bet. He'd recognized neither of the lawmen up on Willow Run, so he didn't think they were from Arapaho Creek. He didn't think that Marshal Stoveville had any deputies, as the town was small and relatively quiet. Without a doubt, Dupree would follow Lonnie there—possibly all the way to the town and maybe even right on up to the doorstep of Marshal Dwight Stoveville, whom Lonnie would warn ahead of time.

Lonnie looked out between the barn doors.

It was still good dark. Maybe around three, three-thirty. It wasn't safe to ride out in the dark, but he was too eager to get to Arapaho Creek to wait around for dawn. He certainly wouldn't be able to sleep anymore tonight. Besides, the moon would light the northeastern trail until the sun rose in a couple of hours.

As quietly as he could, his heart drumming anxiously in his ears,

Lonnie saddled General Sherman. He set the saddlebags filled with Dupree's precious loot over the top of another pair of saddlebags filled with trail supplies. Lonnie hung his cavvy sack, filled with cooking paraphernalia, from his saddle horn. There was no telling how long he'd have to be away from home.

Lonnie led the General out of the yard, wincing with each of the big horse's heavy footfalls. When he was a hundred yards beyond, he mounted up and put the horse into a spanking trot. Lonnie headed along the northern trail while casting anxious glances behind at the eerily silent ranch yard growing smaller and smaller until it disappeared altogether, and he was very much alone.

ELEVEN

LATER THAT DAY, after he'd ridden a good ten miles from the Circle G, Lonnie sat on a rock by the small fire he'd built.

He fished a blackened tin cup from the canvas cavvy sack on the ground by his feet and used a small leather swatch to pad the hot handle while he poured coffee from the dented pot. The dark-brown brew sent its fragrant steam wafting into his face with small white ashes from the burning pine branches.

The smell was one of the best Lonnie knew. It complemented the forest smells. He sipped the coffee and then opened the two-pound bag of jerky his mother had packed, and started eating. When he finished a ragged strip of jerky, he ate a biscuit. When he'd had two strips of jerky and three small biscuits, he poured a fresh cup of coffee.

The General whinnied. Lonnie jerked with a start, and the hot coffee sloshed over the brim to burn his hand through his leather glove.

He winced as he jerked his head up, looking around.

The General was craning his neck to look behind him, edgily switching his tail.

Lonnie had left the main trail that ran through the bottom of the canyon to set up camp here on the side of the ridge, out of sight from the trail. He hadn't wanted to be pestered. The trail was a hundred yards back down the slope, but now Lonnie heard what the General's keen ears had picked up—the slow thuds of approaching horses.

A man said something. The thuds grew louder. There was the clang of a shod hoof kicking a rock. Still looking behind him through the trees toward the bottom of the canyon, the General whinnied again. Lonnie reached for the carbine leaning against a tree to his left, and, rising from the rock, slowly levered a live cartridge into the action.

He glanced at the saddlebags containing the stolen money. They sat at the base of a tree on the other side of the fire, near the General, one pouch slumped against the other. Both pouches bulged curiously. Lonnie wanted to run over and hide the bags in some shrubs, but he could see three horseback riders approaching along the shoulder of the slope behind the General. If Lonnie tried to hide the bags now, they'd see him and grow suspicious of what he was hiding.

Lonnie's pulse throbbed in his fingers.

Three riders . . .

He stepped back away from the fire and over to where he could get a better look at the men approaching. His knees were warm and weak. For a second, he thought they would buckle from the overwhelming wave of fear washing over him. Then he saw that it was not Dupree. The lead rider had long, dark-brown hair and a mustache. The man behind him was older and potbellied and he wore an old, ratty, bullet-crowned, broad-brimmed hat. He was old—maybe in his fifties, even older.

The man behind the old one was younger. He was older than Lonnie but not by much, and he was blond and wild-looking, with bright green eyes and thick lips stretched back from small, brown teeth. His face was heavily freckled. He looked like he might have been soft in the head.

Lonnie knew most of the men who lived and worked in these mountains, but he'd never seen these three. When he'd first seen that they weren't Dupree's bunch, he'd been relieved. Now that relief was tempered by a healthy, natural apprehension.

All types moved through the Never Summers, including cutthroats on the run from the law. The mountains were a haven for cattle rustlers who preyed on the ranchers' herds, like human coyotes. And that's what these three appeared to be—even the young, freckle-faced one.

Coyotes. Only more dangerous because they all wore at least one holstered pistol. Rifles jutted from leather sheaths strapped to their saddles. Lonnie thought he could see the glint of a running iron strapped to the third rider's horse, partly concealed by the young man's bedroll and saddlebags.

That marked them as rustlers, sure enough. Running irons were used to doctor cattle brands.

The first man, the one with the long hair, stopped his horse about twenty yards from Lonnie. The man looked Lonnie up and down, paying special attention to the cocked rifle in the boy's gloved hands. The first man glanced behind at the old man, who reined his sorrel gelding to a halt about five yards behind the first man.

"It's a kid," the long-haired man said.

Then he turned his attention to General Sherman. So did the old man. There was a conniving hunger in their eyes. And Lonnie felt a rock drop in his gut.

The three newcomers, looking around curiously, let their gazes linger on the General, shrewdly appraising the valuable stallion.

The old man said, "You alone, boy?"

"Nope."

The three looked around again from the backs of their horses. The long-haired man said, "Who's with you?"

"That horse and this rifle," Lonnie said, resting the Winchester on his right shoulder.

He eyed the three strangers directly, keeping his expression bland, his gaze resolute. There was no point in letting them know they'd spooked him. He wanted them to ride on. If they saw the saddlebags containing the money, all hell could very well break loose.

Lonnie wasn't about to turn the money over to them. It wasn't theirs any more than it was Dupree's. Besides, he wouldn't be robbed. Of his horse, the money, or of anything else. He considered the money his own until he could turn it over to the town marshal in Arapaho Creek, who would make sure it was returned to wherever it had come from.

The long-haired man, who looked particularly mean, grinned and looked at the old man and the blond young man. They all laughed, their eyes glinting at Lonnie holding his carbine on his shoulder, as though he'd told a joke they'd found amusing. The old man looked at the fire behind Lonnie and to his left. Lonnie wondered if the man's eyes had found the bulging saddlebags, as well.

His chest was tight with the possibility.

"Say, now, you got a pot of coffee on. Mind if we join you?"

"Sure smells good," said the blond young man, cutting his eyes devilishly between the old man and the long-haired man. Then he looked at

General Sherman. For the time being, the young man's main concern was Lonnie's horse.

Lonnie felt another cold rock drop in his gut. It was the custom of the country to allow men to join you around your cook fire, and to share food as well as coffee. Not to allow it would be to commit an unforgiveable sin and to beckon trouble.

These men knew it. And Lonnie knew it.

They had him.

Lonnie faked a welcoming smile, but he opened and closed his hand around the neck of the rifle resting on his shoulder as he said, "Light and sit a spell. I've a pot of coffee on the fire, and you're welcome to what's left. When that's gone, I'll make more." He was saying the words automatically. They were the words he'd heard over and over again, and he'd been expected to say them, so he'd said them.

But if these men thought they were going to rob him of his horse or anything else, they had a big surprise in store.

At least, that's what he told himself.

"That's mighty kindly, partner," the old man said, grunting as he swung heavily down from his sorrel's back. "We'll take you up on that."

He tied his horse's reins to a branch sticking up from a deadfall tree. As he did, he cut his eyes again toward General Sherman, who was eying all three strangers and their horses cautiously, twitching his ears and stomping his right front foot. The old man's sorrel returned the General's belligerent look with ears up and his tail curled.

When the other three had tied their own horses, they reached into their saddlebags for tin cups, and Lonnie met them at the fire, standing near where he'd been sitting on the rock, holding his rifle across his knees and continuing to gaze at the newcomers blandly. He felt a hard defiance and a cold anger, for he knew what they were after, and he kept telling himself over and over they weren't going to get his horse or the saddlebags.

He wasn't sure any of the three had seen the bags yet, but they were bound to. The strangers were within ten feet of where the pouches leaned against the tree near the General. They'd see Lonnie's second set of bags near the fire, and they'd wonder about that. It wasn't common to carry two sets of saddlebags.

Lonnie silently cursed himself for a fool for not having hidden the saddlebags before he'd built the fire. The fire is likely what had attracted these men. They'd likely smelled the smoke from below though Lonnie had chosen this place because he'd thought it was upwind from the canyon floor.

The old man grinned at Lonnie, said, "Much obliged, boy."

He reached down and with the leather swatch lifted the pot off the rock Lonnie had placed it on near the flames, and splashed some into his cup and then into the cups of the other two.

He grinned again at Lonnie as he shook the pot, and said, "Reckon we cleaned ya out," and then set the pot on one of the rocks forming the ring around the fire.

"Like I said," Lonnie said, "I'll make more."

But he merely sat down on the rock he'd been sitting on before and held his carbine across his thighs. He had no intention of making more coffee because that would mean he'd have to set his rifle down.

The three strangers, each holding a smoking cup, squatted on the other side of the fire—the old man to Lonnie's right, the young, blond-headed man in the middle and a ways back, and the long-haired gent on Lonnie's left. They formed a half circle around Lonnie, on the far side of the fire.

The long-haired man had two pistols holstered on his hips. The old man wore a big horse pistol in a holster over his belly. The blond young man wore what appeared to be a Remington .44 in a holster thonged low on his right thigh, as though he fancied himself a gunslinger.

Maybe he was...

Lonnie stared at the men. He didn't bother trying to make conversation, and neither did his new camp mates, who merely hunkered on their haunches, blowing on and sipping from their steaming cups and regarding Lonnie with expressions ranging from blandness to cool disdain.

The old man glanced over at the bulging saddlebags, raised his brows knowingly, and said, "Lookee there! Them bags is mighty full. You must be on a long trip! Say, what you got in there, anyway?"

TWELVE

THE OTHER TWO strangers kept their eyes on Lonnie. The blond young man grinned, showing his small, rotten teeth. The old man cut his eyes at the bulging saddlebags again, and said, "What you got in 'em?"

"Ain't none of your concern," Lonnie said, his cool, even voice belying his trepidation. He'd found, however, that when he was his most fearful, acting brave edged him in bravery's direction.

He was getting sick and tired of sparring with trouble not of his own making. Sick, tired, and more than a little angry. The anger also helped push back some of the fear. He knew he couldn't take all three of these men if they started shooting, but if they started fiddling, as the saying went, he'd have no choice but to dance.

He'd dance one of them right on over the divide before the others took Lonnie out in a hail of lead...

"Well, I'm right curious," the old man said, glancing at the other two on either side of him, still sipping their coffee. "I'm so curious I think I'm going to go over and have a look inside them bags."

Lonnie's heart thudded.

He ran his tongue along the underside of his upper lip and said, "Those are my bags. Stay out of 'em." He drew a deep, calming breath and, squeezing the carbine in his hands, said, "Or you'll be sorry."

The old man laughed. "I'll be sorry, will I?" He glanced at the other two in turn. "What do you fellas think? Will I be sorry?"

"Nah," said the long-haired man whose cold eyes reminded Lonnie of Shannon Dupree's eyes. "Go on over and have a look inside, Wade. See what the kid's carryin'. See what's so valuable he's willin' to die to hold onto it."

Lonnie grew dizzy. He fought against it. He also fought against involuntarily spurting pee down his leg. He drew another breath, said, "Them's my bags. Stay out of 'em. I gave you coffee. Finish it and skedaddle."

"Skedaddle, huh?" the blond-headed young man said, chuckling through his teeth. "I like that. *Skedaddle!*"

"Your ma teach you that, boy?" said the long-haired gent, scowling over the small, leaping flames at Lonnie. He gave his left hand a sudden flick, tossing coffee out of his cup. It splattered over a rock.

In a near tree bough, a squirrel began chittering angrily. For some reason, the squirrel's reprimand caused Lonnie to feel ever more nervous. Cold sweat was dripping under his arms.

The long-haired gent dropped his cup straight down to the ground between his brown boots, rested his wrists on his knees, and said, "Skedaddle on over there, Wade, and see what the boy's carryin' that's so precious."

"Should I?"

"I said you should, didn't I?"

"Well, okay, then," Wade said, rising slowly, staring directly into Lonnie's eyes.

"I wouldn't," Lonnie said, keeping his voice hard and cold though every fiber of his being was trembling like an autumn leaf in a chill wind.

The squirrel was chittering loudly now. The unceasing sound seemed to fill Lonnie's head.

Keeping his eyes on Lonnie's with open challenge, the old man began sidestepping toward the saddlebags. His heart banging inside his ears, Lonnie watched him. He cast frequent glances toward the other two, in case they should suddenly pull their guns.

But as the squirrel kept reading them all the riot act, those two remained on their haunches, both staring at Lonnie—the long-haired gent's eyes dark and threatening, the blond-headed young man's eyes brightly mocking but also threatening in their own way.

The old man continued holding Lonnie's gaze as he edged slowly over to the saddlebags. As Wade began to reach down toward the flap of the first pouch, a rifle crackled loudly, shutting the squirrel up and tearing a fist-sized chunk of bark out of the tree about six inches left of the old man's shoulder.

Lonnie blinked as the old man yelped and hooked an arm up as though to shield himself.

Lonnie glanced down in surprise to see that he was holding his carbine straight out at the old man, and that gray smoke was curling from its barrel. Then he remembered squeezing the trigger, but it felt as though someone else had squeezed it. Automatically, he pumped a fresh cartridge into the chamber, but before he'd even gotten the cocking lever rammed up against the underside of the rifle's breech, the two men by the fire jerked to their feet and reached for their pistols.

Lonnie knew instantly he was a goner. They were both fast, and Lonnie was still turned toward Wade. When the shooting started, Lonnie felt himself being punched back—either by bullets or fear of bullets—until his boots clipped a log and he fell hard on his butt.

He glanced to his right, to where the old man was pulling the big horse pistol out of the soft, brown leather holster over his belly. As he stared at something above and behind Lonnie, Wade got a weird, terrified look on his face.

He dropped the pistol and went dancing off down the slope as though with some invisible partner before dropping to the ground and rolling.

The shooting stopped.

Lonnie blinked. He shifted his gaze from where Wade had fallen toward the other two men. They were down, as well. Dark-red blood oozed from several places in both of them.

Lonnie looked down at himself, expecting to see red oozing from his own body, as well. But he saw no such thing. He wasn't so much grateful at that instant as he was surprised. And then he remembered that Wade had been staring at something behind Lonnie, who twisted around to gaze up the wooded slope toward the ridge.

A man in a broad-brimmed hat was straightening from a crouch and slowly lowering the smoking rifle in his hands.

THIRTEEN

LONNIE LOOKED around him at the dead men once more. He looked at himself, wondering if he, too, was dead but for some reason didn't know it yet. But, no, there was no blood on him. His heart was still beating and he was still raking air in and out of his lungs.

He felt as disoriented as if he'd been hit in the back of the head with a two-by-four. But he was alive, all right.

He looked behind him. The man who'd shot the three strangers was walking down the slope toward Lonnie's smoldering fire. He carried what appeared to be an old-model rifle in both hands up high across his chest.

He was a medium-tall, bandy-legged man wearing a broad-brimmed gray hat so old and weathered it appeared a dusty cream color. It was torn, and the brim flopped. It looked like the kind of hat Lonnie had seen some Confederate soldiers wearing when they'd returned home from the War Between the States. The man's badly faded and patched gray trousers were from the same type of uniform, though the man's calico shirt and his boots appeared newer. He wore a brace of old pistols in soft, black holsters on his hips.

"Any of 'em still movin'?" the man asked as he approached the camp, staring beyond Lonnie at the men he'd shot. He waved a gloved hand at a fly buzzing around in front of his face, which was lean and craggy and trimmed with a thick, salt-and-pepper goatee and mustache.

He spat a wad of chaw on a rock to his left, brushed a sleeve of his shirt across his mouth, and continued moving forward, his pale-blue eyes dancing around deep in their bony, heavily ridged sockets.

"Who...who are you?" Lonnie had climbed to his feet and was staring in awe at the man who'd saved his life, still trying to work his mind around all that had happened.

The man walked past him, not saying anything. He walked around the fire, the mule ears of his boots flapping, audibly sucking and working the wad of chaw bulging out his left cheek. He looked down at the long-haired gent, then moved to the young, blond-headed man. Apparently satisfied he'd get no more trouble out of either of those two he walked down the slope a ways to where the old man lay tangled up against a pine stump.

Lonnie's most recent visitor stared down at the old man, spat a wad of chew to the side, wiped his mouth, and leaned his rifle against a tree. He dropped to both knees beside the old man and started rummaging around in the old-timer's pockets. He grumbled and muttered unhappily to himself, apparently not satisfied with anything he found, until he pulled a knife out of a sheath strapped against the old man's hip.

The newcomer studied the knife, pooched out his tobacco-brown lips, and nodded his approval. Turning to Lonnie, he held up the knife and said in a thick Southern accent, "This might be worth a spud or two. You want it?"

Lonnie shook his head.

The newcomer frowned and then poked his knife in the direction of the other two dead men. "You might as well check 'em out, pull anythin' off 'em you can use. They won't be needed it where they're headed, and they were within about one blink of reintroducin' you to your Maker."

"Were you a Confederate soldier?"

The newcomer stared at Lonnie, mildly befuddled. He rose to his feet and shoved his new knife down behind his cartridge belt. He picked up his rifle and walked up the slope toward the other two dead men.

"I reckon you could say that," he said with a dry chuckle. "Once a Grayback, always a Grayback."

"My pa fought in the war," Lonnie said. He supposed it sounded like a stupid thing to say under the circumstances, but it was the only thing his brain could spit out. It still hadn't quite wrapped itself around the three dead men, nor around the fact that he very nearly had been, as the Confederate had said, reintroduced to his Maker.

Twice in twenty-four hours. Three if you considered Dupree's nearly strangling him the night before.

"What side?" the Confederate asked as he poked around in the pockets of the blond-headed young man.

"What's that?"

"What side did your pa fight on durin' the War of Northern Aggression?"

"Oh," Lonnie said, his thoughts still sluggish. "He fought for the North."

"Figures."

The Confederate pulled a gold-washed watch out of the breast pocket of the long-haired man's bloody shirt. He wiped the watch on the dead man's denim trouser leg and flipped the lid and held the piece up to his hear. "Still runs," he said. "I reckon I'll take it. First come, first served is how I see it. Besides"—the Confederate gave Lonnie a slit-eyed grin—"your old man's a blue belly."

He stood and looked around. His gaze caught on something, and he turned to Lonnie. "Them's yours?"

Lonnie followed the man's gaze to the overstuffed saddlebags. The boy's heart gave a hiccup. Amidst all the gunfire and death and destruction, he'd forgotten about Dupree's money. When Lonnie started to wonder if he'd been thrown out of the frying pan and into the fire, the Confederate grinned and came around the fire to stand in front of Lonnie. He whistled.

"You're stocked for a long trip." The man's smile faded from his deep-set, dark-blue eyes. "You best keep those hid if you aim to make a man one day."

"Yeah, I reckon," Lonnie said with chagrin.

The Confederate pocketed the watch, rested his rifle on his shoulder, and began slouching up the slope in the same direction from which he'd come. Lonnie watched him, puzzled. He wasn't sure why, but he was reluctant for the man to leave him alone with the three dead men.

The man had saved Lonnie's life, after all.

"Hey," the boy called. "What's your name?"

The Confederate stopped and slanted a wily look over his shoulder and down the hill. "What's yours?"

Lonnie got the message.

The Grayback winked and then continued trudging up the hill through the trees.

FOURTEEN

WHEN THE SOUTHERNER was gone from view, Lonnie turned reluctantly toward his camp littered with dead men. Though he still felt as though he'd been kicked in the belly by an angry mule, and the dead repulsed him, he couldn't help walking over to the other side of the fire and having a look.

There was something oddly fascinating about the dead. Fascinating as well as horrifying. Lonnie had seen his father after he'd died in bed of an apparent heart stroke, Calvin Gentry's face twisted in horror, his slitted eyes downcast.

Lonnie had also seen a young man Lonnie's own age after the boy had been kicked in the head by a calf he'd been trying to brand. The calf's hard, sharp hoof had cracked young George Perry's skull above his right ear, and Lonnie and the others had gathered around the branding fire to pay their respects to the dead youngster. Young George had seemed to be smiling up at those gathered around him, his upper lip curled, eyes heavy-lidded but open, almost as though he now knew the answer to a secret that the living could only guess at, and he was gloating about it.

That would have been just like George.

Lonnie stared down at the long-haired gent who appeared to have learned no such secret. His eyes were bulging in their sockets, and his tongue was poking out the right side of his mouth. He looked as though he were strangling. His face was pale, turning blue at the nubs of his cheeks. The sight of him and the blond young man made Lonnie feel wobbly-kneed and heavy-gutted, and he turned away quickly.

He kicked dirt on his fire and packed up his gear. He set the money-bags over General Sherman's back, tightened the buckskin's saddle cinch, and pushed the bridle bit back into the General's mouth. When he had the horse ready to go, Lonnie unsaddled the dead men's three horses and turned them loose. They ran off down the slope toward the canyon bottom, buck-kicking and shaking their heads, eager to be a long way from the smell of their dead, bloody riders.

Lonnie didn't blame them. He stuffed his carbine down into the General's saddle boot and headed the buckskin in the same direction.

It was dusk when Lonnie reined General Sherman up on the crest of a hill and stared toward the north.

The town of Arapaho Creek was a fuzzy gray mass at the bottom of a rise of snow-tipped mountains. The snow shone brightly against the otherwise dark ridge crest, the edges of the glaciers limned in the salmon rays of the fast-falling sun.

The only way that Lonnie could tell that a town lay a half mile ahead was by the cluster of yellow and orange lights flickering against the velvet brown ridge beyond it. And by the occasional whoops and yells of men as well as women, by the barking of a dog, and by the jocular fiddling emanating from that direction, as well.

Arapaho Creek wasn't much of a town, but it was a mining town that also provided supplies for local ranches, and while Lonnie had never visited the settlement at night, it obviously came alive when the sun went down. He glanced over his shoulder to make sure the saddlebags filled with loot were still draped across the General's hindquarters, over Lonnie's own saddlebags.

Riding into town with as much as he was carrying made him nervous, but he had to get the loot to the town marshal some way, and how else could he do it? He supposed he could hide the saddlebags out here some-where, and lead Dwight Stoveville out for it later, but the way Lonnie's luck was going, he'd probably forget where he hid it. Or someone would come along and take it.

Lonnie glanced behind him. At no time during the day had he detected sign of anyone following. That made the boy uneasy for his mother, but it had made getting to Arapaho Creek a whole lot easier despite his run-in with the three men who were now most likely feeding the wildcats and wolves.

Uneasiness like a heavy, laughing monkey straddling his already burdened shoulders, Lonnie touched spurs to the General's flanks. Horse and rider trotted on down the hill and along the trail that was a fast-dimming butterscotch line before them. They crossed Arapaho Creek via a wooden bridge, the General's hooves clomping hollowly on the planks. The bubbling stream was a black-and-silver skin flashing beneath Lonnie, the water chuckling and gurgling.

The air over the river was humid and sweet-smelling.

And when they left the bridge, they were in the town of Arapaho Creek itself where the sweet smell was gone, replaced by the smell of fires and the stench of privies and rotting trash heaps.

Lonnie reined up at the edge of the business district and looked around, getting his bearings. The main street was broad and dark, but the lamplight pushing through the windows of saloons and the still-open shops helped. Silhouetted men shifted around the streets, crossing and recrossing to saloons or to the mercantile or drugstore or to one of the several bawdy houses that were usually shuttered and silent when Lonnie and his mother had journeyed here for supplies or to sell their eggs.

Remembering that the town marshal's office sat on the far side of the town, on the street's west side, Lonnie gigged the General out from under the sprawling cottonwood he'd stopped under, and headed into the fray.

FIFTEEN

AS LONNIE PASSED saloons and parlor houses, he heard men laughing and women singing.

The fiddle music seemed to be coming from somewhere on Lonnie's left. Men and women were clomping and clapping to the raucous music. They were having a good time. Lonnie found himself absently envying their lack of care as he put the General ahead, trying to avoid the largest clusters of men along the street, trying to ride through the town as inconspicuously as possible, hoping that no one would see the overstuffed saddlebags resting behind the cantle of his saddle.

He didn't want to have to explain anything to anyone except Marshal Stoveville. And when that was done, he'd ride back out of town the way he'd come and head for the line shack, as his mother had instructed, and wait for his trail to cool.

A couple of dogs were fighting over a bone in the street before the jailhouse, so Lonnie swung the General wide around them and put the horse up to the hitch rack to the right of the steps that climbed the dilapidated front stoop. The jailhouse itself was a rectangular, block-like stone barrack behind the wooden stoop. A sign over the veranda announced simply TOWN MARSHAL.

The front door was propped open with a rifle.

Lonnie looked around him. There were only a few men on this end of the street. One of the fighting dogs gave a sudden yip and wheeled away from the other one, a German Cherokeeherd, with its tail down. Lonnie swung down from the General's back. He tied the reins around the worn hitching post and then went back and pulled the saddlebags down from the General's hindquarters.

He slung the bags over a shoulder, tipped his hat down low over his eyes, and mounted the porch steps, his spurs ringing, the rotting steps creaking beneath his boots. He paused at the top of the steps when he heard a woman chuckling from inside the place, the laughter echoing faintly off the stone walls. A man said something that made Lonnie's ears warm, and the woman laughed harder.

Lonnie cleared his throat to give the pair ample warning and walked across the stoop, loudly stomping his boots and ringing his spurs, before stopping just outside the front door and glancing inside.

The office was lit by a couple of lamps, one on a cluttered rolltop desk left of the door, another bracketed on the back wall in which three jail cells were set. A long wooden table stood in the middle of the room beyond a potbelly stove that pushed its large, tin pipe through the ceiling above Lonnie. At the table cluttered with the paraphernalia of a recent meal as well as bottles, glasses, and playing cards, a man was sitting with a large, dark-haired, brown-eyed woman wearing a red dress. The woman was perched on the man's knee and she was lolling back against the man's shoulder.

The dress revealed as much of the female form as Lonnie had ever seen, and more, and it was startling as well as shocking to see so much exposed flesh. The woman's eyes snapped wide at the boy in the doorway, and she scrambled off the man's knee to drop into a chair beside him, flushing and laughing and saying, "Looks like you got a customer, Chase!"

She glanced at the man, who was wearing a five-pointed star on his blue shirt. The man was not Stoveville. That puzzled Lonnie; touched the boy with apprehension. He'd thought there was only one lawman in Arapaho Creek, and that lawman was Marshal Stoveville. Though he was sitting down, this lawman appeared tall and lean, with a high forehead from which thin strands of sandy-brown hair were swept straight back. He had a black mole as large as a silver dollar on his left cheek.

Scowling at Lonnie as though peeved at the interruption in his affairs, the lawman—Lonnie saw that his badge said "Deputy Town Marshal"—removed a smoldering cigarette from between his teeth, and blew smoke at the open doorway. "Hey, kid, I think I heard your mom callin'. Suppertime!"

The large woman in the skimpy red dress closed her upper teeth over her bottom lip as though to stifle a snicker.

Lonnie looked around the room. They were the only two here.

The boy adjusted the heavy bags on his shoulders and said, "I'm lookin' for Marshal Stoveville."

The woman looked at the man, who took a drag from the quirley, slitting his eyes against the rising smoke, and said, "Over at the Ace of Diamonds." He blew out another long smoke plume toward Lonnie. His eyes, which were the same color as the mole on his cheek, glittered with mockery.

The boy said, "Obliged," and, anxiety eating at him—he hadn't thought Stoveville *had* any deputies—turned and walked back down the porch steps. Behind him, the woman snickered. The boy looked down the street on his right, saw a collection of jostling shadows in a large pool of light spilling out of a building a block away, and patted the General's wither.

Quietly, he said, "Stay, boy. I'll be back soon. I'm gonna get shed of these bags, and we'll get shed of this trash heap."

He could have left the bags with the man who was presumably Stoveville's deputy, but Lonnie didn't trust anyone except the town marshal himself. Besides, he hadn't liked the look in the deputy's eyes. They'd been cold and cunning, sort of like Shannon Dupree's eyes.

Dupree...

Lonnie looked around for the outlaw and his "the boys" once more. He couldn't see much of anything except shadows on the street, but none appeared to be moving toward Lonnie. He adjusted the saddlebags on his shoulder again, and drew a deep breath, steeling himself for his journey into the crowded saloon but also buoyed by the thought that Stoveville would soon relieve him of his burden.

Lonnie moved through a cluster of men gathered in front of the saloon's batwing doors. The men looked at him strangely, frowning curiously at the bags on Lonnie's shoulder. Lonnie kept his head down and kept moving, pushing through the doors and into the saloon which assaulted him instantly with the nearly overwhelming stench of alcohol and tobacco fumes laced liberally with the smell of unwashed bodies and stale sweat and women's perfume.

There were between a dozen and twenty men in the place, and three or four ladies...if you could call them ladies, dressed as they were. They were all obscured by dull light and shadows and the wafting webs of tobacco smoke. Lonnie couldn't pick Dwight Stoveville out of the crowd.

Several faces turned toward Lonnie as he made his way over to the bar. The man behind the bar was large and as round as a rain barrel, with a soiled green apron straining across his waist. He'd been drawing beer from a tap and frowning curiously at Lonnie, who stopped between two men much taller than he at the bar, and stretched his gaze over the edge of the bar to meet the barman's quizzical gaze.

"I'm lookin' for the marshal."

The barman couldn't hear above the din, so Lonnie had to repeat himself. Deep lines stretched across the barman's forehead. He glanced at the two men nearest Lonnie who were staring down at the boy with expressions similar to the barman's.

Then the barman said, *"Stoveville?"*

"That's right."

"Stoveville's in the gamblin' den," the barman said after glancing once more at the two patrons standing in front of Lonnie, both now smirking down at him. "Gamblin' den," the barman repeated, canting his large head toward the back of the room.

Lonnie moved off down the bar. He didn't look at any of the men lined up to his right, leaning against the bar top. All were glancing back and down at the boy with the bulging saddlebags draped over his right shoulder. Lonnie was going to feel light as a feather as soon as he turned Dupree's loot over to Stoveville. He was so eager to do that, in fact, that he had to fight off the urge to sprint to the back of the room and into the gambling den, where Stoveville was likely playing poker with his cronies.

The closed door at the back of the room, behind the stairs that climbed to the saloon's second story where only God knew what went on, opened suddenly. Two well-dressed gents stepped out, both setting their bowler hats on their heads. They had grave expressions and they were talking amongst themselves, both shaking their heads, but they stopped the instant they saw Lonnie.

SIXTEEN

THE TWO WELL-DRESSED gents scowled down at the boy, who ignored them as he stepped around them and strode through the half-open door.

He vaguely heard several snickers behind him, but he couldn't hear much of anything above the ringing in his ears as he stared into the gambling den that was rife with the stale smells of tobacco smoke, liquor, and varnish and was furnished with several baize-covered tables and a roulette wheel. What had caught the brunt of Lonnie's attention, however, were the two pine coffins sitting on either side of the room, each straddling two abutting billiard tables.

A girl in a black dress and a small straw black hat with a veil of black lace sat near the coffin on the right. She had her head down and she was quietly sobbing into a white handkerchief. She wore black gloves, and her hair was pulled behind her head in a thick braid of sorts. A French braid, Lonnie thought it was called.

On the floor to her left, a man's dark-green Stetson sat crown down. Green bills poked up around the sweatband. A collection hat.

Lonnie again felt his blood quicken and his throat turn dry. He stood frozen inside the doorway, looking around for Stoveville, the ringing in his ears gradually growing louder as he started moving slowly forward. He tried to step as lightly as he could, so that his heels wouldn't thud too loudly on the wooden floor, and his spurs wouldn't ching.

He stared into the casket nearest the girl. When the corpse's face became visible, Lonnie stopped and stared, aghast. The man in the casket was Marshal Stoveville. The marshal wore a dark-blue suit over a white cotton shirt with a celluloid collar and a string tie, and his light-gray hair was combed sideways across his head. His brushy mustache nearly hid the thin, purple line of his mouth. His large hands that looked waxy beneath their deep tan were crossed on the bulge of his belly.

Most startling to Lonnie were the two large silver coins that had been placed over his eyes. Beneath the rose petals, the man's eyes appeared not quite closed, as though Stoveville were merely pretending he was dead. A foxy smile quirked his mouth corners.

He was not pretending to be dead, though. The man whom Lonnie had ridden all this way to deliver the money to was really, truly dead.

As the girl continued to sob quietly into her hanky, Lonnie stepped over to the other casket. His eyes had no sooner found the face of the second corpse with the puckered purple hole in the pale band around the dead man's forehead just above his eyes, than Lonnie took one loud, stumbling step backward, and said much louder than he would have liked, *"Oh, God!"*

He may have only gotten a fleeting look at the face of the man he'd inadvertently killed, back when he'd killed him, but he knew that he was getting a much longer look at him here, in his casket. This man had a pink, sunburned face and shaggy brown mustache and goatee, but now his face looked waxy behind the burn. His eyes were also covered with coins.

To Lonnie's right, the girl stopped sobbing. She sniffed, cleared her throat, and said, "Who're you?"

Her voice had sounded far, far away. Lonnie's mind was spinning so fast that it took him nearly fifteen seconds after he'd turned toward the girl to realize that the face peering at him from behind the black lace veil was beautiful. Lightly freckled and tanned behind the mourning veil, with expressive hazel eyes and a straight, fine nose.

He recognized her. He'd seen her in McGuffin's Mercantile several times, but it had only taken him one time, his first time, to have fallen head over heels in love with the girl, whom he guessed was close to his own age, maybe a little older. Of course, he'd never introduced himself or inquired about her name. There'd be no way he could have ever spoken to a girl as beautiful and self-possessed and assured as she had always seemed.

He'd admired her from afar, looking forward to each infrequent visit to town, so he could lay his eyes on her again in the mercantile and fantasize about her someday being his.

Seeing her here, with these dead men, merely added to Lonnie's confusion.

He must have been staring at her like a nitwit, because as she gazed back at him from behind her veil, her gold-blonde brows became more and more furled until she said slowly, annunciating each word clearly, as though she were speaking to a half-wit, "Your name. I asked you your *name*. And what on God's green earth do you have in those *saddlebags*?"

"In what?"

The girl studied Lonnie through the veil and then turned her head slowly toward the casket containing the body of the man he'd killed. "Sorry about Willie," she said. "He was a good man, I reckon. Anyways, Pa seemed to think he was worth his salt as a part-time deputy." She paused. "How did you know him?"

"Oh, I...uh...just knew him," Lonnie said, wondering if the saddlebags were visibly leaping up and down on his shoulder from the mad beating of his heart. "Just knew him...that's all." He could think of little else except pulling his picket pin as fast he could, before he ran into the other deputy —the one who was still alive and would most likely recognize Lonnie. He hadn't recognized the deputy with the mole on his cheek. The boy didn't think he'd been the one with Willie.

When had Stoveville hired three deputies, and why?

"I'm sorry if he was your friend. You looked pretty shocked, seein' him there."

"Yeah." Lonnie raked his gaze away from the man he'd killed, toward the girl. He tried not to betray the fact that he was shaking in his boots. "You're Stoveville's..."

"I'm his daughter. Casey. Who're you? I know I've seen you before but I can't place you. Maybe it's those big bags you're totin' around. If you're not careful, you're gonna tip over under all that weight."

"I'll manage," Lonnie said, shifting the bags on his shoulder. "I'm Lonnie Gentry."

"Ah. Your ma has an account over at the mercantile."

"That's right."

"I work there."

"I know."

Behind the gauzy, black veil, the girl's lipped quirked slightly in acknowledgment of that. Her eyes turned beleaguered once more as she shifted her head toward the coffin containing the marshal. Tears oozed out from their corners to dribble down her cheeks.

If he didn't find a way out of there soon, Lonnie thought he was going to start bawling, as well.

SEVENTEEN

CURIOSITY HELD Lonnie in that horrible room with the two dead men—Marshal Stoveville and the deputy Lonnie had killed—and Stoveville's pretty daughter.

The boy cleared his throat and asked Casey, "How did...how did your pa...?"

The girl sniffed. "Figured everybody knew by now. The bank in Golden was robbed. Pa got the telegram sayin' the robbers were headin' northwest. Him, two of his deputies, Willie Drake and Lou Dempsey, and a couple of other men from town rode out to cut 'em off at the southern pass. They cut 'em off, all right. But they didn't stop 'em. Pa was shot out of his saddle. Willie an' Dempsey kept after the robbers. This afternoon, Dempsey returned to Arapaho Creek with Willie shot in the head. Said they were bushwhacked by one of Dupree's gang."

Lonnie was sweating. The saddlebags were growing as heavy as a blacksmith's anvil on his shoulders. He looked from Stoveville's casket to the casket containing the man he'd killed.

The man he'd killed . . .

"What you got in them saddlebags?" Casey Stoveville asked him.

Lonnie jerked a startled look at her. His nerves were leaping like striking diamondbacks. He wondered if word about his mother and Dupree had worked its way as far as Arapaho Creek yet. It likely hadn't, or

Lonnie would have been eyed with suspicion, and so far, even carrying the bulging saddlebags, he hadn't.

He turned to the gambling parlor's half-open door through which the low roar of the drinkers in the main saloon emanated. He hurried over to the door, closed it, and walked back to stand in front of the girl, the words exploding out of him like Fourth of July firecrackers detonating in his mouth.

"This here's the money them robbers stole," he told the girl, eager to remove the weight from his exhausted shoulders. Suddenly, Lonnie couldn't speak fast enough as he said, "I found it up at our old line shack on Eagle Ridge. I came here lookin' for your pa, because I figured he was the only one I could trust to unload it on, but now..." He let his voice trail off. "I never realized he had so many deputies..."

The girl rose from her chair and said woodenly as she stared at the saddlebags, "He hired 'em last month, right after gold was discovered south of town...and a bad element started driftin' in...started driftin' in from Denver." She looked at Lonnie, beetling her pretty brows. "How on earth did you—?"

The door burst open. Lonnie jerked his head around to see the deputy from the marshal's office, and another man also wearing a badge stride into the gambling den. Lonnie almost fainted when he realized that the second man was the other deputy from up on Willow Run.

"Yep, that's him, all right," the second deputy said, stopping about six feet from Lonnie, cocking a hip, and folding his arms across his chest. He was tall, with long arms, like an ape, and relatively short legs. His beard was thick and pewter-colored, and he had one green and one blue eye. He wore a brown bowler hat and a wool vest over a white shirt, and patched broadcloth trousers.

He sneered at Lonnie. "That there's the kid who bushwhacked Willie —why, you little *demon!*"

"*What?*" exclaimed Casey Stoveville.

Lonnie's heart dropped into his boots. At the same time, righteous indignation swept through the boy like a wildfire, and he yelled, "That ain't true an' you know it! You two was takin' potshots at me. I tried to get away and you kept comin', and then I dropped my rifle in the stream, and..."

Lonnie let his voice trail off. The deputy he'd seen in the marshal's office, Chase, and the second deputy, Lou Dempsey, were coming at him hard and fast, gritting their teeth, eyes fiery. Behind them, the other men from the saloon were pushing through the open door to get a look at what was happening in the gambling parlor.

"This little jasper killed Willie!" Dempsey shouted at the top of his lungs.

He and the deputy Lonnie knew only as Chase were all over Lonnie, grabbing his arms. Lonnie didn't know what to do. Chase and Dempsey had kill-crazy gleams in their eyes while the men crowded together in the doorway and spilling into the room behind them looked grim, grave, angry.

Lonnie jerked free of the two men's grips. Dempsey was likely lying because he didn't want anyone to know that he and Willie Drake had shot at a thirteen-year-old boy first. That would make them look stupid and inept, which both obviously were. Or, at least, Willie *had been,* before Lonnie had drilled him. Lonnie knew that no one would likely listen to his story, however. He looked wildly around for another way out of the gambling parlor.

But there was only one door, and it was filled with head-wagging townsmen holding beer mugs or shot glasses and, in some cases, burning cigars. Even if Lonnie could get to the door, he'd never get through it.

As Lonnie backed into a billiard table at the front of the room, Dempsey and Chase still coming at him, he held his arms up, palms out. He had no choice but to try to explain himself. "Hold on!" he yelled. "Let me tell it the way it *really* happened, galldangit!"

"Save if for the circuit judge," snarled Dempsey, gritting his teeth as he grabbed Lonnie's right arm while Chase grabbed the boy's other arm.

"That kid's Lonnie Gentry!" a man's voice thundered at the back of the room. The beefy bartender was pointing at Lonnie with one arm while planting his other fist on a broad, apron-clad hip, his face as red as a well-stoked fire. "He's Calvin Gentry's boy! Calvin's widow's been shackin' up with Shannon Dupree for over a year now!" The barman snarled like an angry mountain lion. "When he ain't been off robbin' banks, that is! Apparently, he's taken Calvin's boy down the garden path!"

The onlookers muttered their shock, eyes widening in sudden understanding.

"I thought I recognized that kid!" yelled one of the other townsmen, looking over the shoulders of several others in front of him.

Another townsman shouted, "Sure enough, I seen May Gentry ridin' with Dupree in a buggy up near Bachelor Gulch. May's kid threw in with Dupree and his thievin' killin' ways! Oh, how could ya *do it,* boy?"

"I didn't throw in with Dupree!" Lonnie screamed, trying in vain to pull his arms free of the much larger, beefier deputies. "If I threw in with him, what am I doin' here in town...*with the money he stole from Golden?*"

One of the townsmen stepped away from the crowd and crouched over the saddlebags that Lonnie had dropped on the floor near where Casey Stoveville was standing with her back to her father's casket. The girl appeared to be in stone-faced shock. The townsman glanced darkly up at Lonnie, frowning, then he unbuckled the strap on one of the saddlebag pouches.

He lifted the flap and dipped his hand carefully inside, looking tense, as though he was afraid the pouch was filled with rattlesnakes. Slowly, he pulled out his hand filled with a green pack of bills.

"Sure enough," the man said, staring in awe at the bills in his hand.

"Crafty," one of the other men from the crowd said, stepping forward. He was short and plump, with long, coarse gray hair tumbling down from his bowler hat. He wore a three-piece butterscotch suit with black patent half boots. "The kid's crafty, all right. Prob'ly double-crossed Dupree and stopped here for grub on his way over the mountain!"

The men around him laughed and roared their agreement.

Dempsey said, "What should we do with him, Mayor?"

The little, plump man officiously rose up on the balls of his half boots and canted his head to one side. "I don't care how young he is. Hang a killin' child and save yourself the trouble of hangin' a killin' man later! Toss him in the hoosegow. I'll cable the judge first thing in the mornin', and we'll try him and hang him in the town square before the week is out!"

The crowd roared.

"Hangin's too good for that little catamount!" a disembodied voice cried.

EIGHTEEN

LONNIE COULDN'T BELIEVE what he was hearing. He wanted to yell back at the men around him, to explain himself, but what good would it do him? They'd never be able to hear him above their own roaring.

Willie Drake must have been roundly liked. The town was out for blood. These men were only too eager to play cat's cradle with Lonnie Gentry's head!

"That don't make sense," Lonnie couldn't help saying as Chase and Dempsey began leading him across the room toward the crowd spread out in front of and around the door. "Why would I bring the money to town if I was in with Dupree?"

He'd been only talking to himself. No one could have heard him above the din.

"Hold on!" a girl's voice sounded behind him and the men holding fast to each of his arms.

Chase and Dempsey stopped and turned Lonnie around. Casey Stoveville stood before Lonnie. Her flushed cheeks were wet with tears. Her hazel eyes were wide and bright with rage. "If you killed Willie," she said through gritted teeth, "you just as easily could've killed my pa!"

Lonnie opened his mouth to protest but before he could get a single word out, the girl cocked her right arm back and swung her balled fist forward. She bunched her lips and winced as she smashed her fist against Lonnie's left cheek.

It wasn't like any punch you'd think a girl would throw. It was a hard, crushing blow. Pain was a railroad spike hammered through Lonnie's jaw and into his brain plate. He flew backward and would have hit the floor if both deputies hadn't been hanging onto him, and kept him upright. Laughing, they turned him around and half dragged him into the parting crowd and through the door of the gambling den.

Lonnie must have passed out for a minute because the next thing he knew he was being dragged along the street, his head hanging so that he could see his boot toes carving slender furrows in the dirt and finely ground horse manure. He couldn't remember being hauled through the saloon's main drinking hall. Then he was being dragged past the General, who gave a shrill, indignant whinny when the horse saw the unceremonious way his rider was being treated.

The deputies jerked Lonnie up the steps of the town marshal's office.

"You little demon!" Dempsey snarled as he and his partner hauled Lonnie to one of the three jail cells lined up along the rear of the dimly lit office. He turned to his partner, cementing his story. "Shot Willie in the head! Never even gave him a chance. You should have seen him in action! Never seen the like! Well, you won't get no chance to grow up, kid, and that's bond!" This last was shouted as Lonnie was shoved into the cell, stumbling and falling onto the cell's hard cot as the deputies slammed the cell door behind him with a rattling *clang!*

Lonnie sat up, touched fingers to his cheek, oily with blood. Chase and Dempsey stared in at him as Dempsey turned the key in the cell door's lock.

"Hah!" Dempsey laughed. "Miss Stoveville got you good, didn't she?" He glanced at Chase. "Did you see that cute little gal wind up on him?"

"Yeah, I seen her," Chase said, laughing. Lonnie found Chase staring at him critically. "Hey, you sure this kid shot Willie, Demps? He don't look like the type that would shoot a man, especially a lawman, from bushwhack."

"I didn't shoot nobody from bushwhack!" Lonnie said sharply, sitting on the edge of the cot, frustrated down to the heels of his boots. "Them two—him and Willie—bushwhacked *me*, just like I said. I ran and tried to get away, but they kept comin'...and shootin'."

"Don't listen to him, Chase." Dempsey tugged at his pewter beard, blinked each of his unmatched eyes in turn. It seemed like his habit to not blink each unmatched eye at the same time, and he appeared to be scowling, even when he laughed. His eyes were deeply shadowed under a heavy brow bone. "He shot at us from bushwhack when we was about to fill our canteens at a spring. I figure Dupree must have sent the kid to check their back trail. When he seen me and Willie, this yellow-toothed little devil laid in with a Winchester."

Lonnie got up and walked to the cell door. "Don't listen to him, Chase. He's lyin'!"

Dempsey glared through the bars at Lonnie. "You shut up, or I'll come in there and lay the strap to you. How would you like that?"

"You just try it!"

"All right—I will!"

Dempsey dropped his hands to his belt buckle, but before he could start unbuckling the belt, Chase swatted his partner's shoulder with the back of his hand. "Forget it. Leave him for the judge. I 'spect we'll be puttin' that gallows together before the week's out." Chase shook his head. "Too bad you an' Willie didn't know about his ma and Dupree. Could have gone right to the cabin, thrown a loop over Dupree and them other two renegades right then and there. The boy's ma, too. 'Stead of lettin' 'em lead you in circles."

Chase had the saddlebags draped over his shoulder. He turned toward the cluttered table that sat in the middle of the dingy, smelly jailhouse office. "Come on—let's see how much loot Dupree took out of the Golden bank."

Lonnie drew a deep breath and sagged back down on the edge of the cot. He probed his cheek with his fingers. Dempsey had been right. Miss Stoveville had really cut into him. He could feel a two-inch gash in the nub of his left cheek. The abrasion wasn't bleeding much, but it burned.

The cheek was the least of his concerns. He looked at the cell's three walls. There was a window in the rear wall, which was solid stone, but the window would have been too small for him to crawl through even if three stout iron bars hadn't crossed it.

Lonnie's goose was cooked.

The boy no longer even felt frustrated and angry. All he felt now was hollowed out and so tired that all he really wanted to do was sleep.

But then he thought about the General, and he looked at Chase and Dempsey, who had poured all the money packets out on the table and were staring down at all those greenbacks in shock.

"Hey, my horse needs tendin'," Lonnie said. "He needs feed and water. Get him over to a livery barn, will ya?"

He could never be so downtrodden that he did not think about the welfare of his horse.

"Shut up, kid," said Dempsey, staring down at the money. All those greenbacks piled up in packets on the table had the deputy riveted. "We'll tend your horse when we're good and ready. Hot diggity—look at all that money!"

"How much you suppose is there?" asked Chase in a hushed tone, fingering the large, dark mole on his cheek. Lonnie thought they were both going to doff their hats, get down on one knee, and cross themselves.

Even the jailed, downtrodden boy admitted there was a lot of dinero strewn about that table. That much money could buy a whole lot of things.

"Let's find out," Dempsey said, pulling a chair out from the opposite side of the table from Chase. He'd sat down and was starting to roll up his shirtsleeves when someone knocked on the jailhouse door.

The first person Lonnie thought of was Dupree, and fear grew in the boy once again.

NINETEEN

DEMPSEY AND CHASE leapt to their feet, drawing their pistols and clicking the hammers back.

Lonnie was glad they were on their toes. If Dupree came calling, as he was bound to do, Lonnie would be dead sooner rather than later. Lonnie didn't put it past the outlaw to storm the jailhouse and kill the deputies...as well as Lonnie...before retaking the loot. Lonnie didn't really know why it mattered how he died—by the rope or by Dupree—but it seemed to.

Maybe he didn't want Dupree to have the satisfaction.

"Who is it?" Chase called, aiming his Colt at the jailhouse door.

"Mayor Teagarden," said the voice on the other side of the door.

"Come on in, Mayor," Dempsey said, letting his pistol sag slightly in his hand though he did not uncock the weapon or holster it.

The door opened and the pudgy little man in the butterscotch suit stepped over the threshold, his fingers in the pockets of his wool vest. He grinned when he saw the money, showing one silver front tooth. "Just...uh...just wanted to make sure the Golden money was secure..."

"Oh, we've secured it, Mister Mayor," Chase said.

"Maybe you'd better lock it up in one of the cells for the night."

"Oh, we will, Mister Mayor," Dempsey assured the man, and grinned. "As soon as we count it. First thing in the mornin', one of us'll saddle up and ride it back to Golden, get it back in the bank where it belongs. We wanna make sure it's all there. Who knows—the kid might've spent some of it or maybe hid some along the trail."

Lonnie rolled his eyes. He was too miserable to do anything else in protest of his predicament.

Mayor Teagarden strolled over to the table and stared down at the money. He whistled. "That'd sure buy someone a trouble-free life—eh, fellas? Easy street all the way. And possibly a long vacation in San Francisco to boot!" The mayor laughed, keeping his sparkling eyes on the money.

"Sure would," said Dempsey, holstering his six-shooter. "No doubt, that's what Shannon Dupree had in mind. Not to worry, though, Mister Mayor. I'll start out for Golden first thing in the mornin', deliver these here greenbacks to the bank."

"Well, you know what, fellas?" the mayor said, rising up and down on the toes of his half boots. "I was headin' over to Golden on business tomorrow. I can throw them saddlebags in my buggy, toss a blanket over 'em to make sure nobody knows what I'm haulin', and I'll have 'em there by the end of the week."

Chase and Dempsey glanced at each other. They held each other's gazes for about three seconds, both men wrinkling the skin above their noses in silent, wistful communication.

Chase said, "Ah, no, no, Mister Mayor. We couldn't ask you to do that. Haulin' stolen money back to its rightful owner is a dangerous job. It's a job for the law. And me an' Dempsey here—with the chief marshal dead now, God rest his soul—are about the only law left in Arapaho Creek. That's a job for one of us."

"Maybe both of us," added Dempsey. "One to carry the loot, one to ride shotgun. It's a good three, four-day ride over the mountains to Golden. Who knows where Shannon Dupree is about now? If the kid double-crossed that outlaw, he's probably on his way to Arapaho Creek."

"Yeah, no, sir, Mister Mayor." Chase walked over and drew the front door open as though inviting the mayor to leave. "Haulin' that loot is a job for armed lawmen. It'll be a dangerous trek over to Golden, but me and Dempsey'll make 'er, all right. That's what we get paid for, after all."

The mayor winced visibly at the proclamation. He studied the money on the table for a time, probing his silver tooth with his tongue, before he glanced at both lawmen suspiciously. "Yes, well, I suppose it would be a job for the law." He chuckled deviously and switched his gaze back and forth between the two deputies. "You boys don't let all this tinder go to your heads now, and do somethin'—well, somethin' *dishonorable,* now, you hear?"

Chase and Dempsey laughed as though it were the funniest joke they'd ever heard. When the mayor had strolled out through the door and Dempsey had closed the door and turned the key in the inside lock, securing the bolt, he turned to Dempsey and said, "Why, that old coot was seriously considerin' makin' off with that loot. I know he was!"

He stared at Chase, who remained standing by the table. The men stared at each other for a long time in silent conversation. Their eyes grew at once brighter and darker as malicious thoughts stole across their brains.

"Uh-oh," Lonnie thought, sitting on the edge of his cot. It wasn't hard to read these two scoundrels' simple minds.

Both deputies turned their heads to regard Lonnie through the cell's barred door. He and Dempsey said at the same time, "What about the kid?"

They turned to each other again, and Chase said with quiet menace, "Well, we're gonna have to keep him good and quiet for a long, long time."

"How we gonna do that?" Dempsey asked.

Chase glowered at Lonnie through the barred door and loosened his pistol in its holster, caressing the hammer with his thumb. "How else?"

TWENTY

LONNIE STARED at Chase's thumb fondling the hammer of the Colt's revolver snugged down in the man's black holster thonged to his right thigh.

Emotion heaved in Lonnie's tired brain and exhausted body, and he couldn't stop himself from running up to the door, wrapping both his hands around the bars, and yelling, "You two can't kill me! You can't steal the bank money!" He was so flabbergasted that he thought his head would explode.

Chase glared back at him from the table, lips stretched slightly back from his teeth.

Lonnie switched his gaze to Dempsey, who remained in front of the door. Dempsey wore an even more savage and cunning look than Chase. Lonnie remembered something he'd heard Dupree say once about most lawmen being a hair's breadth from being outlaws and that most *had been* outlaws at one time and likely would be again.

For some reason, it was the only thing Dupree had ever said that Lonnie had paid much attention to.

The statement had riled Lonnie. He'd wanted to yell at Dupree, "You'd like to think that, but it ain't true! Lawmen are good men! They'd never break the laws they were sworn to enforce! You just want to believe they would so you can feel better about yourself!"

Now, the boy was glad he hadn't said that. What a fool he'd have been.

He could see in the eyes of these unwashed, sweaty, unshaven lawmen that they were every bit as bad as Dupree. And they'd have no more trouble killing a thirteen-year-old boy than they'd have shooting a chicken-thieving coyote.

Lonnie had been about to lay into Dempsey, but he saw now he'd just be wasting his breath. He'd run into lawmen no better than the men who'd stolen the money that his trip to Arapaho Creek had been about returning.

In other words, he'd come to the end of his trail, which was what a friend of his father's had told Lonnie after his father's passing of a heart stroke in bed only four years after he'd fought so hard in the War Between the States.

He'd come to the end of his trail...

The idea wasn't new to Lonnie. He himself had almost died several times in the past day. Still, to be facing the two men who were going to do the dirty deed while he himself was trapped behind bars and helpless, nearly caused him to whiz down his leg. His mouth went dry and his tongue swelled.

He switched his gaze between his two executioners, felt tears well in his eyes, and tried to get control of himself. He wouldn't break down. He wouldn't cry. He had enough sand in his hide, young as it was, to not give up that easy.

"You think we oughta do it, Dempsey?" Chase asked, still staring into the cell at Lonnie. He was opening and closing his fists slowly. His eyes were large and round and white-ringed like the General's when the horse saw a rattler or scented a wildcat on the wind. The big mole had turned black. It appeared to pulsate, like a small heart.

Chase was nervous.

Dempsey sat down at the table and started pawing through the money. "This here's more money than either you or I will ever see again, Chase. We gonna let one thievin', outlaw brat stand in our way of bein' rich?"

"I won't tell," Lonnie said weakly, still holding onto the bars of the door and staring bleakly, forlornly out. "I won't tell no one. You can take the money and go. I won't tell who took it. Besides, they'll know who took it, anyway, even if I'm not alive to tell 'em!"

"They'll know *when* we took it," Dempsey said. "If we leave tonight, head for Mexico, we'll have several hours' head start on a posse."

"It didn't help matters that you done just told him where we're goin'!"

Chase chastised his partner in crime, laughing caustically as he turned away from Lonnie and moved to the table.

"Heck," Lonnie said, "where else would you go? Besides, I'll keep my mouth shut. If you leave right now, you can be in Arizona by the end of the week! No one will even find me in here until then! Lock the door! I'll keep quiet!"

"Nah," Dempsey said, spreading out the packets of banded bills. He was blinking each eye hard. "My plan is to leave a note, say Dupree came and stole the money from us, and we went after him. That'll give us several days' head start. Folks might think the story's a mite fishy, but they won't inform the marshal over in Camp Collins for several days, after we don't return. Hell, we'll probably be across the border by then."

Chase sat down across from Dempsey, chuckling. "Sorry, kid. I reckon there's no other way."

Anger burned in Lonnie. He squeezed the bars, trying to twist them. "You two ever killed a kid before? A thirteen-year-old boy with his whole life ahead of him? You really think you got the spleen to do somethin' that mean and low-down and just plain nasty? Why, every time you spend a penny of that there money, you're gonna remember the kid you killed so's you could make a clean break with it!"

"Shut up, kid," Dempsey growled, blinking. "Or I'll shoot you right now, tell anyone who asks that you were tryin' to escape."

Chase was counting the bills but paused to say, "And no one'll shed a tear. Not for the thievin' brat of a woman who took up with a curly wolf like Shannon Dupree."

Then he went back to counting.

Lonnie watched them for a time, stricken. Distantly, he heard them say they'd ride out at midnight, after the rest of the town had gone to bed. They'd take Lonnie out of town, shoot him, and toss him into a deep ravine where the wolves would pick his young bones clean.

Feeling choked as though by a hangman's noose, Lonnie backed up to the cot and sagged down on top of it, helpless. His only chance, he figured, was to try and make a break for it when they opened the cell door. It was a long shot but probably the only shot he'd get.

He was younger than they and fast on his feet. General Sherman was still outside. If Lonnie could get onto his horse, he'd point the General in the direction of the far hills, slap the spurs to him, and never return to the cesspool that was Arapaho Creek ever again.

A long shot, but it was the only chance he had...

There was a cuckoo clock on the otherwise unadorned stone wall over Stoveville's desk. At the top of each hour, a blue-headed yellow bird stepped out onto the door that opened for it, and chirped once with tooth-gnashing shrillness for each hour of the day.

The deputies must have been accustomed to the bird. They didn't seem to mind it chirping like that, like a door on rusty hinges being opened quickly several times in a row. Or maybe they were too immersed in the poker game they'd started playing with their newfound wealth after they'd finished counting the money and finding they were now each worth a little over thirty thousand dollars apiece.

They sat back in their chairs, playing poker and grinning and taking pulls from the bottle they'd hauled out of Stoveville's desk, and smoked cigars they'd found in the desk, as well. While they played, they talked over their plans for a life of leisure down in Mexico. Sometimes they sang or whistled absently or told a dirty joke while they puffed their cigars and threw back the whiskey. Occasionally, they chuckled in anticipation of midnight, when, rich men, they'd ride on out of Arapaho Creek forever.

After they'd silence the kid, of course.

TWENTY-ONE

LONNIE GOT SO that he hated the cuckoo bird so much he'd have shot it off its perch if he'd had his rifle.

Of course, it wasn't just the bird making him nervous as a cat in an attic full of rocking chairs. He was going to die tonight, sometime after midnight, and no one would ever know how it had happened or why, and they'd never find a body to take home to his ma for burial.

His ma...

He wondered what had happened when Dupree had discovered his money gone.

Dupree...

Where were Dupree and "the boys", anyway? Lonnie almost wouldn't have minded seeing the outlaw. At least, Dupree would throw a wrench into the lawmen's plans for the boy, though Dupree's intentions for Lonnie likely wouldn't be any rosier than those of Deputies Dempsey and Chase.

At the last chirp of midnight, Lonnie's heart stopped beating. At least, it felt like it stopped. Then, as Chase and Dempsey shoved all the money back into the saddlebags, and Dempsey headed out to fetch a couple of horses from a livery barn, Lonnie's heart turned two hard somersaults.

He looked at the small window high in the cell's back wall. He was compelled to jump up and start screaming for help through the window, but he doubted anyone would hear through the small opening and from behind the thick stone walls. Besides, Chase, who was finishing shoving some gear into a war bag for the trail ahead, would likely make good on his promise to shoot Lonnie right here and tell anyone who cared to ask that the outlaw boy had been trying to make a break for it.

Make a break for it...

Lonnie sat on the edge of the cot, waiting. He looked at the jailhouse's main door. As soon as either deputy opened the cell door, Lonnie would turn himself into a human arrow flying toward that outside door and freedom waiting beyond.

And, ten minutes later, that's what he did.

When Dempsey opened the cell door, Lonnie bounded off his heels and threw himself straight at Dempsey. But the last thing he saw before everything went black was Dempsey's smiling face and the cell door slamming toward Lonnie's head.

The next thing Lonnie knew, he was watching a night-dark trail slide past his outstretched fingers. His stomach and ribs ached, as though a giant were sitting on his hips. His head ached as though he'd been bludgeoned with a sledgehammer. Blinking and shaking away the cobwebs that had grown up thick as gypsum weed inside his head, he saw that what was crushing his guts against his spine was his own saddle.

Dempsey and Chase had thrown Lonnie belly-down across the General's back, and he was riding with his head hanging down the buckskin's right side while his legs and boots dangled down the General's left side. Ropes were tied around his wrists. The ropes stretched beneath the General's belly, and, while Lonnie couldn't see his ankles from his unfortunate position, he could feel that they were tied.

Tied to his wrists beneath the buckskin's belly.

He was being hauled through the night like a tied-down load of freight.

A load of human freight that would soon be nothing more than a midnight snack for the carrion eaters...

He turned his face to stare ahead along the trail. He could see the rumps of two horses and two jostling tails about ten yards beyond. It was a dark night but there was enough light from the stars that he could see that Dempsey was leading the General by the bridle reins. The two men rode slowly along the trail, their horses' hooves thumping dully in the well-churned dust.

Around Lonnie were dark pines reaching toward the stars. He could feel the cool, high-country air ensconcing him, making him shiver, and smell the tang of pine resin.

Vaguely, he wondered where they were. They seemed to be climbing, probably toward a southern pass. Soon the men would stop and do away with Lonnie. They were likely waiting until they were far enough from Arapaho Creek that no one in town would hear the shot, and remote enough that no one would ever find Lonnie's body.

No one but the wolves that stalked this stretch of the Never Summers.

Lonnie rode, wincing with each jarring step of his horse. He felt as though his spine was going to saw into his belly from the back side, and as though the jostling of the ride was going to pound the boy's brains to such pulp inside his skull that they'd ooze out his ears.

Finally, mercifully, the General stopped.

The misery in Lonnie's belly and head tapered off a little.

Then, not so mercifully, Chase climbed down from his horse and walked back to where Lonnie's head hung down the General's side.

"Sorry, junior," the deputy-turned-outlaw said, "but you've come to the end of your trail."

He took out a big knife and sawed through the ropes.

TWENTY-TWO

WHEN THE ROPES fell away from Lonnic's wrists and ankles, his first thought was to slide off his horse and to run as fast as he could. But before he could start to work himself off the General's back, he was "helped" down by Dempsey from behind.

The deputy dug his hand into the waistband of Lonnie's denim trousers, and gave a wicked pull. The boy grunted loudly as he fell from the horse like a fifty-pound sack of chicken feed. He hit the ground on his spurs and fell on his butt only to be picked up again by his collar, and thrust off the trail and away from the horses. He was so weak from his run-in with the cell door that he dropped to his knees, his head pounding.

Fear had covered him from head to toe with cold sweat.

He looked around.

They were in a clearing ringed with the arrow shapes of pine tops silhouetted against the starry sky. The quarter moon was climbing, offering wan light below the level of the trees but beginning to dim the stars. A flame-shaped mountain was silhouetted against the moon's violet glow, straight ahead of Lonnie.

The air was cool enough up here that Lonnie could see his breath. The chill didn't stop him from sweating. It just made the perspiration colder as it dripped down from between his shoulder blades to cause his shirt to cling to his lower back.

He thought he could see a cabin about a hundred yards ahead and on his right. The moonlight touched its flat roof. Abandoned, no doubt. For some reason it made this clearing feel all the emptier, lonelier. A wolf's howl emanating from somewhere on that black, velvet, flame-shaped mountain added menace to the emptiness and loneliness.

So this was where he would take his last breath. He'd wondered about his end on cold winter nights when he hadn't had enough work the previous day to tire him out. So, here it was.

From behind he could hear boots crunching grass and sage branches raking trouser cuffs. Chase's voice said in a drunken slur, "Get up, kid. Move out there a ways."

"What's the matter, Chase?" Dempsey said, also dragging his words though not as badly as Chase. His tone was slightly mocking. "Don't want him to be too close when you put a bullet in him?"

"I don't care how close he is," Chase snarled at his partner. "I don't want the shot to scare the horses."

"Oh, good thinkin'," Dempsey said with the same note of mockery.

"Hey, you wanna do it?"

"I would do it," Dempsey said, "but we flipped for it, remember? You lost."

Lonnie's heart turned another couple of somersaults as he looked around again and saw that even if he could bring himself to run—his boots felt as though they'd been filled with dry mud—he couldn't see any sheltering tree within fifty yards. All that was out here were trees and the cabin that was way off across the clearing.

Chase pressed the barrel of his pistol against the back of Lonnie's head. "Come on, kid. Get movin'. You're only drawin' this out."

Lonnie climbed wearily to his feet. Sweat dripped under his arms. He heard his voice quiver as he said, "I'm gonna come back and haunt you two. I'm gonna come back and haunt you two until you get heart strokes and die like my pa died—in your *beds!* And then you're both gonna take that long walk down them warm, stone steps until you're in Hell shakin' hands with the *Devil!*"

That thought made Lonnie feel better.

"I said get movin'!" Chase yelled.

"No!" Lonnie spat through gritted teeth. He wheeled to face Chase and Dempsey. "If you're gonna kill me, you're gonna have to do it straight on and close up!" He balled his fists at his sides and leaned forward at the waist, his rage overwhelming him. "Come on, you yellow-livered coward!"

"Why, you...!" Chase clicked the hammer of his Colt back and aimed the barrel at Lonnie's forehead.

The gun barked.

The sudden explosion caused Lonnie to stumble straight back. His spurs raked the ground. He tripped and fell on his rump and found himself, apparently with his skull still intact, staring at Chase who'd given a yelp and twisted around as though a snake had bitten his leg.

Chase's revolver popped and flashed. The bullet slammed into the ground between the outlaw and Lonnie, and dust and grass blew up over Lonnie's boots.

"What in the—?"

Another thundering crash cut Dempsey off.

He yelped and threw away the pistol he'd drawn as though it were a hot skillet handle. He cursed and grabbed his right forearm.

The report of what Lonnie now recognized as a rifle sounded again, knifing across the otherwise silent clearing. This shot took Chase down, howling and kicking. There was another flash in the forest to Lonnie's left, and the bullet spanged off a rock to warm the air just off his own right cheek.

The boy threw himself belly-down and buried his head in his arms as he thought, *"Dupree!"*

The rifle crashed several more times, the shots spaced about two seconds apart, and a voice called, crisp and clear on the suddenly quiet air, "Lonnie!"

Lonnie lifted his head slightly. He blinked. He could have sworn the voice had been a girl's. Nah. His ears were ringing from fear and the clamor of the rifle.

"Lonnie, I didn't hit you, did I?"

No, it was a girl's voice, all right.

Befuddled, Lonnie lowered his arms and raised his head higher. He looked off to where the gun had flashed in the dark mass of the trees, and he said uncertainly and not loudly, "I reckon I'll be all right if you hold your fire...whoever you are."

"It's Casey!"

"Casey?"

"Casey Stoveville. Stay where you are and keep your head down in case I have to start shootin' again!"

"All right," Lonnie said, again uncertainly.

Nearby, Chase and Dempsey were moaning and groaning.

Dempsey shouted hoarsely, "Hold your fire! Hold your fire! Who in tarnation you think you're shootin' at, little girl?"

There was another hiccupping cough and a rifle flash. The bullet plumed dust in front of Dempsey, who threw his head back on the ground, covered it with his arms, and cursed loudly.

His angry screams echoed shrilly around the clearing.

TWENTY-THREE

LONNIE LOOKED toward where the shots had been fired, and he could see a pale-tan silhouette taking shape against the trees.

The crunch of footsteps grew gradually louder. Just as gradually, the pale-tan silhouette took the shape of a short, slender person walking toward Lonnie and his two moaning, groaning assailants. The pale-tan shape became a tan canvas coat that hung to thighs clad in dark-blue denim trousers and calf-high boots.

Casey Stoveville's gold-blonde hair hung down from her man's tan hat to spill across her shoulders. Her eyes caught the starlight beneath the brim of her hat, and glistened. The starlight winked off the barrel of the Winchester carbine she held in her hands, downward slanted, ready to raise in an instant again if needed.

Dempsey spat and shouted, "Who you think you're shootin' at, you fool girl? Don't you know it's me—Dempsey and Chase, your pa's deputies—out here?"

The rifle belched and flashed again.

Dempsey cursed again, shrilly, as the bullet blew dirt and rocks over him.

"Who're you callin' a fool girl, you dung beetle?" Casey said as she stopped about ten feet from the two men writhing on the ground near Lonnie. "I heard all about your big plans for the stolen money through the jailhouse door."

"Hey, that's my rifle!" Lonnie said, recognizing the carbine in the girl's hands.

"Thanks for lettin' me borrow it out of your saddle sheath," Casey said. "It came in right handy. I would have requested help from some of the men in Arapaho Creek, but when I got to thinkin' about it, I could think of nary a one I could trust any more than I could trust my father's deputies."

She glanced at Lonnie. "Are you all right?"

Lonnie sat up and brushed his sleeve across his dirt-pelted face. "I'll live."

"Pa taught me how to shoot but it's been a while since I've had a practice session," she said.

"You did all right," Lonnie said.

"Sorry about your cheek."

"Like I said, I'll live."

Casey took another step forward, aiming the carbine at Chase and Dempsey while saying to Lonnie, "Get their guns." She raised her voice to the outlaws: "If either of you makes any sudden moves, I'm gonna cut loose with this Winchester again, and I'm close enough now to do some damage."

"You already shot us up, you fool girl!" This from Chase.

"If I hear one more 'fool girl' out of either one of you, you'll never say it again...or anythin' else."

The two deputies glanced at each other and didn't say anything.

Lonnie gained his feet. He walked cautiously over to Dempsey and Chase. Both of their revolvers were on the ground, glistening dully in the starlight. Lonnie picked them up, shoved one of the Colts behind his belt, and backed away from the men, cocking the second pistol and aiming it at the deputies.

He was still breathing hard and sweating. His vision swam. He was giddy to be alive after hovering so close to death.

He never wanted to get that close again.

Dempsey and Chase didn't look too badly hurt, despite their caterwauling. They looked as though Casey's bullets had mostly grazed their arms and legs. They were hurting, but neither one looked as though death were imminent. Not that Lonnie cared about either one of the scalawags.

Casey said, "Get up, both of you. Head on over to the horses."

"I don't think I can get up," Chase said. "You drilled a bullet through my thigh, you foo... I mean, Miss Casey."

Lonnie had to smile at that as he kept his pistol aimed at the pair.

"Much better," Casey said. "I like that. But if you can't stand, I'm goin' to shoot you where you sit. So you best get to your feet any way you can, and haul your fool self over to your horse."

"If you got these two covered, I'll fetch the mounts," Lonnie said.

"I got 'em," Casey said assuredly. "My horse is tied in the trees behind me."

Lonnie depressed the Colt's hammer and headed back toward the trail. The horses were spread out a good ways apart, having spooked at the shooting. General Sherman was nearest Lonnie, so Lonnie swung up onto the General's back and rode ahead to gather Chase and Dempsey's horses.

When he'd retrieved Casey's chestnut filly from the trees behind her, he rode out to where Chase and Dempsey had gotten to their feet and stood with their hands up, heads down, like schoolboys who'd been caught turning frogs loose in the girls' privy.

"They probably have some handcuffs in their saddlebags," Casey said.

Lonnie swung down from the General's back and rummaged around in Chase's saddlebags. He'd just wrapped his hand around something that felt like metal, when Casey screamed.

Lonnie whipped around.

Dempsey had lunged at the girl. As the outlaw, who was two heads taller than Casey, and twice as wide, fought the girl for the rifle, the carbine exploded.

Flames lapped skyward.

Dempsey ripped the rifle out of the girl's hands and clubbed her with the rifle's rear stock. Casey groaned and fell hard, rolling once, dust rising around her. Meanwhile, Dempsey cocked the carbine and swung toward Lonnie.

Lonnie had already drawn one of the two Colts he'd taken off the deputies. Without so much as thinking about it, he raised the weapon in both hands, clicked the hammer back, and aimed at Dempsey's murky shadow.

The pistol leaped and roared in Lonnie's hand.

Dempsey grunted and stepped straight back, his dark shadow hard to see against the line of black trees behind him. Dempsey lowered Lonnie's carbine, and flames stabbed from the barrel as the outlaw triggered the weapon into the ground. Dust flew up around his ankles.

Dempsey took another step back and dropped like a felled tree.

Lonnie clicked the Colt's hammer back and swung the pistol at Chase who had started to lunge toward Lonnie.

"You want some o' this?" the boy asked the deputy turned outlaw.

Chase jerked back, holding his hands up, palm out. He shook his head back and forth. "Nope, I sure don't."

TWENTY-FOUR

"I FIGURED YOU PROBABLY DIDN'T," Lonnie told Chase, grinning boldly. It felt good to be the one in control.

Lonnie looked at Dempsey, who was writhing on the ground, spurs ringing as they scratched the gravelly turf.

The spurs stopped ringing. Dempsey stopped writhing. Lonnie kept his pistol aimed at the fallen deputy. He rolled his eyes toward Casey, who was climbing to her feet with a grunt.

"You all right?" he asked the girl.

She was rubbing her right shoulder. "Yeah," she said, staring awfully down at the unmoving Dempsey. "Is...is he dead?"

"I don't know. Why don't you check? Don't worry, I'll cover you." To Chase, Lonnie said, "My trigger finger itches somethin' awful, so you best hold yourself real still. If you even think about tryin' what your friend tried, you'll end up like him."

"Kid," Chase snarled, "you got no respect for your elders."

"Only them that deserve it. I've run into precious few o' them."

Casey stood over Dempsey. "He looks dead to me," the girl said, her voice quaking slightly. It was also a little higher pitched than before. "Yeah, I'm pretty sure he's dead. I don't wanna touch him."

"That's all right," Lonnie said. "He looks dead to me, too."

Casey turned to Lonnie, her chest rising and falling sharply as she breathed. She swept her thick, blonde hair out of her face as she said, "Yep, you blew his lamp out, all right."

"Congratulations," Chase said. "That's your second lawman in two days."

"You wanna be my third?" Lonnie asked him, aiming the Colt at him.

Chase took another fearful step back, shaking his head. "Nope, I sure don't, kid."

———

LATER, when they were riding back toward Arapaho Creek, Lonnie turned to Casey riding her chestnut filly beside him. "What're we gonna do with this fella?" He canted his head toward Chase riding ahead of them.

Casey had secured the deputy's own handcuffs to the man's wrists behind his back while Lonnie had held his carbine on him. Now the lawman-turned-outlaw rode slouched in his saddle, sullen and silent. He occasionally grunted from the pain of his injuries, and spat to one side in frustration, but that was the extent of Chase's acting out.

Casey said levelly, "Throw him in my father's jail. Only place for such a polecat as that. First thing tomorrow, I'll send a cable to the deputy United States marshal over in Camp Collins. He'll probably ride over here and see to Chase and the bank loot himself."

The girl looked at Lonnie. "Sorry you had to do that. Kill Dempsey, I mean."

"It ain't like he didn't deserve it." Lonnie didn't feel as sick in his gut about shooting Dempsey as he had about the other deputy, Willie. Dempsey had been about to shoot Casey. Still, he knew he'd never forget these past couple of days as long as he lived.

"Was he right?" Casey asked him, her voice hesitant. "About...you shootin' Willie?"

Lonnie couldn't help feeling more than a little defensive. "I ain't no cold-blooded killer, Miss Casey, if that's what you mean."

"Don't get your neck in a hump," she said, ducking under a pine branch that bowed low over the trail. They were gradually dropping down into the canyon in which Arapaho Creek lay. Lonnie could tell they were approaching the town from the smell of the privies and the barking of a dog. "I wasn't beratin' you about it. I just wanted to know."

"Shootin' Willie wasn't what I had in mind when I started the day yesterday. If I hadn't shot him, I wouldn't be here. And neither, probably, would Dempsey and Willie. Them two would likely be headin' for Mexico about right now."

"I believe you."

Again, Lonnie looked at her riding to his left, her hair bouncing on her shoulders. So much had happened to him recently that he still hadn't quite worked his mind around the presence of a girl he'd fancied from afar. When that happened, his tongue would likely tie itself into a tight knot.

For the moment, however, he was too tired and hungry and anxious to be bashful around a pretty girl. "How come you've decided to believe me?" he asked her.

"After I got to thinkin' about it, I realized you wouldn't have come to town for any reason if you'd really been in with Shannon Dupree. I realized it after I left the saloon and started thinkin' it through. I went over to the jailhouse to talk to Chase and Dempsey, and I heard 'em talkin' through the door, discussin' their plans. So I went home, saddled Miss Abigail here"—she patted the chestnut's neck—"and waited for them to make their move."

Casey turned to Lonnie, and a smile caused her eyes to glitter in the light of the moon kiting over the tops of the pines lining both sides of the trail. "I'm right glad they didn't decide to kill you in the jail. Otherwise, I reckon..."

"I'd be dead."

"Somethin' like that," she said, gazing at him, her full, pink lips quirking a playful smile.

"I'm obliged to you, Miss Casey," he said.

Now it was happening, darn it. Casey's smile and that frank, humorous gaze through those pretty, hazel eyes were making his tongue start to thicken up, and he was having a hard time looking at her. He found it beguiling how her upper lip was a little thicker than her lower one, and how it curled up slightly, making it hard for him not to wonder what kissing her would be like, though he'd never kissed a girl before.

Casey had a very small mole about two inches beneath her right eye, and Lonnie found that nearly as enticing and mysterious as her lips.

"Well, I reckon you returned the favor back in the clearin'," the girl said, and Lonnie was relieved when she turned her head to stare forward along the trail.

General Sherman whickered and shook his head. Fear pricked the short hairs along the back of Lonnie's neck. He hipped around in his saddle, staring along the pale ribbon of trail curving away behind him.

"Did you hear somethin'?" he asked Casey.

She glanced behind. "I didn't hear anythin'. What'd you hear?"

"Not so much me as the General."

Casey stared along their back trail and then, apparently satisfied they were alone out here, she arched a brow at General Sherman. "That stallion of yours is probably admirin' Miss Abigail." She turned her head forward and said snootily, "Men."

Lonnie's heart thudded. He liked this girl even more than he'd realized. He couldn't let on, though. He wasn't sure why he couldn't, but he couldn't. Something about being smitten with her embarrassed him.

Besides, she'd think he was tough, like a man, if he pretended he wasn't interested. Wasn't that how it worked?

They rode on into the dark town, Chase in the lead. The outlaw sat sullenly in his saddle as Casey and Lonnie swung down from their horses in front of the dark, silent jailhouse. The stone building was pale in the moonlight.

Casey cast wary looks at the building, and for a few seconds, Lonnie felt his blood turn cold. Was she thinking Dupree was waiting inside? But then he realized that this was a meaningful place for the girl, since her father had likely spent a lot of time here.

It was her father's ghost she was sensing. She was remembering only a few days back, when he was alive. Lonnie felt sorry for her. He knew how hard it was to lose someone, wishing they would come back so you could see them one more time. Losing someone was like a saddle gall, only it was inside your soul where you couldn't put salve on it.

The girl didn't sob, however. Instead, she pulled her revolver out of her coat pocket, clicked the hammer back, and aimed it with both hands at Chase. "Climb down off of there, you owl hoot. Get inside."

TWENTY-FIVE

CHASE GLOWERED AT CASEY. He glanced at Lonnie, who stayed back a ways. This was the girl's territory. Lonnie would back her if she needed backing. He doubted she'd need it. She was a tough nut, and instead of pining for her father, she was trying to fill his boots.

Lonnie looked around, keeping an eye out for Dupree.

Chase said, "If you two kids think you're gonna hold me in that jail, you're soft in your thinker boxes. I'm too much for you. Let me go, and I'll ride on out of here, and you'll never see me again. Hell, you got the money!"

Casey licked her lips and there was only a slight quiver in her voice as she said quietly, "You heard me, Chase."

Lonnie held his carbine up high across his chest. He worked the cocking mechanism loudly, seating a cartridge in the rifle's action while staring threateningly at Chase. The metallic rasp was so loud that it started a dog barking somewhere to the east, and a night bird took flight, cawing.

Casey glanced at Lonnie, gave him a half smile, then turned back to Chase.

The deputy sighed, swung his right boot over his saddle horn, and leaped straight down to the ground. He groaned and fell back against his horse, his wounds grieving him.

"Galldarn it," he complained. "I'm gonna need a sawbones take a look at these wounds!"

"In the mornin'," Casey said, waving her gun at him.

When they got Chase inside the jailhouse and Lonnie had lit a lamp so Casey could see to open a cell, she gave the deputy an angry prod with her pistol barrel. Chase stumbled into the far right cell, cursing. He said several nasty things to Casey about her being a girl and him being a man, but he shut up when she poked the gun through the bars and stared at him over the barrel.

She had him turn around so she could remove his handcuffs. Then she ordered him to give her his badge, and when he did, Casey tossed it to Lonnie standing by the door where he could see both inside the office as well as into the street, though it was so dark he couldn't see much out there.

He was feeling spooky about Dupree. The outlaw had to be out there somewhere, waiting for the right time to make a move.

"Consider yourself deputized," Casey said.

Lonnie looked at the five-pointed tin star in the glove of his hand. It was badly tarnished, mostly gray, but the letters were clear: DEPUTY TOWN MARSHAL.

Lonnie felt himself suddenly grow an inch taller, and his shoulders felt fuller and wider.

"Oh, so you two kids are gonna play at lawdoggin' now, huh?" Chase glowered through the bars at them, chuckling caustically.

"That's right," Casey said as she reached into a pocket of her coat.

She pulled a badge like Lonnie's out of the pocket, and pinned it to her left lapel. She stared down at it. It said TOWN MARSHAL. When she gazed up at Lonnie, her eyes were shiny with tears.

"How do I look?" she asked.

Lonnie thought she looked better than anything he'd ever seen in his whole life. "You look wonderful," he blurted, and turned away as his ears started to burn with embarrassment.

Casey brushed a fist across her cheek and hardened her voice as she turned to regard Chase, who was now slumped on his cot. "I'll be over to feed you in the mornin'...if you don't bleed to death in the meantime."

"Hey!" he yelled. "You can't leave me locked up here in the dark, bleedin' like this!"

"I'm goin' to do you a favor and leave the lamp on," Casey said. "And that's more than you deserve."

Chase cursed her and continued to demand a doctor.

As though she hadn't heard him, Casey followed Lonnie outside, and closed and locked the door behind her. She'd left the lamp lit on her father's desk and the orange glow flickered in the windows. Chase continued to curse and yell and to rattle his cell door.

Casey sighed and turned to Lonnie. "Big night for you, huh? I bet you're hungry."

Lonnie shrugged. "I reckon I could eat somethin'."

"Come on," she said, dropping down the porch steps and jerking her chestnut's reins free of the hitch rack. "I'll rustle you somethin' up, and then you can bed down in our spare room."

"You mean we're goin' to your house?" Lonnie said, shocked. "I can throw down in the livery barn."

Casey swung up onto the chestnut's back. "If Dupree's here, he'll find you there." She narrowed a beautiful eye at Lonnie. "And you'll be greased for a sputterin' pan, cowboy."

Lonnie looked around the dark street, suppressing a shudder.

"Come on," Casey said, turning the chestnut away from the jailhouse.

"Hold on."

Casey glanced over her shoulder at him. "Why?"

Lonnie was standing in the stirrups as he stared south along the main street. "Heard somethin'."

Actually, the General had heard something and had twitched one ear and then the other. Then Lonnie had heard it, too. He heard it again now —the murmur of distant voices. Casey must have heard it, too, because she gave a slight gasp as she whipped her head forward.

There was silence for a time, then Lonnie heard a man's low, hard voice as well as the slow clomping of approaching horses. As he stared off toward the south end of town, he saw several shadows jostling in the darkness.

"Come on!" Lonnie said, and reined the General through a break between the jailhouse and the drugstore sitting beside it.

Silently, Casey turned the chestnut after him. Lonnie looked around wildly, feeling his heart starting to beat fast again—his poor, tired heart!— and then he saw Arapaho Creek flashing beyond some cottonwoods and pines. He whistled softly to Casey and spurred the General through the trees and down a gradual slope to the edge of the willows lining the water that gurgled gently over the rocks forming the creek bed.

The boy slipped down off the General's back and tied the reins to a branch of a willow shrub.

"Do you think it's them?" Casey whispered.

"I don't know, but I think we'd best find out."

TWENTY-SIX

LONNIE SHUCKED his carbine from its saddle boot, quietly levered a cartridge into the chamber, and off-cocked the hammer. Casey followed him as he jogged up the slope, the quarter moon lighting his way back through the cottonwoods and pines.

When he'd gained the top of the slope, he turned right and tramped along the rear of several shops before slipping through a narrow break and slowing his pace as he headed toward the main street. When he reached the mouth of the alley that opened onto the street, he dropped behind a rain barrel and shuttled his gaze to the west.

Three riders were making their way toward Lonnie and Casey, who'd dropped to one knee behind Lonnie's left shoulder, so she wouldn't be seen from the street. The riders were little more than silhouettes in the darkness, their faces dark ovals beneath the brims of their hats. Starlight shone in their horses' eyes, glistened off bridle chains and off the silver trimming Shannon Dupree's gaudy Texas saddle.

Lonnie glanced anxiously at Casey and gave her arm a hard tug as he threw himself against the side of the shop on his right. Casey pressed her back to the wall beside Lonnie.

Very quietly, so that it was little louder than a breath, she said, "Is it them?"

Lonnie nodded, staring at her with wide, grave eyes. He'd have recognized that fancy saddle skirt anywhere. Both skirts of Dupree's saddle were decorated with two small, coiled silver riatas, one overlapping the other. Lonnie had heard Dupree once say that he'd won the saddle in a poker game with a Mexican cowboy from west Texas.

Dupree was very proud of that saddle.

Lonnie turned his head so that he could look between the rain barrel and the side of the shop to see the street. The clomping of the horses grew until the dark shapes of the horses and riders were passing in front of Lonnie, roughly fifteen yards away.

"Where you s'pose we're gonna find the little twerp?" one of the men said, his voice loud in the quiet night.

"I don't know, but we'll find him, all right. I'm bettin' the money is in the marshal's office."

Lonnie hardened his jaws at the sound of Dupree's voice. Again, he wondered about his mother.

The low, rumbling voice of Fuego said, "Ain't that the jailhouse up ahead? Look—there's a light in the window."

"Well, I'll be jiggered," Dupree said.

They passed Lonnie and were following a slight curve in the street as they headed toward the marshal's office.

Lonnie turned to Casey. "Did you hear?"

She nodded as she gained her feet and began jogging at a crouch back in the direction from which they'd come. "Come on!"

"Where to?"

"The jailhouse!"

"Why?" Lonnie said, catching up to her as they gained the rear of the shops.

"We left Chase in there!"

"So what?" Lonnie said, running along behind the girl as she headed in the direction of the jailhouse. "We'd best light a shuck out of here, Miss Casey. Town ain't safe no more!"

"It'll be safer if we know where those killers head once they leave the jailhouse!" Casey paused to catch her breath, leaning forward, her hands on her knees. "I wanna know where they're headin' so I can tell Bill Barrows, the deputy US marshal over in Camp Collins. As soon as the Wells Fargo office opens, I'm sendin' that telegram."

She made an angry face, eyes flashing in the starlight. "By God, they're gonna pay for killin' my pa!"

Casey started running again, stopped, and looked back at him. "Are you comin'?"

Lonnie looked toward where they'd left the horses. He really wanted to ride and keep on riding. He never wanted to see Shannon Dupree again. The boy's life grew more and more precious to him every time he nearly lost it, and that was getting to be too many times.

He looked at Casey. She was staring at him, frowning critically. As afraid as he was, how could he run out on Casey Stoveville?

Inwardly, he groaned.

"Yeah," he said, steeling his courage. "Yeah, of course, I am."

They ran.

TWENTY-SEVEN

THERE WAS A LOUD *BANG!*

Running ahead of Lonnie, Casey yelped and fell. For a second, Lonnie thought she'd been shot but then he realized what the sound had been.

Dupree and the other two outlaws had busted the jailhouse door open. Lonnie could hear them stomping around in the building whose rear wall lay just ahead.

Chase's shrill voice called out, "Now, just you wait, Dupree! Just you *wait!*"

Lonnie gave Casey his hand, and he helped her to her feet. Without saying anything, they continued running to the side of the jailhouse. They pressed their backs against the rough, cool stones, one on each side of a sashed window through which flickering orange lamplight slanted out onto the dirt around Lonnie's boots.

The window was partly covered with an old, tattered flour sack curtain. There was a five-inch gap between the two flaps of the curtain. Lonnie held his hat against his chest as he rose onto his boot toes and peered through the window into the jailhouse.

By flickering lamplight, he could see Dupree stepping back from the cell in which Chase stood, the prisoner's hands wrapped around the bars. Dupree cuffed his hat back on his blond head and slacked down into Marshal Stoveville's swivel chair, facing Chase's cell.

"So you tried to make off with the money, did you, *Deputy?*" Dupree said, laughing. "But the kid got the better of you, did he?"

Fuego and Childress were standing near the open door, facing the jail cell. Fuego had a boot propped on a chair near the door and was rolling a cigarette, an elbow propped on a knee. Childress was scraping grit out from under his fingernails with a Barlow knife and grinning in that mocking way of his.

"So where's the money now?" Dupree wanted to know.

"How should I know?" Chase said, his frightened, slightly high-pitched voice echoing around the cave-like room. "That kid of yours and that girl—Stoveville's daughter—took it and lit out. For all I know, they headed to Mexico!"

"That kid ain't mine," Dupree said. "Let me be clear on that. That kid is his mother's and some dead blue-belly Yankee. I never would have fathered a no-account, thievin', sneakin', little jasper like that one."

"Thievin', huh?" Chase's ironic laughter at that was short-lived. Dupree glared at him.

"Stoveville's *daughter,* you say?" the blond outlaw leader said.

"That's right. They're in it together. She's tougher'n she looks. Must take after her pa."

Lonnie glanced at Casey. She didn't return the glance. She was too busy staring through the window, her head a little lower and to the left of his own.

Fuego turned to Dupree. "They're probably over at Stoveville's place."

"Where's the Stoveville house?" Dupree asked Chase.

Chase poked his arm out of the cell door, pointing toward the jail-house's front wall. "Two blocks south. Little frame house with a garden and a buggy shed. Big cottonwood in the front yard. Can't miss it. That's probably where they are, all right. Say, would you fellas mind turnin' me loose?"

"Turn you loose?" Childress said, chuckling and closing his knife.

Chase hesitated. "Yeah, I mean...why not? I ain't no deputy anymore. You got nothin' to worry about from me. I'm gettin' shed of this town first thing in the mornin'!"

"You're gettin' shed of this town right now," Dupree said.

Lonnie hadn't seen Dupree pull his gun, but now the boy saw the gun in Dupree's gloved right hand. There was a loud *pop!* and orange-red flames stabbed from the pistol's barrel in the direction of Chase.

"Oh, my *god!*" Casey screamed, and instantly clamped her hand over her mouth, as shocked and horrified by her own exclamation as by the fact that Dupree had murdered Chase in cold blood.

"Tell me I didn't do that," she whispered to Lonnie.

Lonnie turned back to the window. Dupree was staring at him and Casey through the warped glass. So were Fuego and Childress. Childress threw his arm out toward the window and shouted, "There they are!"

"Oh, yeah, you sure did!" Lonnie said, pushing Casey aside as Dupree snapped his revolver toward the window.

Bang! Bang! Bang-Bang!

The bullets crashed through the window, blowing out the glass and wooden sashes, shredding the curtains and spraying glass and wood in all directions.

"Come on, Casey—run! *Ru-un!*" Lonnie yelled, pulling the girl to her feet and then, holding her hand, lunging into a sprint back toward the rear of the building.

Beyond the jailhouse, the inky shapes of widely scattered cabins and stock pens and outhouses hunched in the darkness. Lonnie swung around behind the jailhouse as a rifle belched behind him, bullets pluming dust at his and Casey's feet. He could hear the outlaws yelling, hear the thuds of their boots and the jangling of their spurs.

Lonnie had released Casey's hand. She was running only slightly behind him, almost as fast as he was, her own spurred boots ringing in sync with his own.

"This way!" Lonnie yelled, and they cut between an abandoned cabin and a small warehouse, running hard to the north.

He wanted to get back to the horses but he wanted to lose Dupree and "the boys" first, because it was going to take him and Casey a minute or so to get mounted and get across the stream and into the mountains. There was a lot of open ground across the stream and a ways up onto the first ridge to the east, and open ground meant that he and the girl could be cut down by rifle fire.

Lonnie heard a hard thud. Casey groaned and fell, rolling. Lonnie stopped and ran back to her. She was sitting up and leaning forward across her knees, clutching her left ankle near the stone she'd apparently tripped over.

Lonnie saw a small stack of grayed lumber partly hidden amongst the sage they'd been running through as they'd swung to the west and the horses they'd tied by the creek. Lonnie cast an anxious look behind them. He could see the silhouettes of their pursuers coming through the tall pines and the dark cabins. They were close enough that Lonnie heard their rasping breaths and the jingling of their spurs.

"You gotta get up, Casey!" Lonnie said, wrapping a hand around her arm. "Get up and run!"

"You go! Leave me!"

"I ain't leavin' you!" he yelled too loudly.

"There they are!" Childress shouted.

TWENTY-EIGHT

CASEY CURSED and with a groan she pushed to her feet and continued running down the wooded slope to the west.

"Come on!" she called behind her.

"I'll be comin'!" Lonnie said, dropping to a knee and raising his rifle.

He was a little startled at how easy shooting at men had gotten to be. But it seemed just as easy for men to stalk him with the intention of killing him...as well as the girl he fancied.

Lonnie aimed in the general direction of the shadows dancing amongst the trees and cabins, and snapped off three quick shots, his rifle crashing loudly, the echoes leaping toward the moon. He heard one of the men yowl. The others stopped running to take cover, and Lonnie wheeled and ran after Casey.

He ran hard, pausing twice to look behind. His shots seemed to have slowed Dupree's pursuit. When Lonnie caught up to Casey, she was limping badly on her left foot.

"I wish you'd leave me," she said.

"If I leave you, they'll kill you."

"They'll kill us both if they catch us."

"They won't catch us!" Lonnie insisted, suppressing a shudder.

Lonnie awkwardly took the girl's right hand.

"What're you doin'?" she said, frowning at him.

"Don't get your back in a hump," Lonnie said, pulling her arm around his neck. "I'm only helpin'."

"Oh." Casey glanced behind before glancing over at Lonnie. "Thanks."

"Don't mention it."

Lonnie led Casey down to the creek and followed it upstream. He wished they hadn't hid the horses so well, because he was really starting to sweat about finding them again when, as they followed a horseshoe-shaped bend, the General whickered.

Relief washed over Lonnie, and he led Casey through the willows to where the horses stood where they'd tied them, nervously switching their tails. He helped Casey climb onto her chestnut, and reached up to give her the bridle reins. Casey was staring back in the direction from which they'd come, looking worried.

"Awful quiet back there," she said.

Lonnie had been so relieved to have found the horses and to have gotten Casey safely onto her chestnut's back that he hadn't noticed that he hadn't heard anything behind them since he'd opened up on their pursuers with the Winchester.

He was torn. He'd wanted to shed them from his trail, but the ensuing silence was ominous. He might have hit one, but he certainly hadn't hit them all.

And Dupree wouldn't stop following him and the stolen money unless the outlaw was dead. He doubted Dupree was dead. He was coming, all right. He was likely being sneaky about it.

Lonnie swung up onto the General's back and looked around. The stream glistened in the dark like a snakeskin. The willows formed a thick, ragged line along the stream bank, and a sudden, light breeze ruffled them. The swishing sounds would cover the footfalls of anyone approaching.

Lonnie looked across the stream and the dark, fir-covered ridges rising toward higher, darker mountains beyond. He glanced at Casey.

"We'd best ford the stream, head up into the mountains. It's the only way we're gonna lose 'em."

"That's how I figured," she said, keeping her voice low. Lonnie could hear the worry in it.

"Best ride slow," he said, booting the General up along the stream bank, looking for a way off the bank and into the water. "Try to keep our noise down."

"Right."

Lonnie followed a game path through the willows and into the water. He winced at the plops of the General's shod hooves, at the hollow rushing sound of the water swirling around the horse's hocks.

He was sure that even as slowly as he and Casey were riding, they could be heard from a couple of hundred yards away on so quiet a night. And they were probably backlit by the starlight reflecting off the surface of the creek.

Ducks. They were like ducks on a millpond waiting to be shot, plucked, dressed out, and tossed into a Dutch oven...

The short hairs were standing up straight on the back of Lonnie's neck. As the General made his way, slipping now and then on the slippery rocks that lay beneath the water's surface, he kept an eye on the dark bank behind them, on the willows dancing in the breeze.

Nothing moved in the darkness. But he was sure that Dupree was back there somewhere. There was no way the outlaw was going to let Lonnie and Casey get far with the money he considered his own. It was also clear that not only did Dupree intend to get his money back, but he intended to kill the kid...or *kids*...who now had it...

It seemed as though a solid month had passed before the General finally reached the creek's opposite bank. Lonnie felt another wave of relief begin to sweep over him as the General lunged up out of the water and through the willows, Casey's filly splashing not far behind him.

The bank they'd left was about sixty yards away. Still there was no movement in the darkness back there.

Lonnie turned his head forward as a bulky figure holding a rifle stepped out from behind a fir tree.

Fuego's teeth showed in the darkness as the stocky outlaw said, "Got me a couple of thievin' urchins for the killin'!"

Fuego glanced back across the creek. "Dupree, I got 'em both over here!"

TWENTY-NINE

LONNIE SHOUTED, "Ah, go flog a boll weevil, you old dung beetle!"

He jerked back sharply on the General's reins and rammed his spurs into the stallion's flanks.

The horse gave a shrill, angry whinny as it reared hard, raising its front, scissoring hooves, kicking the rifle out of Fuego's hands and sending the stout outlaw tumbling.

"Come on, Casey!" Lonnie cried as he smacked his rein ends against the General's flanks and lunged up the slope beyond the creek through the scattered, dark columns of pines and firs.

Gunfire crackled behind him. He glanced over his right shoulder to see Casey hunkered low over her saddle, whipping her chestnut with her own reins and batting her right heel against the mount's right flank. She didn't seem able to do much with her left foot.

Beyond her, the flashes of two guns shone in the darkness on the other side of the stream. Nearer, Lonnie could see Fuego trying to regain his feet, staggering around as though drunk, likely looking for his rifle.

Lonnie had a mind to stop the General, to dismount with his rifle, and pepper the stocky outlaw with .44-caliber rounds. But he nixed the idea. He wasn't such a great hand at killing men yet, and if he got too cocky, he was likely to get filled so full of lead he'd rattle when he walked.

No, his best bet was to flee. To put as much distance as he could between himself and Shannon Dupree. Which he and Casey should be able to do, because he doubted that Dupree's men had their horses.

There were still a couple of hours before dawn. Once Dupree, Fuego, and Childress had collected their mounts, they'd have a hard time tracking Lonnie and Casey until sunup. And by then the boy hoped that he and the marshal's daughter would have put a good, safe distance between themselves and the outlaws.

He and General Sherman rode up over a hump in the steep slope, and then moved downhill from a stony outcropping. At the bottom of the hill, a relatively flat stretch of ground spread out before them in the north, toward the black wall of forested mountain beyond.

The meadow appeared purple in the darkness, mottled with lilac starlight edged in shimmering silver. Sagebrush and small, black spruces and cedars spiked up here and there.

The relatively flat stretch of ground continued for nearly a mile before it began to rise toward densely forested foothills once more. Just before the rise, another, smaller creek stretched across their path, sparkling like a pretty dress.

Lonnie stopped the General, who was breathing hard. The stallion's coat was silvery with sweat, and his lungs sounded like a bellows, his chest expanding and contracting deeply beneath the saddle.

Lonnie swung down from the General's back and loosened the saddle cinch to let the horse breathe easier. He slipped the bit from the stallion's mouth, wrapped his reins around the saddle horn, and stepped aside while the General plunged his front hooves into the creek and immediately began to drink great, slurping draughts of the likely spring-fed water.

"Hey, he'll founder!" Casey warned. She'd dismounted her chestnut and, putting only a little weight on her bum ankle, was holding her horse's bridle tight in her fist.

"What's that?" Lonnie said.

Casey jerked her chin at the General. "You're gonna let that stallion founder...or get colic ...or worse. I'd think a kid from a ranch would know better than to let a hot horse drink his fill like that!"

Lonnie looked at the girl's chestnut filly, who was trying to push forward while staring hungrily at the stream, her nostrils expanding and contracting wildly, hungrily.

"You think wild horses don't take their fill when they're hot and they need it?"

Casey stared at him, incredulous.

"Let her go," Lonnie urged. "Horses need water when they're hot, and I was raised around a passel of 'em, and I've never known a single horse to founder on water. Grain, maybe. Never water. When they're hot they need water even worse than we do."

Casey stared at him. She looked at the General, then at the chestnut. She released her horse's bridle, and the chestnut plunged into the stream beside the stallion and dipped her snout into the rippling water, lapping loudly.

Without the chestnut to hold onto, Casey was having a hard time standing up. Lonnie hurried over to her, wrapped her right arm around his neck, and led her over to lean against a large rock.

"How's the ankle?" he asked.

"I think it's swellin'." Casey glanced across the starlit meadow. "You think they're comin'?"

Lonnie also looked across the meadow. "Oh, they'll be comin', all right. But I figure they'll gather their horses first, and that'll take a while. And they'll have to go slow in the dark, trackin' us. This is pretty big country up here and we could be anywhere."

"What did you tell that fella to do?" Casey asked. "Flog a *boll weevil?*"

Lonnie chuckled. "Don't ask me what it means. An old fella who worked at the ranch one fall used to say it when he was mad at one of the other hands. I think he was doin' all he could to not take the Lord's name in vain, or somethin'."

Casey laughed. "He was right creative."

Lonnie pointed at Casey's left foot. "You want me to take a look at that ankle?"

"Why? You a doctor or somethin'?"

"Not official, but I've doctored plenty of horses' feet. The General tends to go lame in his right front hock from time to time, but I used an old Indian cure, and—"

"I'm not a horse, kid."

"All right."

They were quiet for a minute, then Casey said, "Sorry. I'm feelin' a little off my feed." She turned to gaze worriedly behind them once again.

"Yeah, me too."

"You didn't lose your pa."

"I did a few years back."

"Yeah, I heard," she said. "Sorry about that."

"I suppose you feel like I had somethin' to do with your pa, on account of Dupree's been stayin' out at our place from time to time. I promise you, Miss Stoveville, I didn't have nothin' to do with it."

"Oh, hell, I know that." Casey turned her mouth corners down, lowered her eyes sheepishly. "Like I said, I'm just feelin' owly. I reckon you're caught up in this as bad as I am. Why don't you head on back to your ranch? I'll get the money over the mountains to the marshal. No point in us both goin'."

Lonnie thought about his mother. He felt a hard push to get back to her, to see if Dupree had hurt her, but he couldn't leave Casey. Not with killers on her trail.

"Nah, you got a bum ankle," Lonnie said. "You'll need help gettin' the money over mountains."

"Kid?"

Lonnie looked at her.

She gazed at him for a few seconds, then placed a gloved fist on a hip as she said, "I'm older than you by a significant degree. And I am not currently in the market for a sweetheart. Especially a kid from the country. You have no chance with me. None. So why don't you stop showin' off and go home to your mother and let me get the money over the mountains to the marshal?"

She punctuated that with an arched brow.

THIRTY

LONNIE'S CHEEKS and ears turned so hot that for a second he thought they'd burst into flame. Showing *off?*

Embarrassment mixed with rage, and he had to suck a hot breath down before saying in as deep and calm a voice as he could muster, "I do declare you got a mighty high opinion of yourself, Miss Stoveville. Rocked me back on my heels to see your true colors so sudden-like. Now, I'd be right happy to let you take that money over the mountains to the marshal, but truth be told, I don't think you're up to it. And since my reputation's sort of tied up with them saddlebags you got on the chestnut's back, I'll be showin' off for you for the next few days, I reckon."

Lonnie drew another deep, calming breath and started walking toward the General but stopped and turned back to her. "Less'n you'd like to go on back to town and let me ride on alone, that is. I could make better time if I didn't have you taggin' along with your clubfoot."

Casey drew her own deep breath and lifted her chin, looking down her nose at him. "Yes, well, since I'm the town marshal now and you are merely my deputy, I'll be leadin' up this expedition, *Deputy* Gentry. Now, if you wouldn't mind, I and my *clubfoot* will be needin' assistance in gettin' mounted."

"Yeah, I figured that," Lonnie said, and helped her into her saddle.

In a way, he was grateful for her high-hatted tone. As he'd helped her into her saddle, he hadn't felt nearly as self-conscious. He felt as cool and calm as a big, twelve-point mule deer buck in a herd of does and fawns. Because now that he'd seen who Casey Stoveville really was, he realized he'd been a fool to have set so much store by the girl!

No, he didn't like Casey Stoveville one damn bit and she'd better be able to keep up to him or he was going to leave her behind, eating the General's dust!

He was thinking all that while he tightened the stallion's saddle cinch, shoved the bit back into the General's teeth, mounted up, and continued riding east toward the black mountains rising before him, blotting out the stars.

They were pretty high in the mountains by the time the sun rose. It was cool up here. Lonnie could see patches of frost, like tufts of gray fur some wolf had shed, lying here and there about the floor of the forest they were riding through. The frost glittered like diamonds, turning clear around the edges when buttery shafts of sunlight found it.

Lonnie and Casey were climbing ever higher toward Storm Peak Pass, which was about the only way over the range to Camp Collins. At least, it was the only route that Lonnie knew. He'd been over the pass only once, when he'd accompanied one of his mother's hired men last year to push a small herd of two-year-old cattle over to sell to a buyer in Camp Collins, where they could put the cows on the railroad for shipment to Chicago.

The Storm Peak Pass trail was an old Indian hunting and warring trail. More recently, white fur trappers and prospectors had used it. Freighting outfits still used it shipping gold and silver from west to east over the divide. The pass route was shorter than swinging north or south around the Never Summers, over flatter terrain around the vast, outer bulwarks of the mountains, and then cutting east through narrow valleys.

Such a trip would add a good week's worth of travel. The Storm Peak Pass route was harder but generally shorter, if you didn't get bogged down by snow in the fall or struck by lightning in the summer.

After October first of every year, snow made the trail impassable until July of the next year.

Another, often worse hazard were outlaws. The remote, high, rugged terrain around the pass was known to hide many a wanted man. Men like Shannon Dupree and "the boys", though Dupree had likely cut around the range's southern end of his run from Golden, which lay over near Denver.

Outlaws were something Lonnie didn't want to think about. He'd had his fill of outlaws. He also preferred not to think about the area being called home to some of the largest, meanest grizzly bears anywhere in northern Colorado...

No, best not to think about outlaws and grizzlies. Best just to think about putting as much ground behind him as he could.

When the sun was about at its nine o'clock spot in the sky, Lonnie reined the General up at a creek that snaked through a clearing surrounded by the low humps of pine-carpeted ridges.

He swung down from the stallion's back and fixed the General's rigging like before so he could freely drink from the slow-running stream. Lonnie didn't look at Casey until after she'd done the same, letting the chestnut walk into the stream to get her fill.

Lonnie hadn't looked at the girl because, one, he was mad at her for talking down to him. Two, he felt guilty for being mad at her. She'd just recently lost her pa, after all, and she was probably more alone in the world than Lonnie was. At least, he had his ma. He'd heard that Casey's ma had died when Casey had been a little girl.

She couldn't be expected to follow every word of the politeness book, he reckoned.

Now when he looked at her, he saw that she was shivering and pale. Her long, canvas coat must not be enough to keep the mountain cold out, and her ankle was likely grieving her. Lonnie also realized that Casey had tied no bedroll onto her horse, behind the saddle. She only had the money-filled saddlebags riding there. She hadn't expected to be out all night, much less heading over Storm Peak Pass to deliver the money to the marshal in Camp Collins.

Dupree's spying her and Lonnie outside the jailhouse had changed all that. Now they had nowhere to go but Camp Collins. There was no turning back.

Lonnie untied his bedroll—two wool blankets stitched together along one side to form a sack of sorts—and took it over to where Casey sat in the grass beside the stream, gently removing one of her riding boots.

"Here," Lonnie said, holding out the blanket.

"What's that for?"

"You're cold. Should have said somethin'." She'd likely been shivering all night.

She was miffed at him, just as he was miffed at her. He could see it in her eyes. That rankled him, and he was disappointed that he could be affected again by how she felt about him.

She took the blanket and draped it over her shoulders. "Thanks, kid."

Lonnie ground his jaws at "kid".

"Don't mention it, Miss Stoveville."

He wheeled and walked away from her, not liking her again.

THIRTY-ONE

LONNIE KNEW it was best not to worry too much about Casey Stoveville.

He was stuck with this uppity town girl, so he might as well get used to the idea. No use worrying what she thought about him, because he knew that already. He'd likely be stuck with her for the next two days, because that's how long it usually took to get over the pass. It might take him and her longer, because they might be wise to at least partly avoid the main trail and sort of skirt the sides of it.

Of course, they could head for Golden, but that was a longer ride. Lonnie wanted to get the money to the US marshal as soon as possible.

Dupree would likely look for them on the main trail, which Lonnie was hoping they'd run into soon. He wasn't sure, but he figured that he and Casey were somewhere south of it. They should be able to see it snaking over the higher ridges soon. Once on the trail for a time, they might run into a freight outfit they could buy some food from.

Food...

Lonnie hadn't eaten since before he'd ridden into Arapaho Creek. He realized he felt as hollow as an old stump. His belly growled at the thought of a big steak and fried potatoes smothered in steak gravy. He had trail grub in his saddlebags and cavvy sack. Soon, he and Casey would have to stop and think about getting some of that food in their bellies. This was a tough ride, and you needed a bellyful to make it.

As he looked in the direction from which they'd come, the direction from which Dupree would likely be showing himself soon, he knew he couldn't take the time to eat yet.

Steeling himself against his anger at the girl he was riding with, he moved back to the horses and led the General out of the stream. As he did, he saw Casey sitting on the bank, bathing her bare foot in the water. At the sight of her bare flesh, he turned away. A boy didn't look at a girl's ankles. Doctoring her was one thing, ogling her was another.

He glanced at her foot once more quickly, then he reached under the General's belly to tighten his saddle cinch.

"How's it look?" he asked the girl.

"I don't think it's broken."

"If it was broke, you'd know it. Probably pulled the tendons in there."

"Thanks, Doctor," she said, pulling her sock back on.

Lonnie ground his jaws at that. She'd lost her father. Girls could be cranky for no reason, and here she had a reason and he was blaming her for it.

Still, he felt miffed at her again when he had more important things to worry about. It was just that she seemed to keep taking potshots at his pride, which he'd never realized was so tender.

Because he wanted them to get moving as soon as possible, he walked out into the creek and fetched her chestnut back onto the bank. He slipped the filly's bit back into her mouth, adjusted the bridle straps to sit evenly over her ears and then tightened the cinch beneath her belly.

"Here ya go," Lonnie said. "Miss Abigail's ready for ya."

As he turned around to face Casey, she limped up to him, wrapped her arms around his neck, drew him against her warm, supple body, and planted a semi-wet kiss on his cheek.

"Thanks," she said, sort of crossing her eyes as she smiled at him, pulling that full upper lip back slightly. Her hazel eyes and her blonde hair glistened in the high-country sunlight.

She draped the blankets he'd given her over his own shoulder.

Lonnie's heart turned a backward flip in his chest.

His ears rang.

The boy had no words with which to respond to the girl's inexplicable behavior. He stood there, lower jaw hanging to his chest, while she used a rock humping out of the creek bank to get seated on the chestnut's back.

She rode out away from the creek and called behind her, "Let's make camp soon, huh? If it's safe? I don't know about you but I'm hungry."

———

A CABIN SAT in another clearing ringed with fir-covered slopes.

It was an old, gray log affair with a shake-shingled roof missing shingles the way an old man misses teeth. The shingles that remained were as gray as the hovel's weathered logs, and they were blue-green with moss. A dented tin chimney pipe angled up out of the roof, and a rusty coffee can had been turned upside down over the end of the pipe to prevent birds from nesting inside.

The windows were shuttered. A deep, packed-dirt depression lay in the ground before the front door. Rain and snow must have collected in the depression and rotted away part of the doorsill. A backless chair sat left of the door, a rock propping up one of the front legs to level the chair on the uneven ground.

A doorless privy flanked the cabin, and to the cabin's right squatted a small log stable whose roof had collapsed. Only a few rails remained of the peeled pine log corral that surrounded the stable on three sides.

"Looks abandoned," Casey said, sitting her chestnut beside Lonnie as they inspected what appeared to be an old miner's headquarters.

Lonnie said, "Let's see if it has a stove. If so, I'll try to snare us a rabbit. Nothin' like fresh meat to fuel a long ride."

She glanced at Lonnie who kept his eyes roaming around the dilapidated buildings. "Sounds good to me. I'm so hungry my stomach thinks my throat's been cut."

Lonnie jerked a surprised look at her.

"You heard me." She smiled brashly. "I know that wasn't ladylike, but out here, who's to wash my mouth out with soap?" She pulled his hat brim down, teasing him. *"You?"*

"Nah, you can talk however you want around me, Miss Casey. I ain't no saint—that's for sure." Lonnie poked his hat back up on his forehead, and swung nimbly down from the General's back. "But I don't reckon we'd best stop here for long. You can dismount and lead your chestnut around, though. If your ankle doesn't hurt too bad, I mean. Make as many tracks as you can."

He dropped the General's reins and walked up to the cabin's front door.

Behind him, Casey frowned. "Why?"

"Just do as I say, Miss Casey. I'll tell you later."

"Hey, I don't take orders from you, kid," Casey said, and eased down from her saddle, keeping her cool gaze on him. She was miffed again. "Remember, I'm the marshal. And just because we're on the trail together, and I gave you that kiss, don't go thinkin' we're married!"

THIRTY-TWO

THE GIRL'S fickle moods were too much of a puzzle for Lonnie. He kept his mind on what lay before him, which at the moment was the cabin door.

He tripped the steel and leather latch, which clicked. The door slackened in its frame. The leather hinges squawked. When Lonnie pushed the door open a foot, the door sagged to the cabin floor, which was nothing more than hard-packed dirt. He sidled through the opening and walked on into the cabin, which was about one quarter the size of the cabin in which he and his mother lived at the Circle G.

There was little inside the place except an old table, another backless chair, and a small sheet-iron stove in the cabin's far right corner. A wood box sat beside the stove. It had a few chunks of rotted wood and a squirrel's nest inside it.

There were a few shelves on the wall opposite where the table sat. Three airtight tins sat on the shelf. Inspecting their badly faded and water-stained labels, Lonnie saw that one held tomatoes, one held pinto beans, and the third one held sweetened apricot slices.

Lonnie's stomach growled. He salivated just thinking about chewing up a sweetened apricot . . .

He looked around once more. Obviously, judging by the lack of anything but rotted wood and the squirrel's nest in the wood box and the several layers of undisturbed dust on the table, no one had visited this place in at least a year, maybe more. Lonnie had a feeling the place had long ago been a miner's cabin. It might now serve as a line shack for an area rancher—so infrequently that Lonnie didn't think that he should feel overly guilty about confiscating the three tin cans of food.

He and Casey needed the food more than the squirrels did, and they didn't have time to cook anything.

He took all three cans down off the shelf, went out, and closed the rickety door behind him. Casey was limping around, leading the filly. She stopped and turned to Lonnie, frowning.

"What do you have there?"

Lonnie grinned. "I got pinto beans, tomatoes, and apricots!"

"Hooray!"

"Hold on, hold on!" Lonnie hurried over to where General Sherman stood ground-tied, and dropped the cans into his saddlebags.

Casey gaped at him. "Kid, you got a mean streak—you know that?"

"We can't stay here," Lonnie said, glancing back in the direction from which they'd come. "We don't know how far away Dupree is, but we have to assume he's a better tracker than I think he is and that he's only a mile or so behind us. I know he won't stop lookin' for us until he gets the loot back."

"He couldn't have tracked us in the dark."

"No, but he's had plenty of time to make up for the time he lost before daylight."

"So what're we stoppin' here for?"

"I'm thinkin' that if he's still on our trail, it'll lead him here. Now, maybe we can confuse him a little, maybe lose him for good."

"How?"

Lonnie walked over and helped her back up onto the chestnut's back. "Just follow me."

"You're enjoyin' playin' mountain man, aren't you, kid?" she asked, glowering at him from her saddle.

Lonnie didn't let her see him blushing as he swung up onto General Sherman's back. Yeah, he was showing off. But he figured he had a good reason. If Dupree caught up to them, they were dead.

"Come on, Miss Casey," he said, booting the General northward out of the yard. "Let's make some tracks!"

The General lunged into a lope.

"Hey, wait for me, goll darnit!" Casey yelled behind him. "Don't make me regret givin' you that peck on the cheek back there, Lonnie Gentry!"

Lonnie felt his lips spread a grin.

That was the first time she'd used his proper name.

THIRTY-THREE

LONNIE LED Casey on probably what seemed a wild-goose chase to the girl.

Without following any trail, and with no seeming rhyme or reason, Lonnie galloped the General to the edge of the clearing in which the abandoned cabin sat. He slowed the horse as they entered the forest and descended a gentle hill. About halfway down the hill, Lonnie turned General Sherman onto a deer trail that ran perpendicular to the slope before dropping gradually toward the hill's bottom.

Lonnie glanced behind to see Casey following on her chestnut filly, the girl scowling after him, her hair blowing out behind her in the wind or bouncing across her shoulders. The brim of her man's hat rippled, and the chin thong danced against her chest. Just as Lonnie had to do, she occasionally ducked under low pine boughs.

At the bottom of the slope ran a stream. Lonnie crossed the stream and put the General up through the forest on the other side.

At the bottom of the next hill lay another stream. Lonnie glanced back once more to make sure Casey was keeping up with him. The girl was handling her horse in such rugged terrain well for a gal who spent most of her time clerking in a mercantile. But her suntanned cheeks and hands attested to her likely riding the chestnut any chance she got—maybe after work or on weekends.

Lonnie enjoyed showing off his own riding ability, but he was also glad she was able to keep up with him. If she hadn't been able to ride handily, Dupree was sure to catch up to them sooner or later.

"Where in tarnation, Lonnie Gentry, are we goin'?" Casey demanded behind him, as Lonnie put the General into the stream.

Instead of crossing to the other side, Lonnie rode the General right down the center of the stream, going against the current. Water splashed up over his stirrups, soaking his boots. He said nothing but kept riding. He'd explain later. Besides, he was enjoying keeping her in suspense though he knew it was a devilish thing to do. The uppity town girl deserved it.

When they'd followed the creek around several bends, Lonnie put the General up the north bank. He stopped the horse to let Casey catch up, and when she'd mounted the bank to stop the chestnut beside him, she said, "You're loco!"

"You're keepin' up right well."

"Is this a test or somethin'?"

"Yeah, somethin' like that," he said, enjoying himself. He doubted she'd be looking down her nose at him for much longer.

Lonnie chuckled and reined the General sharply away from her, but as the General lunged up another, fir-stippled slope, a pine bough swept toward him in a dark-brown, lime-green blur. The boy snapped his eyes wide in surprise and started to duck—too late.

The bough caught him across his upper chest and shoulders. He had sense enough to kick free of his stirrups so he wouldn't snap both his ankles, and then, as the horse continued trotting forward under the branch, Lonnie fell back hard and turned a backward somersault over the General's burr-prickly tail.

Lonnie hit the ground with a thump and a loud "Ghahhh!" as the air was pounded out of his lungs.

He'd landed on his back, and now he lay spread-eagle on the ground, staring up through the forest canopy at bits of blue sky and fringes of white clouds beyond the arrow-straight tops of the evergreens.

A church bell was ringing loudly from nearby, and little white birds were fluttering around in front of Lonnie's face, obscuring his vision. Only, after a moment he realized the birds were actually *inside* his head. The church bells were in the same region. He lifted his head, hearing himself grunt raspily, loudly as he tried to suck a breath back into his lungs that were having none of it.

He lay his head down and arched his back, trying again to draw a breath. As he did, Casey entered his field of vision, her pretty face staring down at him from between him and the pine tops and the small scallops of blue sky beyond her. She turned her mouth corners down and shook her head, crossing her arms on her chest and cocking one hip.

"A fool and his horse are soon parted," she said. "My father told me that when he was first teachin' me to ride."

"Wise...wise man," Lonnie croaked out. He tried to push himself up, but Casey set a boot on his chest and pressed him back down to the ground. "Just lay there a minute. You got the wind knocked out of you. If you've broken anythin', I'm leavin' you here. You best know that, Lonnie Gentry. The bobcats can have you."

When Lonnie was finally able to draw a full breath and the tolling of the bells in his ears had died somewhat, he said, "How come you seem so fond of my name all of a sudden?"

"I don't know. It's a nice name, I reckon." Then she cracked a grin, and she laughed. "Better than you deserve, you foolish child!"

"That's more like it," Lonnie said, his ears ringing again but this time with embarrassment.

She helped him to his feet. He couldn't look at her.

"Are you all right?" she asked, kind of snootily, he thought.

He turned away from her and then stooped to scoop his hat off the ground. He muttered something under his breath though even he wasn't sure what it was.

"Are you sure you didn't break anythin'?" Casey asked him.

Lonnie swatted his hat against his thigh, ridding it of dirt and pine needles and little round bits of squirrel scat. His back and shoulders and the back of his head ached like holy blazes, but he didn't think anything was broken. If anything *was* broken, he figured he deserved it.

In fact, he deserved to be put down like a rabid dog for acting like such a copper-riveted fool.

He wished the ground would open up and swallow him.

"I'm all right," he grouched. "I...just didn't see that dang pine branch, that's all. What the heck's it hangin' so low for?"

Hearing Casey give a snort behind him, he set his hat on his head and stumbled stiffly up to where the General stood about thirty yards beyond, head lowered and eyeing his fallen rider skeptically.

"Oh, hobble your lip, General," Lonnie said, grabbing the buckskin's reins. He groaned as he heaved his aching body back up into the saddle.

"Come on," he told Casey, whose amused gaze he could still feel on his back, making the back of his neck burn. "No time to dally, girl!"

He touched spurs to the General's flanks.

But he proceeded a little more slowly and carefully this time.

THIRTY-FOUR

LONNIE STOPPED the General along a deer trail running along the shoulder of a grassy mountaintop clearing, at the edge of fringe of mixed pines and aspens. He eased carefully out of the saddle, for his head ached from the braining he'd taken earlier.

Not to mention that his back and shoulders felt as though he'd been beaten with a shovel.

As Casey reined up her chestnut behind the General, Lonnie dug into his saddlebags for his spyglass, which resided in a small, deer-hide sack with a rawhide thong stitched around its mouth. Looping the thong around his neck, the boy climbed the steep slope, his boots sliding on the short, slick grass and crusted layer of dirt and pebbles. Several times he had to lean forward and push off the ground with his hands.

Near the top of the hill, he got down and crawled until he could see over the top of the ridge and over another, lower, pine-carpeted ridge beyond. Beyond that ridge lay a valley with a clearing, a willow-lined creek curving around the clearing's left end.

Lonnie got out his spyglass, telescoped it, and turned the wooden ring around the brass casing, bringing the clearing below into focus. He heard Casey climbing the slope behind him, breathing hard. When he turned toward her, she got down and started crawling until she lay belly-down beside him.

"Where are we?" she asked. The breeze brushed against them, scudding cloud shadows over the top of the otherwise sun-splashed hill before them.

"Guess?" Lonnie said.

"You don't know, do you? With all that runnin' around, you got us lost! Do you know where the trail to the pass is?"

"Sure do." Lonnie was trying to get some of his pride back, which he'd lost in his tumble from the General's saddle. At least, he was trying to sound confident again, though he was beginning to learn that prideful confidence could be a dangerous thing.

Just as showing off for a girl could get you killed faster than Dupree could do it.

"Well," Casey said skeptically. "Where is it?"

Lonnie rolled over onto his back and sat up on his butt, bending his knees slightly out to both sides. He rolled his neck, trying to loosen some of the kinks, and poked his hat back off his forehead.

"See that big, dark mountain humping up there, higher than the two to either side of it? It's got some snow on the left side of the peak."

"Yeah, I see it."

"That's Storm Peak Pass. The trail to the pass is beyond that lower ridge there. We'll get to it sometime tomorrow, I think."

"Are you *sure* you know where we are?"

Lonnie kept his face plain as he held out the spyglass to her. "Have a look for yourself."

"At what?"

"The clearin' down there beyond the ridge in front of us."

Casey narrowed a skeptical eye at the boy. She took the spyglass and lay belly-down again, propped on her elbows, and lifted the glass to her right eye. She twisted the canister to bring the clearing into focus.

"There's a cabin down there."

"Right. The abandoned one. See the stable beside it, the privy behind it?"

Casey lowered the glass and turned to him in disgust. "You mean we've been ridin' in *circles?*"

"One big circle."

Casey gave a slow blink. "Why have we been ridin' in one big circle, Lonnie? It's the pass we should be headed for. Remember, we're tryin' to get that money to the deputy marshal in Camp Collins."

Lonnie took the spyglass back from her and leaned on his elbows again, raising the glass to his eyes to examine the clearing in which the cabin hunched. "First, I wanna see if Dupree is on our trail. If he is, he should be headin' for the cabin soon. He should also pick up our tracks there and head into the trees east of it, the way we went. Then he'll likely swing south."

"And then what?"

"He'll lose our trail."

"Why?"

"Because I fixed it so he would."

Lonnie lowered the spyglass. "He'll lose our tracks in the creek we followed upstream. The current has likely washed the hoofprints away by now. It would take a darn good tracker—probably no one but a good *Injun* tracker—to pick them up again where we left the water. Not the way we went. I picked the hardest ground for leavin' a print. Even if he picked up our trail where we left that first creek, it ain't likely he'll pick it up where we left the second creek . . . over them rocks. No one except maybe an Injun can track a horse over rocks."

"Okay," Casey said, nodding slowly, thoughtfully, "that was pretty smart."

Lonnie grinned as he continued appraising the clearing through the spyglass.

"I said 'pretty smart'," Casey said. "Maybe you forgot one thing."

"What's that?"

"He likely knows where we're headed. Most folks around know about the marshal stationed in Camp Collins."

"He's figured out where we're headed, all right," Lonnie said. "Dupree's dumb and mean, but he ain't *that* stupid. But I figure as long as he ain't dodgin' our every step, he'll keep wonderin' if he's figured us right, and he won't catch up to us. Especially if we don't stick to the pass trail long but skirt the edges of it where we have to."

"How long we gonna wait for 'em?"

Lonnie shrugged. "If they're not to the cabin in an hour, I'd say they're far enough behind us we won't have to worry about 'em. They'll never catch up to us before we make Camp Collins."

"And if they reach the cabin inside of an hour?" Casey asked.

"Then we'd best pull our picket pins, and ride. I still don't think they'll catch up to us, because they'll lose our trail, but there's no point in takin' any chances."

Lonnie returned the spyglass to its pouch and rose to his knees. "Any way you figure it, we'll get to Camp Collins ahead of Dupree, and deliver the money to the marshal before them cutthroats can get their hands on it."

He removed the spyglass pouch from around his neck and gave it to Casey. "Keep an eye on the clearin'. I'll be right back."

"You're orderin' me around again like we were married or somethin'!"

"Don't get your hopes up." Lonnie rose and began walking back down the slope toward the horses. "Town girls are too snooty for this cowboy." He winked and pinched his hat brim to her.

Casey snorted.

"Where you goin'?" she called after him.

"I don't know about you, but I'm hungry."

Lonnie returned to the hill clutching the three airtight tins to his chest. Casey, who'd been watching the clearing for Dupree, lowered the spyglass and grinned. "You might just do yet, kid."

"See anythin' over there?" Lonnie asked as he sat down beside Casey and pulled his folding Barlow knife out of his jeans pocket. Just as he rarely strayed very far from his horse, he never went anywhere without his knife.

"Nothin'."

Lonnie indicated the cans spread out between him and Casey. "Which do you want first?"

"All of 'em!"

Lonnie chuckled. "Boy, you're hungrier'n a blue-ribbon bull! I better stay back a ways so you don't eat my arm off!"

He set the point of his knife against the top of one of the tins, and punched the end of the knife with the heel of his hand. The blade ground through the lid, and Lonnie sawed it along the edge of the top of the can until he was able to pry up the lid, leaving only a small portion of it attached.

He held up the bean can to Casey. "Girls first. I didn't bring up my spoon, so I hope you're not squeamish."

"Not when I'm this hungry."

Casey scooped out a handful of beans, shoved them in a most unlady-like fashion into her mouth, and chewed. Lonnie did the same and passed the can back to Casey. In a little over a minute they'd emptied the can of every last bean, and the bean juice was running down the corners of their mouths.

They shared a look and laughed at each other.

Lonnie set the point of his knife against the top of the tomato tin. "How 'bout we save the apricots for dessert?"

"Well, ain't you civilized?"

Lonnie punched the blade into the tomato can and then he and Casey were shoving the juicy, red, delicious tomatoes into their mouths like little kids going to work on a frosting bowl. They devoured the tomatoes inside of another minute, and Lonnie opened the apricot tin.

The apricots were sweet, the sugary syrup sliding down Lonnie's throat like an elixir. Suddenly, his aches and pains didn't ache half as much as they had only moments before.

He and Casey had eaten half the sugary fruit slices before Casey said, "Uh-oh."

She was staring over the next ridge and into the clearing to the west.

THIRTY-FIVE

SPYING movement over the next ridge, Lonnie pressed the spyglass to his right eye and adjusted the focus. In the single sphere of magnified vision, he watched three horseback riders trot their horses from left to right, heading for the cabin.

He continued to adjust the glass's focus until he could more clearly see that the lead rider was Shannon Dupree, by the blond hair hanging down beneath the brim of the lead cutthroat's brown Stetson, and by the blond, brushy mustache residing above his mouth.

Dupree rode standing up in his stirrups and staring toward the cabin. The hard set of his shoulders told Lonnie the man was wary, cautious. Dupree cast several quick glances at the ground beside his horse, obviously following Lonnie and Casey's tracks, which they'd made about two hours earlier.

The blond outlaw rode with his right hand on the butt of his Colt revolver positioned for the cross draw on his left hip.

Behind Dupree rode Fuego with Childress bringing up the rear. Both men held rifles across their saddlebows.

Lonnie's heart thudded as he watched the three stop their horses in front of the cabin, Fuego swinging his head from left to right as he inspected the ground where Casey had led the chestnut, trying to confuse the sign a little, make it look as though Lonnie and Casey had spent more time there than they actually had and were not very far ahead of their stalkers.

Anything they could do to confuse the outlaws was in their best interest, Lonnie thought.

"Let me see," Casey said, holding out her hand for the glass.

Lonnie gave it to her. She trained it on the clearing, then lowered it, and looked at Lonnie. Her eyes were wide, her face a little pale.

"Well, now we know," she said. "They're on our trail."

"I didn't doubt it much. At least we know for sure. Let's finish these apricots."

Lonnie pinched out one of the dark-yellow chunks of fruit, and dropped it into his mouth.

"You go ahead," Casey said, lifting the spyglass once more. "I'm not so hungry anymore."

Lonnie said, "Yeah, me, neither."

Not wanting to waste the food, Lonnie ate the last two apricots and gathered up the cans. The mountains didn't need his trash.

He and Casey rose carefully. There was no way they could be seen up here without Dupree training a spyglass or pair of binoculars on them, but Lonnie felt a cold rush of fear return to his veins. He sensed the same thing in Casey as they slipped and slid back down the hill to their horses.

Lonnie dropped the empty tins into his cavvy sack, tightened and rearranged the General's rigging, and swung up into the saddle. He looked at Casey as she did the same, limping only slightly now on her ankle.

"Don't worry, Casey," he said. "They won't be able to track us. I made sure of that."

"Maybe not, kid, but they're still behind us, and that makes me not to want to waste a whole lot of time if you get my drift..." She looked around at the maze of pines and mountains rising around them. "My gosh—awfully big country out here. I think I just realized that." She looked at Lonnie. "I'm startin' to feel a little queasy. Which way?"

"The pass trail's northeast, so I reckon we'll head northeast," Lonnie said, reining the General to the left and into a stand of pines covering the downslope of the mountain shoulder they were on.

They rode down the mountain to the bottom and then climbed the mountain beyond it. This mountain was higher, but the climb was more gradual, and they crossed a creek and a clearing to a windy, treeless knob. Here they rested the horses as well as themselves, and Lonnie couldn't resist casting another look through his spyglass along their back trail.

He wasn't surprised to see no sign of Dupree. Even if Dupree was able to find the tracks Lonnie had tried so hard to hide from the outlaws, the outlaws would still be a long ways behind their quarry.

The fact that Dupree was still after him, however, caused Lonnie's chest to tighten and his breath to grow shallow. Just knowing a man who wanted him dead was following him, maybe only a mile away as the crow flies, with Lonnie's blood on his mind . . .

He and Casey continued riding, crossing one more steep, windy ridge and dropping down the other side as the giant, golden ball of the sun tumbled behind western ridges. They set up camp along another creek that wended along the bottom of the narrow valley that formed a trough between pine-studded ridges.

Lonnie used the twine he kept in his saddlebags along with a hook he'd fashioned from a baling needle that he kept in a sewing kit, also stowed in his saddlebags, to rig a fishing line. He'd attached a small red button to the hook, to attract trout whenever he was out on the range and felt like a meal of fresh fish.

He found some grubs under a rotten log, and impaled a couple of these on the end of the hook and dropped the hook into the creek that was about two feet deep and so clear it didn't even return his reflection but magnified the small rocks forming a bed on the sandy bottom. He tossed the baited hook out several times, and watched it ride along the current before dragging it back and tossing it out again, hoping a fish happened by and saw the flash of the red button.

Meanwhile, Lonnie could smell the smoke from the fire that Casey was building from the wood that Lonnie had scrounged while the girl had bathed her tender ankle in the cool stream water. He glanced back to see Casey on her knees, fanning the growing flames. Blue smoke rose and glinted in the last, orange light angling into the canyon from the west.

His and the girl's gear was piled around the camp. Fortunately, since he'd figured on spending some time at the line shack on Eagle Ridge, Lonnie had packed his camping gear. His fry pan and coffeepot would come in handy for preparing a tasty, fortifying meal for him and Casey.

If any fish took his bait, that was...

While he tossed the bait and retrieved it, he glanced back several times at Casey tending the fire. Her long, wavy blonde hair glowed like sunlit honey in the last light. She'd tucked it out of the way behind her ears. She had a line of ash across her right, lightly tanned cheek. Somehow, that line of ash accentuated how pretty she was. And while Lonnie didn't like her sometimes when she seemed to have a secret that she was holding over him, the girl made his heart ache a little almost all of the time.

He couldn't deny the fact that he was taken with her. She was the only thing that made this current trouble tolerable—the fact that she was in it with him, and they were riding together, supporting each other.

Almost like they were married or something...

That thought made him wince with embarrassment, and he tried to turn his mind back to his fishing, but not two minutes later he found himself casting another look back over his shoulder toward the camp.

Casey was sitting on a rock on the other side of the fire from Lonnie, facing him. She was leaning forward, elbows on her knees, and she was looking toward him. Immediately, she jerked her head back to the fire and began prodding the flames with the long, forked stick in her hand.

Lonnie turned quickly back to the stream, his heart thudding.

Could she be thinking the same sort of things that he was thinking? That it might be kind of nice to stay together even after all this trouble was over...?

Then he cursed under his breath. He was only thirteen. She was fifteen. At their ages, two years were as long as a whole century. Besides, she'd made it clear she wasn't interested in a country boy.

His heart ached harder. It was a dull ache, like two of his ribs were pushing against his ticker from opposite sides.

The fishing line tightened in Lonnie's fingers. It jerked slightly, suddenly. Lonnie jerked back on the line and then it fell slack against the water.

The fish had gotten away. But only a minute or so later a second one did not. The ten-inch red-throated trout was flopping around on the grassy bank when Lonnie caught another, much smaller trout which he threw back to let grow another year, replacing it with another one about ten minutes later that was almost a foot long.

He dressed out the fish with his Barlow knife, tossing the guts into the stream, and carried his two trophies on a single stick proudly back to the camp. Casey was tending the coffeepot, which had come to a boil on the hot coals, and when she saw the fish she arched her brows, impressed.

"Never figured you for a fisherman, Lonnie."

"A fella gets tired of beef now an' then," was all he said, and pulled his frying pan out of his cavvy sack.

He'd set both fish, still cold from the creek, into the pan, which he'd greased with lard, when General Sherman gave a testy whicker and turned to look behind him. The chestnut shook her head and stomped.

Casey gasped as she looked toward the horses.

Lonnie grabbed his rifle from where it leaned against a log, and pumped a cartridge into the chamber.

THIRTY-SIX

"WHAT ARE THEY ACTIN' so skittish about?" Casey asked, standing tensely by the fire and staring toward the horses.

Lonnie held his Winchester up high across his chest and licked his lips as he stared past the horses tied to a single rope strung between two pines. "Heard somethin'. I'm gonna check it out. You stay here."

"You think it's Dupree?"

"I reckon I'll know soon enough."

Lonnie walked out around the horses, running a hand along the General's side as he did. He walked through the forest, pine needles and bits of cones crunching softly beneath his boots. The forest floor was soft, almost like walking on a rug.

It was also eerily quiet now at twilight.

A couple of small birds flitted here and there amongst the branches. Farther off, a squirrel chittered.

Suddenly, that silence was broken by a long, mewling, bugling sound. It sounded like someone blowing a massive bullhorn. The cry rolled up sharply and ended in a high-pitched wail that echoed. The echoes died above the top of a stony ridge looming on the valley's far side, maybe a hundred yards away.

Lonnie stared at the ridge. The short hairs pricked along the back of his neck at the eerie sound. Then relief somewhat eased the tension between his shoulders. The bugling had likely been made by an elk.

Possibly a bear, which wouldn't have been good—especially if it were a *grizzly bear*—but most likely an elk. Lonnie had heard the calls before though they usually came much later in the year, when elk bugled to define their territory and to call in mates.

But sometimes, like humans, animals got confused.

The cry came again, not as loud this time. Whatever the beast was—Lonnie was almost certain it was an elk, which posed no threat to him and Casey—it seemed to be on the other side of the dark-brown sandstone ridge that he could see through the pines and up a slight rise. And, judging by the diminishing sound, the beast seemed to be moving away from the ridge.

Behind Lonnie, the General gave another low whicker.

Lonnie turned. The General was looking back past Lonnie, twitching his ears and switching his tail. The chestnut stared ahead, seemingly no longer bothered.

"It's all right, General," Lonnie said as he walked past the horse, patting the General's rump. "Just an elk who forgot what time of year it is."

Casey looked relieved. She still stood by the fire, the orange flames dancing and the smoke rising behind her. "You're sure it's not a bear? I've heard grizzlies callin' from the ridges around Arapaho Creek." She shuddered and crossed her arms on her chest. "I sure wouldn't wanna come face-to-face with a big grizzly bear out here, Lonnie."

Lonnie leaned his rifle against the log. "I'm pretty sure it's an elk," he said. "Besides, it's in the next valley over. A big ridge between us and him."

"If you say so."

Lonnie glanced once more toward the ridge. He wished he could be absolutely certain that what he'd heard hadn't been a grizzly, but he wasn't. As he set to work looking for mushrooms to slice into the frying pan with his fish, however, he forgot about the bugling.

Night sank slowly into the valley, and soon there was only a little faint, emerald light in the sky beyond the pine tops. Coyotes called distantly, and the creek chuckled over its stony bed. The fish fried slowly in the lard with wild mushrooms he'd sliced, and two corn cakes he'd whipped together from his possibles, and the fire gave off a pleasant warmth as the air grew sharp with a mountain chill.

An almost intoxicating tranquility had descended with the darkness and the stars kindling in the sky straight above.

Lonnie and Casey sat on opposite sides of the fire, which they kept small in case Dupree was closer than Lonnie figured he was to this valley. Lonnie's mind grew slow and peaceful as he ate the tender, flakey fish and mushrooms and nicely browned cake, and washed the food down with frequent sips of the hot, black coffee.

"You catch right good fish, Mister Lonnie Gentry," Casey said as she gathered up their tin plates, wooden handled forks, and coffee cups, and carried them over to the creek for cleaning.

"Why, thank you, Miss Casey."

"Don't mention it," she said back over her shoulder.

While she was gone, Lonnie gathered more fallen branches from the trees along the creek. He didn't want to make the fire too large, so that Dupree or anyone else skulking around the valley at night might see it. If he were alone, he'd probably let it die out altogether. But Casey probably wasn't as accustomed to sleeping out in the high-and-rocky as he was, and the mountains got cold this high. There might even be a little frost on the ground come morning.

For her, he'd try to keep the fire small. He should probably try to stay awake and keep watch for Dupree, but he was dead-dog tired. It was a weariness he could feel making his deepest bones and muscles ache. He'd probably never make it through the night without nodding off. If he did, he'd probably fall off his horse tomorrow along the trail somewhere, and break his neck.

When he returned to the fire with a second armload of wood, Casey was already curled up in Lonnie's bedroll, which he'd insisted she use. He'd even arranged pine boughs for her, to soften the cold, hard ground. His coat was good enough for Lonnie. She lay on her side, knees drawn up halfway to her belly. She'd left her boots on, and they poked out from beneath the blankets. Her blonde hair spilled prettily across her saddle. Already she appeared cold, for she'd drawn one of the two blankets halfway over her face that the fire's orange flames caressed lovingly.

Seeing her so peaceful made Lonnie even more tired. He quietly set a couple of small branches on the fire, then walked off to tend to nature. He came back, spread out some pine boughs for a makeshift mattress, in front of his saddle, on the side of the fire opposite Casey, and slacked down onto one of the fragrant branches. He scrunched himself deep inside his heavy wool mackinaw, whose collar he pulled up around his cheeks.

Lonnie lay staring up through the treetops at the stars for a time.

Dupree was a constant worry nibbling at the edges of his mind. He was glad he wasn't alone. He'd spent many nights alone out on the Circle G range over the past couple of years, when his mother had deemed him old enough to do so. Some late afternoons he was too far away to bother riding all the way back to the cabin at night when he'd only have to saddle up and ride out as far again in the morning. Sometimes he'd sleep out alone in a canyon or at the old line shack.

The first couple of times he'd been a little frightened, lying awake and making mountains out of the molehills of every night sound he heard. The slightest rustle of some burrowing creature would become a stalking, red-eyed wolf in his mind. But he'd quickly gotten accustomed to sleeping out in the mountains alone, and had even come to enjoy it.

He didn't think he'd enjoy it tonight, however. Or maybe that's because three killers were stalking him, and maybe because he was enjoying Casey's company so much.

Thinking back, he realized she hadn't called him "kid" for several hours. Heck, a few minutes ago she'd even called him "Mister".

Lonnie smiled at the twinkling sky. He glanced across the fire at Casey. He could hear her breathing softly beneath her blankets. Lonnie's eyelids grew heavy. Weariness was like a fast-working drug. For a short time, he was vaguely aware of his own soft snores before sleep pulled him deep down into its gauzy depths, turning the world dark and empty, soothing in its silence.

He had no idea how much time had passed before that silence was shattered by Casey's ear-rattling scream.

THIRTY-SEVEN

LONNIE SAT BOLT UPRIGHT, heart thudding, as the girl's scream echoed around the dark encampment.

Only vaguely did he become aware that he had not built up the fire as he'd intended but had let it go out completely. His mind was slow to catch up to the scream, as well, and he realized, as the wail died, that Casey had screamed, *"Daddy!"*

Now, silence.

Lonnie stared across the fire, his eyes growing accustomed to the darkness relieved by starlight and a small snippet of moon angling up over the valley. Then he heard Casey sobbing. Getting oriented—at first, he'd thought he was at the line shack—he reached over to where he'd leaned his rifle against a tree, and fumbled around until he'd gotten a cartridge seated in the chamber.

He looked around, expecting to see three shadows jouncing, trying to drag Casey out of her bedroll. He could hear little above the girl's scream still echoing around inside his head and the ratcheting thunder of his own hammering heart.

Distantly, he could hear her sobbing, and he quietly called her name.

There was no reply.

He jumped to his feet and tramped around the fire in his stocking feet, shivering fearfully and looking around in the shadows flanking her. She was sitting up, her face a pale oval framed by the messy spill of her honey-blonde hair.

"Casey, what is it?"

"Lonnie!"

He dropped to a knee, still looking around behind her. One of the horses whickered nervously, but he was sure the mount had only been frightened by Casey's scream. "Yeah, I'm here. What is it? Why'd you scream? Nightmare?"

Casey sobbed quietly. "Yeah." Her shoulders jerked as she crossed her arms on her chest and lowered her chin.

Her reply tempered the boy's own anxiety. His heart slowed, and his palms stopped sweating. He held the rifle's hammer back with his thumb, pulled the trigger, releasing the action, and eased the hammer down to the firing pin. Still holding the rifle in one hand, he placed his other hand on one of Casey's, and squeezed.

"About your pa?"

Keeping her head down, Casey nodded. She gave another sob and lifted one hand to wipe away a tear rolling down her cheek.

Her breath was ragged. "I dreamt he was callin' me. I was inside our house and he was outside and callin' and askin' me to let him in, and I was runnin' around the house. The house was dark and I was tryin' to find the door, but nothin' in the house seemed to be where it should be, and it was like there was no door.

"Pa kept me callin' me, askin' me to let him in, and I was tryin' to yell back at him that I was tryin' to let him in, but I couldn't get the words out. It was like there was a rag in my mouth. It was so frustratin'! I couldn't call to him, and I was afraid that if he didn't know I was there, lookin' for the door, he'd go away and I'd never see him again!"

"It's all right, Casey."

She lowered her head again and said in a voice pinched with emotion: "That's when I woke up and heard myself screamin'. Then I realized it was only a dream, and that Pa was gone. I'd never really heard him callin', and I'd never hear him callin' me again."

Her head bobbed and her shoulders shook as she bawled for a short time.

"I'm never gonna see him again. He's gone forever, and I will live my whole life without ever seein' him again, and I want to so much that sometimes, aside from Dupree and the money, it's all I can think about!"

"Yeah, I know how that is."

She looked at him, frowning, her eyes wet with tears. "You do?"

"Sure."

"Oh," she said. "Your pa."

When Lonnie said nothing, Casey said, "It's an awful ache, isn't it?"

"Yeah, it hurts like hell. At least, I got my ma. You got somebody else who'll take care of you, Casey?"

Casey raised her knees to her chest, wrapped her arms around them. She sniffed, ran the back of her hand across her cheek again. "Pa said that if anythin' happened to him that I should find my aunt in Denver. Pa's sister. He said he thought she'd take me in, though I don't think he'd heard from her in a long time. Other than that—no, I don't have anyone."

Imagining how alone the girl must feel, Lonnie felt a frightening hollowness inside him. He imagined what life would have been like without his ma and the ranch—a place to call home—and he had to suppress a shudder. He also had to force himself to not consider the possibility that he might be in the same boat that Casey was in.

"When we get this money to Camp Collins," Lonnie said, "you can come back to the ranch with me. We got an extra room. You can be part of our family—Ma's and mine."

That seemed to warm Casey somewhat. She gave him a lopsided smile. "Thanks, Lonnie. You're a good friend. I gotta keep my job in town, though—if I still have it when I get back, I mean. I have to work, so I can keep the house. If I lose the house...well, then I reckon I might have to consider takin' you up on your offer."

"You'll work it out so's you can keep your house. You're tough for a girl. Tough as most boys I've known."

"Thank you, Lonnie."

Suddenly, Lonnie's ears burned with shame. "Oh," he said, stammering. "I...I didn't mean no insult by that, Casey. I didn't mean you were like a boy. Just tough like one." His tongue felt as though it had doubled in size, and he was having trouble forming words with it. "But you're a girl. Anybody'd see that. I mean, not that I was lookin' or thinkin' about it or nothin', but—"

"Lonnie?"

He looked at her.

"Do me a favor? Fetch your bed and drag it over here by mine?"

Lonnie's heart hammered. Now his hands and feet also seemed to have doubled in size. "Miss Casey," Lonnie said, whispering so no one else could hear though he was relatively certain no one else was near. At least, he hoped they weren't. "Are you askin' me to...?" The possibility seemed both wonderful and horrible.

Casey laughed. "Don't get your drawers in a twist, cowboy. I just wanna lay close to you tonight, that's all. Go on—fetch your stuff." She laughed. "Fetch, boy!"

Lonnie scrambled back around the fire. When he'd dragged his gear, including his rifle, over to Casey's side of the fire and had arranged his saddle beside hers, he lay down on the spruce branches, resting his head against the wool underside of the saddle. He lay for a time, aware of Casey lying curled beside him. He stared up at the stars splattered like baking powder across the firmament.

Finally, she scuttled up close to him, wrapped an arm around his belly, and lay her head on his chest. Lonnie stopped breathing. He wasn't sure what to do with his arms.

"Is this all right?" Casey asked softly. "I mean—it don't make you too uncomfortable, does it? I know how boys are."

"No, it's all right," Lonnie lied.

"You can put your arms around me," she said. "I'd like you to."

Awkwardly, Lonnie wrapped his arms around the girl's slender waist and shoulders. She lay warm against him. He could feel her heart beating softly against his chest.

She lifted her head, looked at him, frowning. "You aren't gettin' any devilish ideas, are you?"

"No!" he said, defensively.

"All right, then." Casey lay her head back down on his chest. "Goodnight, Lonnie. Thank you for takin' the money to the marshal."

"Goodnight, Casey. It's no problem."

She chuckled at that, and then Lonnie did, too.

The longer he lay there, with his arms wrapped around this girl he loved, his nerves stopped sputtering, his heart stopped throbbing in his ears, and all seemed—at least, for now—right with this crazy world.

THIRTY-EIGHT

GRADUALLY, the sporadic chittering of a squirrel reached down into Lonnie's unconsciousness and pulled him up into the land of waking.

Before he'd even opened his eyes, he became aware that he was shivering. When he did open his eyes he saw that misty blue light had filled the valley, and fog hung over the creek like smoke. There was a thin, white patina of frost on his coat. He looked at the fire ring, humped with cold, gray ashes.

He'd been so tired that he hadn't awakened during the night to keep the fire built up, as he'd intended.

Casey was curled up tight against his back. Lonnie could feel the warmth of her face and lips pressed against his spine. She was the only warmth he could feel, but her frail body was shivering. She felt good and it was nice, being this close to her, despite the cold, and he hated to awaken her, but that's what happened when he tried to slip out from beneath her arm draped over his hip.

She groaned and removed her arm and pulled her blankets up over her head, curling into a tight ball on her side, shivering.

"I'll have the fire built up in a minute," Lonnie said, rising, shivering inside his coat.

When he'd gotten the fire going, orange flames crackling and sputtering and offering meager warmth, the gray pine smoke peppering his nose, he added a couple of good-sized logs, then took some twine from his saddlebags and went off to see about acquiring the coming night's supper. He didn't want to fire his rifle and possibly alert Dupree to his and Casey's whereabouts, so he'd either have to depend on angling for fish or using his slingshot or the snares he'd fashioned out of twine for bringing down small game, possibly even birds like doves or mountain grouse or wild turkeys.

All of these tools Lonnie carried in his saddlebags or cavvy sack everywhere he rode, because he never knew when he'd get stuck out somewhere away from the cabin and need the food-acquiring implements.

He'd seen some rabbits last night, when he and Casey had ridden up to the creek. Since rabbits usually liked to dine amongst rocks or shrubs that would shield them from the view of predators like coyotes, foxes, wolves, and hawks, Lonnie set his tree snare in the deep, green grass growing among the rocks lining the creek. He bent a springy cottonwood sapling over toward the ground, tied the long end of the snare to its crown, and pinned the snare and also the sapling to the ground with a sharp stick in which he'd cut a trigger notch, setting his trap.

It usually required several hours to gather game like this, and he should have set the trap last night, but he hadn't. So he had to hope that a rabbit, possibly even a fat squirrel, would wander into the snare between now and when he and Casey had swallowed down some breakfast and broken camp.

If not, he'd have to use his slingshot somewhere along today's trail. Lonnie had only the bare minimum of trail supplies in his gear, and he and Casey needed to eat steady meals to keep up their strength and stay alert. It took only one missed meal to cause fatigue and mental dullness, neither of which were fun when you had a full day ahead.

As he finished setting the trap, Lonnie saw strands of smoke from his fire wafting around him. The smoke smelled of pine resin, boiling coffee, and the even-better aroma of frying side pork. Instantly, his mouth began watering.

He walked back to the camp to see Casey up and fully dressed, wearing her coat and gloves against the morning chill. She was crouched over the small, black iron pan in which the side pork sizzled and popped. Lonnie's coffeepot steamed and chugged on a rock around which orange flames danced.

"Breakfast will be ready in a minute, Mister Gentry," she said, adding a couple of baking powder biscuits to the pan. "Hope you're hungry."

"I'm always hungry!"

Lonnie went over and tended the horses, giving them each a handful of grain and untying them from their picket line, so they could freely forage and drink from the creek. When he returned to the camp, Casey had set a couple of side pork sandwiches for him on a tin plate at the fire's perimeter, where they'd stay warm. The girl sat on her saddle, eating a sandwich, which she was washing down with the hot, black coffee steaming in the tin cup at her feet.

The sandwiches were delicious, as was Casey's coffee.

"Lonnie?" Casey said, picking apart her second sandwich with her hands, and frowning. "What's wrong with the horses?"

Lonnie followed Casey's gaze toward where both mounts stood facing east and shaking their heads as though at pesky blackflies. A couple of times General Sherman craned his neck to look back at Lonnie, as though he were communicating his edginess.

"I don't know," Lonnie said, setting down his empty plate and brushing crumbs from his jeans.

He picked up his rifle and walked out to stand beside the two horses. Both mounts continued to stare off toward a low, pine-covered eastern ridge, the top of which was being painted gold by the rising sun. The horses had settled down somewhat, but they continued to stand stiffly, staring with their wide, brown eyes, working their nostrils as they sniffed the breeze.

Lonnie patted the General's neck, then walked a ways out from the camp, looking around cautiously and nervously squeezing the rifle in his hands. He was relieved to find nothing even remotely suspicious anywhere near the camp. It was as much of a relief as he would have liked, however. The horses could detect trouble a lot farther away than Lonnie could.

He remembered the bugling cry and hoped again that it had been made by an elk...

Then he imagined Dupree's gang sneaking up on his and Casey's camp, and he returned to the fire, immediately kicking dirt on it to douse the flames.

"We best pull our picket pins," Lonnie told Casey, unable to keep the uneasiness from his voice. "I don't see nothin' out there, and horses can get cross-grained for reasons of their own, but since they both have burrs under their saddles and they ain't even saddled yet, let's light a shuck!"

When he and Casey had broken camp and saddled both mounts, Lonnie checked his snare. He wasn't surprised to see that it hadn't been sprung. He gathered up the trap to use later, stowed it in his cavvy sack, and swung up onto the General's back.

He and Casey moved out, looking around nervously. A half hour later, they were moving down through the forest stippling the same ridge that the horses had stared at before. Only, Lonnie and Casey were quartering east and hopefully away from any danger the horses had scented.

The hope was short-lived. Just when Lonnie had noted that both horses looked considerably calmer, the General suddenly pricked his ears.

A few seconds later, Lonnie heard what the General must have heard— a loud, bugling cry dripping with savage menace and which seemed to echo forever amongst the pine tops. The cry swirled wildly around Lonnie, disorienting him. It was soon joined by the echoes of cracking, breaking wood and snapping branches, and the thuds of some large, four-legged creature moving toward him.

THIRTY-NINE

THE GENERAL TOSSED his head wildly and loosed another piercing whinny.

Casey's filly, Miss Abigail, joined the stallion a half second later with her own ripping whinny. Lonnie whipped his head around to see what appeared to be a cabin-sized creature moving down the opposite, wooded slope, ahead and on his right and obscured by pines and aspens and occasional tamaracks and spruces.

Sunlight shone on the beast's cinnamon fur that rippled as it ran down the slope, mewling and snarling.

Holding his reins tight in both hands up close to his chest, Lonnie shouted, *"Bear!"*

He meant to add, though of course he hadn't really needed to, that they'd best make a hard run for it. But as though Casey's chestnut was violently offended by the word "Bear", the horse pitched suddenly off her front hooves, lifting her head and fear-sharp eyes and buffeting mane high in the air to Lonnie's right.

Casey screamed, "Lonnie!"

The boy reached for the girl, to try to keep her from falling out of her saddle, but Casey went flying backward off the chestnut's rump. The General gave a similar, sky-clawing pitch onto its rear hooves, causing Lonnie, who'd loosened his grip on his reins and was leaning too far out from his saddle, to lose the reins all together. Knowing that he was going to fall now no matter what, he kicked his boots free of his stirrups and gave a shrill curse that his mother would not have approved of but would no doubt have forgiven him for, under the circumstances.

That was a vague, short-lived thought, gone without a trace before the ground rose sharply at an angle to smack Lonnie on the shoulders and the back of his head. He cursed again as he rolled down the slope they were halfway to the bottom of, wincing as a sharp stick poked his right thigh.

When he rolled up against a thick, half-rotten log, bells tolling in his head and his brains feeling as though they were about to slither out his ears, he looked up. Casey was rolling toward him on his left, her hair and the slack of her coat flying wildly.

The girl's tumble was stopped by a slight, flat shelf in the slope that was heavily padded with forest duff. She lay for a moment, head on the downslope, feet on the upslope, arms and legs akimbo.

The forest was spinning crazily around Lonnie. There was an old leaf in his right eye, causing that eye to burn. There was another one in his ear, and bits of leaves and pine needles in his hair. Some had fallen down the back of his coat and his shirt, raking his skin.

Despite his disorientation, he managed to gain one knee.

Casey was also climbing to her feet, leaves and pine needles falling from her tangled hair and her shoulders.

The mewling and growling continued to grow louder, as did the thuds of the running beast's four feet. Lonnie turned to see that the bear was only a few yards from the bottom of the ravine that was only about a twenty-foot gap between the steep slopes. He turned to Casey at the same time that Casey turned to him, her mouth and eyes wide, and they screamed each other's names at the same time.

Lonnie turned toward where he'd been thrown off the General's back. Both horses had fled into the ravine and were now galloping out of sight, the General leading the chestnut, both horses trailing their reins, until they were gone from view altogether.

Not only were both horses gone, but Lonnie's Winchester was gone, as well.

"General, you gall-blasted son of a worthless cayuse!"

Lonnie grabbed his hat off the ground and scrambled up the slope and over to Casey. As he did, he cast another look down the slope at the bear.

The bruin wasn't cabin-sized, Lonnie could see now that it was closer. But it was at least as large as a good-sized freight wagon. It would probably have dressed out close to a thousand pounds. Its long, shaggy, cinnamon fur was silver-tipped across the hump behind its head, forming a silver swath down its back to its broad rump.

It was now lumbering up the slope in the direction of Lonnie and Casey, shaking its heart-shaped head with one straight and one ragged, flopping ear, and opening and closing its mouth as though showing off its long, yellow, razor-edged teeth, one strategic swipe of which could very likely tear Lonnie in two...

The sun flashed off its large, glassy brown-black eyes, which owned the mind-numbing, cold-blooded savagery of the wild primeval. The grizzly was like the cold soul of the universe that would kill you without thinking only because, if it thought about it all, it would have regarded life as nothing more than silly ornament.

Lonnie locked gazes with the beast for a single moment, and the universe yawned at the boy. His belly tumbled into his boots. The beast's mindlessly brutal eyes silently vowed to impersonally, without malice, rip Lonnie limb from limb and to devour every inch of him and to chew his bones clean afterwards, simply because he was hungry or because his territory had been invaded, or merely because he *could*.

That gaze almost caused the boy's knees to turn to warm mud and to buckle.

Leaving both him and Casey a sure, easy meal for the charging bruin...

Lonnie shook himself out of the trance. Feeling a cold sweat bathing every inch of him beneath his clothes, he charged up the slope, grabbed Casey's hand, jerked her brusquely to her feet, and then turned and started running toward some rocks he'd only half taken note of.

Many of the rocks appeared to be boulders. They'd probably tumbled long ago from the ridge crest and now rested haphazardly and like giant, fossilized dinosaur eggs amongst the trees. Lonnie thought that he and Casey might be able to find sanctuary somewhere amongst those rocks though he had no idea where, exactly. Maybe they could climb one of the boulders, some of which appeared nearly as large as a two-story house.

Lonnie knew that grizzlies—and the big boy after him and Casey was surely a silvertip griz, if it was anything and not a rabbit!—could climb trees large enough to hold their weight, or could tear down the tree that couldn't hold them but which housed their prey.

Could they climb rocks, as well?

As Lonnie ran, breathing hard, he felt Casey pulling back on his hand. He turned toward her. She was limping badly.

"Casey, come on, we gotta—!"

"It's my ankle again!" she screamed as she dropped to a knee. "I'm sorry, Lonnie!"

She glanced back at the bear charging up the slope behind them. The big, shaggy, snarling beast was within seventy yards and closing fast. The bruin might have been large and ungainly, but it seemed to be running as fast as General Sherman could gallop when given his head.

The ground rumbled beneath Lonnie's boots. As the morning breeze swirled, it filled Lonnie's nose with the beast's heavy, sickly sweet fetor. It was the stink of a large, dead, vermin-infested, shaggy thing wrapped in the rotten cucumber stench of a rattlesnake den.

Casey peeled Lonnie's hand from around her wrist. "Run, Lonnie—for godsakes, let me go, and *run!*"

"Not a chance!" Lonnie hollered, crouching to drag Casey's squirming body over his shoulder.

He turned toward the upslope and amazed himself by how fast the ground seemed to be passing beneath his hammering boots. By how quickly the jumble of scattered, gray boulders was growing larger ahead and above him . . .

"Lonnie, you damn fool!" Casey screamed, punching his back with the ends of her fists.

Lonnie figured that Casey weighed maybe only ten or fifteen pounds less than he did, but with his heart's fierce pumping and the weird, powerful energy surging through his veins, the girl seemed to weigh nothing at all.

Lonnie gained the stone escarpment jutting out of the side of the slope, and without even pausing to plan his course, he headed for a narrow, dark cleft in the bulging stone wall ahead of him. If the cleft went nowhere, and was shallow enough for the bear to reach in for them, Lonnie and Casey would be bear bait.

Fortunately, while the cleft was indeed only about six feet deep, it didn't dead-end. Its ceiling opened onto more, higher rocks, and Lonnie thrust Casey up through the open ceiling and onto what appeared to be a granite ledge above them.

Lonnie could smell the bear's ghastly stench so strongly now that his eyes were watering and his lungs were contracting against it. He didn't bother to look back, because he didn't want to see what he knew he would. But in the periphery of his vision he saw the raging bull griz run up to the cleft, shutting out the light and filling the natural closet in the rocks with dark, stinky shadows and the ear-piercing echoes of its enraged roars.

The beast was so close to Lonnie that the boy could feel the heat of its dead-fish breath. He winced as one or two of the beast's razor-edged claws—as long as pitchfork tines—tore into his back with one clean swipe through his coat and his shirt.

"Ow, goddangit!" Lonnie yelped.

"Lonnie!" Casey screamed, looking down at him from the ledge above him. Her blonde hair hung toward him, nearly grazing his forehead. She thrust her right hand down toward him, as well.

Lonnie ignored it and leaped up for a handhold on the opposite side of the cleft from Casey. He found one, found small cracks and ledges in which to stick his boot toes, and began climbing the eight-foot wall. He climbed in a mad, horror-stricken frenzy, feeling the bruin's paws swiping at his boot heels. Lonnie hoisted himself over the edge and rolled clear of the dark cleft in which the bear's roars continued to echo so loudly that they seemed to be originating from inside Lonnie's own head.

The bear stench wafted up through the hole in the escarpment, between Lonnie and Casey on the other side of it, and for a quick second Lonnie thought of the ground giving way to vent the enraged screams of demons trapped in Hell...

Lonnie closed his eyes, relieved to be out of the beast's reach. Gradually, his heart slowed.

But then Casey groaned. "Oh, no, Lonnie—he's climbin' up here!"

FORTY

CASEY WAS KNEELING on the escarpment, on the other side of the cleft up through which she and Lonnie had come. She wasn't looking into the hole, however, but down the front side of the escarpment.

Lonnie leaped to his feet and ran to the edge of the large mound of rock he was on, and stumbled back a step when he saw the large grizzly standing on its hind feet, snarling up at Casey.

"Casey, get back!" Lonnie shouted.

But he hadn't needed to. The bear lunged toward Casey, smashing its broad belly and shoulders against the side of the escarpment and thrusting its paws with extended black claws toward the girl, who gave a horrified scream and fell back on her rump, slapping a hand to her chest. Her pale face was mottle pink, her blue eyes sharp with mind-numbing fear.

The bear leaped up off its hind feet, trying to climb over the lip of the ridge and get to Casey, who scuttled back on her rump until she was pressing her back up against another boulder, knees drawn to her chest.

"He can't get up here, can he, Lonnie? Oh, please tell me he can't climb rock!"

Lonnie dropped to a knee to look down at the bruin shaking its head furiously. Lonnie saw that not only was one of the cross-grained beast's ears shredded, but it had three long, dark-pink scars forming pale streaks down the left side of its face, beneath the left eye, which drooped a little. More signs of a violent past. The lip of the scarp was higher here than back where Lonnie had climbed up through the cleft. It was a good three feet above the bear's head, and frustrating the bruin no end.

The beast kept lunging at the rock wall. It wasn't showing much grace, however. And, thankfully, its timing was poor. Each time it lunged at the wall, its jump was off enough to keep it from being able to hook its paws over the lip of the rock. Lonnie didn't know how much strength the bear had in its front legs—or were they arms?

Could it pull itself up over the rock if it managed to leap high enough?

In case it could, Lonnie looked around. The escarpment continued to rise behind him and Casey—one stone ledge after another. A few cedars grew between the stone slabs that formed the scarp.

"Casey!" Lonnie called. "Climb up as far as you can! Keep climbin' until you can't climb any farther!"

He had a feeling that if the bear could climb up to where he and Casey were now, it could probably climb all the way to the top of the scarp. But there was no point in the girl staying this close when she didn't have to.

Moving gingerly on her injured ankle, Casey began climbing the slabs of mossy-green rock forming the higher scarp beyond the slope that the bear was still on.

"What are you goin' to do?" the girl called over her shoulder, grabbing a twisted cedar, which she used to pull herself up onto the next, table-topped boulder.

Lonnie wasn't sure what he was going to do. But when he'd looked around and found a couple of loose, good-sized rocks, something occurred to him. He grabbed the rocks, returned to the edge of the lip where the bear had gotten a hold and was trying to climb, and slammed one of the rocks down hard on the beast's left paw.

The boy wasn't so sure that that had been such a good idea.

The bruin looked up at him and loosed a bugling growl even louder than before, spittle stringing off its long, curving fangs, its eyes nearly crossing. Lonnie stepped back and slung the rock as hard as he could. It smacked the bear right above its snout that was as wide as a wheel hub and as broad as Lonnie's thigh. That only seemed to enrage the beast even more. It lunged toward Lonnie, turning its head this way and that, mouth wide, roaring.

"Lonnie, get up here!" Casey screamed above and behind him.

Something told Lonnie that the bruin was having enough trouble climbing the rock face that one more slam of a stone across its skull might discourage him, if it was possible to discourage a silvertip.

Lonnie sent the second rock hurling down toward the beast's massive head. The animal had lifted its snout toward Lonnie once more, and the rock smashed into the dead, black, leathery center of it. The beast gave another bone-jarring roar that seemed to fill the whole valley, echoing, causing the escarpment to quiver beneath Lonnie's boots. The beast appeared to jerk slightly, as though something had dawned on it. Lonnie watched in shock as the beast stepped away from the ledge, dropped to all fours, gave another, lower mewling growl, and then lumbered down through the trees away from the scarp.

Pine needles crunched and branches snapped beneath its heavy, running paws.

Lonnie staggered back away from the ledge in shock. His knees went weak, and he dropped to his butt.

Staring after the fleeing bear, Lonnie laughed with relief and said, "Casey—did you see that?"

A man's voice said with sneering menace, "You did good, kid. You did real good."

Lonnie whipped his head around. His heart jerked to life once more, and for a second he thought it would burst when he saw Shannon Dupree hunkered down on the flat-topped boulder beside Casey. The blond, yellow-eyed outlaw leader, wearing a sheepskin vest over his red-and-black-checked shirt, his hat tipped low on his forehead, had one arm wrapped around Casey's shoulders. In his other hand, he held his Winchester rifle, the barrel of which he was pressing up taut against Casey's right cheek.

Casey had gone white as a sheet. She stared dully at Lonnie. Her eyes bore into the boy with a vague, silent pleading as well as with mute apology.

Lonnie lurched to his feet, mind racing. He was still frazzled from the bear attack. To see Dupree squatting there beside Casey—it was all too surreal for his battered mind to wrap itself around, to understand.

"You did all right," Dupree said again with his usual mockery, nodding. He glanced beyond Lonnie. "But I got a feelin' it was Fuego's rifle shot that really discouraged that bruin."

Hoof clomps and the crunching of pine needles rose behind Lonnie. The boy turned, and his gut sank even lower when he saw the stocky, dark Fuego and Jake Childress ride slowly toward him, keeping a tight rein on their mounts that were tossing their heads nervously at the fresh scent of the kill-crazy bear.

Childress was leading Dupree's calico gelding. Both men rode with their rifles across their saddlebows. Fuego's eyes were dark, his mouth beneath his thick, black mustache unsmiling.

Childress was grinning, his too-close, pale-blue eyes glistening maliciously in the golden sunlight angling through the pines.

FORTY-ONE

DUPREE SAID, "Kid, you stay right where you are, or I'll drill a hole through this pretty little miss's head. And you wouldn't want that, now, would you?"

"I ain't goin' anywhere," Lonnie said, rage burning off his mind fog. He clenched his fists at his sides, yearning for his rifle. "You hurt her, I'll kill you, you son of a—!"

"Nuh-uh!" Dupree said, grinning as he rose, making the girl rise with him but pulling his rifle away from her face. "What would your ma say about such barn talk, boy? If you ain't careful, I'm gonna tell May, and she'll wash your mouth out with soap!"

The killer had said this loudly enough that Fuego and Childress could hear. Both men chuckled now, reining their horses to a stop near the bottom of the scarp. Lonnie stood where he was, heart hammering the back side of his breastbone.

"She's still alive, then?" Lonnie asked, knowing the jig was likely up for him and Casey, but still worried sick about his ma. "You didn't...you didn't hurt her?"

"I didn't *what*? Oh, wait!" Dupree said, pretending to ponder the question. "Gee, I don't remember, now. I can't remember if I held it against her that she turned my money...er, I mean, me *and the boys'* money...over to her son so's he could give it back to the very folks I'd taken it from! I mean, if I'd wanted that to happen to all my hard work...er, I mean, me *and the boys'* hard work...I'd have taken it into Arapaho Creek myself!"

"Let me go, you filthy coward!" Casey said, jerking her arm out of the man's grip.

Dupree, who stood close to six feet four inches tall, looked like a tall, blond-headed, slant-eyed ghoul grinning down at her. "You watch your tongue, too, Miss Pretty. Or I'll take a bar of soap and wash your mouth out myself!"

"Just try it!"

"All right, I will," Dupree said. "Just as soon as we get down off this rock." He chuckled and turned to Lonnie with a squint-eyed, suspicious look. "You ain't got a pistol on you—do you, boy?"

"If I had one," Lonnie said, barely able to keep his rage in check, "I'd have used it by now."

He hadn't gotten an honest answer about his ma, and he knew he wouldn't get one. Dupree would only devil him about what he may or may not have done to her. That was the kind of man he was. All Lonnie wanted now was to find some way to get himself and Casey out of this current snare they were in.

Lonnie had thought he'd frightened away the bear, but Fuego's rifle shot had apparently done that. To Lonnie's embarrassment, the very men out to kill him had likely saved him...for now. The rifle's report must have been drowned by the bear's roar. He thought he'd seen the beast flinch a little. Maybe Lonnie wasn't as tough as he thought he was.

Maybe, for how smart he was feeling about brushing Dupree off his trail, this was finally the end of his line.

For himself, he stopped caring. He was plum tuckered out. He felt like an old man. But he didn't want it to be the end of the line for Casey. She was too much girl to be killed by Dupree. More girl than Lonnie had even thought before he'd gotten to know her. He'd fight for her to the very end.

Dupree said, "You think you're tough—don't you, kid?"

"I'm tough enough," Lonnie shot back at the man.

"Lonnie, you hush now!" Casey said, casting him a desperately worried look.

To Casey, Dupree said, shoving her forward, "You go on down there with your boyfriend, Pretty Miss. I'm assumin' you came up this way, so there must be a way *down* this way, too."

Casey crawled gingerly down the boulders to Lonnie, who was waiting for her at the bottom. He took the girl's arm as Dupree followed her down, leaping from rock to rock, keeping his rifle leveled on both of them with one hand, extending the barrel straight out from his hip.

"Well, what're you waitin' for?" Dupree barked, when he was standing over them both. He waved the rifle, angrily. "Let's get down off these rocks, and then we can see about the money."

Lonnie helped Casey back down the way they'd come up—through the cleft in the scarp. Getting down was considerably harder and slower than getting up had been, with the bear snapping its jaws at them. Dupree must have gotten onto the escarpment from the top of the ridge.

When they made it down and were standing outside the cleft, where Fuego and Childress were waiting, sitting on rocks, with their rifles resting across their thighs, Casey was barely able to put any weight at all on her ankle. She had an arm wrapped around Lonnie's neck, while Lonnie had his left arm wrapped around Casey's waist, holding her up.

"All right," Dupree said, stooping as he came striding out of the cleft, his face red from exertion, pressing his rifle against Lonnie's belly. "Where is it? You give me a smart answer, boy, I'll gut shoot you and leave you here for that bear to come back and finish!"

Lonnie chewed on his answer. He could not bring himself to tell Dupree where the money was.

Dupree grinned with menace, showing his long, fang-like eyeteeth and squinting his gray eyes, and loudly cocked his rifle.

"Lonnie!" Casey said. "It's over! We have to give him the money or he'll kill us!"

Lonnie knew it was true. Still, it was hard getting the words out. "It's on my horse. He ran off when the bear hit us." It was true. Lonnie had strapped the money to the stallion's back, so Casey's filly hadn't had to carry the extra weight over the rough terrain.

"Which way?"

"That way."

Dupree looked behind Lonnie and said, "Fuego."

The stocky half-breed rose from his rock, swung up onto his horse's back, and galloped away through the trees.

Childress said, "Maybe I oughta go with him."

Dupree eyed Childress suspiciously. "You stay here with me. He's too stupid to get any ideas himself. But the two of you together might concoct somethin'." He spat to one side. "Somethin' like a double-cross, maybe." He smiled. "I'd be lookin' for you two in Mexico."

"That's just like you, Shannon," Childress said, shaking his head sadly. "Don't got a trustin' bone in your body."

Dupree looked around. He told Childress to gather wood and build a fire. Childress looked at him crossways, and Dupree said, "I'm gonna watch these two lovebirds, make sure they don't go flyin' off together. Neither one of 'em will be out of my sight until we get the money back. So fetch the wood and build the fire before you and me get crossways!"

Lonnie wondered what he meant by "until we get the money back". What would happen once they had the money?

Foolish question. Lonnie knew very well what would happen to both him and Casey. Somehow, he and Casey had to get away.

But how were they going to do that when Casey could put no weight on her ankle, much less run?

When Childress had stomped off to fetch firewood, Dupree said, "You two lovebirds sit down and make yourselves comfortable. Try to run off, I'll tie you to a tree." He grinned at Casey in a way that seared Lonnie with raw fury. "Doesn't look like Miss Pretty's goin' anywhere, though. At least, not very fast."

Casey cursed him in a way that made even Lonnie blush.

Dupree whistled in awe at the girl's finesse with the rougher parts of the English language—the parts that hadn't made it into the dictionary and likely never would.

"You got a mouth on you, Miss Pretty!" Dupree looked at Lonnie. "Kid, you really know how to pick 'em. Where'd you find this one?"

"I'm Casey Stoveville. Marshal Stoveville was my father." Casey spat the words out like unwieldy prune pits. "Until you killed him, you butcher!"

Casey lunged toward Dupree, who took one laughing step back as Casey fell flat on her face with an anguished groan.

"Now, you try that again, Miss Pretty," Dupree said, pressing the barrel of his rifle up against the back of the girl's head, "and this party's gonna be over for you right quick!"

Before Lonnie knew what he was doing, he was lunging for Dupree.

Dupree may have been big, but he was fast. When Lonnie was still three feet away from him, the outlaw shifted his rifle around and rammed its heavy butt into the dead center of Lonnie's belly.

Lonnie stopped in his tracks. His knees buckled as the wind left him in one loud spurt.

Holding his belly, he collapsed in agony.

FORTY-TWO

IT TOOK Lonnie a miserably long time to draw a breath into his lungs. When he finally did, he rolled over onto his back and kept breathing, enjoying the feeling of having air return to his body despite the horrible predicament that he and Casey found themselves in.

When he'd regained his wind as well as his senses, Lonnie realized that Casey had been kneeling beside him the whole time, one hand on his back and scolding Dupree venomously. For his part, the outlaw merely sat on a rock and built a cigarette from the makings sack he wore around his neck, and leisurely smoked it, a smug expression on his face.

When Childress returned with an armload of wood, Dupree continued to smoke while the other outlaw formed a ring with rocks, and built a fire inside the ring. He boiled coffee on the flames, then he and Dupree sat around the fire, drinking coffee to which they added splashes of Old Kentucky Rye and looking downslope every now and then, expecting Fuego and the stolen money.

Lonnie was in no hurry for Fuego to return. When Dupree had what he considered to be his money back, he would have no more use for Lonnie and Casey. In the meantime, Lonnie waited for a chance to make a move on one of the outlaws.

His only hope for survival would be to somehow acquire one of the outlaws' guns, and either shoot them both—he thought he could shoot another man, now, given that it was the only chance he'd have at saving himself and Casey—or disarm them both and keep them pinned down while he and Casey rode off on their horses.

To that end, as one hour passed, and then another, and they all waited for Fuego, Lonnie kept a vigilant eye on the men and their guns. Both were drinking enough coffee and rye while they passed the time that both men left the camp several times to tend nature. Dupree always took his rifle with him, but Childress left his own Winchester leaning against the rock upon which he'd been sitting.

Only, one man always remained in camp. When Childress was gone, Dupree stayed, drinking his spiced coffee and smoking, making any attempt Lonnie might make on Childress's rifle sheer suicide.

Lonnie had seen Dupree wield a rifle several times in the past. The man was not only good with a long gun, but he rarely missed at what he was shooting at, be it gophers or coffee cans perched on fence posts. Once, Lonnie had seen the killer shoot a hawk out of the sky for sport. That was when Lonnie started to hate the man, before he'd ever suspected him of being an outlaw.

Only a no-account vermin would shoot an animal for sport. Real men as well as real women killed animals for food only. Lonnie's father had never believed in mounting an animal's head on the wall, even if the animal had been brought down primarily for food. Doing so was disrespectful to the animal and only proved that the man who did it was a show-off, a soulless tinhorn, a fool.

That's what Dupree was. A fool. Lonnie didn't know why his mother hadn't been able to see that. It was frighteningly clear to Lonnie.

The afternoon was a tense one for Lonnie. He could tell that it was tense for Casey, as well. They sat against the same tree, Casey massaging her swollen ankle. Occasionally they glanced at each other and exchanged wan smiles meant to be encouraging though they really only betrayed the desperation and anxiety percolating inside them both.

Sun-dappled shadows slid around the pair.

Birds piped and squirrels chattered in the branches. The breeze wisped and occasionally moaned amongst the treetops. Sometimes, there was the shrill cry of a hawk hunting high in the sky above camp.

Otherwise, the only sounds were the crackling of the fire, the chugging of the coffeepot, and the occasional murmurs of Dupree and Childress, mostly wondering aloud what was keeping Fuego. Their two hobbled, unsaddled horses munched grass nearby, hooves crunching pine needles as they moved slowly around to forage.

All afternoon, Lonnie's heart beat heavily, and his palms sweated.

Desperation was a living thing inside him, chewing away at his insides. He'd thought he was ready to die. But, now, having had some time to think about it, and to wonder what it would be like, to give up this world for the grave or whatever lay beyond it—would he see his father again, or his mother if she were dead as well?—he realized how badly he wanted to live. To breathe mountain air wind with the scent of pine, to hear a hawk screeching as it hunted, to be close enough to Casey to smell the distinct smell of the girl, to hear her breathing and shifting around beside him.

He knew he was too young to think about such grown-up things, but he thought that he wouldn't mind being married to Casey. He could see them working the ranch together and raising a passel of young'uns.

That, however, was probably not likely to happen...

Lonnie's heart jerked when, in the mid-afternoon, a horse whinnied down the slope behind him. Casey gasped and jerked with a start, as well. Dupree, who'd been sleeping lightly under his hat brim while Childress had been adding more wood to the fire, suddenly poked his hat back on his forehead, and stared down the slope through the pines.

"Here he comes," he said, rising from his rock and resting his rifle on his shoulder.

Lonnie could hear the thuds of an approaching horse. He glanced to Casey on his left. The girl's face was pale again, with a little pink on the nubs of her cheeks. Her face was drawn with worry, lips slightly parted. She slid a plainly frightened glance at Lonnie, and they both turned to stare down the slope where the hoof thuds continued to grow louder until Lonnie could hear the squawk of leather and the faint jingling of a bridle chain.

The stocky Fuego came into view amongst the trees. He rode up to the edge of the camp, and both Dupree and Childress stood regarding the man, frowning curiously.

"I was about ready to saddle up and go lookin' for you," Dupree growled.

"Thought I wasn't comin' back, huh? Maybe headin' for Mexico?" Fuego's dark eyes flashed mockingly. Then he shook his head. "Sorry, boss. I couldn't find that hoss nowheres. Came back because I was so far out I figured it'd get dark on me. No point in stumblin' around after sundown."

Dupree's eyes widened. "No sign of it?"

Fuego shook his head. "None that I could see."

Dupree turned to Lonnie. The other two outlaws turned to the boy, as well, their eyes flat and hard. Dupree walked over and casually pointed his Winchester at the boy's forehead.

"Boy, if you lied to me, I'll kill you right now!"

"He didn't lie!" Casey yelled. "Both our horses ran that way down the ravine. Just because that big idiot can't track..."

The girl let her voice trail off, knowing she was pushing too hard.

Fuego stared at her with flat eyes.

"I wasn't lyin'," Lonnie said. "Both horses ran that way down the ravine. Maybe they turned and ran up the other ridge. I don't know. I didn't see 'em. Had more important things on my mind when they run off. But if Mister Fuego didn't find 'em, that's what they must've done."

"How can I be sure?" Dupree said, staring menacingly down the barrel of his rifle at Lonnie. "How can I be sure you didn't hide the money somewheres along the trail? Maybe you an' Miss Pretty knew me an' the boys was closin' on you, and you didn't want us to catch you with it. Maybe you figured if we caught you without the money we wouldn't kill you, and you could go back for it later."

Dupree blew a caustic snort. "Well, you figured wrong, boy."

Lonnie made a hard effort to stifle his shaking. He raked his gaze from the round maw of the rifle, and said, "How do you figure killin' me an' Casey is gonna get your money back?"

"It ain't," Dupree said, smiling coldly and pressing the rifle barrel against Lonnie's chest, over his heart. "But it'll make me feel a whole lot better." He grinned again. "Best pray, boy. Best pray real hard!"

FORTY-THREE

LONNIE STARED up at the outlaw, speechless. Sweat dribbled down the sides of his face to drip from his chin and dampen the front of his shirt. Even Casey had been rendered speechless by what appeared the dead certainty that Dupree was about to pull his rifle's trigger, and kill Lonnie.

The boy's shoulder was touching the girl's. He could feel Casey breathing as hard as he was.

There was a long silence as Dupree stared down at Lonnie with those snake-like eyes of his.

Finally, Childress said, "No point in killin' him yet, Shannon." The lanky outlaw was nibbling a weed. "Kid had a point. Killin' him ain't gonna get us the money. Let's get the money first, then we'll talk about what we're gonna do with him and the girl."

"Only one thing to do with 'em, either way," Fuego said. "They know all about us. Can't let 'em live."

"Well, I for one would like to consider the situation a little longer," Childress said. "I don't know—killin' kids. I ain't never done that before. Mighty tall order. Maybe we could take 'em with us down to Mexico, set 'em free at the border."

"Travel all that way with a couple of howlin' brats?" Dupree said, still staring at Lonnie. He shook his head.

"Sounds like a good idea to me," Lonnie said after he'd tried to swallow the hard knot in his throat. "We wouldn't be no trouble. None at all. In fact, we could set up and tear down camp for you fellas."

Of course, Lonnie had no hankering to do any such thing. He was trying to buy him and Casey some time.

"Yeah," Casey said. "We could do that. And I can cook, too. No point in killin' us. The law would be extra mad, track you extra hard, if you killed a couple of kids."

Dupree looked at her in that way of his that burned Lonnie deep in his bones. The outlaw lifted his rifle and off-cocked the hammer. He laughed and then said, "We'll track the horses tomorrow, spend the night right here. Let's eat—I'm hungry as a wolf."

While the outlaws laid out their gear, forming a proper camp, Lonnie was sent out to snare a rabbit and gather firewood. Dupree had seen how handy Lonnie was with a rope snare. The outlaws weren't worried that Lonnie would try to run away. They knew he'd stay with Casey. How far could he get on foot, anyway, before they ran him down again?

Lonnie didn't think he'd be able to snare anything before good dark, but he set his trap in the brush well away from the camp. He gathered enough wood for the night, and had built up the fire and put a fresh pot of coffee on to boil. Then they sent him out in search of water. There was a small stream at the bottom of the ravine, so he walked down the slope and filled the men's canteens after taking a long drink himself. A high shriek rose from the direction in which he'd set his snare. Lonnie strode over to find that he'd caught a big jack. He wrung the frightened beast's neck, and brought him back to the fire.

Dupree chuckled and glanced at Fuego and Childress. "Told you the kid was half Injun."

Then he grabbed the rabbit out of Lonnie's hands and set to work, dressing it out, skinning it, and chopping it up for the pot in which beans and bacon bubbled on the fire. Meanwhile, Lonnie gave Casey one of the canteens he'd filled.

She took a long drink. The outlaws didn't seem to mind she was drinking their water. They'd already settled in for the night, drinking their coffee laced with rye and laying out a poker game while a pot bubbled and splattered on the fire. They were distracted, not overly worried about their captives.

That was fine with Lonnie. He hoped they'd stay distracted, so he could make a play for one of their guns.

The men ate but they didn't offer any food to Lonnie or Casey, despite Lonnie's having snared the rabbit to add to their otherwise thin stew. They acted as though the two weren't even there, sitting about ten feet back from the fire. That, too, was all right with Lonnie. He hadn't eaten since breakfast, but he wasn't hungry. He supposed that having been in almost constant jeopardy since he'd awakened that day had something to do with that.

The men ate, and Dupree ordered Lonnie to scrub their dishes. Lonnie didn't see that he had much choice, so he took the utensils down to the stream, and cleaned them. When he returned to the fire, Dupree ordered him to refill their coffee cups and to add a good portion of whiskey to each. The men were sitting on rocks and throwing playing cards down on the ground between them, calling, bluff, and raising.

Lonnie vaguely thought with an inward smirk that it would be nice if one of them drew a "Dead Man's Hand." He wasn't sure what that was, exactly, but he knew it was a poker hand.

He added more wood to the fire, then sat back down with Casey. The men were getting drunker and talking louder, and the fire was burning loudly, too, so he figured they wouldn't hear him and Casey conferring. Still, he kept his voice low as he asked, "How you holdin' up?"

"I'm doin' all right, Lonnie. How're you doin'?"

"I'm all right. How's your ankle?"

"It's feelin' better now. It's not broke or nothin'. I just have to stay off it for a while. I reckon I'll be doin' that real soon, huh?" She'd dragged her voice out ironically, and gave Lonnie a droll look.

What she'd said and the way she'd said it struck Lonnie as funny, and he couldn't help chuckling. That got Casey chuckling, then, too, and they both had to cover their mouths and hold their noses to keep from rolling out the loud guffaws.

Still, Dupree heard them, and he turned to scold them. "You two shut up over there. Go to sleep. I'll be over to tie you up in a minute, so you don't run off in the night."

That sobered them, reminding them of the fix they were in.

They both sat back against the tree. A minute later, Casey slid her hand across the ground and closed it over Lonnie's, and squeezed it. He squeezed hers back. When he looked at her, she was looking down at their entwined hands, her eyelids low. A couple of tears were dribbling down her cheeks, flashing in the umber firelight.

"It'll be okay, Casey," Lonnie said.

She didn't say anything, but dipped her head a little and bit her upper lip as she continued to squeeze his hand.

Lonnie kept an eye on the outlaws' rifles, but they were keeping the long guns close to them. Lonnie was beginning to think of a way he could get his hands on one later, after the outlaws had gone to sleep, when the three men began to confer amongst themselves in low, guttural tones. They seemed to be discussing something of gravity.

Dupree and Fuego glanced over at Lonnie, raked their drink-bright eyes across Casey, then Childress looked at Lonnie and said something to his partners.

Dupree threw his cards down, and rose with a grunt, saying, "No—it's gotta be done. Might as well do it now as save it for the mornin'."

Dupree stooped to fish around inside one of his saddlebags, pulling out a small coil of rope. Neither Childress nor Fuego said anything as Dupree staggered around the fire. Lonnie could smell the alcohol reek of the man as he stood over his two captives, his heavy shoulders rising and falling as he breathed.

The sick feeling in Lonnie's belly got worse.

Dupree dropped to a knee and began rapping the rope around both of Casey's ankles.

"Gonna tie you up, girl. You'll be goin' with us in the mornin'."

Casey looked sharply at Lonnie.

"What do you mean 'I' am?" Casey asked, her shrill voice quaking with trepidation. "What about Lonnie?"

"Don't got no more use for him. He's about as useless as his mother." As Dupree brusquely grabbed Casey's arm and rolled her onto her belly, he gave Lonnie an evil smirk, adding, "God rest the stupid woman's soul."

Lonnie looked down at the pistol jutting up on Dupree's left hip, the walnut handle angled back toward his belly. Lonnie's heart started hiccupping and lurching every which way as he imagined making a grab for the pistol.

As Dupree began wrapping an end of the rope around Casey's wrists, hog-tying the girl belly-down on the ground, Lonnie bounded up onto his feet and lurched forward, wrapping his hand around the big Colt on Dupree's hip. The boy gave a loud grunt as he jerked the revolver free of the keeper thong and out of its holster.

Dupree cursed loudly and grabbed at the gun, almost tearing it from the boy's grip before Lonnie jerked it back away from him. As he did,

Dupree growled, "Why, you cussed little *snip!*" and grabbed for his second Colt holstered low on his right thigh.

Dupree's hand was moving in a blur. He was fast. Too fast for Lonnie. The boy had no time to consider his actions, so he didn't bother.

He merely ratcheted the Colt's hammer back, took quick aim at the center of the outlaw's broad chest, and fired.

FORTY-FOUR

THE PISTOL'S report sounded like a shotgun blast in the quiet night.

Smoke wafted in the air between Lonnie and Dupree, peppering the boy's nose with the smell of cordite, making his eyes water.

Dupree froze, dipped his chin to look down in shock at his lower left side. His back was angled toward the fire, so Lonnie couldn't see much of the man's front, but he thought he saw a dark hole in the flap of the man's sheepskin vest. Dupree stood a little to one side, and as Lonnie realized that his bullet must have plowed through the man's vest and merely grazed the man's left side—if he'd hit him where he'd thought he'd hit him, he wouldn't still be living much less standing—Lonnie took another step back and cocked the Colt once more.

"Why, you little dung beetle!" Dupree bellowed, lurching for Lonnie and throwing his arms up as he thrust his left boot forward and sideways.

The boot swept Lonnie's feet out under from him. As Lonnie became airborne, he inadvertently triggered the Colt straight up at the stars that glowed dully beyond the firelight.

"Lonnie!" Casey screamed as Lonnie's old friend, the ground, came up to greet him once more without ceremony.

Again, Lonnie's wind was pummeled from his battered lungs, and he lay on his side, legs scissored, groaning and trying with little success to suck air back into his chest. He looked at his right hand, which was thrown high over his head and lying against the ground. The Colt lay several feet beyond it, half buried in the finely churned dirt and pine needles.

Dupree was holding his hand against his side as he stepped over to Lonnie.

"No!" Casey cried from where she lay belly-down on the ground, wrists tied to her ankles behind her back.

"Kid, I thought this was gonna be hard for me," Dupree savagely barked, bending at the waist to glower down at Lonnie still trying to suck a clean breath. "But it just got a whole lot easier."

He slanted his Colt down at Lonnie, clicked back the hammer.

The gun barked. Only, it didn't flash or stab flames toward Lonnie. And it hadn't really so much *barked* as made a *pinging* noise, and gave off a spark somewhere up near the cylinder.

"Ach!" Dupree yelped, tossed the gun away as though it were a hot potato.

Dupree grabbed the hand that had been holding the gun and looked at it with a curious mixture of outrage and befuddlement. "What the *hell?*" he yelled, lifting his head to cast his demon-eyed gaze into the woods behind Lonnie.

In the sudden silence that followed, a mild voice owning the soft twang of a Southern accent said, "Now, that ain't no way to treat a young'un an' you know it, sir."

Both Fuego and Childress were standing. They both reached for their rifles at the same time. The pistol in the woods barked two more times.

In the periphery of Lonnie's vision, he saw the flash of the flames in the darkness of the downslope trees, and he also saw, to his other side, both Fuego and Childress lose their hats. Each hat leaped off its owner's head, one after the other, and flew back behind them in the darkness beyond the fire.

Losing their hats seemed to take all the sap out of the two outlaws' demeanors. They left their rifles where they were, and tensed, stared fearfully across the fire and into the darkness beyond Lonnie and Dupree, who was still standing where he'd been standing before, clutching his hand to his belly and grunting painfully, grinding his jaws.

The strangely slow, mild voice rose again from the forest. "Anyone reaches for another shootin' iron, they're gonna acquire a third eye—one they can't see out of—right quick. Now, ya'll stay where you are so I can keep these old hog legs quiet."

Boots crunched pine needles until the figure appeared at the edge of the firelight—a lanky gent whose clothes seemed to hang on his gaunt, bony frame. The battered and torn Confederate gray cavalry hat was tipped low over the craggy, severe-featured face that Lonnie had seen somewhere before, though he couldn't remember exactly where. The stranger held not one pistol but two old-model, cap-and-ball pistols in his gloved hands. One pistol was aimed at Dupree, the other was angled in the general direction of Fuego and Childress.

The stranger looked down at Lonnie. "Son," he said, "you got the gall-darnedest worst luck of any shaver I ever known. Can you stand?"

"Can I what?" Lonnie said tightly, still unable to take a full breath.

"Can you stand? You know—get up and walk around? I'm thinkin' you should do that if you can." The man turned his head to one side and spat out a long stream of chaw onto a rock. "The girl, too—if'n she wants to ride out of here."

The severe-featured face belonged to the old Confederate—at least, Lonnie figured he was in his forties or so, maybe even older—who'd saved Lonnie's bacon back before the boy had reached Arapaho Creek.

Dupree winced against the pain in his bloody hand, and let his eyes bore into the lanky gent holding the old-model pistols on him. "You know who you're messin' with here, Grayback?"

"No," the mild-voiced stranger said while Lonnie climbed to his feet. "But I gotta feelin' you're gonna tell me."

"Shannon Dupree!" The tall, blond outlaw held out his bloody right hand clutched in the other one. "And it's my hand you just shredded with that old horse pistol, Grayback!"

The bearded stranger's severe brows drooped over his deep-set, dark-blue eyes, and he shook his head as he said, "Dupree, huh? Well, I do apologize. Don't recollect the name. It's a tall one, huh?"

"A hell of a lot taller than you, my soon-to-be-dead Rebel friend!"

"That's no way to talk to a man bearin' down on you. Now, I could understand you talkin' that way if *you* was the one holdin' the pistols, but you ain't." The Confederate glanced at Lonnie, who, standing, was still trying to drag a breath deep into his lungs. "Boy, I ain't gettin' any younger and neither is this night, and I got your horses waitin', so I sure would appreciate it if you'd take that big-talkin' Yankee's knife out of his boot and use it to cut that girl loose."

Lonnie's eyes brightened when he turned to regard the stranger. "You got our horses?"

The stranger gave a slow dip of his chin. Switching his gaze from Casey to Dupree, he pursed his lips and shook his head. "That's no way to treat a girl, neither. Tyin' her up such as that. What was you thinkin', Yankee? You think she's a calf for the brandin'? Why, I never seen the like! Boy, take his knife and cut her loose! Don't worry—if he so much as twitches, I'll give him a pill he can't digest!"

Lonnie looked at the knife handle sticking up out of Dupree's right boot. He crouched down and slipped the Bowie knife out of the sheath sewn into the boot. Lonnie didn't look at Dupree while he did, though he could feel the outlaw's devil eyes boring into his back.

Knife in hand, Lonnie hurried over to Casey, and sawed through the ropes, freeing her wrists from her ankles. Casey rolled over, flinging the ropes away with a grunt. Lonnie tossed away the knife, leaned down, and wrapped his right arm around Casey's waist, helping the girl to her feet.

"You two young'uns head on back behind me. You'll see your horses there with mine, ole Stonewall—the big cream. Steer clear of Stonewall, as he'll tear your shirt, you get close, as he can smell Yankees from ten miles away!" The old Confederate chuckled at that. "Mount up and ride north along the bottom of that ravine. I'll catch up to you as soon as I've made sure we won't have no shadowers."

Lonnie glanced once more at Dupree, who was eyeing him darkly, then Lonnie helped the girl into the trees. They headed downslope together. As they did, the General gave a bugling whinny, and Lonnie grinned broadly. The big buckskin had scented its owner, or maybe had heard his voice, and that had been the General's vigorous greeting. Another whinny followed the General's, and Lonnie saw the cream standing about ten feet away from where the General stood with Casey's chestnut, about fifty yards down the slope.

The outlaws' horses were tied straight south of the camp, up higher on the slope and nearer the rocks capping the ridge crest.

"Hey, you big chicken," Lonnie greeted the buckskin, which gave its young rider a vaguely sheepish look and then bobbed its head unctuously. "Thanks for runnin' out on me. I really appreciate that."

Both the stallion and the roan were tied to one tree while the Confederate's stallion, named after an opposing general, was tied to another tree several yards away. As Lonnie helped Casey up onto the chestnut's back, he saw with relief that the second pair of saddlebags, containing the money, were still draped over the General's back, where Lonnie had strapped them to his saddle skirt.

"Lonnie, do you know that man?" Casey asked as Lonnie untied their mounts.

"Seen him once before," Lonnie said, tossing Casey her bridle reins. "Don't ask me his name, but I reckon I've acquired a Confederate for a guardian angel. Don't that beat all?"

"Well, its beats somethin', anyway," Casey said, glancing up the dark slope toward where the fire glowed amongst the tall, black pines.

As Lonnie stepped up onto the General's back, he looked up the slope, as well. The old Confederate stood silhouetted against the firelight, just off its far right side. Lonnie could tell Dupree by the man's considerable height. He could hear the Confederate talking, and then, as Lonnie turned General Sherman toward the downslope, he saw the Confederate's gray shadow move away from the fire and toward the outlaws' horses, which they'd tied to a picket line.

Lonnie let the General pick his own way down the slope. Casey's chestnut clomped along behind, occasionally snorting and whickering. Both horses sensed the edginess of their riders. As Lonnie touched heels to the General's flanks, urging more speed when they'd gained the bottom of the ravine, the boy jerked with a start as a pistol popped once, twice, three times.

"Git on!" he heard the old Confederate yell amidst the thudding of the outlaws' horses' hooves. "Git along there, you Yankee cayuses, or I'll shoot you and leave you to the possums!"

The horses were jostling shadows against the side of the slope, scattering as they headed straight for the bottom, dodging trees. There was one more pistol crack, and then a shrill, wild Rebel yell—*"Heee-ee-yahhhh!"* —vaulted over the still night that was as tense as a held breath.

That high-pitched, echoing yell caused the hair on the back of Lonnie's neck to stand on end. He had a feeling he'd just heard what his father and so many other Yankees had heard and what had turned their knees to mush on so many Southern battlefields during the war. Behind Lonnie, the sound of fast-moving hooves rose quickly, and then, as Lonnie and Casey followed the creek meandering along the bottom of the ravine up and over a low divide, the old Confederate on the cream stallion he called Stonewall shot past them in a streak of gray lightning.

"Come on, young'uns!" he called. "We's aburnin' moonlight!"

"Lonnie?" Casey said, as they both put their horses into lopes down a broad, grassy hill, the large, silver moon quartering over them, silvering the forest on both sides of the meadow.

"What is it?" Lonnie asked, pulling his hat low over his forehead, so it wouldn't blow off.

"Why do I have the feelin' we just jumped out of the fryin' pan and into the fire again?"

FORTY-FIVE

NEARLY AN HOUR of hard riding later, through forest and over low divides and into this narrow canyon heavy with the smell of the creek running through it, and ferns and rich, green grass, Lonnie checked the General down.

The horse was silver with its own sweat lather. As Casey stopped the filly off Lonnie's left stirrup, Lonnie stared through the trees at what appeared to be a cabin sitting about thirty yards back from the creek. The cabin was a black silhouette against the slope rising behind it, but the starlight reflecting off the tin chimney pipe poking up out of the hovel's roof told Lonnie it was a cabin, all right.

His Grayback guardian angel had stopped his own cream stallion in front of the place, and was stepping down from his saddle. He turned toward Lonnie and Casey sitting a cautious several yards away, and he said, "Well, come on, then. You Yankee children don't like roofs over your heads?"

Lonnie studied the man and the surroundings. He didn't know who this gent was other than he was an ex-Confederate and good with his old Confederate pistols. Lonnie had watched him kill three men as easily as swatting flies, and he'd also watched him stare down Shannon Dupree. He was a killer, all right. Lonnie knew that for sure. What else he was, Lonnie didn't know. Maybe whatever it was, was good. But maybe it was bad, too, and that's what had given the boy pause.

That's what had given Casey pause, too.

"All right, then," the stranger said, removing his stallion's bridle and slipping its saddle, rifle scabbard, and bedroll off its back. He took the gear over to what appeared to be a dilapidated lean-to stable with connecting corral, and set it on the corral's rail fence. Then he went on into the cabin, and soon Lonnie saw a wan amber light burning in one of the windows.

"Gonna get cold out here, I reckon." Lonnie continued to look around, cautious. "And it looks like the money's still here on the General's back."

"Did you count it?"

Casey knew he hadn't had time to count the money. It was her way of saying they shouldn't assume they could trust this old Confederate, uncommonly good with a cap-and-ball pistol, because he'd saved their lives. But the more they both thought it through, the more they both saw it from a different angle. The man *had* saved them and he hadn't taken the loot, which he very easily could have done, so they were probably being foolish, mooning around out here like a pair of stray pups.

At least, that's the angle Lonnie saw it from, and he could tell by Casey's shrug that she'd come to that conclusion, too. They both dismounted, and stripped the gear from their horses and set it near the Confederate's. Since the stranger hadn't stabled his mount or hobbled or tied it, Lonnie figured the General and the chestnut could safely forage freely, as well. Both the General as well as the chestnut got down and began rolling, which the stranger's stallion had done, as well, rubbing the lather off their backs.

Hoping that the two stallions wouldn't fight over Casey's filly, Lonnie draped the stolen money over his right shoulder and carried his rifle in his right hand as he helped Casey over to the cabin. He knocked on the door that was so rickety it bounced and groaned in its frame. Lantern light seeped through the cracks between the planks.

"It's open an' nothin' in here's gonna bite, so come on in, and light."

Lonnie opened the door and peered inside. He'd been a little worried there might be more like the Confederate in here, but he was alone, all right, sitting at a wooden table that had seen far better days. The strange old man was lighting a porcelain-bowled pipe. He sat with one mule-eared boot hiked atop the other knee. The little monkey stove behind him rattled with a freshly laid fire, and a coffeepot was chugging on top of it.

He'd set his battered gray hat on the table. His head was long and narrow, with a bulbous forehead. His hair was gray-streaked chestnut along the sides, curling over the collar of his calico shirt, but there were only a handful of strands angling back over the top of his age-spotted dome. A worm-shaped white scar knotted his cheek only a few inches from his left ear. A bayonet wound, Lonnie silently opined as he stepped inside the earthen-floored place, which was little larger than the kitchen of his own cabin.

"This your place?" he asked the man, who was drawing on his pipe, causing the flame in his hand to leap and flutter, sparking in his dark-blue eyes.

"It is now, I reckon. Go on and set your loot down on the floor there, and pull up a chair. I won't promise you they won't cave in under you, cause they're both older'n Jehosophat's cat, but if they do, we'll burn 'em in the stove. I'm almost out of wood, anyways."

He lifted his mouth corners with amusement as he continued to blow smoke into the air around his craggy head.

Lonnie set the saddlebags down and pulled two of the three extra chairs up from the wall. He helped Casey into one directly across from the old Confederate. Then Lonnie eased down into the chair to Casey's left.

He didn't like the way it creaked and groaned beneath his weight. When he leaned forward to place his arms on the scarred table, the chair sank precariously down in front and to the right, and for a minute Lonnie thought it would break and take him to the floor with it.

But once it was down on its shorter right front leg, it held firm.

Lonnie leaned forward on his arms. He realized he was still wearing his hat, so he took it off and set it on the table before him. He looked around quickly to see that the cabin was furnished by little more than the table and chairs and the stove and a few old fruit crates so old that the labels had faded and were nearly illegible. There was a cot on the wall to Lonnie's right, with a moth-eaten wool blanket on it. A tied bedroll lay nearby. A coffee sack served as a pillow.

The place smelled of pipe tobacco, of course, but also of old, rotting wood and mouse droppings. A rusty bullseye railroad lantern hung from a wire over the table, casting a watery umber light amongst the shack's heavy shadows.

Except for the gurgling coffeepot, deep silence hung over the place. The old Confederate sat sideways to the table, his right profile to Lonnie and Casey, his elbow on the table, puffing his cigar and staring toward the door. Lonnie thought of him as old, because he had an old way about him, and he was still wearing the old gray hat and uniform trousers. But here where the boy could get a good look at him, he didn't otherwise seem all that old. At least, he probably wasn't far into his forties. Not young, to be sure, but he wouldn't necessarily be considered an "old man".

Lonnie felt fidgety with all the silence. Casey was fidgeting around beside him, also uncomfortable. The old Confederate seemed to not even realize that he had company, for all the conversation he was trying to make.

Wasn't he curious about the money? He must have opened the saddlebag flaps and seen it. Or...maybe he hadn't. Lonnie knew that it was probably not to his own credit that he likely would have snooped through the gear, had the tables been turned.

Lonnie glanced at Casey. She returned the glance, giving her brows an incredulous arch. She was as uncomfortable as Lonnie was.

Finally, the boy cleared his throat, and to fill the silence as much as anything else, he slid his hand across the table and said, "I'm Lonnie Gentry."

The old Confederate removed the pipe from his mouth and regarded Lonnie cryptically. He looked down at the boy's open hand, then slipped his pipe into his left hand, and closed his large, gnarled, brown right hand around the boy's, giving it a squeeze. He had the grip of a strong man. He scrutinized Lonnie and Casey from beneath furled brows, hesitating, and then he said in his gravelly, heavily accented voice, "Wilbur Calhoun."

Casey slid her own hand across the table. "Casey Stoveville. Pleased to make your acquaintance, Mister Calhoun."

Calhoun nodded, regarding the girl curiously, as though trying to puzzle her out, as if maybe he didn't believe she was really whom she'd said she was.

Casey gave Lonnie a nervous, self-conscious glance, then looked around and said, by way of making conversation, "So...this your place?"

"Nope," Calhoun said, not bothering to explain whose it was. His mind seemed to be somewhere else as he studied Casey through a haze of wafting pipe smoke. Then he said in his slow, gravelly fashion, "Stoveville. That's the name of the marshal down to Arapaho Creek, ain't it?"

"It was," Casey said. "Marshal Stoveville was my father." She sucked her bottom lip and stared down at the table. "He was killed last week."

"You don't say," Calhoun said with interest.

His eyes flicked toward the saddlebags resting on the floor behind Casey. Lonnie knew then that the man had opened the flaps and seen the money. He was curious, but it wasn't his way to seem so. It was the

Western way to not ask questions. Lonnie's father had explained that the custom had probably come about because so many people in the West were on the run from something back east. Not all, of course, but enough to make asking too many questions dangerous. An overly inquisitive sort might just get drilled with a .44 slug—if he asked the wrong question of the wrong person, that was.

Lonnie wanted to clear the issue of the money up fast, so the old Confederate didn't get the wrong idea.

"The money's stolen, Mister Calhoun. It was stolen out of the bank over in Golden. It was stolen by the men you met tonight. That big, tall one—the blond-headed one with the devil's eyes—he's Shannon Dupree. He's courtin' my ma." The boy lowered his voice in shame, staring down at the hands he was entwining on the table. "Leastways, he was. He..." He cleared his throat, having trouble explaining the horrible facts of the situation. "He...or one of the other two—the half-breed Fuego or Childress— killed Casey's pa after they got over on the west side of the Never Summers, and Marshal Stoveville formed a posse out of Arapaho Creek to go after 'em."

Calhoun suddenly looked interested. He'd turned toward the table now, laid a rigidly veined hand down on the rough aspen boards while he held the pipe in his mouth with the other one. "How'd the two of you come to be packin' all that money?"

"Let's just say my ma didn't want it around the cabin," Lonnie said.

"Ah." Calhoun nodded, smiled shrewdly. "She was tryin' to save that curly wolf from himself, that it?"

"That's about the size of it."

"That'll happen. Sometimes women see what they wanna see in a man, whether it's there or not. Men do the same with women." Calhoun added that last sentence with a wry snort, as if he knew plenty enough about the topic. He puffed his pipe and pondered what he'd been told. "Where you two headed?"

Casey said, "To Camp Collins. We're gonna turn the loot over to the deputy United States marshal there. Figure he'll return it to the bank over in Golden."

"You figure to ride all that way," Calhoun said, scowling his dismay, "with Shannon Dupree on your trail?"

Lonnie said, "You sound like you heard of him before, Mister Calhoun."

"Prob'ly ain't too many around the Front Range who haven't heard of that low-down dirty dog. It's a shame your ma put such stock in that cottonmouth."

"I reckon word of him hasn't traveled all the way to the back side of the Never Summers," Lonnie said, crestfallen. "But even if it had, well...Ma's been lonely since my pa died."

"The Yankee?" Calhoun said with another shrewd glint in his eye.

Lonnie gave his shoulder a sheepish shrug and cut his eyes at Casey, who returned the look with a skeptical one of her own. Then she shuttled a cautious look at the old Confederate sitting across from her.

"Helkatoot!" Calhoun said, knocking the dottle out of his pipe and sweeping it off the table and onto the floor. "The war's long since over, young'uns. The past is gone. Confederates and Yankees—we're all one an' the same—Americans!"

He set his pipe down, pushed up out of his chair, and walked around the table to drop to one knee beside Casey. "Let me see that foot, little miss. What you packin' there—a break or a knot?"

"I think it's just twisted," Casey said, casting Lonnie another wary glance. "It'll be all right, Mister Calhoun. Thank you, anyway."

"Oh, come on—show the ole Reb your ankle, Miss Casey. I learned some doctorin' skills back durin' the War of Northern Aggression, there bein' few enough medicos providin' for the wounded on our side." Calhoun slapped his thigh. "Put it right up there, and let me take a gander and see what kind a hurt you're packin'."

Casey fidgeted around, embarrassed, and then finally turned in her creaky chair, facing Calhoun. She hesitated some more, and then placed her boot on Calhoun's thigh. Gently, the old soldier slid the boot off her foot, looking up at her concernedly as the girl sucked a sharp breath through her teeth, her cheeks turning crimson from the pain.

"Hurt, does it?" Calhoun asked, moving even more gently.

"A little," Casey raked out.

When Calhoun had Casey's boot off, he rolled her sock down to inspect her swollen, purple ankle. He manipulated her foot a little and then released it, sank back on his heel, and said, "Helkatoot—I've hurt myself worse gettin' out of bed! What you need to do is soak that limb in the creek out yonder. It's good and cold—spring-fed. Bring the swellin' down. Boy, help her out there. I'll start some vittles cookin', what little I got, then I'll come out and wrap some rawhide around that limb of yours. The rawhide'll shrink while it dries and give that wing the support it needs to mend."

Casey shrugged. Since it appeared good advice to her, Lonnie helped her up out of her chair. She wrapped around his neck and sort of skip-hopped over to the front door, which Lonnie opened.

Two red eyes glowed at him and Casey from the darkness outside the door.

An animal gave a deep growl.

Casey screamed.

FORTY-SIX

LONNIE SLAMMED the door and he and Casey stumbled back.

"What is it?" Calhoun said, sliding one of his pistols out of its holster fast as lightning and smooth as silk. He clicked the hammer back and walked boldly up to the closed door.

"There's somethin' out there—a wolf, maybe," Lonnie said.

"Wolf?"

Calhoun chuckled as he depressed his pistol's hammer, and opened the door. "Cherokee, that you?"

The two red eyes moved closer until the lamp flickering over the table showed a large, shaggy, brown-and-white collie dog holding a large, limp rabbit by the neck between its jaws. The dog was eyeing Lonnie and Casey and growling deep in its throat in more of an apprehensive, curious way than an angry one.

"Hidy, Cherokee!" Calhoun intoned. Then, to Lonnie and Casey: "Don't mind him—that's my ole collie. I call him Cherokee cause I couldn't think of nothin' else to call him when he wandered into my camp a few years back, skinnier'n a boiled chicken. He looked like a collie dog we called Cherokee back to home in Tennessee, and I always been partial to collie dogs. Smarter'n most humans I ever known." He added with another wry snort, "Heckuva lot more loyal, too."

Calhoun turned to the dog. "Drop, Cherokee."

Cherokee opened his jaws and the rabbit rolled out from between the dog's jaws to land with a thud on the earthen floor. "Just in time, my good friend. I was fixin' to prepare supper, late as it is. Meet our guests, Mister Lonnie Gentry and Miss Casey Stoveville from out Arapaho Creek way."

The dog wagged his tail and stepped forward to sniff the newcomers, but when Lonnie leaned down to pet the animal, Cherokee gave a groan and stepped back, head and tail low.

Calhoun said, "He takes some warmin' up to, Cherokee does."

Casey looked skeptically at Calhoun. "So...he hunts...game...for you, Mister Calhoun?"

"Sure enough. I don't like to fire no shots, so...I mean, I'm kinda colicky about expendin' ammunition when it's so gallblamed hard to find way up here in the high-and-rocky, and Cherokee fell to it naturally—huntin', I mean. He eats his share and brings what he don't eat back to my camp, and, well, I reckon we got us a partnership."

Calhoun held the rabbit up by its rear legs. It was long and plump, with a charcoal coat and long, broad, mule-like ears. "That's some jack there, Cherokee. You done good, old son. I'll fry him up with some wild onions and canned tomatoes, and we'll have us a nice meal to turn in on." The Confederate rubbed his concave belly, both hipbones protruding beneath it. "Myself, I can't sleep when I go to bed with no paddin' between my ribs. You two go on out and soak that foot, and I'll get the vittles started."

"Thanks, Mister Calhoun," Casey said.

"Yeah, we appreciate the grub, Mister Calhoun," Lonnie chimed in.

"Helkatoot," Calhoun said, tossing the big jack onto the table and pulling a big skinning knife from his belt sheath. "Besides, it wasn't me that fetched it. It was Cherokee!"

"Thanks Cherokee," Lonnie said, as he and Lonnie continued on out the door.

The dog followed Lonnie and the hobbling Casey across the grassy yard toward the creek that flashed in the light of the moon kiting high over the canyon, casting shadows every which way. The dog followed closely, sniffing, mewling deep in his throat, wary of strangers. He reminded Lonnie of his master in that way.

When Casey was sitting on the creek's grassy bank, and soaking her foot in the cold spring water that gurgled pleasantly over rocks and down a beaver dam a little ways upstream, she turned to Lonnie, who'd sat down against a tree close by. She opened her mouth to speak, stopped, and glanced at the cabin.

Calhoun was moving around behind the windows, cooking supper.

She turned to Lonnie again and kept her voice low and confidential as she said, "Remember what I said about us maybe fallin' out of the fryin' pan and into the fire again?"

Lonnie glanced toward the cabin. "You think Mister Calhoun's dangerous? I think he's been livin' alone a little too long." He looked at the dog that sat a ways upstream from Lonnie and Casey, staring at the newcomers in much the way that Calhoun had while he'd smoked his pipe—wary in the way that people get when they're alone a lot, and maybe got a little mushy in the head from it. "Livin' alone with just his dog for company."

Lonnie held his hand out toward the dog, trying to lure it up to be petted. Cherokee stretched out belly-down on the ground and gave a soft cry of frustration, not sure if he should trust the boy or not. The crooked white streak angling down the top of his otherwise brown head glowed in the moonlight.

Casey shook her head. "It's not that at all, Lonnie. It took me a while to remember where I'd heard Calhoun's name before, after he introduced himself. But before he came around the table to inspect my foot, I remembered. A few months back, Pa was visited by Marshal Barrows from Camp Collins. Barrows had a wanted poster, and I saw it. It had the name..."

Casey paused and glanced back at the cabin once more. Lonnie could hear Calhoun whistling in there as he chopped up the rabbit's carcass on the kitchen table.

"It had the name Wilbur Calhoun splashed in big, black letters across the top of it," Casey said, whispering and shielding her mouth with her hand. "He's a *train robber!*"

"A *train robber?*"

"*Shhhh!*"

Lonnie gritted his teeth and turned to the cabin again. Calhoun was still whistling while he worked.

"A train robber?" Lonnie asked again, much lower this time.

Casey nodded. "The marshal said some prospectors had seen him campin' alone in the Never Summers. Said the man had a list of train robberies as long as his leg. He'd been robbin' trains since after the Civil War, and often took to remote mountains between holdups. The marshal was out lookin' for Calhoun but when he talked to Pa, he hadn't seen hide nor hair of him, but he wanted Pa to keep an eye skinned for him." She glanced back at the cabin as she added, "He said Calhoun was fast as greased lightnin' with his old Confederate pistols. A cold-blooded killer, with a hefty reward on his head."

She slowly kicked her foot in the water, making gurgling sounds. She turned back to Lonnie, looking grave. "And you know what else?"

"Ah, heck," Lonnie groaned. "I don't think I wanna hear any more."

Casey stopped kicking her foot in the water, and swallowed. "Just after the war, he killed his wife. That's when he came west and started robbin' trains."

Lonnie stared at Casey in disbelief. He could still hear Calhoun whistling, and he could hear meat frying in a pan. "You mean, that old man in there did that?"

"Well, he probably wasn't so old back then. And did you see how easily he blew those outlaws' hats off their heads? Those weren't accidental hits. I mean, if he'd been aimin' a little lower—well, you get my drift. And he stared down Dupree like he was no more of a danger than a cottontail rabbit!"

Lonnie pondered the information as again he felt his shoulder tighten with trepidation. He glanced a couple more times back at the cabin, then he said, half to himself, "Well, I reckon that's why he's so suspicious of strangers. Probably been one step ahead of one lawman or another since the war ended. But what I don't understand is this, Casey."

"What don't you understand?"

Lonnie hooked a thumb over his shoulder, indicating the cabin. "He could have run off with that money, and he didn't. He could have run off with it *twice* now and he didn't!"

"Yeah," Casey said, slowing nodding. "And he saved your life twice and mine once." She shook her head and resumed kicking her foot in the cold spring water gurgling along the creek. "No figurin' some people, I reckon."

She turned to Lonnie. "What do you figure we should do?"

"I think we oughta pull out first thing in the mornin'." Lonnie felt something brush up against his right thigh and saw that Cherokee had hunkered down beside him, slapping his tail against the ground. "Hey, look—his dog's right friendly!"

"Yeah, but Calhoun killed his wife, Lonnie. And he's a train robber. Imagine how many innocent people he killed!"

They both pondered that while Lonnie stroked the dog's burr-laden coat that smelled a little gamey.

"What if..." Casey seemed to ruminate on continuing, and then she decided to go ahead: "What if he's one of those crazy killers you hear so much about, wanderin' the mountains lookin' for innocent blood to spill?"

"Innocent blood to spill?"

"Yeah, like in the stories you read about in *Policeman's Gazette.*"

"Oh," Lonnie said, nodding. "Pa used to bring them rags home from town once in a while. I wasn't supposed to, but I'd read 'em out in the barn. You think them stories are true?"

"I don't know, but I hope we don't become the makin's of one of those stories tonight, Lonnie. I sure don't. I'm not sure I want Mister Calhoun close enough to me to wrap my foot with rawhide." Casey looked at Lonnie, her eyes glinting worriedly.

"Yeah, I know what you mean. Under the circumstances, I don't think I would, neither."

The cabin door scraped open and thudded shut. "All right, young'uns," Calhoun called, striding toward the creek. "Time to doctor that foot and make you good as new again, Miss Casey!"

FORTY-SEVEN

CHEROKEE BARKED as his master walked toward the creek.

Casey looked at Lonnie and gasped. "What am I gonna do?"

Lonnie didn't know what to say to that. He didn't have his rifle near, if he should need it. There wasn't much he could do except sit there as Calhoun knelt down beside Casey and pulled her foot out of the water. Lonnie saw that the man was wearing both his pistols and the knife he'd dressed the rabbit with, too.

If the old Confederate should go crazy and start shooting and stabbing, there'd be nothing Lonnie could do about it.

Wilbur Calhoun didn't, however, go crazy and start stabbing or shooting. He very gently set Casey's bare foot on his thigh again. He slowly and with painstaking gentleness wrapped the back of the girl's foot and ankle halfway up to her shin with the rawhide, tying and knotting it and professing, "There—you'll be good as new in a few days, or I'll return the shoat!"

Calhoun chuckled at that. When neither Lonnie nor Casey said anything, and both seemed not to understand, the old Confederate gave them a wink and, patting the head of Cherokee who'd taken a seat close to his master, tongue lolling, said, "That's an old Southern expression. Back before the war, many folks paid for their doctorin' with pigs or other animals. Maybe they still do. I wouldn't know. Been a while since I been back to the old home country."

Calhoun cleared his throat, and, rising, his old knees popping, said, "Yes, ma'am—that ankle'll be good as new in no time. Soak it once more with the rawhide on, and then come on in and get warm by the fire. The hide'll shrink up and form a cast of sorts, hold the tendons tight so they can heal." As he tramped on back to the cabin, Cherokee following close on his heels, the old Southerner said, "Come on inside, now, young'uns. Gettin' cold in this holler, and supper's on. No hominy, gallblast it, but it's a good one, just the same!"

He cackled and went on inside while the dog laid out by the front door, though Lonnie could only see his white spots in the darkness in front of the low-slung hovel.

Lonnie looked at Casey. Neither said as much, but they didn't know what to make of old Calhoun. But the smell of the man's rabbit stew and coffee had drifted out over the canyon, and Lonnie's stomach was rumbling. He and Casey hadn't eaten since breakfast, and their bellies were getting way too cozy with their backbones.

Their concerns about the man's past being overpowered by the pangs of their hunger, Lonnie climbed to his feet. He helped Casey to hers, and, arm in arm, they made their way back to the cabin, past Cherokee now curled into a tight ball near the door, and on inside to one of the best meals Lonnie could remember devouring.

Of course, most meals probably tasted that good when they sated a hunger as big and lumbering as the one Lonnie was harboring, but the old Southerner's cooking was still good. Especially given that it was composed of the bare minimum of ingredients—the rabbit, canned tomatoes, and a few wild onions. There were no spices for seasoning. The coffee was hot and black, and as Lonnie tossed the last of it back, Calhoun cleared his own plate with a thick finger and poked it into his mouth.

He looked up, shuttled his gaze from Lonnie to Casey, and chuckled. Both had already cleaned their plates. Casey looked a little sheepish, sitting back from her own nearly spotless plate and empty coffee cup, her hands in her lap.

"You young'uns get enough?" asked the old Confederate.

Lonnie stifled a belch with his fist.

Casey said, "That was absolutely heavenly, Mister Calhoun." Lonnie wanted to kick her under the table to forestall what she said next, but he didn't know the headstrong girl was going to say what she did until the words were half out of her mouth.

Casey probably didn't, either. "You're a right good cook, for a man.

You ever have a woman cook for you, Mister Calhoun? I mean, besides your mother, of course..."

She flushed a little, vaguely ashamed, while she slid a furtive glance over at Lonnie. Obviously, she was probing the man.

"A man gets to be my age, he's usually suffered havin' a female around the place, time or two," Calhoun said with a caustic chuff, piling up the empty plates on the table before him and rising. Then he stopped, gave Casey a sly grin, and winked at her. The girl blushed. The man's jovial retort seemed to shame the girl more than a straight-out admonishment for prying so boldly into his past would have done.

"I'll wash those, Mister Calhoun," Casey said, apparently feeling the need for penance.

"And strain that injured wing? I'll say you won't. You best get to sleep, little girl. You, too, boy. I'll take care of the cleanin' up. Miss Casey, you sleep right down there on the mat. It smells a little skunky, as skunk's what was likely livin' here before me an' Cherokee moved in. But that hotroll there came with the place—some pilgrim must've forgot it—and it's fresh. The boy an' me'll sleep outside—give you plenty of peace and quiet from our snorin'—eh, boy?"

Calhoun guffawed and headed out to the creek with the plates.

Casey looked at Lonnie. "Whoops," she said.

"Good goin', girl," Lonnie said, genuinely peeved at her. "If he goes loony on me out there, I'll have you to thank."

Casey stuck out her tongue at him.

Lonnie checked on the horses, contentedly grazing. Lonnie didn't think he'd have to tie or hobble them. Calhoun had told him that the canyon, with its steep ridge walls, served as a nearly enclosed corral of sorts. Besides, the horses were tired from all the running they'd done. Calhoun had also assured Lonnie that he didn't need to worry about Dupree catching up to him and Casey here.

At least, not tonight.

Not only would the outlaws have to run their horses down first, which would take considerable time, the canyon was hidden well and virtually impossible to find on even a moonlit night to someone who didn't know it was even here. Calhoun doubted that more than a few handfuls of folks over the past couple of hundred years had known of the canyon's where-abouts, and most of them, besides the old prospector or sheepherder who'd built the place, had likely been Arapaho Indians, who'd called the

Never Summers home not all that long ago. A couple of wandering bands still did.

Feeling as secure as possible given the situation, and considering what he now knew about Calhoun himself, the boy threw his gear down in the soft grass and ferns by the creek. When Calhoun was done working around the cabin, the old-timer spread out his own bedroll and saddle near Lonnie. While the old Confederate was asleep nearly as soon as his head hit the soft underside of his saddle, Lonnie fidgeted and rolled from side to side. His nerves were still popping like miniature lightning bolts inside him.

As he'd started to drift off, he'd imagine a bear's roar or the demon-like face of Dupree would reveal itself, ominously shadowed by imagined firelight.

Guns would pop and hooves would pound inside the boy's weary head.

Also, Calhoun snored. Lonnie had never heard a man snore as loudly as the old Confederate. He sounded like ripsaw trying to cleave solid rock, only louder. And the snores weren't steady and predictable, which somehow made them worse. They were as irregular as the thunder in a slowly swirling storm.

Eventually, however, the soft hand of sleep rose up out of the primordial soup of unconsciousness, and swept Lonnie away. When he awoke, it took him nearly a full minute to remember where he was and what he was doing there. He sat up suddenly, squinting at the blinding sun pillaring on and around him through the canopy of the towering firs and aspens.

He shielded his eyes against the light with his hand, and sucked a sharp breath through his teeth. The sun was not only high, but it seemed to be starting its slow shift to the west!

He blinked sleep from his eyes and looked around, getting his bearings. Straight across the creek and beyond the trees, he could see three horses—General Sherman, Casey's chestnut, and Calhoun's cream stallion grazing in a small clearing bright with sunshine gilding the green grass. Beyond the horses and more trees rose a tall, gray crag of ridge wall maybe a thousand feet tall.

The air was warm. Not hot but warm. A light breeze blew.

There was a splashing sound, and Lonnie turned to look upstream. Calhoun was sitting on the beaver dam about sixty yards away. The old Confederate was slowly kicking his bare feet in the water and holding a willow fishing pole against his thigh, the line angling down the dam and into a dark, gently rippling pool in which a cork bobbed gently. The collie dog, Cherokee, was scrounging around on the bank, head down, tail curled over his back.

Suddenly, the dog pitched back onto his hind paws, coiling like a spring. Then, bounding high and forward, Cherokee formed a near-perfect brown-and-white arc over the grass before he slammed his front paws down on the ground, burying his head for a second in a thick patch of ferns before pulling it back up with a mouse squealing between his jaws.

The dog flipped the mouse high in the air and then plunged after it again, playing.

"Cherokee, stop tormentin' that poor creature and either eat it or leave it alone!" Calhoun beseeched the dog. The man turned his bearded face, shaded by his old cavalry hat, toward Lonnie and said, "Good mornin', sunshine!"

"It ain't mornin' no more, is it?" Lonnie asked, dreadfully. He'd wanted him and Casey to get an early start. They needed to stay ahead of Dupree and to get the loot to Camp Collins pronto.

Calhoun squinted up at the sun and then casually pulled a gold watch from the pocket of his calico shirt. "Accordin' to this old timepiece I acquired thanks to you, it's nigh onto one-thirty."

"Holy moly," Lonnie said, bewildered. "Half the day is gone."

He looked around for Casey. There was no sign of the girl.

He looked at Calhoun, who was grinning at him like the cat that ate the canary.

That grin caused a cold stone to drop deep, deep down into the deep well of the boy's soul.

Casey...

FORTY-EIGHT

"WHAT?" Calhoun asked. "You think I ate her or somethin'?"

Lonnie hadn't realized he'd called the girl's name.

Calhoun chuckled, dropped his chin as he looked toward the cabin. "There she is now."

Lonnie turned to the cabin. Casey was fully clothed but she was standing in the open doorway, staring out and blinking as though she, too, had just awakened.

"What time is it?" she asked in a sleep-gravelly voice.

Calhoun said, "Well, you're both late for breakfast *and* lunch. Now, I reckon you'll have to wait for supper. I'm tryin' to catch it right now. Ain't havin' much luck." He scowled at the cork floating in the pool. "Never was much of an angler, and that's a bonded fact."

"We gotta get movin', Casey an' me," Lonnie said, shrugging off his blankets and climbing stiffly to his feet.

"You'd best rest up today. You two young'uns been through a lot. Rest up the rest of the day and get a clean start in the mornin'."

"What about Dupree?" Casey said, gazing apprehensively back the way they'd ridden into the canyon.

"He's likely fetched his horses by now, and him and them other two curly wolves are most like scourin' the country for you." The old Confederate pulled in his bait, inspected the worm dangling from the hook, and tossed it and the cork back into the stream again. "He won't find you here. I went back and scratched out any sign we left last night. There's only about one time of the day a fella can see the entrance to this canyon clear, from the western valley, on account of the way the light and shadows sit, and that time's done come and gone. There's a way in from the north, but it's a long ride around. You're safe here. Tomorrow, you can ride out bright and early. You'll both have some good rest behind you, good vittles in your bellies."

Calhoun scowled down at the unmoving cork in the water, and shook his head. "Leastways, I hope you do..."

Lonnie shuttled his gaze upstream. He'd had visions of Dupree and Fuego and Childress riding Lonnie and Casey down last night, and those phantoms lingered, needling the boy. He went over to the cabin and helped Casey hobble out to the creek, where she sat down to bathe her foot. He found a stout branch for the girl to use as a cane to help her get around, then he rolled his blankets.

"Helkatoot," Calhoun said, retrieving his line. "If there's any fish in this stream, they ain't hungry. Never have been hungry long as I been here. This old Reb can't abide a finicky fish." He gained his feet and began walking carefully down off the beaver dam. With Cherokee dogging his heels, he strode back to the cabin bathed in midday sunshine.

Lonnie sat down on the bank near Casey, still drowsy from her long slumber, and chewed a weed stem. His dreams about Dupree would not leave him. A few minutes later, Calhoun called his stallion into the yard, and saddled him. Then the old Rebel swung up into the leather, turned the horse downstream, and galloped off, the collie dog running along behind but swerving this way and that to investigate brush clumps or to give brief chase to rabbits and squirrels.

When Calhoun had followed the stream around a wide, right-swinging bend and had disappeared amongst the firs and aspens, Casey said, "Wonder where he's goin'."

She and Lonnie jerked worried looks at each other.

Lonnie leaped to his feet and went running to the cabin. He tripped the latch and nearly tore the door off its frame, lunging inside, and stopped just over the threshold, breathing hard. Relief lightened the load of worry that had been pressing on his shoulders.

The saddlebags still sat against the front wall, near the chair Casey had occupied last night. When he'd crouched down to inspect each bag, making certain that none of the money had been removed, Lonnie walked back out to where Casey faced him on her knees, concern showing in her eyes.

"I'll be hanged if it ain't all still there," Lonnie said.

"And he didn't shoot you or knife you," Casey said, only half-ironically, staring downstream toward where the old Confederate had disappeared. "All he done to me was tend my foot, and it feels better already. Maybe he's not who I thought he was at all."

"Maybe not."

"I know that's the name I saw on the Wanted circular, though. I got a good memory."

"Well, maybe some zebras can change their stripes."

"Maybe," Casey said. "I wonder where he's goin'."

"I don't know, but I'm gonna ride back and check out the mouth of this canyon." Lonnie lifted his saddle and tied bedroll onto his shoulder. "Not that I don't believe what he said about it bein' hard to find, but I reckon it's best if we don't over trust nobody. Especially when we got Dupree and his boys shadowin' us."

"You're not gonna leave me here alone, are you, Lonnie?"

Casey turned to the girl. She looked so plump-faced and morning pretty, with a splash of freckles across her nose and the nubs of her cheeks, her hair still tangled around her ears, that Lonnie couldn't help himself.

He leaned forward and kissed her on the mouth.

Her lips were warm and pliant. When he pulled away, Casey wrapped her arms around the boy's neck, drew him to her once more, and kissed him, long and deep.

Lonnie could feel the passion in the girl's body.

He could feel it in his own, as well. It made the tips of his ears burn hot as a skillet over a stoked fire.

They released each other at the same time. Casey smiled warmly at him. Lonnie didn't know what to say. It was as though every word in the English language he'd learned over the past thirteen years had suddenly left him, until he finally managed to sputter, "I won't be gone long. Give a holler if you get scared. I'll hear and come runnin'."

He started walking over to the corral, his mind still foggy from the kiss. He paused to whistle for General Sherman, who was now grazing on the near side of the stream with Casey's chestnut.

When he'd saddled the horse, Lonnie rode upstream, in the opposite direction from which Calhoun had ridden. As he left the sunlit yard and gained the shadows of the forest he turned back to Casey, who was bathing both her feet in the stream now. She'd turned to look after Lonnie. She was smiling.

Her mouth opened and closed, and Lonnie heard her yell barely loudly enough to be heard above the thudding of the General's hooves: "I love you Lonnie Gentry!"

At least, that's what Lonnie thought she'd yelled.

He turned his head forward as the General stretched his stride into a lope. Lonnie's brows hooded his eyes. The boy was in deep thought.

At least...that's what he *thought* she'd said.

"Nah, couldn't be," he muttered as the General picked up a faint game trail twisting amongst the pines. He'd just heard what he'd wanted to hear. *No town girl as wonderful as Casey Stoveville could love a raggedy-heeled mountain kid like Lonnie Gentry...*

FORTY-NINE

LONNIE FOLLOWED the game trail up a low grade through the forest, occasionally skirting the creek, for what he figured was a good mile or so. When the game path appeared to dead-end in a stand of piñon pines and juniper, near the base of a craggy, gray stone wall leaning back against the southwestern sky that bore not a single cloud, Lonnie reined the General to a halt and swung down from the saddle.

He dropped the stallion's reins, slid his rifle from its scabbard, racked a round into the chamber, just in case, and then off-cocked the hammer. He followed the game trail, littered here and there with deer and elk scat, up into the trees.

Continuing to follow the trail through the trees, Lonnie saw that it did not end at all. It meandered between junipers and pines that were not as closely spaced as they'd appeared from where Lonnie had left the General, and continued through a broad gap in the mountain wall.

At the gap in the wall, which was maybe thirty feet wide and which Lonnie vaguely remembered riding through the night before though it had looked much different in the moonlight than it did in the full light of the sun, Lonnie stopped and dropped to one knee. He saw why this mouth to the canyon in which Calhoun's cabin sat would be so hard to find from the adjacent valley.

The game trail dropped down and away from him into the valley, quickly intersecting several other game trails. There were trees to the right and left, and a jumble of boulders inside the line of trees on the right. Shade was creeping over Lonnie from the towering rock walls on either side of him, and he could sense that this opening, which sat crookedly atop the slope he was on, probably looked like solid stone from only a few yards down the slope that dropped into the valley. He didn't want to check it out and risk being seen or leaving tracks, but he was fairly certain this was so, that few people had ever gone beyond where Lonnie knelt.

It would take a man who'd spent a lot of time traveling around these mountains to happen upon such a gap as the one Lonnie was in. A former Confederate train robber, who had a lot of time for traveling remote mountains ranges as he stayed ahead of the law, would be such a person.

Feeling better, more secure, Lonnie walked back to where General Sherman stood ground-reined, and swung up into the saddle. He turned the horse around and loped back in the direction from which he'd come.

After he'd ridden fifty or so yards, he stopped, swung down, found an aspen branch with a few dead leaves on it, and used the branch to carefully, subtly scratch out his trail but leaving the deer and elk scat and a mound of what appeared coyote dung bristling with chokecherry seeds and rabbit fur.

Lonnie tossed away the branch, mounted the General once more, and returned to the cabin.

When he'd unsaddled the stallion, he rubbed him down and curried him thoroughly, and then he gave the same treatment to Casey's chestnut. With her gimpy ankle, the girl couldn't tend the horse herself, but Casey hobbled up from the creek and sat on a corral post, watching Lonnie work. She didn't say anything more about love or anything even similar, if she ever had, but merely looked around and chewed a weed and watched Lonnie work with a warm, self-satisfied half smile on her face.

She seemed to be enjoying the day of rest from travel, as was Lonnie.

Occasionally, when they heard the breeze scrape branches together or they heard birds light from the trees, they turned to see if Calhoun was returning. When the old Confederate hadn't returned by the time Lonnie was done tending both horses and rubbing some bear grease into his and Casey's tack, the two stripped down to their underwear, and waded around in the creek, skipping stones and splashing each other playfully.

After a while, they swam in the cool, deep pool beneath the beaver dam, and then lay together on the bank, drying out in the sun.

They didn't hear the thuds of a single rider until well after the sun had gone down, filling the canyon with deep-purple shadows. Lonnie and Casey, both dry now, had dressed and were gathering wood for a fire, when Calhoun returned with a croaker sack tied from his saddle horn and hanging down over his left stirrup fender. Cherokee followed him, tongue hanging but his ears up and eyes smiling. The dog was wet and dirty, as though he'd taken several swims in the stream.

The ex-Confederate cast a bright, toothy smile toward the youngsters gathering wood near the creek, and then, whistling, stripped the tack from his horse and carried the croaker sack inside the cabin.

"What do you suppose he's got in the sack?" Lonnie asked Casey, as the boy dug a shallow hole in which to build a fire against the canyon's growing chill.

"I don't know. Why don't you go in and fine out?" Casey nudged him with her hip.

"Why don't you?"

"Chicken!"

The door to the shack opened then, and Calhoun asked Lonnie to fetch him some wood from a pile behind the cabin. Turning the outdoor fire-starting duties to Casey, Lonnie gave the girl a conspiratorial wink—he'd find out what was in the sack now—then strode around behind the cabin. He found a few pine logs under an old, moldy tarp that didn't look too soft, and split them with a mallet. When he had an armful of relatively well-seasoned wood, he took it into the cabin, stopping inside the door in shock.

On the table was a fat, dead chicken, appearing freshly killed, and two potatoes, a handful of carrots, and a large turnip. All the vegetables appeared to have been freshly harvested, as they were all still wearing a moist skin of soil though the bright orange of the carrots couldn't help but shine through the dirt. On the table was also a fresh-baked pie, a small stone crock filled with only the Lord knew what, and a loaf of crusty, dark-brown bread.

There was also a bottle on the table, with its cork resting on the table beside it. Wilbur Calhoun was crouched in front of the small stove, shoving bits of paper and kindling and feather sticks into the firebox.

"Holy moly, Mister Calhoun—where'd you get all that grub?"

Calhoun turned to Lonnie. He hesitated slightly, the nubs of his craggy, red-brown cheeks turning a tad darker, and said, "Oh, this stuff here? Oh...well...I...uh...I got me an old prospector friend livin' downstream a couple miles. I told him I had guests and needed some possibles, and he...uh...well, he obliged...seein' as how he owed me a favor or two."

The old Confederate took the wood from Lonnie and set it on the floor outside the stove's open door. "Much obliged, young'un! Run along, now! I'll call you and the pretty li'l gal when supper's ready! Hope you're hungry!"

He winked and saluted Lonnie with the bottle and took a long drink.

Lonnie headed back outside, his stomach already rumbling at the sight of all that food, and filled Casey in on the details. As it was getting colder the darker it got, they both hunkered down on either side of the fire Casey had built, and enjoyed how the fading light played on the stream, and how the smoke issuing from the cabin's stovepipe grew more and more fragrant with the smell of cooking food.

About an hour later, Calhoun called them to supper, and Lonnie had a hard time holding himself back and not running ahead of Casey, whom he had to help hobble across the yard to the cabin. Once inside, they both stopped again in shock at what the table displayed—three battered tin plates covered in thick, light-tan chicken stew colored with the white of fresh potatoes and turnips and the bright orange of fresh carrots.

Tin cups of milk sat at the head of two plates. The bread sat in the middle of the table, near the stone crock that was no longer wearing its lid so that Lonnie could tell it was filled with fresh-whipped butter!

The pie sat at the far end of the table, fairly screaming to be cut into.

"Well, I never seen such polite children-folk—waitin' to be asked to sit down to table," Calhoun said, leaning over the table to cut the bread loaf into slices. Lonnie noticed that the level of the whiskey had gone down by about a third. Calhoun laughed and beckoned. "We don't stand on form here at the Calhoun plantation, young'uns. Come on in, belly up to the bar, and get to shovelin' before it gets cold!"

There were crunching sounds, and Lonnie looked under the table to see Cherokee under there, chowing down contentedly on a big heap of chicken bones.

The old Confederate laughed again, heartily, and took another deep pull from the bottle.

FIFTY

LONNIE AND CASEY and Wilbur Calhoun made short work of the chicken stew and bread lathered in thick, fresh-whipped butter and the apple pie dessert, while Cherokee crunched bones beneath the table.

The old Confederate had slacked off on the whiskey bottle, switching to coffee for the meal, and Lonnie was glad he had. There was a certain untethered, hell-for-leather quality about the old man's spirit, which, while charming when the man was sober, could possibly turn into something dark with too much skull pop under his belt. Lonnie didn't think consciously about this, but, having been around drunk, mean men enough times in his short life, it did occur to him instinctively, and it caused an all-too-familiar apprehension in the boy.

Men were too darn big, physically, and they wielded too much power and were too well armed for Lonnie to feel safe around them when they were drinking.

He didn't like it when, after the meal, Calhoun freshened his coffee with the stuff. Lonnie thanked the man for the wonderful meal and rose from the table, wiping his mouth with the back of his hand and excusing himself.

"Hold on, boy."

Lonnie inwardly cringed as he looked across the table at the old Confederate. Casey, having insisted her ankle was much better, was washing the dishes out at the creek. The dog, having taken to the two young strangers, had followed her out there, and Lonnie could hear her talking to the dog while she scrubbed the plates and cups and the dog scampered around the brush.

Calhoun had filled his pipe. He tamped the chopped tobacco down inside the bowl, and plucked a long stove match off the table between his thumb and index finger, so ingrained with dirt that both appeared nearly black, as did nearly all the deep-cut age lines in his skin.

"Yes, Mister Calhoun?" Lonnie said.

"Wilbur."

"Beg your pardon?"

"Sit down there, and call me Wilbur."

Lonnie didn't know what to say to that. It didn't feel right, calling a man as old as Calhoun by his first name. It didn't sound right at all. In fact, it sounded almost as bad as cursing. It sounded *worse* than cursing.

Calhoun struck the match to life atop the table. The flame chuffed and blossomed and then settled down against the end of the match, which the old Confederate held over the bowl of his pipe. "You really," he said, sucking the flame down into the bowl and blowing the smoke out the side of his mouth, "you really...gonna take all that loot...back to the marshal in Camp Collins...?"

He continued to suck at the flame and blow the smoke, his gaze focused on the pipe bowl.

"Yes, sir," Lonnie said, frowning at the man, not sure what his point was. "It belongs to the bank over in Golden."

"Bank money, boy," Calhoun said, flipping the match onto the floor and turning his slightly watery, drink-bleary eyes to Lonnie over the smoldering bowl of his pipe, "is money meant to be taken by them it don't belong to."

Lonnie wasn't quite sure he'd heard the man correctly. He felt the impulse to poke his fingers in his ears, to clean the wax out of them, but then he realized that he'd heard the man correctly, after all.

"I don't know what you mean, Mister Calhoun," was all that the boy could think of to say.

"I mean, son, that whoever belongs to that money has by now forgotten about it. Leastways, they've probably written it off their books, or the bank has made up for it. Most likely, rich people own that money. Rich *Yankees*. People who ain't gonna miss it none." He paused, let more smoke billow out the side of his mouth. "Folks that got enough money to lock up in a bank got enough money to lose, is what I'm sayin'."

Calhoun stopped and regarded Lonnie levelly over the smoldering bowl of his pipe. Lonnie sat frozen, waiting for the man to continue though he really didn't want him to.

"If I was you," Calhoun continued, puffing his pipe, "I'd take that money, and I'd start a life for myself somewhere a long, long way from here. New Mexico, maybe. Or maybe *Old* Mexico. Son, the senoritas down there...why, they'll..." His bearded face gained a sheepish look, and he let his voice trail off. He'd been about to gesture in the air with his hands, but he thought twice about that, too, sitting back in his chair and returning the pipe to his mouth. "Son, what I'm sayin' is this is a dog-eat-dog world. We gotta get ahead any way we can. If that means bein' stronger than the next fella, and takin' what's his and makin' it yours—why, then, that's what you gotta do."

"That ain't how I been taught it, Mister Calhoun."

"No, of course not. They don't teach you that." The old Confederate lowered his pipe once more, squared his shoulders, and leaned forward on the table, his eyes growing large and passionate. "The so-called *Good Book*...our parents...*school marms*—they wanna keep you weak, keep you cowerin' to everybody else. Cowerin' to the ones who done figured it out and learned how to make this short life we have down here on this miserable scratch of dirt somethin' worth livin'. All for the sake of bein' *civilized*. But we *ain't* civilized, boy. We're savages. All of us is savage through an' through, and hidin' that fact is plain foolish and prideful."

Calhoun laughed without humor. "It's the toughest savage that survives. It's the savviest savage that has an easy ride. Why, hell, I rode with Jesse James for a time...after the war. Him and me didn't get along—we was both the same kinda savage, I reckon—so we parted ways. But Jesse—he knew what I done just told you. You see, the war was a good teacher in that regard to us Graybacks."

Calhoun knocked the dottle from his pipe out onto the table. "No, no...you an' that girl take that money. It's yours now. You'd be fools not to take it and make a good life for yourselves."

Lonnie stared at the old Southerner who sat blaze-eyed across from him. The old man's words had grown wings and they were flying around between the boy's ears. Lonnie's palms were slick with sweat. He looked down at the overstuffed saddlebags leaning against the wall. Thousands of dollars in those two pouches. Enough so that he could go home and turn his cabin into a nice, big place, and decorate it nice, too, like he'd seen in the catalogs at the mercantile in Arapaho Creek.

He'd give his ma a nice place to grow old in, keep her mind off men that hurt her and Lonnie. Give her enough so that she wouldn't need any such man to make her happy. Because her son would make her happy.

Make her and the baby she was carrying happy. Maybelline Gentry would be wealthy and happy in her old age. If she was still alive, that was.

If Shannon Dupree hadn't killed her...

Lonnie was starting to breathe hard, as though he'd run a long way up a steep hill.

If his mother was gone, Lonnie would be alone. Maybe he had Casey, maybe he didn't. If he did, they'd need a nest egg to make a fresh start for themselves...

Maybe Calhoun was right. Maybe he should take the money. He'd never had a dime, and he at only thirteen years old worked himself to the bone, rolled into his bed every night feeling as beaten-down as an old man. Hell, none of his three pairs of socks didn't have holes in them!

Who if not Lonnie Gentry deserved such wealth that had suddenly fallen into his lap?

The door hinges squawked. Casey had left the door partway open to let the stove heat out while she'd washed the dishes at the creek. Now she nudged it wide and stood in the open doorway, holding the freshly washed plates and cooking pans, with silverware and tin cups propped on top. She was staring at Lonnie from beneath rumpled brows. She turned her head partly to one side, and narrowed her eyes reprovingly.

"Don't you listen to him, Lonnie. Don't you dare!"

FIFTY-ONE

"NOW, YOU LOOK HERE, LITTLE MISS—!"

"You look here, you old train robber," Casey said, slamming the dishes and silverware down on the end of the table and casting Calhoun one of her spine-melting glares, her smooth, suntanned cheeks flushing with fury. "How dare you try puttin' evil thoughts in Lonnie's head!"

Before Calhoun could interrupt her, she swung toward the boy. "Don't you listen to a word of his blarney. He's an old train robber and a killer. He killed his own wife! Shot her in the back! Is this the kind of man you want to be, Lonnie?"

Lonnie sat back in his chair, feeling his lower jaw becoming unhinged. Both Calhoun's words as well as Casey's had taken manic flight between his ears. He wasn't sure what to think about it all, much less what to say.

Calhoun answered for him. "He'll make up his own mind. Where I come from, a boy big as him's a man. Hell, I had friends as well as kin who fought for the Confederacy when they was no bigger'n Master Gentry there. I'm tellin' it the way this old world works, and you oughta listen, too, little miss!"

Casey stomped her good foot down hard on the floor. "Stop callin' me 'little miss'! Why, you're nothin' but a common outlaw. A ne'er-do-well and a scoundrel. You're an old rogue wolf hidin' up here from them tryin' to exterminate you. My pa worked hard to run your ilk to ground so the

West could grow and become a civilized place—a place folks who lived here could feel proud callin' their home!"

"Yeah, well, how'd that work out for your pa? What'd it get him 'cept an early grave?" Calhoun slapped a big hand down hard on the table. "I'm tellin' it right—you two best take that money and carve a life out of this miserable rock while you can. Laws and whatnot—why they're written by the scared and the weak. Them laws're meant to be broken by them strong enough to carve a life for themselves without workin' themselves to the bone to do it! Only the weak follow the laws, cause only they *have to!*"

"You old fool!" Casey screamed, slapping her own hand down hard on the table. "How dare you spew your evil blather to an innocent boy?"

"He ain't so innocent. He might be young, but he's bein' hunted like a full-grown man. That grows a child up right fast—shows him what the world's *really* all about! And *fool* am I?"

Calhoun rose, kicking his chair back and wobbling a little, drunkenly, on his feet. For a second, Lonnie thought he was going to fall into the table. "You don't know nothin' about me, little miss! I fought hard in that war, and what did it get me? Nothin' more than graves to visit when I finally got back home with so much Yankee metal in my back—bedsprings an' screws an' nails—that I jingled when I walked. And when I finally did get home, I learned my wife hadn't been pinin' away for me half as much as she was tellin' me in the letters she wrote. Ah, hell, no—she weren't pinin' at all. In fact, she was makin' time with a rich man from town— Virgil Boatwright, the town banker's son. One afternoon I come back early from sellin' eggs and I caught 'em together!"

Lonnie had been riveted to every word both Calhoun and Casey had said. Now, staring up numbly at the old Confederate, sensing the anguish in the old Rebel's heart, he said, "That... that when you killed her?"

Tears dribbled down the old man's cheeks, soaking his beard. "No." His voice cracked on that, and he turned away, giving Lonnie and Casey his back.

He lifted his head and ran a hand back over the nearly bald top of his head. "I didn't kill her, though I might as well have. June's dead on account o' me. It was a mistake. I loved her. I *still* love her. I shot Boatwright! I reckon I only clipped him though I heard he died later, but before he expired, he grabbed his old LeMat off the dresser...and...June moved between us...and he shot her in the back."

The old Confederate sobbed as he lowered his head, staggered toward the other end of the cabin, and took his face in his hands. His shoulders jerked as he cried. "There wasn't nothin' I could do for her, an' I heard a neighbor yellin' from his field, and I went crazy with shame an' fear, an' I ran. And, oh, Lord, I'm still runnin'."

Calhoun turned back toward Lonnie and Casey.

"That was the end of civilized life for me. I reckon I missed it more than I thought. Leastways, the family part of that life. Been nice havin' you two young'uns here...to cook for... to listen to you talkin' out by the creek, sparkin' each other, fallin' in love, like me and June... back before the war."

Lonnie flushed. He glanced at Casey. The girl stared stony-faced at Calhoun though Lonnie could tell by a slight softening in her eyes that the man's story had reached through her anger.

"Hell," Calhoun said, chuckling though tears continued to dribble down his cheek and into his beard, "I went out and stole grub for you, didn't I?" He chuckled again.

There was a short, heavy silence, then Casey said tonelessly, "What?"

"Helkatoot," Calhoun exclaimed. "I never did no prospectors any favors. I stole that food you ate tonight. There's a little shotgun settlement, three cabins and some stables down along Eagle Creek, and I raided their garden and keeper shed, took a chicken out of their coop." The old Confederate's tone was buoyant with mockery. "Pretty darn good vittles even if they was stolen, wasn't they? Hell, those rock breakers ain't gonna miss none of it. They got more than they can eat, anyways, and a man'd be a fool to go hungry up here when he's got their chickens and gardens down there!"

He turned to Lonnie. "You see what I mean, boy? Why work like a dog when you don't have to? We're savages! All of us." He leaned forward and tapped his temple. "It's the smart savages that know how to make the plows pull for *them!*"

Lonnie couldn't move from his chair. He didn't know what to make of all he'd heard, but he knew one thing—Calhoun's story, however horrible, had been fascinating. And Lonnie wasn't sure he didn't agree with the old Confederate's life philosophy, either...

Why shouldn't he do what Calhoun had recommended—take the money and make a good life for himself? Why should he struggle when he didn't have to? Casey obviously didn't agree with Calhoun, but she was still under the influence of her father, the town marshal of Arapaho Creek.

Calhoun had been right: Marshal Stoveville's efforts at holding the lawbreakers at bay had been rewarded by only a premature death and an orphaned daughter.

"You go ahead and sit here and listen to this scoundrel as long as you want, Lonnie," Casey said in that same disdainfully toneless voice. "But I'm goin' to bed." She picked up the saddlebags, drew them over her shoulder with a grunt. "And I'll be pullin' out with the money first thing in the mornin'."

She stopped at the door to glare once more at Calhoun. "I'll be takin' it back to where it rightly belongs."

She opened the door and headed out, stepping around Cherokee who sat beyond the doorway, mewling his discomfort at the raised voices and the tension.

"Casey, hold on!" Lonnie said, rising from his chair but getting his boot hung up on a corner of the table, and tripping. He was drunk on the possibilities of a new, rich life. He made his way through the door and swerved around Cherokee. He caught up to Casey easily, as she was still hobbling on her injured ankle.

"Casey, stop!" Lonnie pleaded, grabbing the girl's arm.

She stopped and swung toward him, her eyes ablaze with anger.

"What're you gonna do when you go back to Arapaho Creek?" Lonnie asked her. "You gonna go back to work for that mercantile? You know how much you're gonna have to work to keep your house? And what if you lose it? Then, what're you gonna do?"

Lonnie knew that the frontier was a harsh, cruel place for young women without families. Casey knew it, too. Lonnie could see the fear in her eyes. Her gaze grew less angry and more pensive, and then, as though ashamed by what she was thinking, Casey swung around again and continued favoring her sprained ankle as she strode toward where the fire by the creek had burned down to faint, umber ashes.

She sat down and, keeping the saddlebags draped over her shoulder, raised a knee and wrapped her arms around it. She studied the darkness straight out across the murmuring creek for a time, and then she said softly, "So, what are you thinkin', Lonnie? What're you thinkin' we should do with this money?"

Lonnie sat down beside her. His mind was swimming with possibilities. He could hardly catch his breath. "We could take it back home. I could build up the ranch, and we could—"

"Get married?"

Lonnie hiked his shoulder. "Why not? You don't have nobody,

and...and Ma...she might or might not be at the ranch when I get back." The horror of that possibility struck the boy like a blow. So much had happened, and he'd been so distracted trying to stay ahead of Dupree, of trying to keep himself and Casey alive, that he really hadn't allowed himself to consider what life would be like for him if his mother was dead.

If both his parents were dead, and, like Casey, he had no one.

Suddenly, he realized that Casey was staring at him sympathetically, as though she knew what he was thinking. She sighed, shook her head. "Damn you, Lonnie, for listenin' to that old train robber...and for makin' me actually consider doin' such a low-down dirty thing."

She set the saddlebags aside, gently pulled off her boots, and rolled up in her bedroll. She turned her back to Lonnie.

Lonnie wandered off and tended nature, then he came back to the fire, built the flames up a little with pine branches. Then, he, too, curled up in his blankets. But he was too distracted with swirling thoughts about the money to fall asleep right away. Money and shame, money and shame—he was caught in a cyclone of those two conflicting ideas.

He could hear Casey over on the other side of the fire, rolling and thrashing this way and that, for a long, long time, before sleep finally claimed him.

He woke abruptly, lifting his head from his saddle. He blinked and looked around, heart pumping.

Something had awakened him. Then he realized what it had been, because he heard it again—Casey screaming from a long ways away: "Lonnie! Help me!" There was a slight pause as the girl's cries echoed around the canyon touched with the pearl light of dawn.

Then Casey screamed something Lonnie couldn't hear, because it was muffled with distance and partly drowned by the morning chirping of birds.

And then she screamed something Lonnie could hear:

"Dupreeeee!"

FIFTY-TWO

TWO HOURS LATER, after the sun had cleared the horizon but the valley in which the boy found himself was still cloaked in cool shadows, Lonnie abruptly stopped the General on the side of a sparsely wooded ridge.

He stared straight ahead, his eyes wide. His pulse hammered in his ears as he stared at something pale in the ferns and small spruce saplings growing around a deadfall tree about thirty yards away.

Lonnie couldn't move. His boots were glued to his stirrups. He could not bring himself to dismount and walk over and take a look at the pale object obscured by the brush.

He knew what he would find there if he did.

Dupree, Fuego, and Childress had killed Casey and thrown her body there like trash.

Finally, knowing that he had to confirm his suspicions, the boy climbed slowly, heavily down from General Sherman's back. He dropped the horse's reins and walked slowly forward, setting each spurred boot down slowly, the lighthearted ringing of the spurs seeming to mock the boy's growing dread.

The long, pale object that he knew would be Casey, killed by Dupree, grew gradually larger before him. The boy's stomach felt as though someone had rammed a railroad spike through it. Tears were oozing over his eyes. He blinked them away, rubbed his cheek with a gloved hand, swallowed hard to keep the vomit down.

When he stepped into the ferns and saw that what lay before him was not Casey, after all, but the pale carcass of a freshly killed mule deer fawn lying with its pale belly facing Lonnie, the brown eyes regarding him blandly, the boy's knees nearly buckled with relief.

The fawn had likely been killed by a wolf or a mountain lion last night, partly eaten, and then dragged here to be chewed on later.

Lonnie turned and strode quickly back to his horse. His relief at not finding Casey dead was quickly obliterated by the growing possibility that he would still find her that way.

He looked down at the tracks of four horses. He'd cut the sign about a half a mile downstream from Calhoun's cabin, in the opposite direction from which Lonnie, Calhoun, and Casey had first entered the canyon two days ago. The tracks continued through a small notch in the ridge wall and on down the eastern side of the mountain, following a faint trail that was probably an old game path as well as a trace once used by the Arapahos for traveling from one valley to another within the Never Summer range.

Lonnie hadn't been on it long before he'd realized that it was probably an alternate route, probably an easier route than Storm Peak Pass, especially in bad weather, over the mountains to the eastern plains.

Earlier, it hadn't taken Lonnie long, once he'd shaken off the cobwebs of sleep, to realize what had happened to Casey. She must have awakened well before dawn and, deciding that she had to take the money to the deputy US marshal in Camp Collins herself, because she thought she could no longer trust Lonnie to help her, she'd quietly saddled her chestnut and ridden out alone along the stream and, not long after leaving Calhoun's cabin, into the hands of Dupree, Fuego, and Childress.

Lonnie had seen the tracks where the four horses had come together. Forming a group, they'd headed southeast. Two of the horses had been ridden close together, which told Lonnie that Casey's horse was likely being led. The girl was now Dupree's prisoner. For whatever reason, the outlaw and his two partners had taken her captive.

And, of course, they had the money, too.

Lonnie was vaguely surprised to discover that he was no longer concerned about the money. What made his heart pound until he thought it would crash through his breastbone was Casey.

As he rode down the slope and then followed a winding watercourse through a crease between heavily timbered ridges, he also reflected that as much as he might have wanted to, he couldn't have taken the bank loot any more than he could have sprouted wings and flown.

That was all clear to him now, wedged in between thoughts of getting Casey back unharmed. He was no more like Wilbur Calhoun than Wilbur Calhoun was like Lonnie Gentry—a good kid on his way to becoming a man of integrity no matter what the cost.

Lonnie wished he would have realized that last night, because it might have saved Casey's life as well as him a whole heap of trouble.

Better late than never.

Lonnie held the General to a fast pace as he followed the tracks of the four shod horses ahead of him. As he did, he looked around warily.

He wouldn't put it past Dupree to set a trap for him, to try to blow him out of his saddle from ambush. Lonnie wished that Calhoun were riding with him. The old Confederate may have been many things, most of them bad things, but he was also good with a gun, and he was trail-savvy. Lonnie wasn't too proud to admit that he could have used the old man's help now, with Casey's life on the line.

When Lonnie had raced into the cabin earlier, after he'd heard Casey's scream, he'd tried to awaken the old Confederate, but there'd been no doing. Lonnie had found not only one but two empty bottles on the floor. Calhoun had stirred and mumbled and called for June, sobbing, then rolled over and cried himself back to sleep on his bunk.

Late in the day, when the sun was tumbling over the mountains jutting up behind Lonnie, several strands of wood smoke touched the boy's nose. He checked the General down where two shallow washes intersected, and tied the horse to an old root angling out the northern bank.

He was out of the mountains now, on the north side of the Never Summers, in a relatively flat, dry area relieved by widely spaced bluffs and low mesas. The ground was thin and sandy and not able to grow much except for short, brown grass and clumps of prickly pear and yucca. There were few trees except a light peppering of scrub cedars, junipers, and piñons.

The sky above Lonnie was a velvety lime-green. He glanced toward the Never Summers towering darkly behind him to see the glowing, crimson sun being cleaved by a high, black peak shaped like an ax blade. The sun was falling quickly behind that blade toward the west side of the range.

Lonnie climbed up out of the forking ravines, doffed his hat near the top of the bank, and stopped beneath the bank's crest. Slowly, continuing to smell the smoke, he edged a look over the top of the bank. He pulled his head down quickly, pulse quickening. He nervously licked his lips and then edged another look over the top of the bank, and held himself steady despite his nervousness.

He was staring out over a broad table of ground rising gradually toward a low, sandstone mesa rimmed with bulging rock from which a few hardy cedars twisted. The crest of the mesa stood maybe three hundred feet above the land below it and on which a low, gray cabin and barn and corral sat behind a windmill, whose blades lazily twisted in the warm, dry breeze blowing over the mountains.

In the corral fashioned from peeled pine poles, five horses ate from a hay crib, lazily swishing their tails. Lonnie recognized Casey's chestnut.

Gray smoke curled from a stone chimney rising up the cabin's far right end. Voices emanated from inside the cabin. Mostly men's voices. Then Lonnie heard a girl's voice.

Casey's voice. She gave a harsh retort to something one of the men said.

There was a sharp *crack!* The sound of a brutal slap.

One of the men inside the cabin laughed. Then Lonnie almost kicked out of his boots with a start when he saw a slender, denim-clad female figure in a man's wool shirt appear in the cabin's open doorway, the door being propped open with rock. There was a motley-looking porch on the place, crouched on low stone pilings. The figure walked out onto the porch and down the steps and into the weakening sunlight, which flashed off Casey's gold-blonde hair.

The girl limped around the side of the cabin, gathering wood from a low stack around the chimney, and carried the wood back into the cabin. She'd moved with her head and shoulders angled low with fear and defeat.

Lonnie watched the black, open doorway through which Casey had disappeared.

He watched it for a long time as he tried to calm himself down and gather his thoughts.

Then, his lips set in a hard, straight line, Lonnie eased back down the bank, shucked his Winchester from his saddle sheath, and pumped a cartridge into the chamber.

FIFTY-THREE

LONNIE TOLD himself he had to wait until dark to approach the cabin.

But that was a very difficult thing for him to do. The farther the sun dropped, and the darker the tableland got as well as the shallow wash in which Lonnie waited with General Sherman, the quieter everything got.

At least, the quieter everything except the cabin got.

Lonnie could hear Dupree and the other men talking loudly in there. Their voices gradually grew louder and louder. They were accompanied by the occasional violent jingle of coins being thrown down on a table, and the clinking of bottles. They were obviously playing poker.

Lonnie could also hear the clatter of pans. The smoke from the chimney grew thicker. The men had Casey cooking for them while they played cards and drank. Lonnie had to get the girl out of there. The more the men drank, the more dangerous they would get.

But he had to wait until dark. At least twilight. There was very little cover anywhere around the cabin, so if he tried to approach the hovel while it was still light, someone inside the cabin would probably see him, and Lonnie would acquire a two-ounce chunk of lead for his efforts. Worse, he'd let Casey down.

There was no telling what Dupree and the others might do to her after dark, when they were good and drunk. Lonnie didn't want to think about it. He wanted to get her out of there.

Lonnie sat on his butt on the bottom of the wash, his back to the bank, his rifle across his thighs. He'd unbuckled the General's latigo strap, and both ends of the strap were hanging free beneath the horse's belly. Lonnie had also let the horse drink water from his hat, and he'd fed him a handful of grain, as well. Now the horse stood only a few feet from Lonnie, facing his rider, head up, twitching his ears, listening.

The General knew something of great gravity was about to happen, and he was waiting with anticipation, as was Lonnie.

When there was only a little light left—sort of a soft blue fog touched lightly with the blush of salmon—Lonnie rose and took a long drink from his canteen. He patted the General's neck, and strode quickly along the wash. He followed the wash to the east, and when an even shallower wash intersected the main one from the north, he tramped through this lesser, feeder wash that was likely dry except during monsoons or when the snow was melting in the mountains.

This wash was choked with spindly sage, yucca, rocks, prickly pear, a few bleached bones of long-dead animals. As Lonnie had admonished himself to be mindful of rattlesnakes, he heard one give its high, eerie rattle. He stopped to see the diamondback, little thicker than a rope but as deadly as one twice its size, slither off amongst the rocks and shrubs, likely heading for its hole.

Lonnie paused to steady his nerves. Then hefted his rifle in his hands, holding it up high across his chest, and continued moving north along the shallow wash. He paused twice more to peer carefully over the crest of the wash, to see where he was in relation to the cabin, and then, ten minutes later, he ran up and over the crest of the wash toward the cabin's east wall. He ran hard, crouching low, holding his rifle in his right hand and swerving around occasional tufts of buck brush and sage.

There was only one window in the side of the shack facing Lonnie, to the right of the large, stone chimney and near the rear of the cabin. That was likely a bedroom window. No one was probably back there yet. A least, Lonnie hoped they weren't. There was a curtain over that small window but it was partly open.

Lonnie dropped to a knee and pressed his shoulder against the cabin's log wall, behind the chimney and the woodpile. He was breathing hard, sweating. It had warmed considerably when he'd dropped out of the mountains, and he'd wrapped his coat around his bedroll. His shirt was pasted to his back.

He mopped his brow with his shirtsleeve. He could hear the voices more clearly now. Mostly, he heard the more talkative Dupree and Childress. He knew Fuego was in there, however, because he'd seen the man's brown-and-white pinto. He wondered who the fifth horse belonged to.

Lonnie rose, drew another deep breath—here it goes—and started moving around the chimney. He'd gotten as far as the woodpile on the chimney's other side, when he heard someone walk out onto the stoop and come down the steps. Lonnie dropped back down to a knee with a gasp, and very slowly, quietly ratcheted back the Winchester's hammer, lifting the stock to his shoulder.

A figure came toward him, and he tightened his finger on the trigger.

Then he eased the tension when Casey stopped before him, rocked back on her heels, and slapped a hand to her shirt. "Lonnie!" she exclaimed.

She'd been too startled to whisper it. Immediately, she realized her mistake, and turned her head quickly toward the cabin.

Dupree yelled from inside, "What's out there, girl?"

Casey whipped her head and stricken gaze toward Lonnie. Lonnie's heart hammered his sternum until he almost couldn't breathe. Fresh sweat broke out on his back and inside his gloves.

"Girl!" Dupree yelled. "What's out there?"

Lonnie gritted his teeth when he heard a chair scrape back across the rough wooden floor. He looked up at Casey standing over him, and very quietly whispered, "Snake."

Casey turned her chin toward the front of the cabin. "Just a snake. Shocked me's all! He's gone now!"

Lonnie was glad to hear a chair squeak as Dupree's weight settled back into it. "Well, hurry it up with that wood! You try to make a run for it, Fuego here'll shoot you. Fuego can shoot the wing off a fly at a thousand yards—can't you Fuego?"

Childress and someone else laughed, though Lonnie didn't think the someone else was Fuego.

Casey turned her anxious gaze back to Lonnie, who stood and squeezed her right hand encouragingly. "Now, tell 'em you're comin'," Lonnie said.

She frowned at him curiously, anxiously, but then she did as Lonnie had instructed.

"Sit down, now," Lonnie said. "Keep your head down."

Casey grabbed his arm, dug her fingers in. "What're you gonna—?"

"I'm gonna end this right here," Lonnie said. "Sit down and keep your head down."

"Forget the money. Lonnie, let's just run!"

Lonnie gazed straight into her eyes, hardened his jaws, and said firmly, "No."

Casey shook her head slowly, dreadfully, then she slowly sank down against the cabin wall, behind the chimney.

Lonnie turned his head forward. He pulled his hat down a little lower on his forehead, and then walked around the cabin's front corner. Keeping his head down, so that anyone looking out the door couldn't glimpse his face and see that he wasn't Casey, he moved up the porch steps, crossed the half-rotten boards of the stoop and stepped inside.

He stopped suddenly, raised his rifle to his shoulder. He aimed at Dupree, sitting at the left end of a small, rectangular table on which dirty tin plates and cups and several bottles were cluttered. Two lamps burned where they hung from nails on square-hewn ceiling support posts. The fireplace was to Lonnie's far right, but he didn't look at the small fire whose heat he could feel pushing against him.

He blinked once as he kept his gaze on Dupree, who sat back in his chair, his left boot hiked up onto his right knee. His hat was off but his longish, blond hair showed the marks of it. His left hand was wrapped with a bloody bandage. He had another bloody bandage around his ribs. He clutched his wounded hand against his belly, and he was glowering demonically at Lonnie.

The boy could tell by the deep lines carved around Dupree's eyes, and by the sweat beading his cheeks, that his wounds were grieving him.

"Hey, Squirrel!" he said. "Been waitin' on you. What took you so long?"

Fuego sat facing Lonnie on the other side of the table, leaning forward, a cigarette smoldering in his right hand. He was absently fingering his wolf-tooth necklace with his left hand. The half-breed wasn't wearing his hat, either. Neither was Childress, who sat with his back to Lonnie, half smiling over his right shoulder at the boy, his close-set, pale-blue eyes glistening mockingly in the flickering lamplight.

They'd all settled in for the night.

Lonnie swallowed, tried to keep his voice from quavering as he said, "Toss your guns onto the table there. One fast move, and I'll drill ya."

"Balderdash!" intoned Dupree, laughing, showing all his large, white teeth. "Put the Winchester down, kid, before you get hurt." He held up his bandaged hand, which shook like a leaf in the wind. "I wanna talk to you about this hand"—he dropped his gaze to the bloody bandage around his ribs—"and about this here."

Too late, Lonnie heard a boot thud on the floor behind him. The stench of sweat filled Lonnie's nostrils. A man grunted loudly as he wrapped his big, bare, hairy arms around Lonnie's waist from behind, and, laughing, lifted the boy two feet off the floor.

Lonnie gave a loud groaning *chuff!* as the bear hug squeezed the air out of his lungs. He inadvertently triggered the Winchester into a ceiling beam. The three outlaws at the table started laughing as they watched wood sliver and dirt sift down from the ceiling.

Lonnie gave a loud, enraged yell, and swung his right boot forward before thrusting it straight back, hard, ramming his spurred heel into the kneecap of the man who was holding him above the floor.

The man bellowed loudly. The thick arms dropped away from Lonnie's waist. Lonnie dropped nearly straight down to the floor, and pivoted on his hips.

He saw the man who'd lifted him—a big, barrel-waisted hombre with a long, tangled, cinnamon beard and a thick, food-stained mustache. The man's hands appeared large as plowshares. He glared through narrowed eyes at Lonnie as he cupped one hand over his bloody left knee. He bulled forward, swinging his thick, right fist toward Lonnie, who flipped the Winchester around, and smashed the stock against the underside of the man's chin.

The man flew back out the open door, bellowing raucously. When he got his boots under him, Lonnie rammed the stock of his Winchester into the man's bulging gut. The man groaned and dropped to his knees, and Lonnie slammed the rifle butt down hard on the back of his head, laying him out cold.

Guns roared behind Lonnie, who turned, cocking the Winchester as slugs sizzled through the air on either side of his head. Both Dupree and Fuego were standing and extending pistols at Lonnie, trying to aim around Childress. Childress was falling drunkenly back against the table.

Lonnie looked past Childress at Dupree, who was leveling his pistol on Lonnie once more, and Lonnie triggered the Winchester.

As Dupree crumpled, firing his revolver into the table, shattering a whiskey bottle, Lonnie stepped hard to his left in time to avoid a bullet triggered by Fuego, whom Lonnie shot next. Fuego groaned and clapped a hand to his left temple as he twisted around, tripped over his chair, and hit the floor with a loud *boom!*

Childress was still trying to get his revolver out of his holster. He stopped when he saw the Winchester aimed at his throat. He looked at the round maw only six inches away from him, and took his hand away from his gun, swallowed, and raised both hands in the air.

FIFTY-FOUR

LONNIE WAVED the barrel of his Winchester around in the air before him, expecting one of the other men to take another shot at him. But Dupree was lying beyond the end of the table, unmoving, his lips stretched painfully back from his teeth. Blood welled from the bullet hole in the center of the man's chest. The outlaw's cold, gray eyes stared lifelessly at the ceiling.

Dupree had robbed his last bank. Absently, Lonnie wondered what his mother would think about that, if she were still living.

Fuego lay on his side, writhing and groaning as he cupped both his hands to his bloody left temple. Childress stood with his hands raised, scowling at Lonnie.

"What're you gonna do now, kid?" Childress asked. "You think you know?"

"Yeah, I know," Lonnie said, glaring back at the man. "I know exactly what I'm gonna do."

A floorboard squawked behind Lonnie.

He swung around, but it was Casey this time. She stepped slowly over the unmoving figure of the man who'd grabbed Lonnie from behind, and into the cabin. Lonnie stepped back away from Childress, giving himself plenty of room, keeping his rifle aimed at Childress's head.

Casey looked around as though in a daze.

"Get their guns, Casey," Lonnie said. "Get every gun and knife you can find, and haul 'em all outside. Then we're gonna need some rope. Lots of rope."

When Casey had relieved the outlaws of all their weapons, and had tied Childress and the painfully grunting Fuego to ceiling support posts, Lonnie wagged his rifle at the big, unconscious man on the porch.

"Who's that?" he asked Casey.

"Fellow who runs this little outlaw camp," Casey said. She had a coil of rope on her shoulder. "They called him Hansen. An old partner of Dupree's."

"Best tie him, too," Lonnie said, stepping outside and keeping his Winchester aimed at the big, unconscious gent with the thick, bare arms. When Casey had hog-tied the man in much the same way that she'd hog-tied the others, making certain there was no way they could work lose, Lonnie walked back inside, found the saddlebags lying near the dead Dupree, and drew them over his shoulder. He swept the money from the table into one of the pouches. Now the bags felt as heavy as before.

"Best get these out of there," Lonnie said as he stepped out, resting his Winchester on his shoulder. "I'll stow 'em in the stable until mornin'."

Casey stood at the bottom of the porch steps. The big gent was waking up now and groaning as he lay belly-down against the porch floor, hands tied to his ankles behind his broad back.

"Oh, my head," he bellowed. "Oh, Lord o' mercy—my *head!*"

"That's the least of your troubles, partner," Lonnie said as he stepped over the man and descended the porch steps.

Casey smiled crookedly at the boy, and arched a brow. "You clean up right well. Ever think of becomin' a lawman?"

Lonnie shrugged. "You all right?"

"I've seen better days," Casey said. "And I'll see more, I reckon." She paused and looked brightly up at Lonnie. "Your mother's alive, Lonnie. I heard Dupree talkin' to the others. I reckon even he couldn't hurt a woman with child."

Lonnie sighed and leaned back against a porch post in relief.

Casey moved closer to him, crossed her arms on her chest, and cocked her hip. She looked at the saddlebags draped over Lonnie's shoulder. "What're we gonna do with those, come mornin'?"

"Same thing we were always gonna do with 'em. Take 'em to the same place we're gonna take them two inside and that Hansen fella. To Marshal Barrows in Camp Collins."

"My pa'd be right proud of you."

Lonnie ran a hand across the saddlebags, considering. "Casey, I..."

"You don't have to say anythin', Lonnie. I know who you are. You may have lost track for a little while. Heck, I lost track of myself. I reckon we all do from time to time. But I know who I am now. And I know exactly who you are, too."

"Oh, yeah?" Lonnie said, a little sheepish. "Who's that?"

Casey wrapped her arms around his neck and kissed him. "You're the man I love."

THE CURSE OF SKULL CANYON

For Bill and Amy Schmidt
longtime friends from the old home country.
For their daughter Olivia,
who I hope enjoys this one, too.

ONE

FOURTEEN-YEAR-OLD LONNIE GENTRY didn't care if he never heard another gunshot again in his life.

In fact, after his many recent near-death experiences at the hands of the outlaw, Shannon Dupree, who'd hunted him and Casey Stoveville like game through the Never Summer Mountains a year ago, he hoped he'd *never* hear the blast of another rifle.

But now as he stopped his buckskin stallion, General Sherman, on a high-mountain trail not far from timberline, and cocked an ear, he was sure that the raking, echoing cough he'd just heard was gunfire indeed.

What else could it be? Surely not thunder, for there wasn't a cloud in sight against the high, dry arch of cerulean blue.

Lonnie looked at his horse. General Sherman had turned his head to stare toward a granite-capped outcropping jutting several yards upslope and behind a ways. The General's eyes were wide, and those dark copper orbs were twitching. The black nostrils worked as the stallion sniffed the breeze.

"Ah, heck," Lonnie said, his gut tightening with anxiety. "Let's head on down the mountain, General. I think we've done found all the bogged cows we're gonna find today."

With that, Lonnie clucked and touched spurs to the General's flanks. The sleek buckskin seemed to want to hightail it as much as Lonnie did. The General gave an agreeable snort and broke into a trot, following the game trail they'd been on for the past several hours, on down the steep slope and into the cool shade of firs, pines, tamaracks, and a salting of white-stemmed, verdant-smelling aspens.

This day and the day before, Lonnie and the General had been scouring this neck of their mountain range for any cows or calves that had gotten left behind last week, when Lonnie had moved his and his mother's herd to another range in the southern reaches of the Never Summers. Now, he'd head on back to the line shack and call it a day, maybe return here for one more look early tomorrow.

He had work to do on the corral flanking the shack, anyway, and besides, he didn't want to be anywhere around where there was shooting.

Even if it was just someone shooting at elk or deer.

No, he'd had enough of shooting, thank you very much.

Lonnie gave the General his head, and they made good time descending the slope. They reached the bottom of a ravine through which a creek ran. As they were about to turn onto an intersecting game trail that would take them even lower toward where the line shack sat at the base of Eagle Ridge, an eerie buzzing sounded just off Lonnie's right ear.

Then there was a loud *thud!* as what could only have been a bullet smashed into a fir bole just ahead and to Lonnie's right.

The rifle's blasting, echoing report followed a half a second later.

"Jesus!" Lonnie shouted, ducking instinctively and then glancing back over his left shoulder.

A cold stone dropped in his belly.

Four horseback riders were galloping toward him, spread out side by side and weaving amongst the columnar pines. One was just now aiming the carbine in his hands, pumping a fresh cartridge into the rifle's breech. The carbine's dark maw blossomed smoke and fire.

The bullet screeched toward Lonnie before searing a hot path of torn cloth over his right shoulder. His right arm went instantly numb. The bullet continued past Lonnie and over the General's head to bark loudly into a granite boulder.

As the rifle's report reached Lonnie's ears, the General whinnied shrilly and pitched sharply up off his front hooves. Lonnie had grabbed at his right shoulder, dropping the rein he'd been holding in that hand, and hadn't been prepared for the horse's sudden, violent buck.

"Ah, *hell!*" Lonnie cried as, kicking free of his stirrups, he felt himself being hurled back over the General's left hip.

The sloping ground came up to slap him hard about the head and shoulders. Lonnie heard his breath slammed out of him in a loud *"Ghah-hh!"* of expelled breath. As the General galloped on down the mountain, stepping on his trailing bridle reins, Lonnie rolled, losing his hat and cursing.

Unfortunately, he'd been through this before. So, when he'd stopped rolling and found himself still alive and able to use his limbs, he heaved himself to his feet. With one quick look behind him to see the four galloping riders closing on him fast—one shouting, "Get him!"—Lonnie took off running as fast and as hard as he could, trying to ignore the aching burn in his right arm.

He'd been through this before, all right, but he didn't have time to reflect on the bad turn of his luck. He could now feel the reverberations of the galloping horses through his boots as he sprinted for an outcropping of black granite rising ahead of him.

He hadn't planned to head for the rock. But, then again, he hadn't planned on getting bushwhacked again in these mountains, either—nearly exactly a year since the first time!

As Lonnie ran, he could hear the horses growing near—hear the squawk of tack and bridle chains, the raking of the air in and out of the horses' straining lungs. Guns popped. The bullets tore into trees around Lonnie and chewed up the turf around his hammering boots.

Lonnie glanced back once more. The riders were fifty yards away now and closing fast.

Another bullet burned across the nub of Lonnie's right cheek.

The boy sucked a sharp, pained breath and turned his head forward. He gained the escarpment and fairly hurled himself up into the first nook he saw—leaping and throwing his hands up to grab for hidden holds. He found the holds he was looking for and hoisted himself up into a natural flue in the side of the outcropping. Breathing hard, in a frozen-blooded panic, the boy continued climbing—scrambling, really—following the natural route that opened before him.

"There he is!" one of the men now below him shouted.

Two more rifles blasted. The bullets slammed into the rock around Lonnie, peppering him with stone shards. Another rifle belched. The slug slammed into the heel of Lonnie's boot as the boy pulled himself over the top of the outcropping and hurled himself across the rock and out of sight from below.

Lonnie lifted his right foot to look at his boot heel. The bullet was poking its evil head out of it. Lonnie swiped at it, trying to dislodge the malicious thing, but it was in there solid. He didn't have time to worry about bullets that weren't in his hide, anyway. He fell back against the escarpment, catching his breath.

Air sawed in and out of him loudly. His heart thudded in his ears.

He was shaking.

He could have lay there a long time, the sky swirling over him, but a horse whinnied below the scarp. A man said, his voice pinched with fury, "Get after him, Jeb!"

"Why me?" Jeb asked.

"I got twenty years on you, you son of a buck! Get after him and kill him!"

A man cussed. Boots scraped against rock. Someone was climbing up the scarp.

Lonnie heaved himself to his feet and looked around. The scarp was nearly solid rock with only a few tufts of grass and wiry brush cropping up occasionally A few irregular stone formations jutted from its surface, speckled white and gray with what Lonnie figured were bones of some kind. Ancient bones of animals or maybe men. He'd seen them before throughout the Never Summers.

But the only bones he was concerned about now, however, were his own.

He ran across the uneven surface of the escarpment. It shelved downward after several yards, and several stone corridors opened around him. Lonnie considered taking cover in one of these, but if the man after him found him, he'd be trapped.

He glanced over his right shoulder.

The man was behind him, all right. He was behind him and just now aiming a rifle at Lonnie, cheek snugged up to the rifle's rear stock.

Lonnie lurched forward. The rifle thundered. Lonnie tripped over a thump of stone rising from the escarpment floor and stumbled wildly forward before falling and rolling.

Lonnie gained his feet in mid roll and continued running. Behind him, the rifle thundered again. The slug spanged shrilly off a rock to Lonnie's left.

He ran hard. The escarpment floor dropped more and more. He ran down a steep decline through a narrow corridor.

When he came out on the other side, he saw a narrow gap in a rise of black stone to his left. Instinctively, knowing he didn't have much time, he threw himself into the gap, vaguely hoping it was more than a nook or a cranny without another exit but had a back door to somewhere...

To anywhere but where he was now, with a man out to kill him hot on his heels.

Lonnie had hoped in vain.

The gap, only about three feet wide, was only about five feet deep.

Lonnie found himself staring at a cold stone wall of solid rock streaked with bird droppings.

Boots thudded behind Lonnie. The boy winced as the raking breaths of his approaching pursuer grew louder and louder.

TWO

LONNIE WHIPPED around to face the mouth of the gap.

The boot thuds grew louder. Spurs trilled softly.

Lonnie slid slowly down the rear wall of the gap until he was sitting on his butt, making himself as small as possible. He brushed his fist across the bullet burn on his cheek, wrapped his arms around his knees, and sat staring out of the gap.

His heart tattooed a desperate rhythm against his breastbone.

His stalker moved slowly into view from Lonnie's right. Lonnie tightened his jaws. He hugged his knees tighter, vaguely wishing the stone floor would open and swallow him.

The man was tall and lean and unshaven. He wore a long, black duster and a low-crowned hat with a thong dangling beneath his chin which was sharply spade-shaped and carpeted in lusterless brown whiskers. That angry chin gave a mean, belligerent cast to his face—at least to his profile, which was all that Lonnie could see from his angle.

He held a Winchester carbine up high across his chest as he continued moving from Lonnie's right to his left. As he did, he limped on one foot, as though he'd injured himself on his run across the irregular floor of the escarpment.

He turned his head as he looked around the stone knob. All he had to do at this moment, now that he was directly out in front of Lonnie, was turn his head a little more to the left. Then he'd see Lonnie cowering in the shadowy gap.

The man lurched to a standstill.

Here it comes, Lonnie thought. *Now he'll see me and after two or three quick blasts of his carbine, that will be the end. Ma will never know what happened to me, because once this fella drills me, he'll leave me here in this gap and I won't be found till someone finds a reason to scout around up here, which, given the remoteness and ruggedness of the place, will likely be never.*

I'll molder here alone...

Ma will die wondering what happened to her fourteen-year-old son, Lonnie Gentry. She'll likely leave the ranch and move to town because if there was one true thing about Ma it was that she hated being alone. She'll likely find a man in town and...

Lonnie let the fast train of his half-conscious thoughts trail off. The man before him wheeled away from Lonnie and went limping back the way he'd come, cursing and lowering his rifle to his side.

Lonnie blinked in shock. He couldn't believe the man was giving up on him. All he'd needed to do was turn a little more to the left, and *bam-bam!*

Lonnie listened to the man's spur-trilling footsteps fade to silence.

Lonnie couldn't believe his luck. Was it too good to be true? The man might be setting a trap for him. Did he want Lonnie to believe he'd given up and gone back to his kill-crazy partners? Then, when Lonnie showed himself, the lead would fly.

Lonnie sat there a long time. It was as though he had turned to stone. His heart slowed, the hammering in his ears grew less and less violent. An hour must have passed, for the shadows in the gap grew thicker and thicker and Lonnie detected a cooling in the air that sharpened the smell of forest duff and pine resin.

From somewhere that Lonnie couldn't see, a hawk gave its ratcheting cry. The ratcheting came and faded several times as the bird glided across the skies, hunting the forest floor for mice or squirrels.

Lonnie heaved himself to his feet. His boots feeling like lead, he stepped up to the mouth of the gap and slid a cautious gaze around the wall on his right. He stared in the direction his pursuer had gone, half believing that the man would be squatting there only a few yards away, carbine ready.

Nothing.

The only sounds were the hawk's cry and the breeze playing in the forest canopy surrounding the escarpment.

Lonnie moved out of the gap and looked around. Should he go back the way he'd come? No. The three shooters might be waiting for him at the base of the scarp. Of course, they might have fanned out and were waiting for him at various points around the scarp but returning the way he'd come seemed the least desirable of his options.

His instincts told him to try to find another way off the knob.

Crouching, keeping his head low so that he wouldn't be seen from the forest floor, he moved off along the scarp, following what was now a gradual drop toward the ground. The scarp continued to drop until Lonnie found himself at the edge of it, crouching, sweeping his gaze across the forest floor only ten or so feet beneath him now. The pines were spread six or seven feet apart, affording little cover for anyone waiting for Lonnie to show himself.

Deciding—or at least hoping—that his pursuers had given up on him —Lonnie dropped to his butt, turned to face the scarp, and crabbed his way down the wall, using small cracks and fissures for hand- and footholds. When he reached the ground, he dropped to his butt once more and pressed his back to the wall he'd just descended and held very still as he again surveyed the forest around him.

After a couple of minutes of seeing no more movement beyond that of squirrels, chickadees, and nuthatches flicking amongst the branches, Lonnie rose and began moving down the slope toward the east. He had no intention of moving back directly toward where he hoped to find General Sherman, because his pursuers might be looking for him there, possibly even using the buckskin stallion as bait.

Instead, he decided to move in a roundabout way in that general direction, watching, listening, and sniffing the breeze. Lonnie had a good sniffer on him, and he could smell horse or man sweat from fifty yards away. He wasn't sure how his senses had become so keen. Probably because his youth made him vulnerable, and he spent a lot of time alone in these rugged, remote mountains, moving cows around and hunting calf-killing coyotes and wolves—and even the occasional grizzly—while his mother tended the ranch headquarters and her newborn baby, little Jeremiah, several miles away and at least a thousand feet below.

Lonnie Gentry had developed an unusual sharpness to his senses out of necessity.

Without it, he might very well be dead by now.

He made his way around the base of a stone ridge, the wall towering a couple of hundred feet above. Eventually, the wall opened on his left, forming a forty- or fifty-foot gateway into a canyon. As Lonnie stepped into this gateway, which was the mouth of the canyon, he heard something that ran a chill up his spine and caused chicken flesh to rise between his shoulder blades.

"Help me," a man was calling, half moaning. "Help me...please. Someone...please...help me!"

THREE

LONNIE STARED INTO THE CANYON, his lower jaw hanging.

The man's moaning pleas had died, so all he heard now was the eerie soughing of the breeze and the occasional, soft thud of a pinecone tumbling from a tree.

Another moaning sound rose from deep inside the canyon. A louder sound than the soughing sound of the breeze or the previous moaning of the injured man. This sound was made by occasional gusts of late-day wind blowing through a high, porous, distant ridge at the west end of the canyon and then funneling down the canyon's sloping floor toward where Lonnie stood now.

The wind carried with it that eerie, hollow, ratcheting lament that sounded like the agonized moaning of a dying man.

Another chill slid deep into Lonnie's bones despite his knowing that the moaning was not that of a dying man but merely the wind as it sluiced through a rock formation. That formation, standing tall atop the far ridge that Lonnie couldn't see from this vantage, bizarrely resembled a giant human skull.

Thus, the canyon's name.

Skull Canyon.

Lonnie had always tried to avoid the canyon when possible, though occasionally he'd had to ride into it looking for lost cows and calves he hadn't been able to find elsewhere. Over the years, he'd found three or four cows inside the canyon, and never dallied but had hazed the befuddled beasts back out of the canyon and down the mountain.

Few people around here dared enter Skull Canyon, for it was said—and had been said for generations of non-Indian settlers throughout this neck of the Never Summers—that Skull Canyon had been cursed long ago by a young Indian brave who'd sought refuge inside the canyon and had perished there after he'd been run down and tortured for several long days and nights by the mountain-man husband of the Indian's white lover.

The white lover had been a young Norwegian girl named Ingrid, a pretty blonde with cornflower-blue eyes. Thus, the name of the creek curling down out of Skull Canyon to form falls farther on down the mountain—Ingrid Creek. The dying brave had summoned a dark Indian spirit who had conjured the curse that was said to cause any man who saw the sun go down in the canyon to suffer shortly thereafter a violent death.

Of course, most folks didn't give the legend much credence. Such stories abounded throughout not only the Rockies but across the entire frontier. The story had probably been made up by some old-timer who'd discovered gold in the canyon and had merely wanted to frighten others away from his mine.

He'd probably been inspired by the skull formation at the canyon's far end, and the eerie sound the wind made as it passed through and around the giant skull.

Lonnie hadn't taken the legend overly seriously, either, though his young imagination was vivid enough to make him want to stay as far away from the canyon as possible whenever he could. He'd noted, however, that the cows he'd found lost inside the canyon had seemed unusually nervous and afraid and had seemed relieved when they'd been hazed on out of it.

But that might have been Lonnie's overactive imagination, too. Most beasts—whether they be with four feet or two—did not enjoy being lost.

Just as the cries he'd heard only a few minutes ago had likely been a trick of his imagination, fired to a frenzy by his recent, harrowing escape from the four men who had been determined to kill him. They'd most likely been rustlers worried he'd spied them at work with their running irons—branding irons long-loopers used to doctor the brands of the cattle they stole. Rustling was a hanging offense. Lonnie's hunters had likely felt the desperate need—even if that need meant shooting an innocent young cowboy—to keep the law from playing cat's cradle with their heads.

That was all he'd heard, Lonnie decided. Merely the wind playing its usual tricks in Skull Canyon.

Relieved, Lonnie swung around and started back down the mountain, deciding to follow the narrow, bubbling creek to the falls, where he'd fill his canteens and water the General, and then continue riding down into the lower reaches.

"Help!" a man yelled behind him.

Lonnie swung back around to stare once more up into the canyon, his heart thudding with exasperation.

"No," he told himself, shaking his head. "It's...it's the wind, galldangit."

"Help me!" the man cried, louder.

Then Lonnie saw him. The man was maybe a hundred yards away, stumbling through the knee-high grass along the creek, tracing the bend the creek made as he continued stumbling toward Lonnie.

"Help me!" the man yelled, his voice strangely clear now in the cool, dry, high-country air, aided by the canyon's good acoustics. "I've been injured. I need a hand!"

His arms were crossed on his lower belly.

He took three or four more steps and then he dropped to his knees and pitched forward. He was hidden now in the tall grass behind a thicket of chokecherry shrubs sheathed in brightly flowered wild peas and columbine.

Lonnie hesitated only for a second and then strode forward, into the canyon. He was wary of this place and all the more so because of what he'd just been through. Still, a man was injured. He needed help. It didn't occur to Lonnie that the men who'd been out to kill him might be laying a trap for him until he was within ten feet of the man lying before him.

The possibility hit Lonnie like a slap across his bullet-burned cheek.

He stopped and looked around, half expecting to see the smoke and flames of guns opening up on him.

But there was nothing anywhere around him. Only this man lying on his back, breathing hard, his hands pressed to his belly rising and falling sharply.

"Help," the man cried, squeezing his eyes closed and lifting his head and hardening his jaws as he looked down at his bloody hands and his bloody belly. "Help me. You gotta...help me!"

It was as though he were speaking only to himself believing that no one else were here.

Lonnie moved forward. He stepped around the chokecherry thicket, the creek murmuring to his left, and stood over the man who'd laid his head down again now, squeezing his eyes closed. Sweat glistened on his forehead and cheeks, which were very smooth and from which very thin strands of beard stubble sprouted like down.

He was young. Maybe only a few years older than Lonnie. He was dressed, like Lonnie, in the trail-worn gear of the working cowboy—checked shirt, suspenders, faded denims, and brush-scarred chaps.

Lonnie cleared his throat, which felt like sandpaper from all the running he'd done. "I'm...here...mister."

At first, the young man did not open his eyes. It was as though it took some time for Lonnie's words to make their way into his consciousness. Then, when they did, the eyes opened, slitted against the sun quartering westward over Lonnie edging toward the ridge jutting on the far side of the creek.

"I'm hurt," the man said, wincing with the anguish of his wound. "My stomach...hurts real bad."

"What happened?"

"Gut shot."

"I see that. By who?"

"Some jaspers...who didn't want me lurkin' around here...I reckon. Didn't see 'em."

"Were there four?"

"I didn't see 'em close enough to count. They shot me an' rode away, took off after my partner, Dwight Halsey. I thought maybe you was him, when I first seen you. Dwight...he's prob'ly dead now."

Lonnie looked around, a nearly palpable sense of danger closing around him once more. The men who'd ambushed him must have thought he'd been Halsey. He doubted it would matter now if they found out he wasn't Halsey. They'd kill him to keep him quiet about shooting this man, whom they'd likely finish off, to boot, though it didn't seem necessary.

The man was bleeding bad. He'd already lost a lot of blood, judging by the crimson weeds charting his path down the canyon. He was due to lose a lot more unless that wound was closed.

"What's your name?" the man asked, squinting against the sun again.

Lonnie glanced around once more then dropped to one knee beside the man. "Lonnie Gentry."

"Cade McLory."

"Pleased to make your acquaintance. Wish it were under more favorable circumstances. You got a horse around here, McLory?"

The wounded man lifted his head to glance around. "Well, I did. But I ain't seen hide nor hair of him since they shot me out my saddle."

"Why'd they do that? Why'd they shoot you out of your saddle, McLory?"

McLory tensed as pain rippled through him. Then he licked his dry, chapped lips. "I reckon that's a long story. Don't reckon I got time to tell it...less'n we can figure out some way to stop the bleedin'."

"Are they rustlers?"

McLory merely shook his head and shrugged.

Berating himself for not having done so sooner, Lonnie untied the man's billowy green bandanna from around McLory's neck, took it over to the creek, soaked it, and returned. He pressed the bandanna down hard against the wound.

McLory lifted his head, cursing. "Ah, Jesus that hurts!"

"You're gonna have to press down on that until we can figure another way to get the blood stopped."

"Mister Lonnie," McLory said, "do you think you'd do me the favor of helpin' me over to the creek so I can get a drink of water? I'm powerful thirsty."

"I don't know. If you move around too much..."

"I'd very much appreciate it. I'm so galldarned thirsty that gettin' that drink is about the only thing I can think about right now." McLory gave a bleak, choking laugh. "Reckon I can't say's I even care if it kills me!"

Lonnie looked around. He couldn't see anyone else out here.

There was only that moaning wind as it sawed down from the giant skull. It seemed to be giving voice to Cade McLory's own agony. But then it always seemed to be giving voice to *someone's* agony.

Maybe it was giving voice to Lonnie's own agony, now, too—the agonizing fear of what would happen if the four riders returned, which they might very well do before he could get the wounded man to cover.

FOUR

"CAN YOU STAND?" Lonnie asked McLory.

McLory rolled onto his belly and then climbed to one knee. "Let's give it a shot."

Lonnie wrapped the man's left arm around his shoulders and helped him to his feet. "There," McLory said. "That wasn't so hard—now, was it?"

Lonnie helped McLory walk through the high grass. McLory put a good bit of weight on Lonnie, who grunted with the effort of holding the bigger man up. McClory was about four inches taller than Lonnie, and he probably outweighed Lonnie by at least thirty pounds.

When they'd reached the creek, McLory dropped to his knees and groaned miserably, clutching his hands to his belly again. He leaned forward. For a moment, Lonnie thought he'd pass out. But then McLory lifted his head, crawled a foot or so nearer the creek, and lowered his head to the water, cupping the cool, running liquid to his lips.

When he had his fill, he lifted his head, smiled with satisfaction, and then, his eyelids growing heavy, swayed from side to side. Lonnie crouched beside him and wrapped an arm around him to keep him from falling forward into the water.

"Look, McLory," Lonnie said, glancing back toward the mouth of the canyon. "We'd best get you somewhere safe. We're too exposed out here. If them shooters come back..."

"Yeah, I know," McLory said. "We'd be sittin' ducks."

Lonnie looked around. His gaze gravitated toward the western ridge wall, which was strewn with gravel, boulders, pines, and cedars. Above and behind a nest of boulders, there appeared a black, oval-shaped gap in the ridge wall. Possibly a cave.

Lonnie's eyes swept the creek. When he saw a shallow place atop a natural shelf over which the water dropped, Lonnie said, "Let's get you up into them rocks yonder. I see a place where we can ford the creek without gettin' too wet. Think you can make it?"

McLory nodded dully. He appeared to be only about half conscious. He was no longer pressing the bandanna to the belly wound. Fresh blood glistened in the waning sunlight, the stain over the young man's belly growing larger and darker.

Lonnie helped McLory to his feet once more. He led the young man upstream a ways, and then they crossed, the cool water just covering their boots and inching up toward their ankles. Once across the creek, Lonnie led the cowboy up the gradual slope rising to the base of the ridge.

From there, the walk got harder, for they had to negotiate the steep slope up through and around behind the sandstone-colored boulders. Loose scree caused them both to slip and slide, both going down once on their knees.

When they'd finished negotiating the hazardous trail, Lonnie was glad to see that the trip had been worth the effort. There was indeed a cave behind the boulder, which shielded the cave from the canyon floor.

The cave was about five feet high and maybe twice that long. The scat and tracks inside told Lonnie that rabbits and a bobcat or two had called the place home within the last few weeks. There didn't appear to be any fresh sign, which meant the place wasn't currently occupied. The last thing Lonnie wanted this hectic day was to be fending off a bobcat or, worse, a mountain lion.

He had no gun, as he'd left his Winchester in the boot strapped to his saddle. He'd already taken note that McLory's holster, which sat high on his right hip, was empty. He'd probably lost the pistol when he'd been shot off his own mount.

Lonnie helped McLory sit down inside the cave. Then he removed his own, navy-blue bandanna, and gave it to the wounded man. "Take this. Press it hard against your belly or you'll bleed out. I'm gonna see if I can't fetch my horse. I have a few medical supplies in my saddlebags, and a small bottle of whiskey. We need to get that wound tended."

McLory leaned his head back against the cave wall and grinned through his misery. "Whiskey, huh? I didn't take you for an imbiber, Master Gentry."

"It's medicine," Lonnie said, though he knew the man was only pulling his leg. "Best thing for cleanin' cuts and wounds and bad rope burns, and I get plenty of all that out here."

"You got a nice cut across your cheek."

"I got another across my shoulder. Compliments the same rustlers that shot you, most like."

McLory studied him. "Young cowboy, are ya?"

"That's right."

"Live around here, then?"

"My ma and I own the Circle G down in the valley."

McLory shook his head. "Don't know it."

"You're not from around here, then."

Again, McLory shook his head. "Not by a long shot. Texas, born and raised."

"What're you doin' here? What're you doin' in the canyon? I thought maybe you rode for one of the other outfits."

Before McLory could open his mouth to respond, Lonnie said, "Never mind. Save your strength. I'd best get off after my horse before it gets too dark to see him."

McLory looked at Lonnie. His face was slick with sweat and the color of parchment paper. The walk up here had taken it out of him. "You really have to go?"

Lonnie looked at him, vaguely puzzled.

McLory licked his lips. "It's just that...I don't... I don't wanna die alone. I'm really afraid of...dyin' alone, for some reason. Never knew it till I thought I was all alone out here. I reckon that's why I was makin' such a fuss. Lost my head." He swallowed, sucked a sharp breath, wincing against the pain it caused him. "Don't wanna die alone, that's all."

"You ain't gonna die." Lonnie wanted to believe that was true, but he wasn't sure. "Not if I fetch my horse and bring some cloth back for bandages. That whiskey'll clean out the wound till we can get you to the sawbones in Arapaho Creek."

Lonnie placed a hand on McLory's shoulder, trying to comfort the young man. "I won't be long."

McLory nodded, though Lonnie could see the darkness of fear mixing with the pain in his eyes. "All right. You go ahead. I'm sorry for the trouble, Master Gentry."

"I'll get a fire goin' as soon as I get back. I'll boil some coffee."

"Good on ya, good on ya."

Lonnie stepped back out of the cave and straightened. He looked once more at McLory, who rested his blond head back against the cave wall.

He was breathing hard and sweating though he appeared to be losing more and more color from his face. For a moment, Lonnie hesitated, wondering if he'd made the right decision to go after the General.

What if McLory died while he was gone?

That would be an awful thing, his having left him while knowing how fearful he was of dying alone.

But then Lonnie told himself that while the Texan looked bad, he didn't look like he was about to die. Not within the next hour, anyway. And Lonnie would give himself only an hour to look for the General. If he hadn't found the buckskin in that time, he'd head on back to the cave though he sure didn't like the idea of spending the night in Skull Canyon.

FIVE

LONNIE FOUND the General grazing near the pool beneath the falls that Ingrid Creek made as it dropped over a granite cliff.

At first, the horse ran, still skittish from the shooting. He couldn't hear Lonnie's voice above the falls' loud pattering. When Lonnie worked his way upwind of the stallion, the General recognized the scent of his rider and came running, dragging his reins, one of which the horse had stepped on and broke.

Lonnie was relieved that he hadn't run into the four trigger-happy riders. But his caution had caused his excursion out from Skull Canyon to take longer than an hour. By the time he rode the General back through the gap into the canyon, he judged by the low angle of the sun that he'd been gone a good ninety minutes.

He remembered the curse.

He remembered McLory's fear of dying alone.

Anxiety rippled through him as he galloped the General across the creek and around behind the boulders a ways up the steeply slanting ridge base. He leaped down from the stallion's back before he was fully stopped, dropped the reins, and ran up the gravelly shelf and into the cave.

His spine turned to ice when he saw McLory lying on his side at the base of the cave wall, where Lonnie had left him. The young man's eyes were closed. His chest was not rising and falling. His face looked waxen.

Trembling, horrified that McLory might have drifted off while he'd been alone here, with no one to comfort him, Lonnie dropped to a knee. He placed a trembling hand on the young Texan's shoulder. McLory did not respond. Lonnie thought his flesh felt cold beneath the flannel cloth of his shirtsleeve.

Lonnie nudged the young Texan. "McLory?"

He was about to say the young man's name once more when McLory turned his head toward Lonnie. He opened his eyes and looked up at the young cowboy. For a moment, it was as though McLory were trying to place him.

Then he glanced around and pushed up off his shoulder with a rattling sigh. "Reckon I done drifted off."

Relief washed through Lonnie though he didn't like the amount of blood that McLory had left on the cave floor, where he'd been lying. "How you feelin'?"

McLory smiled, his gray-blue eyes slanting devilishly. "Never better. Where's the girls? Ain't it Saturday night? Me—I'm ready to dance, Master Gentry!"

"I don't think you'll be doin' any dancin' anytime soon, McLory," Lonnie said, straightening but keeping his head bowed so the low ceiling wouldn't scrape his hat off his head. "But I found my horse, so I'll fetch my possibles."

"Don't forget the whiskey!" McLory raked out as Lonnie ran down the steep gravelly slope to where the General waited for him. "Uh...for medicinal purposes only, ya understand."

Lonnie retrieved his saddlebags and canvas war bag and hustled back up into the cave. He dug around in the saddlebags, found his flat bottle wrapped in burlap, and handed it to McLory, who took it and, struggling a little with the cork, tipped it back.

McLory took two hard swallows and then pulled the bottle down, blinking and turning even whiter than before. "Oh, jeepers," McLory said. "Oh, boy...maybe that wasn't such a good idea."

"Burns?"

"Yeah."

"Better go easy on it."

McLory scrunched his face up and stiffened and then gradually relaxed and rested his head back against the cave wall. "I'm...better now. Once the liquor gets into my blood...it eases the pain."

"But when it hits your belly, it probably kicks like a mule."

"There you have it." McLory held the bottle up to Lonnie. "Snort?"

Lonnie shook his head as he rummaged around in his bags for his flannel wrappings and the small, buckskin pouch of ointments his mother had prepared for him when, here and there throughout the year, he'd begun spending several nights by himself in the line shack, when he was working their herd.

"You don't drink?" McLory asked him.

"Nope."

"Good for you." McLory took another, small sip from the bottle and winced as the fiery liquid seared its way into his belly. "Many a desperate man has turned to drink for comfort . . . only to find it's about as much comfort as a woman. No comfort at all when the chips are down."

"Speak from experience, do you?" Lonnie asked him.

"Sure do."

"You've had bad experiences with both, then, I take it."

Lonnie was unbuttoning McLory's shirt. McLory put a hand on Lonnie's, stopping him and narrowing one eye. He already seemed drunk. "Kid, when you're as old as I am, you'll get savvy to the ways of men and women...and firewater. And you'll learn the two don't go together."

"How so?" Lonnie was genuinely curious despite his urgency at wanting to get the young Texan's belly bandaged, the blood stopped.

McLory merely shook his head. Releasing Lonnie's hand, he took another drink from the bottle.

"Best save some of that for the wound," Lonnie said. "I'm gonna need some for the cleanin'."

"Don't bother."

"What's that?"

"I'm a goner, kid."

Lonnie looked at McLory. McLory was staring hard at Lonnie. He was trying to be tough just as he'd been trying to talk tough and sound worldly. But a fear blazed through that hard stare, giving the lie to the young man's braggadocio. He was young and sick to death with the fear of dying, with the fear of leaving this world before he'd really had the chance to experience it.

Lonnie knew that fear himself. He'd experienced it last year with Shannon Dupree, and he'd experienced it just a couple of hours ago, when he'd nearly been blown out of his saddle.

"It's gonna be okay, McLory," Lonnie said. "I'm gonna patch you up.

Then I'll take you down to our cabin and send for the sawbones in Arapaho Creek."

McLory looked at him, and now his gaze was even more fearful than before.

Finally, McLory rested his head back against the cave wall and let his gaze slide past Lonnie and into space as his fears set to work on him with even more intensity, chewing away at him the way the whiskey probably was.

SIX

LONNIE CLEANED and bandaged McLory's wound, but it continued to bleed. Lonnie could see the blood staining the flannel pad he'd placed over the wound and held in place with a long, slender strip of flannel he'd wrapped around the young Texan's lower torso.

If McLory noticed the blood, he didn't let on.

He sat back against the cave wall, dozing as Lonnie fed and watered the General then gathered wood and built a fire in the middle of the cave, far back enough that the flames wouldn't be seen from the canyon floor. Lonnie emptied his war bag and brewed a pot of coffee.

While the coffee cooked, he tended his own wounds, cleaning them with a flannel swatch dipped in whiskey. Neither was bad enough to require a bandage.

When the coffee was bubbling over, the smell awakened McLory.

Lonnie filled him a cup and gave him a bacon-and-biscuit sandwich that Lonnie had made earlier that day, before he'd left the line shack. It was his favorite food to nibble on throughout the day, until he could head back to the shack and cook a pot of pinto beans with a rabbit from one of his snares. Though only fourteen, Lonnie Gentry was an impeccable if rudimentary cook.

Night descended on the canyon. A metallic chill stitched the air. Mornings up this high, there was usually frost on the ground. Lonnie had given

McLory his bedroll, and the Texan curled up in the sewn-together blankets, his head resting back against the wool underside of Lonnie's saddle.

Lonnie kept the fire built up, knowing the night would grow colder and that McLory needed to stay warm. Even now, he could see the Texan shivering beneath the blankets. McLory's coffee steamed up from where the cup sat beside him on the cave floor. He hadn't drunk much of it. He'd taken only a couple of small bites from the biscuit Lonnie had given him.

"You want some jerky?" Lonnie offered when he'd returned with another load of firewood. "I got some in the saddlebags there. Help yourself."

McLory shook his head.

"How come you're not drinkin' your coffee?" Lonnie asked him, biting into his second biscuit, and chewing. "You don't like the way I make it?"

McLory didn't respond to the question. He seemed to be staring right through Lonnie from where he lay back against Lonnie's saddle. Lonnie studied him, feeling a little queasy with worry for the young Texan whom he'd found himself taking a liking to.

McLory seemed a lot like Lonnie. In McLory, Lonnie thought he could see something of his later self. Besides, being young, he had a raw fear of death that could probably be attributed to his lack of understanding of death, despite having witnessed it when he'd killed Shannon Dupree and Dupree's two rotten, thieving partners and even having lost his own father to a heart stroke several years ago.

All he really knew about death was that it was a horrible thing, and he wanted nothing to do with it. But now, as he stared back at the dull eyes of Cade McLory, he had the chilling feeling down deep in his bones, that he was staring into the face of death itself. It might have just been his imagination, but he thought that McLory's eyes were sinking deeper into their sockets and that the waxy skin was drawing back tight against his cheekbones. It was as though the young Texan was becoming a skeleton before Lonnie's very eyes.

McLory smiled, then, as though to put the younger man's mind at ease. "You got you a girl, do you, Master Gentry?"

Lonnie felt heat rise into his ears. The topic of the fairer sex always seemed to embarrass him for some reason, though it once did more than it did now. Now he felt a thrill of pride to say, "I reckon you could say that."

"I had a feelin'—a good-lookin' kid like yourself. A neighborin' ranch girl, is she?"

"No. A town girl." Lonnie refilled his coffee cup, using a thick leather swatch he'd fashioned for the maneuver, to keep from burning his hand. "Her name's Casey. Casey Stoveville. She works at Hendrickson's Mercantile in Arapaho Creek." With a touch of pride, he added, "She's sixteen."

"How old are you?"

"Fourteen." Lonnie felt his upper lip curl a grin.

McLory whistled. "An older woman—imagine that!" He looked at Lonnie askance, and Lonnie knew he was being teased now. "She don't...she don't work the cribs on the side, now, does she, Master Gentry?"

"Hell, Casey ain't no parlor girl!" Lonnie felt a sudden burn of anger. He and Casey had been through a lot together, when they'd been trying to take Dupree's stolen money over Storm Peak Pass to the deputy US marshal in Camp Collins, and they'd gotten close. As close as a sister and brother, at first. But then Casey had professed to Lonnie her love for him.

The boy's heart had swollen to the size of a mature pumpkin. It had fairly sprouted wings and flown.

While he hadn't had the chance to visit the girl in a while, her living in town and him living thirty miles up in the mountains, Lonnie held her close in his heart, and he was quick to run to her defense. But then he realized that McLory's mockery was all in fun. The young Texan was merely trying to distract himself from his misery and, most likely, his fear of death.

"Must be nice," McLory said, his gaze growing distant again, pensive. "Havin' a girl all your own. I had me one, once. A couple years back. I was gonna marry up with her, back in Texas, but then her pa, a rich rancher—one of the few rich men in west Texas—steered her in the direction of a man who had a better chance of providin' for her—you know, *long term*."

"She let her pa convince her of that?" Lonnie was incredulous.

"She sure did. The night before we was to be married, she came out to the little shotgun ranch my brother and I were runnin' at the time. She even brought me a bouquet of wildflowers, as if those would soften the blow of what she had to tell me."

Tears glistened in McLory's eyes. Thoughts of the girl still haunted him, obviously. Lonnie could imagine how he felt. He'd likely feel that way if anything like that happened between him and Casey, though he doubted it ever would. They were too close and too much alike.

They'd be married, eventually, when they were both a few years older. Lonnie had it all planned out in his head—how Casey would move out to the ranch with him, and he'd build a cabin just for her and him, separate from his mother and his little brother, who was Shannon Dupree's child.

They'd raise a family out there—Lonnie and Casey.

"Summer."

"What's that?" Lonnie asked McLory.

"Summer was her name. Summer Nulf. It was like her folks gave her such a purty first name to make up for the humble last name. It fit her, too —Summer did. She was purty as a Texas hill country summer—all jasmine eyes and hair like honey. I can still smell her. She smelled like wild cherry blossoms growin' on the banks of the Rio Grande."

McLory paused. He was staring at the ceiling against which the firelight and shadows were playing tag. "I'd like to see her again. Never thought I would. But now, I'd really, really, really like to see my Summer again."

Tears dribbled down the young Texan's cheeks.

Embarrassed, Lonnie turned away. He was surprised to find his throat swollen with emotion. He cleared it and then said, "You'll find someone else. Sounds like she didn't really deserve you, her listenin' to her pa and thinkin' only about money an' such. That ain't how life should be. It's too short. I know that from seein' folks die."

Lonnie stared off for a time. Then he sipped his coffee. Noting that McLory had fallen silent, he turned back to where the young Texan lay back against his saddle, staring dully up at the ceiling. McLory did not blink his eyes. He merely lay there, still, staring at the ceiling.

"McLory?" Lonnie said.

SEVEN

LONNIE SET his coffee down on the ground. He rose slowly from where he sat against the cave wall, on the opposite side of the fire from McLory. His heart was beating hard and fast.

Again, his boots felt like lead.

"McLory?" he repeated.

He walked over and knelt beside the young Texan. McLory's eyes stared nearly straight up at the play of light and shadows on the cave ceiling. He did not blink. Lonnie slowly waved a hand in front of McLory's face.

Still, the Texan didn't blink.

Lonnie set his hand down flat against McLory's chest. He didn't detect even the faintest flutter of McLory's heart. He pulled his hand away quickly, instinctively repelled. He sat back hard on his heels and stared in shock at the Texan, who was now merely the husk of whom he'd been only a minute before.

A minute ago, he'd been a living and breathing man.

Now, suddenly, he was a corpse lying here before Lonnie. There didn't seem anything more hideous to Lonnie than a corpse. His impulse was to hightail it. To leave the cave and set up camp elsewhere.

But then, swallowing, Lonnie made a conscious effort to control himself. McLory was still McLory even if he was dead. Even in death, the Texan needed Lonnie's help.

Lonnie lifted his right hand. It quivered as he slid it out toward McLory's head. Lightly, he ran the tips of his fingers down over the dead man's eyelids, wincing and shuddering at the papery feel of the dead man's skin and the fine prick of his eyelashes. Lonnie gently raked the eyes closed.

Instantly, he felt better. Now McLory looked as though he were merely sleeping, though of course he was just as dead as he'd been before. But those open eyes had been deeply disturbing.

Lonnie stared down at the dead Texan for a long time. Many thoughts ran through him. As his revulsion for the nearness of death faded, they were replaced by sad thoughts of what McLory had lost, dying so young.

McLory's last thoughts had been of the girl who'd spurned him. Now, he'd never be able to see her again or to find another girl and build a life with her. He'd never raise a family. He'd never ride a horse or eat a meal or swim in a creek or know the joy of holding a girl's hand.

Now, he would know only darkness. Or, if the preachers had it right, he'd know Heaven. In that case, he might make out even better than Lonnie, who was still alive and, if all went well, he'd live through this night and eat another meal and ride his horse down out of these mountains. If the preachers had it right, Heaven would be even better than a good life right here on earth.

Heaven seemed like a tall order, but what did Lonnie know about such things? The preachers were older than he was, which meant they were wiser, too, didn't it? Lonnie supposed he was skeptical because he always needed sound reasons for his beliefs, and he couldn't say any grown-ups, preachers included, had ever given him any clear evidence about Heaven.

Enough thinking about all that. What did Lonnie Gentry know about it? He was a cowboy who'd been born in these mountains. He'd likely die in them, too. Just like McLory.

Only, later. He hoped.

Lonnie would see his girl, Casey Stoveville, again soon. That was as close to Heaven as he cared to get for now. In fact, he wanted right now to head down out of these mountains and visit Casey. It seemed the most important thing he could do.

But he could not. He'd see her again soon. First, he had to figure out what to do with McLory.

Lonnie drew McLory's blankets up over the dead man's face. Then Lonnie rose, walked over to the other side of the fire, and sat back against the cave wall, staring toward McLory. The young Texan faded gradually from Lonnie's view as the fire died. It was an eerie sight, seeing him over there, still and silent in death beneath the blankets, his head still tipped back against Lonnie's saddle.

When the fire died down to only three or four small, dancing flames, Lonnie built it back up again. The night was cold. And Lonnie didn't want to be alone in the darkness with McLory's body.

And not with that old Indian's curse on this canyon. He knew he should leave, but it was too dark. He couldn't risk injuring the General on his way out of here. And he couldn't leave McLory.

He had to take his chances that the curse was nothing more than some old prospector's tall tale.

When Lonnie had the fire going again, he sat back against the cave wall, crossed his arms on his chest, and shivered despite the fire's heat. He should take McLory's blankets, but there seemed something rude and crass about doing so, though he needed them more than McLory did now.

Still, he couldn't do it. He'd keep the fire going all night.

But then he opened his eyes and realized that he'd slept there against the cave wall though he hadn't thought he'd be able to. The fire was merely a mounded pile of faintly smoking ashes. False dawn filtered a milky light into the canyon. Birds were chirping and squirrels were chattering.

McLory lay where Lonnie had left him, on the far side of the cave—a dark mound beneath the blankets.

Lonnie shivered. He'd probably been shivering in his sleep all night. But now he shivered at the passing of a young man he'd grown close to in their short time together as well as at his refreshed knowledge of the nearness of death and of having to deal with it somehow.

Lonnie got to his feet. The cold made him feel like an old man. When he'd worked the creaks out of his young bones, he ate a couple of pieces of jerky and washed them down with water from his canteen.

He didn't bother with a fire. He wanted to get out of the canyon as fast as possible. He felt a cold, hard knot of sadness about McLory, but, frankly, the young Texan's body tied Lonnie's nerves in knots.

He decided that he probably couldn't get McLory onto his horse. McLory was too heavy for him. He probably could have found a way to get the dead man onto his horse if he'd been less repelled by him. But he chose to tell himself that it would be best for them both if Lonnie left McLory here, discreetly covered by Lonnie's blankets, while Lonnie fetched the sheriff out from Arapaho Creek.

He owed it to McLory to tell the sheriff about what had happened here, so that the sheriff could find those four rustlers who'd killed him not to mention who'd tried to kill Lonnie. The sheriff would see to it that McLory was taken to town and given a proper burial.

Gently, Lonnie eased his saddle out from beneath McLory's head. He noticed that McLory already appeared to be stiffening. Moving quietly, as though it were possible to wake the dead, Lonnie hauled his gear outside and onto his horse.

The sun had still not risen when Lonnie rode the General out of the canyon, leaving the dead man alone in the cave behind him. He reflected with dread that he had now spent a full night in the canyon.

Did that mean he would join McLory soon?

EIGHT

LONNIE WAS glad when he reached Arapaho Creek around noon that day. During the ride, he'd been wary of being run down again by the same men who'd run him down the day before.

Now as he rode into the bustling mining camp and ranch supply hamlet lying in a shallow valley in the southernmost reaches of the Never Summer range, he continued to look around cautiously. There was a good chance the men who'd ambushed him—likely, the same men who'd killed McLory—had come to town.

Lonnie felt safer here than he had in the mountains, but he was not yet out of the woods.

He headed directly for the sheriff's office. As he trotted the General along the street, Arapaho Street, which occasionally snugged itself up against the creek running through the heart of town, he weaved through the steady traffic of pedestrians and ranch and mining supply wagons and around the occasional bearded prospector and his pick-and-shovel-laden donkey or mule.

The mercantile was coming up on the right side of the street. That was where Lonnie's girl, Casey Stoveville, worked.

As Lonnie always did when he came to town, he scouted the place, hoping for a glimpse of Casey. He didn't have to look hard today. She was sitting out on the front steps running up to the mercantile's broad front porch and loading dock. Casey wasn't alone. She was sitting next to a man in a store-bought three-piece suit and bowler hat.

The gent had a handsome face though his nose was a little short. Dark-brown hair curled onto his celluloid shirt collar. He sported a neatly trimmed goatee and watch chain. Likely a drummer of one sort or another. Salesmen often swarmed the mercantile, imploring the proprietor, Mr. Hendrickson, to stock his shelves with their company's goods.

Mr. Hendrickson was probably out to lunch at the moment. That was likely why the drummer was talking with Casey, who often ran the place for Hendrickson and who knew how to do nearly everything that Hendrickson himself did. But then, as Lonnie started moving on past the mercantile, raising his hand to wave if Casey caught his gaze, Lonnie frowned uncertainly.

There was something about the man sitting with Casey that made Lonnie doubt that he was a drummer, after all. One, he didn't appear to have a sample kit with him. Two, his suit appeared of a better cut than your usual salesman. And it appeared fairly new. Drummers didn't usually earn enough for a new suit of fine quality.

Also, this gent—who appeared to be in maybe his mid twenties—didn't look hungry or desperate enough to be a drummer. In Lonnie's limited experience, salesmen were usually the slick, syrupy-eyed, wolfish sort.

But that wasn't all that Lonnie noted about him. This fellow was sitting so close to Casey on the step that their legs were nearly touching, and he was giving Casey his full attention as he talked, smiling in a groveling way. He seemed to be keeping his voice low, so that no one else could hear. It was an intimate conversation.

Casey sat leaning forward, elbows on her knees, her head turned toward the man beside her, one finger twisting up a long lock of her dark-blonde hair as she sat listening to him, rapt.

Lonnie's gut twisted a little behind his belt buckle. Was this fancy Dan sparking Casey?

The General pulled up sharply and gave an indignant whinny.

"Hey, watch where you're goin', young fella!"

Lonnie whipped his head forward to see a freckle-faced, potbellied man in a soiled bar apron glaring at him. Standing ahead and to one side, the man was holding an armload of firewood.

"This time o' day the street's too damn busy to be ridin' through town with your head in the clouds, boyo!" The barman spoke with a thick Irish accent.

A man coming up on Lonnie in a buckboard ranch wagon, chuckled and shook his head in mockery. The barman, whom Lonnie recognized as Paddy O'Ryan, who ran a shack out of which he sold tin buckets of beer and ran a couple of whores' cribs out back, gave Lonnie one more venomous glare, and said, "You damn near ran me down!"

Then he swung around and, shaking his head, stomped through the open door of his low-slung shop.

Holding the General's reins taut in his gloved hands, Lonnie glanced at Casey and the suited gentleman, who were behind him now, as he'd ridden on past the mercantile. Casey and the fancy Dan were still talking back and forth, smiling and occasionally laughing, so involved in their conversation that neither one seemed to have noticed Lonnie despite Paddy O'Ryan's loud harangue.

Lonnie had never really known jealousy before. But he knew it now. It was an ache down deep inside him. It was like an injury though no bones or muscles were involved.

He rode on. He had more important business to take care of at the moment, though his aching gut felt otherwise. He glanced back over his shoulder once more. The fancy Dan and Casey were still chinning as though they'd known each other for years.

Maybe they had. Maybe they were just friends.

Something told Lonnie that wasn't true. Something told him the fancy Dan wanted to be more than friends with Casey. Lonnie had sort of half consciously been worried about that sort of thing. Casey had filled out nicely in the last year, and she'd acquired a certain mature, self-confident sparkle in her eye that meant she was growing up and getting even prettier than she had been before.

She was becoming a young woman, which somehow didn't seem fair to Lonnie, who was still two years younger. At fourteen, he was still a kid. In the worst way, he wanted to catch up to her, to be her equal.

Lonnie managed to sweep the confounding problem aside for the moment, but not before reflecting briefly on the story that McLory had told him the night before, about McLory's girl spurning him in favor of a gent who'd made more money than he had.

That girl, that heartbreak, had been the last thought, the last image in the young Texan's mind before he'd died.

Lonnie drew up to the sheriff's office, a log cabin supported on low stone pylons near the county courthouse on a side street behind it. Smoke issued from the tin chimney pipe to sweep down low over the porch, rife with the sweet tang of pine.

Two men wearing deputy sheriff badges were lounging on the front porch. Lonnie recognized them, for he recognized most folks in the town as well as around the county, having grown up here and also being curious and observant in the way that boys often are, learning the ways of things.

Lonnie dropped down out of the saddle and tied the General's reins to the hitch rack. As he mounted the front stoop, one of the sheriff's two deputies, Chick Bohannon, said, "Well, look what we have here. Mister Big Britches his own self!"

The other deputy, Randall "Walleye" Miller, laughed as he sat back in his timber-framed, hide-bottom chair, sipping a cup of coffee likely laced with whiskey. It was said that Miller, who'd been fired from several mines in the area, had a problem with who-hit-John. Miller was a big man with a thick, curly beard and one wandering, red-rimmed eye. He had a sawed-off, double-barreled shotgun resting across his fat thighs clad in greasy, torn denim trousers.

"You find any more money out in them mountains, Mister Big Britch-es?" Bohannon asked, referring to the money that Lonnie and Casey had taken over the mountains and delivered to the deputy US marshal in Camp Collins.

The tall, slender man's tone was fairly dripping with sarcasm. Bohannon's lilac eyes were flat and malicious, and he had long, coarse, yellow hair streaked with mud brown.

Lonnie knew from the way he'd been glared at and spoken to in town over the past year that some folks around here still thought, as had originally been suspected, that he'd been part of Shannon Dupree's holdup gang. He wasn't sure how they coupled that notion to the fact that he and Casey had returned the stolen bank money to the rightful authorities.

Lonnie had inadvertently shot one of the sheriff's deputies who'd ambushed him in the mountains. That deputy had been a well-liked man in this area. Lonnie suspected that that was a big reason why it had been hard to change some folks' minds on the subject of Lonnie's part in the initial robbery.

That and the fact that Dupree had been making time with Lonnie's mother, earning not only May Gentry a bad reputation hereabouts, but earning her innocent son a bad reputation, as well.

"Nope, no money today," Lonnie said, trying to keep his tone jovial. "Sheriff Halliday in?"

"What you want him for?" asked Deputy Miller with a suspicious, self-important air, narrowing that odd, wandering eye of his. "The sheriff's too busy to be bothered by the offspring of mountain scrubs."

Lonnie drew a sharp breath, trying to calm himself but finding himself balling his fists at his sides. "My family ain't scrubs, Deputy Miller."

Walleye, who'd been tilted back in his chair, set the chair down with a dull thud, and flared his nostrils at Lonnie.

"Oh, yeah? Well, I say you are. What're you gonna do about it?"

NINE

DEPUTY MILLER slowly gained his feet, his dung-brown eyes riveted on Lonnie though the wandering one rolled slightly to the outside of its socket. The man's swollen nostrils and thick neck gave him the aspect of an angry Brahma bull. Long, grizzled dark hair liberally woven with strands of gray hung down from his slouch hat.

Walleye moved toward Lonnie and stopped. "I asked you a question, Gentry."

Lonnie couldn't believe this. He'd done nothing to provoke this man. He tried not to let his exasperation show as he said, "I'm just lookin' for Sheriff Halliday. That's all. I ain't lookin' for no trouble."

"You Gentrys is always lookin' for trouble. Your pa was a trouble-maker, too. An uppity troublemakin' Yankee."

"I doubt that."

Lonnie's dim memories of his father were of a gentle, good-natured man. The problem was that for some reason or another, Southerners, some of them ex-Rebels from the Old South, outnumbered Yankees in and around the Never Summer Range.

The lingering differences between the two sides often boiled over in hop houses and whiskey saloons—usually after sundown. Lonnie had heard that his father, a well-liked man with many friends and also a decorated war veteran, had occasionally visited the saloons here in Arapaho Creek, and he'd no doubt been involved in a skirmish or two over the lingering disagreements. From what Lonnie had heard about his father, Calvin Gentry had been a man who'd stood up for his principles.

Apparently, Walleye had been involved in one or two of these likely busthead-induced dustups, as well.

Walleye shoved his shotgun out toward Deputy Bohannon, who took it with a laugh and leaned back against the office's front wall. "You callin' me a liar, Gentry?" Walleye asked.

"Whoa, now," Lonnie said, holding up his hands, palms out. "No one called no one a liar. I don't want no trouble, Deputy Miller. I'm just here to..."

"How's your momma doin'?"

Walleye's question surprised Lonnie. He stared up at the big man towering over him. Walleye stood on the porch while Lonnie stood on the middle step leading up to it, a hand on each rail. He didn't like the dark, glowering cast to the big man's eyes coupled, as it had been, with the mention of Lonnie's mother.

"What's that?"

"I asked you how you're momma's doin'. A purty gal like that, livin' out there all alone with a scrappy shaver to look after, and with her outlaw boyfriend dead...she must get lonely."

Again, Bohannon laughed. Louder this time. He said, "I heard she gave birth to Dupree's child, to boot!"

Walleye said, "You tell your momma, boy Gentry, that if she gets *too* lonely, I'm right here. She can come knockin' on my door—"

"Shut up!" The words were out of Lonnie's mouth before he knew it. His ears were burning with sudden fury.

Walleye lurched forward, jaws hard. "What'd you say to me, boy?"

"I told you to shut up, you fat son of a bitch!"

Lonnie was suddenly so riled that his innate common sense slithered out his ears. He was ready to fight this big, gutter-brained peckerwood, never mind that the man outweighed him by close to two hundred pounds and was nearly twice as tall as Lonnie. As Walleye started down the steps, Lonnie tried to hold his ground, but Walleye lunged like a cat, snatching him up in his arms, and fight as he might, there was little that Lonnie could do.

Within seconds, Lonnie found himself upside down. His hat went tumbling off his head. Walleye was holding Lonnie by his ankles and jerking him up and down, so that the ground came up so close to Lonnie's face that Lonnie could see every rock, pebble, strand of hay, and fleck of horse manure.

Walleye jerked Lonnie down sharply.

The ground came up to slam the top of Lonnie's head, stunning the boy. His arms fell slack, hands in the dirt. Then Walleye carried Lonnie over to the stock trough behind the hitch rack. He raised Lonnie up and over the hay-flecked trough and then lowered him. Before Lonnie could suck a complete breath, his head was plunged into the trough, cold water engulfing his head and seeping into his ears.

Lonnie's heart was a drum beating away in his ears as the water rushed in to make the drumming even louder.

Lonnie sucked water into his lungs. He convulsed, blowing bubbles around his head as he thrashed his arms and kicked his legs, trying to free himself of the burly Walleye. Just when Lonnie thought his head would explode, Walleye lifted him out of the trough but dangled him in the air above it, his head about three inches above the water.

The General was whinnying and stomping his front hooves, threatening Walleye from the other side of the hitch rack. Walleye was hugging Lonnie's knees hard against his chest.

Walleye glared at the General, and yelled, "Shut up, you mangy cayuse, or I'll put a bullet in you!" He looked down at Lonnie, who continued to thrash while coughing water up out of his battered lungs. "You ready to say you're sorry, boy?" Lonnie's nose and eyes were on fire.

He looked up at the big man towering over him and clenched his fists. "You go to hell, you big son of a—!"

Before Lonnie could finish his sentence, Walleye plunged Lonnie's head into the trough once more. Again, Lonnie inhaled water. He strangled, thrashing, his head swelling, his heart hammering like an Apache war drum in his ears. When he didn't think he could go another half second without a breath, his head growing so light he thought he was about to pass out, Walleye lifted him clear of the trough once more.

Above the General's enraged whinnying and hoof stomping, Walleye said, "How 'bout now, boy? If not, you're gonna—"

"Turn him loose, Miller."

Lonnie had only vaguely heard the voice above the General's caterwauling and his own strangling sounds. Then he saw Frank Halliday step out onto the porch and move up to stand beside Chick Bohannon, fingers in the pockets of his brown wool vest, which he wore beneath a black, claw hammer frock coat. His shiny, five-pointed sheriff's star was pinned to the lapel of his coat—up high where everybody could see it.

Pursing his lips, looking like a schoolmaster only mildly annoyed with the current bout of playground roughhousing, Halliday said, "Put him down."

"Whatever you say, Sheriff."

Grinning, Walleye released Lonnie's legs. Lonnie dropped straight down and headfirst into the trough. His head struck the bottom of the trough, and then his legs splashed into the water, as well.

He grabbed the trough's wooden sides and heaved himself up and out of the water, strangling as he tried to rid his lungs of water while also trying to draw a breath, to keep from passing out. As the sunlit street grew dim around him, Lonnie crawled over the side of the trough, and dropped into the street. He rolled onto his belly and then rose onto his hands and knees, convulsing violently as he fought away the cold, wet hands of what felt like certain death.

As he did, he could feel the General's hot breath against the back of his neck and the occasional, concerned touch of the buckskin's prickly, rubbery snout.

"What's this all about?" Frank Halliday wanted to know.

"The kid comes waltzin' up here, bein' a smart Mcgee, Sheriff," said Chick Bohannon. "You know the Gentrys. Him an' his ma think they're really somethin', when all May Gentry is is a Jane-about-the-mountains."

"Prob'ly shackin' up with another outlaw," said Walleye.

Rage and exasperation continued to boil through Lonnie, but he had no energy with which to vent it, even if he was inclined to bring more trouble onto himself. Walleye likely would have drowned him in the stock trough if Halliday hadn't stepped out of his office.

"Boy," Halliday said, raising his voice so Lonnie could hear above his choking, "what brings you to town?"

TEN

WHEN LONNIE THOUGHT he'd finally coughed most of the water out of his lungs, and could draw at least half a lungful of air, he rolled onto his back. The General lowered his head, sniffing him again with concern.

Lonnie looked up past the horse to where Halliday was standing on the stoop with Chick Bohannon, who just now tossed the shotgun back to Walleye. Walleye caught it one-handed and turned to glower down at Lonnie.

"I found a man wounded in Skull Canyon."

"A wounded man this time," said Chick Bohannon, mockingly. "No stolen bank loot?"

"Maybe you wounded him," grunted Walleye. "Just like you killed Willie Drake. Willie—he was my cousin." Walleye poked his sausage-sized, grime-encrusted thumb against his lumpy chest. "I take it personal that you shot him!"

Lonnie said, "Yeah, well, I take it personal that he was shootin' at me before he got his facts straight."

Walleye bunched his lips and lurched toward Lonnie once more.

"That's enough, Walleye," Halliday said. "Pull your horns in." Halliday produced a long, black cigar from inside his vest, nipped off the end, and stuck the cheroot between his large, pale-yellow teeth. "Tell me about this wounded man you found in Skull Canyon."

"A little...a little older'n me. Name was McLory. Cade McLory."

"What do mean 'was'?"

"He died last night. I tried doctorin' him, but he didn't make it."

"You shoot him?" Walleye asked, accusingly. "By *mistake*—same way you shot my cousin?"

Bohannon laughed.

Lonnie sat up and tried to brush water off his cheek. All he did was smear mud on his face. He was sitting in what had now become a bog around the horse trough. "Hell, no!"

"Don't bring your foul language to town, boy," the sheriff ordered. "You leave it back on your ranch. Your mother may let you get by with talkin' that way, but I won't. Not in my town."

"I'm sorry, Sheriff, but I'm tired of him hound doggin' me!"

"I'll hound dog you, all right!"

"Stand down, Walleye. Get the hump out of your neck." To Lonnie, Halliday said, "Where is this dead man you're talkin' about? You leave him out there?"

"He was too heavy. I didn't think I could get him on my horse. I left him in a cave near the entrance to the canyon. Just inside about a hundred yards, west ridge wall. Behind some boulders." Lonnie rose, his wet clothes heavy on him, his sodden boots squeaking. "Four men tried to run me down before I found McLory. Rustlers, most like. They must've shot McLory and thought I was McLory's partner."

Lonnie didn't like the way Halliday was staring at him. It was a vaguely suspicious look. Mostly, it was menacing. Why it was so, Lonnie had no idea.

He picked up his hat, stuffed it on his head, and looked up at Sheriff Halliday, who was a tall man of middle age, with a neatly trimmed, gray-streaked brown goatee to match his thinning hair. He was an elegant man who spent most of his time in the gambling parlors and hurdy-gurdy houses. Dwight Stoveville, Casey's father, had been the sheriff here until Shannon Dupree had shot him when Stoveville had tried to cut off Dupree's escape from the bank holdup in Golden last year.

Halliday, a wealthy dude from Oklahoma who owned a saloon and a freighting business, knew important men in the area. Those men had gotten him an appointment as sheriff. There would be an official election in September though no one was running against him. It was said that no one dared. It was also said that Halliday had gotten rich by sinister means and that he intended to use his position as sheriff to continue cashing in on his sinister ways.

Suddenly, Lonnie wished he hadn't involved Halliday and his no-account deputies. He thought he'd been doing the right thing for both himself and Cade McLory, but now he was starting to feel incriminated in McLory's death, for all three lawmen were regarding him skeptically.

Halliday took a long drag off his black cheroot, blew the smoke out into the wind, and then, keeping his gray-eyed gaze on Lonnie, said, "Walleye, Bohannon—saddle up and check it out. Bring the body back to town. I want a look at it."

Walleye frowned at Halliday. "Skull Canyon's supposed to be cursed, boss."

Bohannon laughed as he dropped lightly down the porch steps, spurs jingling. Halliday looked at Walleye as though he'd just broken wind. Walleye flushed and then, setting his shotgun on his shoulder, followed Bohannon off in the direction of the Federated Livery Stable.

Halliday returned his hard, gray eyes to Lonnie. He didn't say anything for a time. It was as though he were probing the boy's deepest thoughts and motivations with his gaze.

Then he stuck the cheroot back between his teeth, took another long drag off it, and blew the smoke out as he said, "I know about you, boy. I know about the trouble you and your mother got yourselves into last year. I know all about you and her throwin' in with Shannon Dupree and those two tough nuts he rode with—Childress and Fuego."

"We didn't throw in with 'em, Sheriff. That's just a malicious rumor goin' around. Heck, me an' Casey Stoveville, the sheriff's daughter—"

"I know, I know—I heard that story, too. About how you two took the money to the deputy US marshal over in Camp Collins. But I don't think that's the whole story, is it? I think you did that after you killed that deputy and you saw the writing on the wall—that you were goin' to hang if you didn't do somethin' fast with the money. Somehow you got the drop on Dupree, Childress, and Fuego, and shot them all just to keep them quiet about your part in the robbery."

Exasperated all over again, Lonnie wagged his head.

"Just hold your tongue, boy," Halliday cut him off before he could speak. "I won't take no sass from a no-account mountain boy. I don't know what you and your mother got goin' up there in them mountains, but you best understand I'm gonna keep my eye on both of you. The word goin' around is that your place is a hideout for cattle rustlers."

"What?"

"I told you to hold your tongue, boy!"

"But I'm tellin' you that's a damn lie, Sheriff!"

Halliday pulled his cheroot out of his mouth, lurched down the porch steps, and smashed the back of his hand holding the cigar across Lonnie's right cheek. Cigar ash burned Lonnie's eye as the blow hurled him back to the muddy ground.

The General gave a menacing whicker and shook his head, not at all happy with all the abuse being visited upon his rider.

Halliday poked his cigar threateningly at Lonnie and gritted his teeth. "I done told you I won't allow young folks to talk like drunken Irish miners. Not in my town! Now, you get the hell away from me. When I've investigated the killin' out in Skull Canyon, I'll know where to find you for further questions. If I hear one more word of insolence from you, I'll take the strap to you and throw you in jail for a night!"

Halliday wheeled, marched back up onto the porch, and disappeared into his office.

Lonnie sat up, rubbing his cheek. He glanced around. Several towns-folk—women as well as men—were staring at him. They were regarding him accusingly, muttering among themselves and shaking their heads.

Lonnie cursed under his breath.

He spat mud from between his lips, slogged over to the hitch rail, and untied the General's reins.

He shouldn't have come to town.

He should have kept quiet about Cade McLory. He should have kept quiet about the rustlers who'd tried to kill him. He probably hadn't helped McLory one bit, and he'd only made more trouble for himself.

From now, Lonnie Gentry would make a trip to town once every six weeks for supplies, and that was it. Other than that, he'd stay in the mountains. That was the best place for him.

He heaved his weary self into his saddle. He rode on down the street, back in the direction from which he'd come. He was intending on riding on out of town. He was too beaten up and humiliated to visit Casey.

But then, as he passed the mercantile, he saw her standing on the loading dock waving goodbye to the young fancy Dan she'd been talking to before. The fancy Dan turned abruptly away from Casey, lifting his hat to the girl, and nearly ran smack into the General.

The fancy Dan stopped abruptly, gave Lonnie the hairy eyeball, and said, "For Heaven's sake, boy—watch where you're going, will you?"

Then he waved at Casey once more and strode off down the street.

Casey looked at Lonnie, her eyes raking his soaked, muddy, and generally bedraggled countenance up and down.

The pretty, hazel-eyed blonde planted a fist on her hip, and said, "Lonnie Gentry, what kind of trouble have you gotten yourself into *now?*"

ELEVEN

"THE USUAL," Lonnie said, feeling too downtrodden to defend himself. "The usual trouble, Casey."

He turned the General away from the mercantile and continued down the main street. He no longer cared about seeing Casey. He just wanted to get back up into the mountains and be alone. He was feeling sorry for himself. He wanted to hole up and lick his wounds.

"Lonnie—hold on!"

He couldn't ignore the girl, however. He drew back on the General's reins and turned to see Casey moving on down the porch steps, holding the hem of her checked gingham housedress above her ankles, her long, wavy, gold-blonde hair bouncing on her shoulders.

She moved out into the street and stopped near Lonnie's left stirrup, looking up at him, brows furled with concern. "You look like you were caught in a cyclone. What happened?"

Lonnie spat more mud from his lips and glanced in the direction in which the fancy Dan had gone. "Who was that?"

Casey hiked a shoulder, saying, "A friend. You're soaked. What have you been doin'? You're all mud. And that eye... You're gonna have a nice shiner, there, Lonnie. Did you get into a fight?"

Lonnie could only give a caustic laugh at the question.

"Ride on over to my place. I'm gonna clean you up before you catch your death of cold in those wet clothes."

"Never mind, Casey."

"Lonnie!" She gave him one of those admonishing scowls of hers, both cheeks dimpling, her hazel eyes slitting. He didn't think she was any more beautiful than when she was scowling at him, though he had to admit her warm smiles could turn his heart to putty.

"Casey, you're workin'."

"I was about to close up for lunch. Mister Hendrickson is home sick, though I think it's the bottle flu. I heard he was up all night gamblin' in the Purple Palace. Lonnie, you ride on over to my house. I'll meet you there in a minute. Don't argue with me, Lonnie Gentry!"

Lonnie had to admit if only to himself that the girl's obvious concern for him made him feel a little better about his lot in life. He didn't let on, however. He sighed as though at another bitter defeat and gigged the General on around the corner of the mercantile and down the side street to the south.

He crossed a tributary of Arapaho Creek, picked up another side street, passed several old cabins—the original cabins of Arapaho Creek, from a time when the town had not been named yet and was only a small, seedy mining camp. The cabins slouched beneath their shake roofs pocked with moss. An ancient, bearded old man in pinstriped overalls sat out front of one, blindly staring toward the far peaks, a shaggy dog asleep in the shade beside him. A stick he'd been whittling lay across his lap.

Lonnie passed a giant cottonwood rattling its leaves in the warm, dry breeze and rode into the yard of the neat, white clapboard house in which Casey Stoveville now lived alone. There was a small stable and corral behind the house, as well as a buggy shed. Lonnie rode around back and after releasing the General's belly strap and slipping his bit, Lonnie led him into the corral and closed the gate.

By the time Lonnie walked back around to the front of the house, Casey was walking into the yard, having followed a shortcut over the creek from the mercantile. She wore a long, faded denim jacket over the dress, and a gray felt Stetson, the chin thong dangling down her chest.

She stopped in front of Lonnie and reached up to touch two fingers to the swelling area around his eye. "That hurt?"

"Startin' to fuss a little."

"Compliments of whom?"

"Walleye Miller."

Casey grimaced as she turned away and started up the steps of the small, white porch fronting the house that was in need of a fresh coat of paint. The mountain winters were hard on clapboard houses. A floorboard was missing from the porch, as well, and there was a small crack in a front windowpane.

"How on earth did you get mixed up with Walleye Miller?" Casey asked. "You know he's a tough nut who couldn't keep a ranch job because of all the fights he got into."

"Kind of hard to see the sheriff without seein' Walleye first," Lonnie said, following Casey into the house. "You know how all he and Bohannon do is sit out on the sheriff's front stoop, sharpenin' matchsticks and drinkin' coffee spiced with busthead. It sure is a different office without your pa runnin' it."

Immediately, Lonnie wished he hadn't mentioned Casey's father. His murder was still an open wound.

Lonnie saw Casey's cheek blanch slightly and her shoulders tighten as she went to the kitchen sink and pumped water into a tin coffee can. She shook her hair out of her eyes and glanced at Lonnie. "Have a seat, killer. I'll try to get you cleaned up."

Lonnie stood on the rope mat just inside the door. He was trying to pull a boot off.

"Don't worry about your boots," Casey told him, pumping water. "I sort of miss havin' a man to clean up after around here...on occasion."

She gave Lonnie a faint, wan smile then turned away, letting her hair drop down to cover her face.

"Sorry," Lonnie said. "I shouldn't have said that...about your old man."

"My father is dead," Casey said, setting the filled can on the table and then turning to open a cupboard door. "I miss him, but I'm used to it."

She came back over to the table and sat down beside Lonnie, turning her chair to face him. She dipped one of the flannel cloths into the can and wrung it out. "It's just that...times are tough."

"How do you mean?"

Casey reached forward and began lightly wiping mud from around Lonnie's eye. "I might lose the house."

Lonnie grabbed her hand, frowning. "Why?"

"Taxes. And I'm havin' trouble keepin' up with the payments. Pa was a good provider, but he didn't save much. I was able to get through the first eight months all right, but now I'm startin' to backslide. I don't make enough at the mercantile. That's not Mister Hendrickson's fault. He pays me all he can." Casey shook her head as she dabbed at Lonnie's lip. "Still, it's not enough."

As she continued cleaning Lonnie's face, taking special care with the area around his eye and the bullet burn across his cheek, she said, "The house needs a new roof and fresh paint."

"I can shingle the roof for you. And I can paint for you, too. For free."

Again, Casey gave a halfhearted smile. "Thanks, Lonnie, but you got your hands full out at the Circle G."

Lonnie grabbed Casey's wrist again and gave it a gentle, reassuring squeeze. "Don't worry, Casey—everythin' will be all right."

"Listen to me go on," Casey said, wringing out the cloth in the can again. "Good Lord—you're the one all soaked and muddy and beaten up. And you haven't even told me why you needed to see the sheriff in the first place."

Lonnie looked at her. At first, all he could see was Cade McLory lying dead in the cave, staring blankly at the ceiling. Another chill swept through Lonnie. He swallowed back his emotion, trying to be strong. But he heard a tremor in his voice as he said, "I saw a man die last night."

TWELVE

CASEY JUST STARED at him for a long moment.

"Good Lord, Lonnie. Where? How?"

"In Skull Canyon."

Casey looked surprised now as well as shocked. "What were you doin' in Skull Canyon? You know the place is cursed."

Lonnie had never known Casey to be the superstitious sort. But then, he hadn't known her all that long. Just since last year. She'd always seemed levelheaded, so for her to believe the old legend about the canyon being cursed made Lonnie all the more unnerved about having spent a whole night in the spooky place.

Half of that night with a dead man . . .

"I was chased by four men on horseback. They tried to kill me. They popped off enough lead to cast a cannon."

"Oh, Lonnie, what in the world have you—?"

Lonnie squeezed her wrist a little harder, to forestall the question. "I got no idea who they were. Rustlers, most likely. I seen one of 'em up close and didn't recognize 'im. I don't think they're from around here. They're probably from Wyomin' or New Mexico. I've seen every range rider from these parts at least once, and I got a mule's memory."

"What about the dead man?"

"When I got away from them four shooters, I was workin' my way back down the mountain to look for the General. I heard a wounded man moanin' and carryin' on. He was in the canyon—Skull Canyon. I didn't see another way, so I went in. He was gut shot. He couldn't walk very far, so I got him into a cave near the canyon entrance. I built a fire and tended him as best I could."

Lonnie swallowed and gave a shudder, remembering last night and wishing some of the vividness had been honed away by time.

"His name was Cade McLory. A nice fella, seemed like. Only a few years older'n me. He was from Texas."

"What was he doin' in Skull Canyon, this Cade McLory?"

"I don't know."

"You didn't ask?"

Lonnie tried to remember. Little but McLory himself and the way he'd died, the way he'd *looked after he'd died,* had stayed clear to Lonnie. The peripheral stuff, what they'd talked about, had turned blurry.

"I don't know. I reckon I did. But...if I did, he didn't tell me. At least, I don't remember what he said, if he said anythin'. He was there with another fella."

"Lonnie, why were those other men chasin' you?"

"I got no idea, Casey. I know what you're thinkin'. You an' Walleye an' Bohannon and Sheriff Halliday."

"Don't throw me in the stable with those worthless—"

"All I know is I was up brush poppin' lost cows an' haulin' 'em out of the mud when those four curly wolves rode at me like the devil's hounds loosed from hell. Then I found McLory. I came to town to report it all to the sheriff, but now I'm wishin' I'd stayed in the mountains. I should know better than to ever leave the mountains. Dang near got drowned in a horse trough, was treated like a killer, slapped by a man three times my size—and all that was only *after* I rode by the mercantile and saw my girl lookin' all starry-eyed at..."

Lonnie let his voice trail off when a knock sounded on the door.

The door opened. Fancy Dan himself poked his head into the kitchen, grinning. The grin faded, however, when his large, copper-brown eyes found Lonnie sitting at Casey's kitchen table, still wet and muddy, with Casey sitting within three feet of him, the two of them holding hands.

"Miss Casey," fancy Dan said, looking bewildered as he slid his gaze from Lonnie to Casey and back again, "I just wanted to stop by and tell you...when the next dance was...out at Vott's Barn, but..."

"Oh, Niles!" Casey lurched to her feet so quickly that she nearly knocked her chair over backwards. She hurried over to the door. Fancy

Dan retreated out onto the porch, and Casey followed him out, drawing the door closed behind her.

The door wasn't much of a buffer, however. Lonnie could hear the fancy Dan also known as Niles say, "Casey, who is that boy? He and his horse nearly ran me over in town, and..."

Casey spoke in a soft, low voice, but Lonnie could still hear the girl say, "Oh...he's...he's just a boy from the mountains, Niles. I see him from time to time. He gets into trouble on occasion and..."

Then they must have moved off down the steps because Casey's voice grew gradually quieter until Lonnie could no longer hear what she was saying.

That was all right.

Lonnie had heard enough.

His bruises no longer ached. At least, they were nothing compared to the driving, burning agony that the invisible fist of Casey Stoveville's hushed words had hammered into his gut.

Lonnie rose unsteadily from his chair.

The kitchen pitched and swayed around him. He felt the way he had when he'd "gentled" half-wild horses to add to his own remuda, riding the green out of them. Those owl-eyed broomtails would use the lean-to shed off the barn to rake Lonnie off their backs and then pummel him down hard in the dust with their hooves.

He felt the same way now. He felt as though he'd had the stuffing kicked out of both ends.

Dragging his heavy feet, Lonnie made his way out of the kitchen, through a curtained doorway, and down a short hall to the house's rear door. He pushed through the door and outside, leaving the door wide behind him. Regaining his balance, he almost ran to the corral, threw the gate open, and ran at the General so fast that the horse whickered and sidestepped from him, neck arched, and tail raised.

"Easy, boy—easy, easy," Lonnie said, moving up on the horse more slowly but with no less urgency.

When he'd slid the bit back into the General's mouth and tightened the latigo strap, Lonnie mounted up and rode out of the corral. He galloped off to the southwest, toward the trail that would take him deep, deep into the mountains where no one else in the world would ever see or hear from him again.

THIRTEEN

CROUCHED behind a boulder sitting like a hat on top of a haystack-shaped bluff, Lonnie slowly pumped a cartridge into his Winchester's chamber and caressed the cocked hammer with his gloved right thumb.

He doffed his hat and edged a look around the boulder.

The trail he'd been following from town snaked around the base of the bluff to climb steeply into pines. A few minutes ago, while Lonnie had been riding deeper and deeper into the mountains, the General had given a warning whicker. Thirty seconds later, Lonnie had heard what the General had heard—the distance muffled hoof thuds of a rider approaching along Lonnie's back trail.

Lonnie had quickly dismounted, led the General off the trail, and climbed the bluff to hide behind the boulder. If he was being followed, he wanted to know by whom and why.

The hoof thuds told him only one man was approaching, but there might be more behind him. Like *three* more. Which would make a total of four—the same number who'd bushwhacked him yesterday afternoon around the same time of day, when his life had exploded like a powder keg.

Now a shadow moved among the pines. Lonnie jerked his head back behind the boulder with a start. Then he slowly slid another peek around the boulder. He drew a short breath and held it.

The rider was moving down out of the trees. He was a lanky man in a tall gray Stetson and long, spruce-green duster. His pinstriped trouser legs were stuffed down into stovepipe, cavalry-style boots. Lonnie couldn't see his face from this angle, for the man was riding down the slope, and he had his chin down, as well, as though he were scrutinizing the tracks in the trail ahead of him.

Lonnie's tracks.

The man rode a speckle-gray horse that lifted its head abruptly and gave a warning whinny. The horse had winded Lonnie. Behind Lonnie, at the base of the bluff, the General answered in kind.

"Dangit, you old hay burner!" Lonnie snarled at the stallion.

The rider jerked his head up, pulling back on his reins, and reaching for the big pistol holstered for the cross draw high on his left hip. Lonnie licked his lips, drew another, calming breath, and stepped out from behind the boulder, aiming his rifle at the big man on the speckle gray.

Trying to keep his voice calm, Lonnie said, "Leave the hog leg in its holster or I'll blow you clear back to sunup."

The man froze and slid his head slightly to the side, his eyes finding Lonnie beneath the broad brim of his tall, gray hat. His long, lean face was sunbaked; his hawk nose was brick red. Long, gray hair curled over his collar. He wore a mustache, goatee, and muttonchop whiskers of the same color. Lonnie thought his eyes beneath his hat brim were frosty blue. They resided in deep sockets around which a meshwork of deep crow's-feet spoked and beneath which heavy, dark bags sagged.

Lonnie said, "Who are you and why're you followin' me?"

The man narrowed his eyes as he took the measure of the rifle-wielding kid before him. "Careful, boy. You don't want that thing to go off."

"Neither do you," Lonnie said, consciously keeping steel in his voice. Just because he was young didn't mean he was gonna take any grief from a grown-up. He'd had enough grief from grown-ups.

The man raised his gloved hands slowly, holding his reins in the right one. "I was only wantin' to ask you a few questions, that's all. I don't know who you are or where you're from, but I figure you're from around here. I'm not."

He raked a thumb across the edge of his duster, peeling the canvas lapel back to reveal a copper moon and star badge. "Name's John Apple-yard. *Deputy US Marshal* John Appleyard. Out of Denver. I'm lookin' for an hombre who goes by the name of Crawford Kinch. Thought maybe you knew him or seen him hereabouts."

Lonnie kept his rifle aimed at the tall man before him though he eased the tension in his trigger finger. He'd shot one lawman last year. He didn't want to go for another lawman this year. Unless he had to, that was. He knew from experience that not all lawmen were lawful. They could kill you just as dead as the worst variety of outlaw.

"I don't know no one named Crawford Kinch," Lonnie said.

"He might be goin' by another name. He's a tall man. About my size, a few years older. Has a gray beard, one blue and one brown eye, and wears a tattoo on his neck. The tattoo is, uh..." The lawman glanced away, vaguely sheepish, before turning back to Lonnie. "The tattoo is a naked lady. Big enough so's you couldn't miss it."

Lonnie flushed a little at the image of the naked lady floating around inside his head. "Never seen him."

"Could you lower that gun, son? You're makin' me nervous. And I *am* a lawman. I don't just wear the badge because it looks nice and shiny on my shirt."

"Just cause a dog has a tail," Lonnie said, "don't mean he wags it."

The man smiled briefly at that and looked away again. "Fair enough." He looked up at Lonnie, narrowing one eye. "You from around here?"

"Yep."

"What's your name?"

Lonnie considered whether he wanted to give the man his name. He supposed it couldn't hurt. He could ask around and find out easily enough. Lonnie told him.

"Would you do me a favor, Lonnie Gentry?" the deputy marshal asked. "If you do happen to see this man, Crawford Kinch, around here some-where, would you please get word to me in Arapaho Creek? I'm stayin' at the boardin'house on Third Avenue."

Lonnie lowered the gun to his side but kept his finger curled through the trigger guard, in case he needed it quickly. "What do you want with this Crawford Kinch fella?"

"Never mind about that. Whatever it is, you'll want to steer clear of it. And you'll want to steer clear of Crawford Kinch, too. But if you do happen to be unfortunate enough to run into him, and live to tell about it, tell me, will you?" Appleyard gave an ironic grin.

Lonnie studied the man, nodded slowly. "All right. I'll get word to you if I see this Crawford Kinch...and live to tell about it."

Lonnie wondered if he should tell the marshal about the four men who'd run him down yesterday, and about Cade McLory. He decided against it. He'd been reminded in town only a couple of hours ago that the less he said to the law, the better. Besides, he hadn't gotten a very good look at three of the four riders yesterday, but he was sure he'd have noted a tattoo on one of them.

Especially one in the shape of a naked lady.

He'd already told Halliday about Cade McLory. He'd done his duty, and he'd suffered the consequences for it, and McLory wasn't going to benefit one way or the other if the men who'd shot him were brought to justice.

Appleyard dipped his chin and pinched his hat brim to Lonnie. "Much obliged, boy. Even from here, your lips look blue. You'd best get yourself warm before you catch your death of cold."

Lonnie didn't say anything. He watched the lawman turn his horse around on the trail and then ride up into the pines, heading back in the direction of town.

Lonnie stared at Appleyard's back growing smaller and smaller until the tree shadows swallowed horse and rider. Lonnie scraped a thumbnail along his smooth jawline and mused softly, "Crawford Kinch, huh? A naked-lady tattoo. Imagine that."

FOURTEEN

LONNIE SHIVERED as he rode higher into the mountains. His clothes were no longer soaked, but they were damp. The dampness had leeched into his bones, muscles, and tendons.

He didn't intend on riding all the way back to the ranch just yet. He didn't feel like seeing his mother and his half-brother, whom May Gentry had named Jeremiah. Jeremiah was the offspring of Shannon Dupree, but Lonnie didn't hold it against the baby, only a few months old.

Still, the kid was loud, and Lonnie needed peace and quiet. He felt like being alone for a while, to lick his wounds both physical and otherwise. He headed for the line shack at the base of Eagle Ridge. His mother wouldn't start to worry about him for another day or so. When coyotes or wolves were around, or when he'd spotted the tracks of a mountain lion on his range, Lonnie often stayed with the herd in the mountains for several days and nights at a time, to try and keep his losses to a minimum.

He was used to being alone. In fact, he was starting to prefer being alone. People were too much trouble.

The trail meandered ever higher into the Never Summers. Finally, when Lonnie was a good hour and a half out of Arapaho Creek, he turned off the main trail and followed an old horse trail through a ravine thick with aspens. Eagle Creek flowed down the middle of the ravine, rippling over beaver dams. The air was spiced with the wine fragrance of the creek and green leaves and wild raspberries.

The line shack sat at the head of this ravine and at the base of the towering granite crag known as Eagle Ridge. The cabin was a low-slung, mossy-roofed log structure that his father had built when he and May Gentry had first settled in these mountains. Mostly, his father had stayed overnight in the cabin only during spring and summer roundups or when predators were on the prowl. He'd limited his time here. He'd loved his family, so he'd stayed close to home.

Lonnie tended and stabled the General out back of the line shack. Then he hauled his gear into the cabin. He climbed up onto the roof and removed the coffee tin which he always placed over the chimney pipe, to keep birds and squirrels out, and then went back inside the cabin and built a fire in the sheet-iron monkey stove.

As the fire got going, Lonnie walked over to where the creek ran over its rocky bed through the aspens. He paused at the edge of the stream, near a cool, dark hole of waist-deep water, doffed his hat, kicked out of his boots, and steeled himself.

He took a deep breath and then plunged feet-first into the pool.

The water, fed by a spring deep beneath Eagle Ridge, was as cold as snowmelt. It was so cold that Lonnie thought his teeth would crack. Still, it was the best way to get himself and his clothes clean.

He thrashed around for a while in the water, shivering and yelling, unable to control the outburst. Oddly the cold felt good. It almost pushed Casey and fancy Dan out of his mind.

Almost, but not quite . . .

When he thought his heart could no longer take the bittersweet torture, Lonnie crawled up onto shore, and gained his feet. Water sluiced off him. He shivered and cursed like a sailor, feeling the luxurious freedom of being able to do so in so remote a place, where the hawks, chickadees, squirrels, owls, and occasionally a skunk or two were his only neighbors.

Once, he'd befriended an orphaned fox cub out here, and named it Red. Red had grown up and gone off on his own, but occasionally Lonnie saw a red fox hunting mice in a near meadow, and he believed—at least, he hoped—the fox was his old pal Red.

As he walked back to the cabin, Lonnie peeled off his wet clothes, leaving a soggy trail of blue denims, socks, long handles, checked shirt and navy-blue neckerchief in a long, wet, twisted line behind him. Gray smoke billowed from the cabin's stovepipe. It was like the fire was beckoning to the shivering youngster.

By the time Lonnie reached the front door, he was naked—dark brown where the sun reached him and as white as flour where it did not, which was almost everywhere except his face, neck, and hands. He went in, closed the door, wrapped a blanket around his shoulders, shoved more pine sticks into the stove, and hunkered close to the open stove door.

The heat pushed against him, hot as a dragon's breath. The fire *whushed* and the stove ticked as the iron grew hot.

Gradually, the chill began to ease its grip on Lonnie though he continued to shiver violently, crouched beneath the blanket. After a time, he rose from the cot, went over to where he'd hastily piled his gear, and rummaged around in a saddlebag pouch. He pulled out the pint bottle of whiskey and held it up to the window.

Still half full.

Lonnie had never had a desire for liquor before. He'd seen what it had done to the likes of Shannon Dupree. It had turned him into an ugly, wild, violent animal. But Lonnie's mother had given it to Lonnie, mixed with hot water and honey, when he'd suffered from colds and sore throats. The busthead had soothed not only the pain of the illness, but it had drawn the chill from his bones, as well.

Lonnie sat back down on the edge of the cot, close to the crackling, popping fire, and pried the cork from the bottle. He took a sip and made a face as the liquor dribbled down his throat, burning harshly all the way down into his belly. A moment later, however, the burn eased. A comforting flush spread out from his belly, rising from his chest and neck and into his cheeks and ears.

Soothing...

He took another sip. That one was too big. It nearly came back up.

Somehow, he managed to keep it down though he thought it would strangle him. He coughed and choked for a brief time, as though someone like Walleye Miller had his hand around his neck. But then the hand eased its grip, and the soothing flush rose once again.

Lonnie looked around. The harsh angles of the cabin softened, and the mountain light slanting through the windows grew less harsh, pleasantly fuzzy.

The chirping of the birds outside in the branches grew keener.

Best of all, the warmth of the fire was finally seeping into his fingers and toes, thawing him out. Still, his heart felt swollen and tender. He doubted any amount of whiskey would heal it.

Casey...

Lonnie corked the bottle and set it on the floor beneath the cot. He chunked another split pine log onto the fire and sat back down on the cot, holding the blanket tight about his shoulders. He was no longer shivering. He just sat there now. Beneath the ache in his chest, he enjoyed being mildly drunk and the feeling of being dry and warm at last.

Outside, the General whinnied.

Lonnie snapped his head up.

Now, what?

Outside, another horse whinnied from the direction of the trail. Hoofs thudded softly as the horse approached. Someone was coming.

Lonnie held the blanket loosely around his shoulders as he scrambled over to his gear and picked up his rifle. He opened the cabin door, cocked the rifle, and held it in one hand straight out from his waist.

No more, he thought. He would be trifled with no more...

Now he could catch glimpses of the sun- and shade-dappled horse and rider moving through the aspens toward the cabin. Lonnie tightened his grip on the rifle, hardened his jaws, and tightened his finger across the trigger.

FIFTEEN

"LONNIE?" Casey yelled as she emerged from the trees, riding her chestnut mare, Miss Abigail.

Lonnie's heart was wrenched one quarter turn in his chest.

Ah, hell.

Casey stopped at the edge of the trees, on the far side of the small clearing in which the cabin sat. Lonnie stepped back inside the cabin door, lowering the rifle and drawing the blanket tighter around his shoulders, very aware that he wasn't wearing a stitch beneath it.

"What the hell're you doin' here?"

Casey looked around at Lonnie's clothes strewn between the creek and the cabin. Then she turned to Lonnie and gigged the mare into a trot, shaking her head. "I'm so sorry, Lonnie."

"Stow it."

Casey rode up to the cabin and dismounted, dropping Miss Abigail's reins. She paused to pick up Lonnie's long handles, which she twisted in her hands, wringing them out, and then moved up to the cabin. She tossed the long handles over the hitch rack and moved closer to Lonnie, her eyes large beneath the brim of her hat.

She raised her arms as though to hug him, but Lonnie stepped back.

"What're you doin' here, Casey? I'm just a boy from the mountains. A boy who gets in trouble a lot. Ain't you just so nice befriendin' such a troubled soul!"

Lonnie swung around, retreating inside the cabin, and sat down on the edge of the cot, keeping the blanket pulled close about him. He saw Casey's shadow slide across the cabin floor as she stopped inside the doorway.

"Lonnie, I'm just awful," Casey said. "If you want me to leave...if you don't want to see me ever again, I understand. I'll ride away right now. But I'd like to explain. I owe you that much."

Lonnie glowered at the floor. "So, who's the fancy Dan?"

"Niles Gilpin."

Lonnie glanced at her over his shoulder. "Gilpin? That's the banker's name."

Casey turned the corners of her mouth down, nodding. "Niles is George Gilpin's son. He was studyin' at a college back east. He graduated last fall and came home to help his father in the bank."

Lonnie chuckled without humor as he turned his head back forward. "Now it's all comin' clear to me."

Casey moved into the cabin. She sat down on the cot beside Lonnie. She took one of his hands in her own. She was wearing riding gloves. She didn't say anything for a moment. Lonnie didn't look at her, but he could feel her gaze on his face.

"Lonnie, I think it's time we faced facts," Casey said finally.

Lonnie turned to her. His cheeks were warm with embarrassment, anger, and jealousy—a nasty concoction that neither the fire's warmth nor the whiskey could alleviate. He steeled himself to keep from crying as he said, "You told me...you told me you loved me."

For some reason, despite his need for Casey's love, the word "love" only aggravated his humiliation. He wasn't sure why it was such a wonderful and repelling word, but it was.

Casey squeezed his hand. "I know I did. And I always will, Lonnie. We've been through a lot together. We almost died together. But we have to face facts."

"What facts are those?" Lonnie said with sarcasm. "That you found yourself a fancy Dan? The banker's son. Hell, Casey, if money means so much to you, we had a whole passel of it last year. For a time, old Wilbur Calhoun had me convinced that we should keep Dupree's loot and head to Mexico—don't you remember? You're the one who convinced me to turn it in!"

"Because that was the right thing to do, Lonnie. That money didn't belong to us."

"What *is* the right thing to do? To go skulkin' around with some fancy Dan behind my back? I'm sorry you didn't take what you said to me as serious as I did, Casey."

"I did take it seriously. I still do. But we're young, Lonnie. Too young to be makin' commitments to each other. The fact is, I'm goin' broke. Every month I get farther and farther behind. Soon, the county is goin' to sell my house because I can't pay the taxes on it."

"Gettin' hitched to the banker would solve that problem, wouldn't it?"

"Yes, I'm not sorry to say, it would."

Lonnie glared at her, hardening his jaws, trying not to cry though he felt on the verge of it. "I didn't think you were like that, Casey."

"Like what? Not wantin' to be put out on the street? Listen, Lonnie, you're a boy. You don't understand how frightenin' life on the frontier can be for a young woman with no prospects. When Pa was killed, he left with me about fifty dollars cash and the house. He was behind on both house payments and taxes. In less than a year, I'll be broke. Do you know what that means for a young woman to be broke on the frontier? *Do you?*"

Now, it was Casey who seemed angry. She squeezed Lonnie's hand harder, until it hurt a little. Lonnie felt his own anger subside. He hadn't been thinking about Casey's welfare. Only his own.

Only his love for the girl.

Lonnie did know what happened to homeless girls on the frontier. They usually ended up either working as fry cooks for miserable hours on end in some sweltering café kitchen, or in hurdy-gurdy houses until they either died in childbirth or some disease took their lives much too soon.

Casey said, "It was easy to commit to each other a year ago. We'd been through a lot together—almost killed by Dupree multiple times, almost eaten by a bear! But we persevered and we did the right thing in returnin' the loot to the deputy US marshal in Camp Collins. But now we're back home. It's day to day. It's real life. And I'm scared, Lonnie. Giles is a good man with a good job and a future. He's warm and gentle and he likes me. You and I—what would we have to look forward to, once you were old enough to marry me? You yourself told me that you and your mother barely made enough to feed yourselves. And now she has a baby, to boot!"

Lonnie stared at her, his lower jaw hanging. He wanted to respond to all that she'd said with a reasonable argument of his own.

But the fact was, Casey was right. Lonnie hadn't been able to see past his love for her, and her love for him, to face the hard, cold facts that he was just too young and poor to marry the girl. And she, being two years older and on the verge of going broke and losing her house, couldn't wait around for him to get his ducks in a row.

Besides, Casey was a town girl. She'd probably never take to living on a remote mountain ranch even if Lonnie had enough money to build them their own cabin, which he did not. He'd need help and materials, not to mention time, to build that cabin.

Really, that cabin was merely a castle in the sky...

He just stared at her, unable to say anything. Finally, he closed his mouth, turned his head back forward, and stared at the flames leaping behind the stove's open door.

Very softly, Casey said, "I'm sorry, Lonnie." Then she kissed his cheek, gave his hand another squeeze, rose from the cot and went outside. When she didn't leave right away, he glanced through the window behind him to see her gathering his clothes between the cabin and the creek.

When she'd gathered them all, she brought them in and hung them to dry from wall pegs and over chair backs.

"You don't have to do that," Lonnie told her, his throat tight with emotion.

Casey swung the chair, over which his denim trousers hung, closer to the stove. Then she turned to Lonnie, her gaze somber, her eyes veiled with tears. She brushed a hand across her cheek, cleared her throat, and said, "I wanted to."

Then she strode out of the cabin, drew the door closed behind her, mounted her horse, and rode away.

Lonnie leaned forward, gnashed his teeth, and ground his knuckles against his temples.

SIXTEEN

LATE THAT NIGHT, lying on the cot in the line shack, Lonnie opened his eyes.

Something had awakened him.

What?

Outside, the General whickered.

More accustomed to danger than most young men his age, Lonnie grabbed his rifle from where it leaned against the wall near his cot and scrambled out of bed. Clad in long handles and socks, he sidled up to the window.

The half-moon was kiting high above the clearing, shedding a milky light that sparkled off the frost-rimed grass. Lonnie looked around, but he couldn't see anything.

Again, the General whickered. The horse's hoofs thudded as the General moved nervously around the corral connected to the stable.

The General might have only winded a skunk or a coyote, but Lonnie had to check it out. Could be a mountain lion, even a grizzly. Or, worse, it could be two-legged predator...

Lonnie dressed quickly, pulled on his boots, pumped a cartridge into his Winchester's chamber, and went out, closing the door quietly and then stepping to his left, around the cabin's left-front corner and out of the moonlight. Pressing his back against the cabin's log wall, Lonnie dropped to a crouch and edged a look back around the front of the cabin and into the clearing beyond.

He glanced over to where the General stood, staring over the corral gate toward where the trail led up out of the trees. The General was nervously switching his tail.

Lonnie dropped to a knee and held still as he stared out toward the trail and the moon-silvered forest. There wasn't a breath of wind. The night was still and silent. It was darker over there at the edge of the clearing, down low where the trees shielded the moonlight from the clearing floor.

It was over there, however, that Lonnie saw a shadow move.

He pulled his head back a little closer to the cabin corner. He held his breath when he saw a man-shaped shadow run out from the trees and into the moonlight. The man was crouched low, his breath pluming in the chill air. The moonlight reflected off something shiny that he was holding down low in his right hand.

A gun.

Lonnie's heart skipped, fluttered.

He licked his dry lips and watched the man take cover behind a boulder where the trail curved up out of the forest and angled toward the cabin.

As Lonnie stared at the boulder, he spied another flicker of movement in the corner of his right eye. He swung his head around to catch a glimpse of what appeared another man-shaped, pearl-limned shadow run out of the forest. Frost-stiff grass crunched softly under the runner's boots. The man ran at an angle toward the back of the cabin, and out of Lonnie's field of vision.

Lonnie's heartbeat increased. The mountain air was cold, but his hands were sweating as he squeezed the Winchester. The hair on the back of his neck pricked with the fear that the second man might circle the cabin and move up behind him.

Lonnie looked toward the boulder behind which the first man had taken cover. The man's hatted head slid out slightly from behind the boulder. The man raised a hand to his mouth. He made what sounded like a soft birdcall though it really didn't sound much like any night bird Lonnie had ever heard.

The second man returned the call with another call that sounded more like an owl. An owl that had smoked too many cigarettes.

Something told Lonnie that the man behind the boulder was going to stay put and let the second man make the first move on the cabin. What they wanted, Lonnie had no idea, but a voice whispered the warning in his head that these two might be from the same pack that had ambushed him yesterday and had set his life spiraling into the hell he now found himself in.

Lonnie pulled back away from the cabin's front corner, swung around, and stole quietly back to the rear. He edged a look around the back of the cabin.

The second man was walking through the moonlight toward Lonnie. He was maybe forty yards away and moving slowly on the balls of his feet, almost hopping. He wasn't wearing spurs, or Lonnie would have heard them trilling. He appeared a big man wearing a bullet-crowned black hat and fur jacket.

He held a rifle in both hands up high across his chest.

Obviously, neither of these men was up to any good.

Lonnie stepped out away from the cabin, raising his rifle to his shoulder and taking aim at the big man walking toward him. "Stop right there."

The man stopped, jerking back with a start. He froze for a second then snapped up his rifle and fired, the explosion cleaving the silent night, red flames lapping from the rifle's barrel. The bullet screeched over Lonnie's right shoulder and hammered the cabin wall behind him.

Jerking back, Lonnie fired his Winchester. He was surprised to hear the big man yelp, for Lonnie had been moving when he'd fired, and he hadn't expected to hit the man. Lonnie fell back against the cabin wall, got his feet beneath him again, and saw the big man lying on the ground, writhing, clutching his left thigh.

"Walleye!" the other man yelled. "Walleye, you hit?"

The wounded man twisted around and shouted with hoarse exasperation, "That loco kid just shot me!"

Pressing his back against the cabin's rear wall, Lonnie muttered, *"Walleye?"*

Inside the boy's head, another voice said, "Oh, no! Oh, no! Oh, no!"
Lonnie Gentry, you just shot another lawman!

Chick Bohannon shouted, "Kid, you hold your fire, now, you hear? You done just shot Walleye Miller! *Deputy Sheriff* Walleye Miller!"

Lonnie slid his gaze around the cabin corner, gazing toward the boulder that the moonlight touched and behind which he could see the head of his other stalker.

"What the hell are you two doin' skulkin' around out here, Bohannon?"

"You step out here where I can see you and put your rifle down, Gentry!"

Lonnie needed only two seconds to think about that. A year ago, he might have followed this lawman's order. But he'd grown a lot in a year. He'd learned a lot about men including lawmen. "So you can shoot me?"

"You're in big trouble, kid!"

"Walleye fired first!"

"He's a deputy sheriff!"

"Get over here and haul him away or I'll shoot him again!" Lonnie shouted, anger beginning to burn brighter than his fear. "Get over here and take him away, or so help me, I'll shoot him again!"

Gritting his teeth in fury, remembering the "swim" he'd taken in the stock trough for all to see in Arapaho Creek, Lonnie swung his rifle toward Walleye, who lay writhing and clutching his leg. He'd lost his hat and his long hair was spread across his shoulders.

"Bohannon!" Walleye shouted, voice pinched with pain. "I'm gonna need a doctor. *Bad!*"

"Kid, I'm comin' over. Don't shoot!"

"Raise your rifle above your head!" Lonnie shouted, suddenly enjoying the power he found himself wielding.

Slowly, Bohannon emerged from the behind the boulder. He raised his rifle in his right hand above his head. He moved slowly out away from the boulder and moved toward where Walleye was writhing and cursing through gritted teeth.

Lonnie kept his rifle leveled on Bohannon, but he kept an eye skinned on Walleye, as well.

The big deputy jerked his enraged, moonlit eyes toward Lonnie. "Kid, if I die, I'm gonna haunt you to your last livin' day—you hear me? I'm gonna come back and I'm gonna watch you *hang!*"

"Talk's cheap," Lonnie said, feeling calmer now, knowing he had the upper hand. "What the hell are you two doin' out here, anyways?"

"We come to have us a little chat about that man you said you found in Skull Canyon," said Bohannon, approaching Walleye.

Lonnie frowned. "What about him?"

"He wasn't there!" Walleye shouted. "You sent us on a wild-goose chase, you lyin' little devil!"

SEVENTEEN

LONNIE STARED at the two deputies, incredulous. "What're you talkin' about? What wild-goose chase?"

"You know what wild-goose chase, you little fang-toothed snot!" barked Walleye, throwing his head back in pain. "Ah, god—it *hurts*. This little boardwalk cur *shot* me!"

Bohannon glared at Lonnie as he said, "Yeah, well, you ain't the first lawman he shot, neither!"

"He wasn't in the cave where I left him?"

The two deputies were ignoring Lonnie.

"Can you stand, Walleye? I'll help you back to your horse," Bohannon said, crouching over his partner.

While Bohannon draped one of Walleye's arms around his neck and helped him rise, Walleye said, "I gotta get to a sawbones, get this bullet dug out of my leg." He looked at Lonnie and snarled, "If I don't bleed out first!"

Lonnie's mind was with Cade McLory. "I left him in a cave. Did you see a cave?"

"We seen a cave, all right," Bohannon yelled as he helped the badly limping Walleye back toward the trees where they must have tied their horses. "The cave was there—the only cave around that part of the canyon. But there wasn't no dead man there. But you know that, don't you? If you think you're gonna make fools of me an' Walleye, you got another think comin', kid!"

Walleye whipped his head toward Lonnie once more. "I'll be back to show you how smart you are, you little cur. You can bet the seed bull on that!"

Lonnie stared at the two as they shuffled off into the darkness of the trees then lowered his rifle and drifted back to the front of the cabin, pondering what the two deputies had told him. How could McLory not have been in the cave?

That wasn't possible. Unless some predator had dragged him out. But if that had happened the deputies would have seen some sign of him. They'd have known a dead man had been there. No predator would have dragged him off intact.

The only explanation Lonnie could figure as he moved back into the line shack and closed the door was that the cork-headed fools, Bohannon and Walleye, had investigated another cave. Apparently, there were at least two caves in that part of the canyon, though Lonnie had only seen one.

That had to be the explanation.

What other explanation could there be?

As Lonnie lay back down on his cot and got himself slowly settled down enough that he thought he might still squeeze a couple more hours of shuteye out of the night, he decided he'd just have to return to Skull Canyon and see about the situation himself.

————

LONNIE WAS up at the first blush of dawn the next morning.

He packed his gear, saddled the General, and rode away from the line shack.

It took him well over an hour of hard riding to reach the entrance to Skull Canyon. When he did, he sat there at the gap in the ridge wall, staring up the brushy ravine that rose steadily and twisted around behind a bulging belly of bald granite and sandstone.

Very faintly, Lonnie could hear that tooth-gnashing whine of the wind funneling through the skull-like formation on the canyon's far end and which gave the canyon its name.

Was the canyon really cursed?

Was that why Bohannon and Walleye hadn't been able to find McLory's body? Was Lonnie now cursed because he'd spent a night in the canyon, and was that why his luck had suddenly gone south? Maybe the reason McLory had met a premature end was because of the canyon's curse...

If so, did Lonnie really want to ride into the canyon again?

No, he sure as hell did not. But the way he figured it, he could probably only be cursed once. So what more harm would another half hour in the canyon do? He wouldn't linger around till sundown again—that was for sure.

Still, the hair under his shirt collar pricked as he gigged the General ahead through the natural gate. He rode up the curving, rocky floor of the ravine and then swung the General west. The buckskin splashed across Ingrid Creek, and five minutes later Lonnie dismounted at the base of the western ridge wall.

He climbed the steep slope that led up to the boulders and wound his way behind the rocks until he found the long, egg-shaped opening in the ridge. Lonnie paused. His neck hairs were standing up even straighter. He wasn't sure what he was more afraid of—finding McLory here or not finding McLory here.

Lonnie crouched to peer into the cave. His lower jaw dropped.

McLory wasn't here. In fact, *nothing* was here. The cave was as empty as it had been when Lonnie had first come upon it the day before.

"Well...I'll be a monkey's uncle," Lonnie heard himself mutter as he dropped to his knees and stared at the place on the cave floor where he'd left McLory, near the fire he'd built and of which no evidence remained!

Lonnie moved on into the cave and looked around in awe.

There were no ashes on the cave floor. Not even a handful. No unburned wood. No charred dirt. No blood from McLory. Not a scrap of anything remaining from the night before last.

It was as though Lonnie and McLory had never been here.

Which must be exactly what someone wanted someone else to believe.

On both counts—*who?*

Who would have taken such pains to scour the area of all sign of the dead man?

Why?

Where was McLory?

Below the cave, the General whickered warningly. Lonnie whipped around to stare out of the brightly sunlit cave opening, his blood whining in his ears. Faintly, he heard men's voices.

Lonnie dashed out of the cave and scrambled down to where he'd left the General. The horse stood between two boulders, making him visible from the canyon floor.

Placing a hand over the buckskin's snout to keep him quiet, Lonnie backed the horse behind the larger of the two boulders, so he wouldn't be seen. Keeping a hand over the General's snout, Lonnie turned to peer through the gap between the boulders, toward the canyon floor beyond the slender, meandering creek.

Men's voices grew louder.

A horse snorted. The clacking of hooves on rock rose to Lonnie's pricked ears.

The young man drew a slow, shallow breath as he watched four horseback riders enter the canyon. He drew back behind the boulder with a startled grunt when he saw that they were the same four men who'd try to run him down and kill him the day before yesterday.

EIGHTEEN

LONNIE EDGED another look around the boulder.

The horses the men were riding told him that these four men now moving up the canyon were the same men who'd tried to kill him. He recognized the brown-and-white pinto of the man who'd scrambled up the outcropping after him, as well as a broad-chested cinnamon dun.

He also recognized the man who'd chased him on foot. He was riding third in the pack, behind two who rode abreast and ahead of the fourth rider, who wore a cream slicker and had long, almost white hair hanging straight down to his shoulders. In profile, Lonnie could see he was a fair-skinned man, and his face was badly sunburned, his long nose almost glowing red. The flaps of his duster were drawn back so that Lonnie could see a big, pearl-gripped, silver-chased pistol jutting from a holster on his left hip.

Lonnie had remembered catching a glimpse of that rider, too, during a brief look behind when the four were bearing down on him.

The first two riders were conversing in low tones as the group rode on past Lonnie, walking their horses up the canyon.

When they'd passed, Lonnie stepped up into the gap between the two boulders, and watched them ride away from him, gradually tracing a curve in the west wall of the canyon and disappeared from sight.

Still, Lonnie stared after them, wondering who they were and why they'd been so determined to kill him.

Had they been the ones who'd removed McLory from the cave?

Why?

More questions reeled through the young man's head to the accompaniment of a low hum of dread in his ears. Obviously, something strange and out of sorts was happening in Skull Canyon. Lonnie's curiosity somehow pushed through his fear. He wanted to ride out of the canyon and forget everything that he'd seen here. He even wanted to forget about the men who'd almost killed him.

But the strong pull of his curiosity wouldn't let him.

He dropped the General's reins, said, "Stay here, boy," then shucked his Winchester from the saddle boot and stole down the steep slope to the canyon floor. He crossed the creek, only dampening his boots, and then jogged along the rocky floor of the canyon littered with apples from one of the passing horses.

He felt a pressing need to find out where the four men were heading and what was in the canyon that had compelled them to kill McLory and to try killing him, Lonnie. They must be holding stolen cattle somewhere in the canyon. What else would compel them to commit murder? If so, some of those cows might be Lonnie's.

Lonnie jogged until he reached a bend in the canyon wall, then catfooted around it, not wanting to run up on the group in case they'd stopped. Once around the bend, he saw the backs of the four riders as they continued riding in the opposite direction—sixty yards away and gradually broadening the gap between themselves and Lonnie.

Just ahead, the canyon narrowed to not more than maybe a hundred feet, with the creek running along the base of the left side wall, with a spring-fed freshet running across the floor from the opposite wall, forming a boggy area. Lonnie tramped on through the soft, muddy ground, and began jogging again, not wanting to get so close to the four that their horses might wind him, but not wanting to lose them, either.

Skull Canyon was a large, deep chasm with several branches. Because of its dark legend, Lonnie had spent as little time in the canyon as possible, but he'd heard from other cowboys who'd grazed cattle in the canyon that it covered a vast, rugged area. Lonnie had also heard that many prospectors had once worked the canyon for gold and silver. Some still might, though he didn't know of any. He thought the legend, widely known throughout the area, probably kept most people out.

Lonnie continued to make his way along the canyon floor, which widened dramatically beyond the bottleneck. As he moved, wishing he'd thought to leave his spurs with the General, it occurred to Lonnie that the four men ahead of him might not be rustlers, after all. They might have discovered gold or silver somewhere in the canyon and were shooting those they thought might be trying to jump their claim.

McLory didn't seem like the claim-jumping type to Lonnie, but he had hardly known the man.

Whatever they were doing was obviously illegal. And whatever they were doing, Lonnie had no idea what he was going to do about it. He wasn't exactly chomping at the bit to pay another visit to Sheriff Halliday. In fact, Halliday might be paying Lonnie a visit soon to talk about the deputy Lonnie had shot.

Lonnie jogged ahead now, trying to gain some ground on the four riders, who had disappeared around another right bend in the canyon floor. The canyon widened even more just ahead, and aspens and birches grew to both sides of the rocky center of the canyon down which a rushing, snowmelt river flowed every spring. Large, clay-colored boulders that had fallen from the steep ridge wall shone among the trees.

As the four riders appeared before Lonnie again, still riding away from him, he jerked with a start at what sounded like a large tree branch snapping. One of the four riders jerked back in his saddle.

The man's horse turned sharply to one side, giving a shrill whinny.

One of the other riders shouted, "What in the—?"

The shouted question was cut abruptly off as the rider who'd been shot fell backward down the side of his saddle to hit the canyon floor in a twisted pile.

Another gun popped among the trees and boulders so that now two rifles were cracking wildly. Lonnie jerked with each shot, as though the bullets were tearing into his own body.

Smoke puffed and gun flames shone in the trees and rocks to each side of the trail. The four riders screamed and bellowed curses as they were blown out of their saddles. They hit the ground and rolled as the rifles continued to crack and belch, gun smoke wafting in the tree branches.

Lonnie stood staring in wide-eyed, hang-jawed shock at the four men rolling on the ground, writhing in pain only to be shot again by the two ambushers. Amidst the belching of the gunfire, Lonnie could hear the quick rasping of the rifles' cocking levers. The four riderless horses galloped, whinnying shrilly, on up the canyon, the last one buck-kicking and stomping on its reins as it fled.

Lonnie stood frozen, as though his boots were stuck to the canyon floor. His eyes were riveted on the four men, all of whom now lay twisted and unmoving on the floor of the canyon, under a large, drifting gun smoke haze.

When he saw two men moving down out of the trees and boulders to each side of the trail, Lonnie swung around and took off running back the way he'd come, breathless fear overpowering his curiosity.

NINETEEN

LONNIE SCRAMBLED up the steep slope to where the General waited, staring at Lonnie through the gap between the boulders. Breathing hard, casting cautious glances back in the direction of the slaughter of the four riders, Lonnie slid his Winchester back into its sheath and swung up onto the buckskin's back.

"Let's split the wind, General!" Lonnie said, whipping his rein ends against the General's hip.

The stallion had heard the shooting. He did not hesitate to oblige his rider. The sure-footed buckskin dropped down the steep incline in two long strides then galloped the rest of the way to the canyon floor. He leaped the creek, bulled through some berry bramble, and swung toward the canyon's yawning mouth.

Lonnie cast another anxious glance behind him and was relieved to see that no one had followed him. He put his head down as the General galloped on through the gate and down the gradual slope through the pines, following the old horse trail along Ingrid Creek.

Lonnie gave the General his head. The horse knew where home was, and that was where Lonnie wanted to get as quickly as possible. He didn't care if he never saw the entrance to Skull Canyon again in this life. In fact, he didn't even want to think about the possibility of his cows straying into the canyon so that he'd have to track them down.

The way he felt about it now, if any of his beef-on-the-hoof strayed into Skull Canyon, they could find their own damn way out!

As the General galloped along the creek that wended its way down the gradual mountain slope, Lonnie kept seeing and hearing the killing of the four riders in his mind's eye. The shooting had sounded like firecrackers popping at a Fourth of July celebration, like the one they had with horse races every year in Arapaho Creek. Only, what Lonnie had just heard and seen had been no celebration.

It had been a slaughter.

Not that he really cared about the four men who'd almost done the same thing to him, but watching their violent demise had Lonnie feeling so shaken that his entire body quivered. He felt so sick to his stomach he thought he might throw up what little he had in his stomach.

Fortunately, it wasn't much.

He was too shaken to think about Skull Canyon right now, or about who might have gunned down the four riders or about who might have taken Cade McLory's body out of the cave.

Lonnie just wanted to get home to the peace, quiet, and safety of his and his mother's ranch headquarters. He just wanted to sit down to a good meal with his mother and then tend his barn chores and then hit the sack for a long, badly needed night's rest in his own bed.

He hoped little Jeremiah would let him sleep and not spend half the night crying for May Gentry's attention. If the latter, Lonnie would go out and sleep in the side shed off the barn, which Lonnie had outfitted with a cot and wool blankets. That's where he slept when Shannon Dupree spent the night with Lonnie's mother in the cabin.

A little over an hour after leaving the canyon, Lonnie rode northeast along the floor of the broad valley in which his ranch lay, at the base of a rise of forested, spruce-green peeks. Lonnie trotted the General through the wooden portal straddling the trail.

The Circle G brand had been proudly burned into the high, wooden crossbar by his father when Calvin Gentry had finished building the barn and cabin from the timber growing along the slopes and mountains flanking the ranch, back when Lonnie had been only two years old and they were all living in a small, temporary shack, waiting for the main cabin to be finished.

Lonnie rode into the finely churned dust of the yard fronting the large, low-slung, shake-roofed log cabin, heading for the stock trough below the windmill whose wooden blades churned lazily in the late-afternoon breeze. As he did, he frowned at the two strange horses standing in the corral attached to the barn's side shed.

One horse was a blue roan, the other a Steel Dust with a black mane and black head except for a long, crooked white stripe running down its snout. The mounts stood forward of the four horses from Lonnie's rough string, which he used mostly to give the General a break during busy spring and autumn roundups.

The two unfamiliar horses stood staring toward the cabin. Their tack straddled the top rail of the corral, to the left of the gate. Two Winchester carbines leaned against a corral post.

Deep lines cut across Lonnie's forehead in a frustrated scowl.

Visitors.

He hadn't figured on that. They rarely had visitors way out here. At least, not since Dupree had bit the dust. Why did they have to have visitors tonight of all nights?

As Lonnie dismounted the General by the windmill and slipped the horse's bit so he could drink freely, Lonnie surveyed the cabin. The west-angling light reflected off the sashed windows. Smoke from a supper fire plumed from the stovepipe.

As Lonnie hauled his gear over to the corral, his mother's muffled laughter rose from inside the cabin. A man's laughter followed. Lonnie glanced over his shoulder at the lodge, and grimaced.

"Oh, no," he said under his breath. "Please, no...not again."

May Gentry was understandably lonely, living way out here without a husband. But that loneliness had led to trouble in the past. Lonnie hoped that kind of trouble hadn't come calling again...

When Lonnie had rubbed the General down, grained, and stabled him, Lonnie crossed the yard to the cabin, slapping his hat against his thighs, causing trail dust to billow. He could hear two men talking with his mother inside the cabin.

He didn't care for the lighthearted tone, but, then again, he was glad there was no trouble.

Lonnie climbed the front porch and saw a pitcher of fresh water sitting on the second shelf of the washstand, beneath the top shelf that held the tin washbasin. A fresh towel hung from the nail beside the mirror hanging slightly askew from the cabin's front wall. Using the cake of lye soap provided, Lonnie scrubbed his face, neck and ears, and used a small bristle brush to scrub the dirt and grime out from beneath his fingernails.

As he washed, he could hear his mother chatting amiably with the men inside the cabin. Hearing the buoyant happiness and faint coquettishness in his mother's voice rubbed him the wrong way though he supposed it shouldn't. She had the right to enjoy the company of men.

The problem was, May Gentry was a nice-looking woman, but she wasn't very discriminating. She'd drawn more than a few rogue male eyes her way, including the eyes of the roguish outlaw, Shannon Dupree.

Lonnie toweled himself dry, combed his damp, close-cropped, light-brown hair in the mirror, ignoring the cowlick, and then flipped the latch of the front door. As the hinges squawked—he had to oil them one of these days—the conversation inside the cabin stopped. Two men sat at the halved-log dining table in the kitchen part of the cabin, straight out from the front door. One man sat at the table's far end, the other adjacent to him, his back to the front wall.

Lonnie's mother stood with her back to the range, rocking the tightly wrapped blanket of Lonnie's little half-brother, Jeremiah, in her arms. The baby was fussing, and May was flushed from the effort of trying to calm him.

"Oh, there you are, honey!" May Gentry intoned. "I've been worried about you, Lonnie. Won't you come in and meet our two supper guests—Bill Brocius and George Madsen? I've offered to let them stay in the bunkhouse out back for a few nights...if they don't mind a few spiders, that is, as the bunkhouse hasn't been used in a month of Sundays!" Beaming, Mrs. Gentry glanced at the two visitors, and said, "Bill, George—this is my son, Lonnie, Jeremiah's big brother."

Brocius was the one sitting at the table's far end. Madsen sat adjacent to Bill, facing Lonnie's mother. Lonnie shook Madsen's hand first and then reached across the far corner of the table to shake Bill Brocius's hand.

"Pleased to meet you," Lonnie said, unable to work up much enthusiasm for the introduction.

"The pleasure's all ours, boy," Madsen said. "Your mother told us a lot about you." He was fair-skinned with dark-brown hair, a dark-brown beard, and bulbous red nose. Brocius was a compact, clean-shaven man with a high forehead and thin, sandy hair combed so that a lock swept down over his right, pale blue eye. Both appeared in their thirties.

The men had washed recently. They had freshly scrubbed looks, and their hair, like Lonnie's, was damp and combed. Lonnie thought he smelled the sweet, cloying odor of pomade on one of them, or maybe both.

Brocius seemed to study Lonnie with a faintly sheepish, devious air, though he kept a smile on his small, thin-lipped mouth. Or maybe Lonnie just imagined the devious gaze, being suspicious of men who got along too well with his mother, especially when they hardly knew her.

Madsen was smiling, too, but he had dark, deep-set eyes that gave him a menacing look.

"Bill and George work for a mining company," May Gentry told Lonnie, rocking the sleeping Jeremiah in her arms. "They're...they're...what did you fellas call it?"

"Geologists," Brocius said. "We're scoutin' around, lookin' at rocks an' such, tryin' to find evidence of any gold or silver in the area."

"I see," Lonnie said, unable to feign interest.

His mind was still up at Skull Canyon, and all he wanted was to shove some vittles into his gullet and then get about his barn chores. He wasn't in the mood for socializing. He had livestock to tend before he could roll into the mattress sack, and he felt deeply fatigued—both mentally and physically.

He looked at his mother. "When's supper, Momma? I feel as empty as a dead man's boot."

"Lonnie Gentry, what a way to talk in front of our new friends!" May scolded. "Why, Bill and George are going to think I didn't raise you to talk proper!"

"Not at all, not all, May," Brocius assured her, chuckling as he sat back in his chair and began rolling a cigarette from the makings sack on the table before him. "I was raised in the country myself. I know what it's like."

Lonnie noticed that Madsen had his head turned to one side, scrutinizing Lonnie. He was trying to look subtle about it, but Lonnie could tell when he was being sized up. Madsen made Lonnie feel uncomfortable. But when he looked at Brocius, he realized Brocius made him feel uncomfortable, too.

"So, Momma," Lonnie said, peering around his mother and noting an iron pot steaming on the range, "when's supper?"

"As soon as the rolls are done, Mister Scowly Face. Look at you. You're in one of your moods again, Lonnie Gentry. Here—why don't you take little Jeremiah outside for a spell. Walk him from one end of the yard to the other while I visit some more with our supper guests. He's been so fussy since you've been gone." To her guests, she said, "Lonnie's so much better at getting the baby settled down—isn't that peculiar?"

To Lonnie again: "By the time you get back, I imagine the rolls will be done, and we can dish up...but only after you've said grace, Mister Scowls. So while you're out there with your little brother, you think up a nice, sweet table prayer and show these gentlemen that you have better language than that you use around the cattle!"

May Gentry had handed over the tightly wrapped bundle of little Jeremiah to Lonnie. The baby's little, red, pinched-up face was turning redder now as the child started to fuss harder.

Lonnie silently cursed as he took the baby in his arms.

He walked outside, silently, bitterly fuming. He kicked a rock and then he turned toward the cabin to see Madsen watching him from the window right of the door. Madsen had that same, dark, speculative look as before.

What did that look mean?

"One thing after another," Lonnie said, as he started walking his squawking brother around the yard, hearing his mother's and her visitors' laughter rise again from inside the cabin. "When will it ever end?"

TWENTY

JEREMIAH DIDN'T SQUAWK LONG after he and Lonnie started walking out toward the ranch portal. Lonnie often took care of the baby, only three months old, when his mother was in one of her nervous states and needed a few minutes alone or was down with the "vapors".

Lonnie had found he'd had a calming effect on the baby. He wasn't sure why, but when Lonnie held Jeremiah, the baby usually stopped crying within a minute or two. Then Jeremiah would either drift to sleep or lie staring up at his big brother as though in fascination, sort of gurgling and sighing contentedly deep in his little chest.

Lonnie walked toward the ranch portal, jostling the baby gently. Though he'd never admitted as much to his mother, and maybe not even to himself, he liked having the kid around. When it had been just Lonnie and May, they'd seemed less like a family than they did now.

The problem was that when staring into the baby's deep-blue eyes, Lonnie often saw the eyes of Shannon Dupree staring back at him. The baby didn't look anything like Dupree now, but Jeremiah would likely take on some of his father's aspects when he grew older.

Lonnie often wondered how he himself would feel about that, reminded constantly that Jeremiah was the son of a man whom Lonnie, his brother, had killed. He also wondered how Jeremiah would feel about that, when he eventually was told. Would he hold the killing of his father against Lonnie?

Lonnie didn't feel guilty about having killed Shannon Dupree. Dupree had been going to kill Lonnie and Casey. Besides, if there was ever a man who needed killing, that man was Dupree. No, Lonnie didn't feel guilty about killing him.

He felt guilty about having killed.

Humming gently as he rocked his brother in his arms, Lonnie turned away from the ranch portal and started back toward the cabin. He hoped his mother had done enough chinning with her supper guests, because Lonnie was damn hungry.

He'd hoped to be able to talk to May alone this evening, but that didn't look like it was going to happen. Judging by the air of revelry inside the cabin, he'd likely turn in long before his mother and Brocius and Madsen did. He'd wanted to tell his mother about all that had happened to him during the past twenty-four hours, to get it off his chest.

But, then again, maybe it was just as well May didn't know. She was not a strong woman. Lonnie had learned that the hard way. If she knew about the men who'd tried to run down and kill her son, and about Cade McLory and the four riders whom Lonnie had seen shot off their horses—who knew what she'd do?

Merely reflecting on it nearly had Lonnie panicking and wanting to run far, far away from here. The only problem was, there was nowhere to go.

He'd just started wondering about the two strangers in his house, when May Gentry opened the cabin door and called him to supper. Lonnie went in, handed the baby over to his mother, who took him into her bedroom to feed him, and then sat down at the opposite end of the table from Bill Brocius.

May had told them to get started, so Lonnie dug into the rabbit stew and fresh bread, grateful that May had apparently forgotten about grace. Brocius and Madsen had apparently forgotten about it, too. Lonnie doubted that either man was in the habit of saying table prayers. They both had a hard, trail-savvy look about them.

If they were really working as geologists for a mining company, he was a monkey's uncle.

He didn't know who they really were or what they were doing here, but he didn't like them. He'd seen too many strangers in the Never Summers over the past two days. And too many of those strangers had tried to kill him. Not only that, but he didn't like the way these two strangers looked at his mother.

Lonnie and his mother's guests ate in silence for a time, all three too involved in padding their bellies to waste time with conversation. That was fine with Lonnie. He had nothing to say to these men—at least, nothing he could say without getting in trouble with his mother.

Then Brocius gave a snort as he set his fork down on his nearly empty plate, brushed a fist across his nose, and split a roll in two. He glanced at Madsen and then turned to Lonnie: "So, sport, you've lived here all your life, I reckon."

Lonnie was buttering his own roll. "That's right."

"You probably know every nook and cranny of these mountains, strappin' lad like yourself."

Lonnie hiked a shoulder as he set his knife down and dipped his roll into the remaining stew on his plate. He bit into the succulent, gravy-soaked, buttery bread.

Madsen looked over his coffee cup at Lonnie. "You probably know a lot of the folks who live in these mountains, too."

Again, Lonnie only shrugged as he continued to shovel stew into his mouth while swabbing the gravy off his plate with his roll. He could tell by their fishing that these men wanted something from him. Well, let them want. Let them fish. Through their questions, Lonnie might learn something about *them*.

"You know anythin' about a stolen army payroll shipment that might have been buried up in these mountains, several years back?" asked Brocius.

Lonnie looked at Brocius who held his steady, penetrating gaze on him. Now that the man had mentioned it, Lonnie had heard about such a shipment.

Lonnie had dismissed the story about the stolen army payroll as just another legend. There were as many legends in these mountains as there were people who lived and *had* lived in and around the Never Summers.

When Lonnie didn't say anything but only returned Brocius's curious gaze, Madsen leaned forward and, keeping his voice down as though to make sure no one else overheard the conversation, said, "You have heard about it, haven't you, boy? Tell us what you know."

Lonnie knew little. But he enjoyed the power he suddenly found himself holding over these two grown-up strangers. "What do you wanna know about it?"

"Has anyone ever found it?" Brocius asked.

Again, Lonnie merely shrugged.

Brocius glanced at Madsen, gave a baleful grin, and returned his cunning gaze to Lonnie. "Come on, kid. Tell us what you know."

"First, tell me what you know about it," Lonnie said, casually helping himself to more stew.

TWENTY-ONE

BROCIUS GAVE A DRY CHUCKLE.

Madsen stared at Lonnie with silent menace.

Lonnie ate his stew, trying not to look at Madsen. Both these men made him nervous, but Madsen more than Brocius. He didn't want either one to see how he felt, however.

"What we know," Brocius said, "was that a strongbox containin' an army payroll was stolen down in Arizona about seventeen years ago. The gang that stole it was goin' to powder the trail to Mexico, but their route was cut off by a contingent of cavalry out of Fort Bowie. So the gang swung north instead.

"They evaded the cavalry, but telegraphs were sent to local lawmen and some deputy US marshals in New Mexico, and these men formed a posse. They chased the gang up into Colorado. Supposedly, they were headin' for the Hole in the Wall in Wyomin'. They didn't make it.

"Their gang was whittled down by the posse as they headed north, until only two men was left. Both of those men were wounded, one badly. He and the other man made it into the Never Summers, where, as the story goes, they hid the strongbox. Then one of the men died. The sole survivor left the Never Summers to get medical attention for himself and was captured by the posse that was still on the scout for him."

Brocius picked up the blue-speckled coffeepot sitting on the table and refilled his stone mug. As he set the pot back down, he said through the steam wafting up from his cup, "That sole survivin' thief never did tell the law where he and the other man had hid the strongbox. But it's long been believed that they hid it somewhere in the Never Summers. Now, some are sayin' it must be in or somewhere around Skull Canyon."

Lonnie had known that part of the story was coming since Brocius had been about halfway through his tale. Still, he literally almost fell off his chair. His shock must have shown in his features, because Madsen, who'd been staring at him with those flat, deep-set brown eyes gave a wry snort.

"Is that where it is, boy?"

Lonnie composed himself, cleared his throat. "Couldn't tell ya."

Brocius dipped his chin and pinned Lonnie with a direct, threatening look. "Can't? Or won't?"

"Can't," Lonnie said quickly, realizing the trouble he was in.

These men were after what all those other men including probably Cade McLory had been after—stolen army loot! Which means that they were likely as kill-crazy desperate as all the others. Again, in his mind's eye, Lonnie watched the four riders get shot out of their saddles.

"Can't," Lonnie repeated with more urgency this time. "I heard some time back about the loot maybe bein' cached somewhere in the Never Summers. But I never knew where. That right there is everythin' I know on the subject."

It was as though Madsen hadn't heard what Lonnie had just said. "Has someone found it? Or is it still out there somewhere?"

Brocius said, "We don't want to waste our time on a wild-goose chase."

"I have no idea," Lonnie said.

Madsen narrowed a suspicious eye at him. "You do know—don't you, boy? You're a lone wolf, wily as a coyote. Most boys like you got their ears to the ground, so to speak. They move around. They're savvy as Apaches. That's you—ain't it, kid? You know more about that loot than you're lettin' on."

"Hell, no!"

"Lonnie Gentry, did I just hear you cuss in front of our guests?"

May Gentry had just stepped out of her bedroom which opened off the parlor part of the cabin. As she quietly latched the bedroom door so as not to awaken little Jeremiah, she came toward the kitchen, frowning.

"Uh...sorry, Momma," Lonnie said. "I don't know what happened. I reckon it just slipped out."

"Oh, we don't mind," Madsen said, leaning over to tussle Lonnie's hair. "He's a green one, this younker. That's all right—the best colts got some pitch in 'em."

May Gentry refilled Madsen's coffee cup, saying, "Lonnie's problem is that he has an ornery streak. Gets a little too full of himself from time to time. I reckon that's my fault. I'm too soft on him." She shook her head and filled her own cup. "A boy needs a man's touch. Lonnie hasn't had that since his father died... God rest his soul."

May Gentry sighed as she sat down near Brocius and across from Madsen. Holding her steaming cup in her hands, she regarded Lonnie with sadness, shaking her head.

Lonnie pushed his plate away and rose from the table. Anger burned in him, but he tried to keep it on a leash. "Thanks for supper, Momma," he muttered, wiping his mouth with his napkin. "I'd best get to my night chores and turn in."

Lonnie felt all eyes on him as he grabbed his hat off a wall peg, opened the door, and went out. He stood at the top of the porch steps, a mix of emotions roiling within him—fear, confusion, and anger. He had to admit that he was also curious about the stolen army payroll loot.

He'd hoped he'd seen his first and last cache of stolen money when he and Casey had delivered the Golden bank loot to the deputy US marshal in Camp Collins.

He'd been wrong.

And now he couldn't help wondering how much loot there was in that army strongbox, and if the loot really was hidden somewhere in Skull Canyon. If so, judging by the number of men looking for it, it hadn't been found.

It must be a sizeable amount to have attracted so many treasure hunters.

As Lonnie's eyes scanned the forested western ridges standing tall and dark before him, the very last of the setting sun's rays gilding the tops of the highest pines and firs, he entertained a brief fantasy of finding that cache himself. He wouldn't take it, because it didn't belong to him. But he'd bet aces against navy beans that after all these years the army was offering a sizeable reward for the return of that strongbox.

He fantasized about cashing that reward note and of riding a long, long ways away from here.

Of leaving this place of so much misery and heartache behind him.

Lonnie heard his mother and Brocius and Madsen talking and laughing in the cabin behind him. He moved down off the porch steps and headed for the barn.

TWENTY-TWO

AS THE LAST light bled out of the sky and the cool mountain night descended on the valley, Lonnie bedded down in the lean-to side shed off the barn.

He was surprised to hear the laughing and obviously pie-eyed Brocius and Madsen leave the cabin only about an hour or so later. Either they'd brought a bottle or Lonnie's mother had broken out the brandy she occasionally uncorked when she couldn't sleep.

Lonnie had thought that they and May, who hadn't had any visitors except for the occasional traveling tinker or drummer in a month of Sundays, would sit up half the night. He'd also been worried one of the men might not leave the cabin till morning.

Lonnie was pleasantly surprised.

Still, he couldn't sleep. Too much was racing through his mind. He kept seeing those blindly staring eyes of Cade McLory as well as the four riders being shot out of their saddles while guns smoked and sparked in the surrounding trees and boulders.

He could hear the screams of those men as they'd died.

Also, he couldn't help imagining digging up that stolen loot himself. Even if there was only a small reward on that payroll cache, it would likely be enough money to give a young man a decent start somewhere he'd have half a chance.

Lonnie had the cold, brittle feeling that he'd run out of chances here in the Never Summers.

Finally, sick of all the unwanted thoughts and images assaulting him, he threw his covers back, drew on his boots and his hat, and left the side shed clad in his long handles and holding a blanket over his shoulders. He found the night's chill pleasantly uncomfortable, distracting him from the barrage of unwanted worries. He sat on a hay rake parked near the corral's front corner and studied the stars that were dimmed by the rising moon.

After a while, a sound drew his attention toward the cabin.

A shadow moved out around the cabin's left-front corner. The shadow slid up to the front of the porch. It mounted the porch, and then Lonnie could hear the light taps of boots on the porch's wooden floorboards.

A light was turned up inside the cabin, causing the kitchen window right of the front door to glow wanly through the gingham curtains. The door opened, and the man-shaped shadow, topped with a Stetson, stooped as he passed through the lit opening.

The door click closed. The light in the window died.

Lonnie wondered which one it was—Madsen or Brocius.

He wasn't surprised that his mother was entertaining one of the men. In fact, it plowed through all his worries to make him feel dull and numb. That was a pleasant feeling after the sharp pangs of anxiety that had been assaulting him only moments ago.

Even if the reward was only a hundred dollars, a hundred dollars would take him far. He could maybe get a job in Denver, say, swamping out saloons or livery barns. He could possibly land a cowboying job if he could convince a ranch owner that he had all the skills, and sometimes more, of cowpunchers twice his age, though that might be a feat.

Few folks thought a boy his age was good for much of anything than lying to him and shooting at him, and—he was thinking of Casey now—of betraying him.

Lonnie's eyelids grew heavy. He felt as withered as an old, dried-up cornstalk. He could probably sleep now.

He went back into the side shed, rolled into his blankets, causing the cot to squawk beneath him. He punched his pillow, laid his head back on it, took a deep breath, and fell asleep...until a sound woke him.

He lifted his head, blinking groggily. He'd been in a deep sleep. Something glinted in the moonlight angling through the side shed windows, in the air before his head. There was a ratcheting sound that he instantly recognized as a gun hammer being cocked.

Then he saw a figure take foggy shape in the moonlight before him.

His heart hiccupped, and he was about to reach for his rifle when the cold, round maw of the revolver was pressed up taut against his forehead.

"One move, and I'll drill you, kid."

Madsen's voice.

Lonnie froze. He squeezed his eyes closed, waiting for the bullet.

"What...what do you want?"

"Just to finish up the conversation from earlier."

"I told you," Lonnie said, his heart racing now, "I don't know anythin' about that payroll."

"I got a feelin' you do."

"That's just 'cause I was actin' cocky at first. I tend to do that. Like Ma says, I tend to get full of myself. But...please believe me...all I ever heard about that loot was that it might have been buried in the Never Summers somewhere. That's it. If it's in Skull Canyon, it's news to me."

Madsen didn't say anything for nearly a minute. He kept the revolver pressed up close to Lonnie's head. It was cold and hard and unforgiving, and Lonnie vaguely wondered if he'd feel the bullet before it blew his brains out, or if he wouldn't feel anything but just pass into Heaven or Hell or wherever it was he was headed.

The gun clicked quietly as Madsen depressed the hammer, let it fall benignly against the firing pin. He pulled the barrel away from Lonnie's head. Lonnie drew a deep, relieved breath and opened his eyes.

Madsen let the gun fall straight down against his right side.

"Kid," he said, "I can't tell if you're really, really smart or really, really stupid."

Lonnie cleared his dry throat. "That makes two of us."

Madsen holstered the big revolver and then drew up the ladderback chair from the small, plankboard eating table near the sheet-iron stove. He slacked into the chair with a weary sigh, doffed his hat, and leaned forward, turning the hat in his hands. He was a dark, man-shaped silhouette against the two moonlit windows behind him. His round, bearded face with deep-set eyes now filled with shadows looked especially sinister in the shadowy moonlight.

Lonnie was glad the man had holstered the pistol, but he wouldn't rest until Madsen had left. Again, Madsen didn't say anything for a time, likely knowing that his silence was causing Lonnie a great deal of anxiety, and likely enjoying it.

"We're Pinkerton agents."

Lonnie blinked, studied the man in the darkness. "What's that?"

"Me an' Brocius," Madsen said. "We're Pinkerton detectives."

TWENTY-THREE

AGAIN, Lonnie blinked at the menacing visage of Madsen sitting before him. "I don't understand."

"You ever hear of the Pinkerton Detective Agency?"

"Yeah."

Lonnie had never been to school, for the nearest school was too far away even if he hadn't been too busy at the ranch to attend. But he'd been bound and determined to not have to "make his mark" with an X every time he needed to sign his name, like so many of the old-timers did.

To that end, he'd acquired a rudimentary, mostly self-taught knowledge of reading and writing. When he rode to town every couple of months for supplies, he scrounged around in trash heaps and privies for newspapers, usually returning to the ranch with a few local papers as well as several issues of the *Rocky Mountain News* out of Denver.

During his reading, he'd stumbled upon stories about the famous Pinkerton Agency founded by Allan Pinkerton and based in Chicago.

But he'd certainly never figured on meeting two detectives from that illustrious company. Especially not out here, at his own ranch...

Madsen said, "The army hired the Pinkertons to find the stolen loot. That's what me an' Brocius are doin' here. The Pinkertons have been lookin' for that strongbox ever since it was stolen, but the detectives workin' the case—there've been several over the years—always came up cold. The company sort of put the case on the back burner...until the outlaw who rode with the gang who stole the gold in the first place broke out of prison three or four weeks ago."

Lonnie remembered the name that Deputy Marshal Appleyard had mentioned. "Crawford Kinch?"

Even in the darkness, Lonnie saw a puzzled frown slice across Madsen's forehead. "How did you...?"

"Like Brocius said, I'm savvy."

"That's the name, all right. You seen him, kid?"

"Nope. And I reckon I don't want to, neither. Or so I've been told."

"That would be right." Madsen paused, sighed, and then leaned a little farther forward. "Look, I've laid my cards on the table. It's time for you to tell me everythin' you know about that loot."

"I've already done that, Mister Madsen." Anger flared in Lonnie suddenly, and he sat up a little in bed. "Do the famous Pinkertons make a habit of holdin' cocked guns to boys' heads?"

"Not officially," Madsen said, sitting back in his chair. "But we do whatever's necessary to get the job done. Pull your horns in, kid. That arguably nasty little tactic worked in your favor."

"How so?"

"I believe that you don't know where the loot is."

"Why didn't you just tell us who you were in the first place?"

"Folks aren't as willin' to talk to detectives as they are, say, geologists. And there's men out lookin' for that gold who would kill others to keep them from findin' it first."

Don't I know! Lonnie wanted to say but didn't.

"I got a proposition for you."

"Look, I can read and write *a little,* but could you chew that up a little finer and spit it out slower? What's a 'proposition'?"

"I got an offer for you. You show me an' Brocius the way to Skull Canyon, and we'll pay you five dollars."

Lonnie shook his head. "I don't want nothin' more to do with that canyon."

"Nothin' more? What do you mean?"

"Nothin'."

"All right, ten dollars."

Lonnie considered it. Ten dollars was a lot of money. "Forget it. I wouldn't do it for twice that much. I don't like the way you came in here, lyin' to me and my ma about who you are. I don't like Brocius bein' in our cabin right now. I don't like havin' a gun pressed to my head."

Madsen quirked a wry, menacing half-smile. "I could do it again."

Lonnie grabbed his rifle from where it leaned against the wall behind him. He cocked the Winchester, aimed it at Madsen's chest. "You've worn out your welcome, Mister Madsen. You'd best leave."

Madsen stared at Lonnie, his shoulders rising and falling slowly as he breathed. "All right, all right. You win, sonny."

Madsen walked to the door then glanced over his shoulder at Lonnie. "For now, you win. You an' me—we'll be talkin' about this later."

"I'll be lookin' forward to it."

Chuckling, Madsen went out.

Still holding the Winchester, Lonnie went to the door, opened it, and watched Madsen retreating in the moonlight, his footsteps sounding crisp and clear in the heavy night silence but dwindling quickly.

Lonnie closed the door and slipped the nail through its hasp, locking the door. He leaned his rifle against the wall and lay back down on the cot with a heavy, weary sigh...only to be awakened again by hoof thuds outside the barn.

Lonnie lifted his head with a frustrated sigh. Fatigue hung heavy on him. He didn't know how long he'd slept.

What now?

He grabbed his rifle, stepped into his boots, and donned his hat. He cracked the door and poked his head out. A horse and rider had just trotted past the barn to stop before the corral to his left. It was still dark, but he recognized the horse as well as the blonde hair tumbling down from the rider's gray felt hat to spill across slender shoulders clad in a short leather jacket.

"Casey?"

Lonnie had kept his voice down. Now as the girl swung down from her saddle, she jerked around with a start.

"Lonnie?" she said, also speaking softly. "You startled me! What're you doin' out here?"

He wasn't too bothered about Casey seeing him in his long handles. She'd seen him in his long handles before, when they were making their run over the mountains together. Besides, she'd seen him in only a blanket just yesterday at the line shack.

"Long story." Lonnie frowned. He still felt more than a little bitter. His heart was still broken though he had even more pressing matters on his mind now. "What're *you* doin' out here?"

Holding the reins of her chestnut mare, Casey walked over to him, glanced at the cabin, as though making sure they were alone, and said, "Lonnie, you're in trouble. Big trouble!" Her breath frosted in the air around Casey's head.

"If you rode all the way out here just to tell me that, you wasted a trip."

"Sheriff Halliday is gettin' a warrant for your arrest."

"Huh? *What?* Because I shot Walleye?"

"What do you *think?* You can't go around shootin' sheriff's deputies without it eventually comin' back to bite you, Lonnie!"

"Walleye shot first! Just like last time with Willie, I was only tryin' to protect myself."

"Walleye and Bohannon said you ambushed them."

Lonnie shook his head. He looked around for a rock and kicked it. "I reckon that doesn't surprise me."

"The sheriff and Bohannon are ridin' out here to arrest you later this mornin', Lonnie. I heard them talkin' out front of the courthouse yesterday evenin'."

Lonnie laced his hands behind his head and looked toward town, as though he might see the two county lawmen riding toward him out of the early-morning darkness. "Well, that tears it!"

Frustration bit him hard. As he'd figured he would, he found himself between a rock and a hard place.

Casey said, "What're you goin' to do?"

"How the hell should I know?"

"Here's what I think you should do, Lonnie. I think you should save the sheriff a trip."

Lonnie swung around in shock. *"What?"*

"It's the only way to take some of the bite out of what's about to happen. Maybe if you ride to town and tell Halliday what you just told me, he'll believe you. At least the judge might be lenient."

Lonnie cocked his head a little and narrowed a suspicious eye at her. "Do *you* believe me, Casey?"

She stared at him for a long moment. Then she moved toward him and stopped just inches away from him, gazing at him levelly. "I know you wouldn't ambush anybody, Lonnie. But I also know you're prone to trouble."

"Prone to trouble, huh?"

"Don't act like it's such a surprise."

Lonnie could give only a caustic chuckle at that.

"Will you please do as I say? Ride to town and try to defuse the situation before it explodes. Tell Halliday what happened. He knows Walleye's own penchant for trouble. He'll probably believe you."

Lonnie swung around again. This time he stared toward the high western peaks standing dark against the fading stars. False dawn was starting. Birds were starting to sing.

Slowly, Lonnie shook his head. "I can't do it, Casey. Last time I was hauled into jail, I was dragged out into the mountains and nearly killed. You remember. Heck, you were the one who saved my bacon."

"Lonnie, I don't see what choice you have."

"I do. You'd best get on back to town."

Lonnie swung around and started back into the barn.

"Not so fast, bucko!" Casey grabbed his arm and turned him back around. "What have you got on your devious mind, Lonnie Gentry?"

"*Devious?* Now, ain't that the pot callin' the kettle black!"

Lonnie jerked his arm loose of the girl's grip and went on into the side shed. Casey stomped in behind him. "I know you're mad at me, Lonnie, but I can't help that. Whatever you might think of me, I still...I still care about you. I don't want you to do anything you're goin' to be sorry for later on."

"Thanks for your concern," Lonnie said as he kicked out of his boots and reached for his pants.

Casey walked to the table and lit the hurricane lamp, turning up the wick and causing shadows to scuttle like rats into the corners. "What're you goin' to do?"

"I rode to town earlier to tell Halliday about a dead man in Skull Canyon. He and the deputies think I lied. They think I sent 'em on a wild-goose chase to make fools of 'em. I reckon they think I'm so bored up here, with nothin' else to do, that I need a laugh bad enough to go to all that trouble."

Lonnie chuffed and shook his head in exasperation. "Maybe *they're* bored, but *I* sure ain't!"

"Lonnie, please don't," Casey urged. "Please ride back to town with me."

Lonnie was stepping into his denims, moving fast and shaking his head. "I need to ride up there and see if I can't find poor McLory. If the sheriff realizes I wasn't lyin' about him bein' in the canyon, maybe he'll realize I'm not lyin' about Walleye and Bohannon scuttlin' like Apaches up to the line shack in the middle of the dang night!"

"Oh, Lonnie." Casey turned around and opened the door.

"Yeah, you get on back to town," Lonnie said.

"I'm not goin' back to town," Casey said, glancing back at him. "I'm goin' with you. Maybe...just maybe...I can keep you from gettin' yourself killed!"

TWENTY-FOUR

LONNIE QUICKLY SADDLED the General and led him out of the barn. As he did, Casey led Miss Abigail up from where she'd been watering the mare at the windmill.

Lonnie glanced at the cabin and felt an urgent need to leave the yard before his mother awakened. Lonnie knew he should tell her where he was going, but she'd only try to stop him. She wouldn't be able to understand what was happening to her son. She'd only think he was up to no good, like everyone else in this neck of the Never Summers.

If he rode out now, May Gentry would think he'd headed back to their summer pastures higher in the mountains. That was just as well. She had her hands full with her overnight "guest" and little Jeremiah.

Lonnie turned to Casey. She was studying him as though reading his mind. She looked a little sad.

Lonnie swung up onto the General's back and, keeping his voice low, said, "You'd best not follow me, Casey. It's too dangerous. You don't know the half of what's been goin' on."

Casey stepped into her saddle and neck-reined the mare around. "Tell me," she said, touching spurs to Miss Abigail's flanks, heading west.

Lonnie rode after her. When they'd passed beneath the ranch portal and were a good distance from the cabin, heading for the main trail, Lonnie rode up beside Casey and started to tell her about the past forty-eight hours.

By the time he was finished filling her in on all that had happened, they were rising through the pine forest high above the ranch, and the big, lemon sun was on the rise behind them, heating the air and stirring the tang of pine resin. Lonnie shrugged out of his denim jacket and wrapped it over his blanket roll.

Riding ahead of Casey, leading the way, Lonnie glanced back over his shoulder at her. She stared straight past him, her eyes wide beneath the brim of her hat, her cheeks pale.

"You all right, Casey?"

Dully, as though she'd suffered a blow to the head, Casey turned to him, but it took her several seconds to find her tongue. "My god, Lonnie —all that happened over *the past two days?*"

"Sure as tootin'."

Lonnie swung the General back to face Casey, who halted Miss Abigail. "*Now* are you ready to head back to Arapaho Creek?" Lonnie asked her.

Casey glanced around cautiously, looking a tad frightened. Then she stared past Lonnie, toward the high ridge of craggy peaks where Skull Canyon lay. Her cheeks turned even a little whiter.

"You wouldn't be chicken," Lonnie assured her. "You'd be smart. I oughta stay away, too, but I don't see as I have many options other than to try to find McLory and haul him to Arapaho Creek."

Casey sighed. "Well, you're gonna need help, Lonnie. If you do find him"—she gave a little shudder of revulsion as she no doubt imagined hefting the body of a dead man onto a horse—"you're gonna need help gettin' him back to town."

"I can find another way," Lonnie said. "I can rig a travois. It'll just take me a little time, that's all."

Casey appeared to consider this. Lonnie thought she was likely imagining the four riders getting shot out of their saddles, as he himself couldn't help replaying inside his head. Finally, Casey shook her hair back behind her shoulders and gigged Miss Abigail up and around Lonnie. "Someone's gotta save you from yourself. Looks like I drew the short straw!"

"What about the mercantile?" Lonnie called after her.

Casey glanced behind as she and the mare trotted up the trail. "Since I pulled double duty for him, Mister Hendrickson gave me the day off. Come on, Lonnie. What is it you always say? We're burnin' daylight!"

Lonnie watched her wavy hair bounce across her slender back as she rode up into the shade of the pines. The sunlight flashed in those blonde tresses like nuggets of pure gold. He didn't want her here, because he knew how dangerous it was.

On the other hand, he wanted her here, close by his side, so badly that he could feel the need in every fiber.

"All right," he said, concealing his great happiness as he spurred the General ahead, "but don't blame me if we get into the same sort of trouble we got into a year ago!"

"Ridin' with you, Lonnie Gentry, there's *always* goin' to be trouble!" Casey yelled behind her.

Lonnie couldn't help snickering a little at that as he galloped the General up the mountain.

———

"THAT'S IT," Lonnie said later, when they'd reached the canyon. "That's the cave where I left McLory."

Lonnie scrambled up the steep slope behind the boulders. When he'd reached the small shelf fronting the egg-shaped cavern, he threw his hand out for Casey making her way up the slope behind him. Casey took Lonnie's hand, and he gave her a tug.

Together, they crouched to stare into the cavern. Direct sunlight reached about five feet beyond the opening, but there was enough indirect light that they could see all the way to the stone wall at the back.

"See—no sign of him," Lonnie said.

"No, there sure isn't." Casey turned to Lonnie. "You sure this was the cave?"

"It's the only cave around."

"You built a fire in there?"

"Yep. Whoever took McLory, wiped the cave clear of all the fire ash, too."

Casey pondered this as she stared into the cave. "So...whoever took McLory out of the cave wanted to make sure that whoever you told about him wouldn't find a lick of any sign of either of you. So they wouldn't believe you about McLory."

"That's about the size of it."

Casey turned to Lonnie. "Why?"

"The only way I can figure it is they didn't want the law snoopin' around and possibly findin' out that they—whoever killed McLory—was out here lookin' for the stolen army payroll. Whoever 'they' are—they probably killed those four riders I told you about, too. And likely hid their bodies. They don't want the law sniffin' around."

"Who could 'they' be?"

"Search me. But they're most likely wanted. That's why they didn't want the law around. Or *were* wanted, at least—if it was one of the four men I saw shot off their horses who shot McLory. I got a hunch there's a couple of different groups searchin' for that gold. One might even be led up by Crawford Kinch himself."

Casey straightened and looked around. "Let's find McLory and get out of here, Lonnie. It isn't safe here."

"You can say that again." Lonnie looked around, too, scouring the terrain around the cave with his eyes. "What would they have done with him?"

"Findin' a dead man around here is goin' to be like lookin' for a needle in a haystack. There's all *kinds* of places they could have hid him, Lonnie." Casey looked at him. "I'm startin' to think this idea of yours is even crazier than I thought it was *before* we reached the canyon. I think we oughta go back to town."

"Yeah, I'll go back to town so Halliday can arrest me, and Walleye can shoot me tryin' to escape." Lonnie chuckled dryly. "No, thanks. I'll take my chances lookin' for McLory."

Lonnie looked around again. "I'm thinkin' they wouldn't have taken him far. No one wants to be haulin' a dead man around for longer than is absolutely necessary. They might have dragged him somewhere nearby and tossed some brush or rocks on him."

Lonnie continued to move on along the base of the ridge, behind the boulders shielding him from the canyon floor.

"You're wastin' your time, Lonnie."

"Maybe so, but at least I still *have* time. In town, I'd be livin' on borrowed ti—*oh, crap!*"

"Lonnie!" Casey screamed.

Lonnie had tripped over a boot-sized rock. Trying to maintain his balance, he'd stepped onto a downward slope covered with talus. That foot slid out from under him. Lonnie hit the ground on his belly and rolled down the slope. It was so steep that there was nothing he could do to stop or even ease his descent.

Fortunately, the slope was only about a twenty-foot drop. There was a boulder at the base of it. Lonnie slammed against the base of the boulder with a dull *smack!*

He grunted.

He found himself lying belly down against the boulder's base, in a small area that rainwater had likely eroded away to form a dip. When Lonnie turned over on his back, groaning at the pain in his limbs and head, he snapped his eyes wide, and gasped.

A pale hand hovered over his face, the dusty fingers curled toward the palm.

"Lonnie!" Casey yelled from atop the slope. "Are you alright?"

Lonnie stared in horror at the stiff hand. Then he eased himself out from under it, gazing at the limb in shock.

"Yeah," Lonnie said dully. "Yeah, I'm all right. But I, uh...I think I found McLory!"

TWENTY-FIVE

WINCING, Lonnie gained his feet and stared down at the arm he'd partially uncovered when he'd rolled up against and sort of under the boulder, where erosion had dug out a crevice beneath it.

Apparently, whoever had found McLory in the cave had shoved him into the crevice and kicked slide rock down on top of him, covering the body. Lonnie saw bits of ash and charred wood, as well. This is also where they'd deposited the remains of the fire.

Casey dropped to her butt and slid down the steep slope behind Lonnie. When she gained the bottom, she crumpled her face as she pointed. "Is...that...what...I think it is?"

"McLory's hand."

"Oh, my gosh."

Lonnie looked at her. "You squeamish?"

Casey nodded. "When it comes to baitin' my own fishhook, no. When it comes to handlin' dead men, yes."

"I'm gonna need help gettin' him out of here, Casey."

Still staring down at the uncovered hand and part of an arm, Casey flopped her hands against her thighs and said blandly, "Well, that's what I came here for."

Reluctantly, Lonnie dropped to his knees and began carefully removing debris from over McLory's body. His heart fluttered as he worked. He felt his innards recoil as he revealed more and more of the dead young man's body. Finally, he removed the last rock and chunk of charred firewood from over the young man's pale, dusty face.

Dust clung to McLory's hair. It was like a thin cap pulled tightly over his head.

Casey removed more debris from over McLory's legs.

She and Lonnie sat back on their heels, regarding the body now fully uncovered before them, a dark stain of blood showing through the remaining dirt and sand.

"Well, at least you weren't hallucinatin', Lonnie," Casey said. "I was beginnin' to wonder."

"Yeah, so was I."

"How're we gonna get him out of that crevice? He looks pretty snug in there."

"Good question."

Lonnie leaned forward and, making a face as he put his hands on Cade McLory's stiff, lifeless body, he tried to pry the man out of the crevice. The body moved a little but didn't budge from the crevice.

"Good question," Lonnie repeated, sitting back on his heels once more.

"Maybe if we dig the dirt out from under him," Casey said.

"Might as well give it a try."

Lonnie and Casey used their gloved hands to scoop the coarse red dirt and gravel out from under McLory. When they'd dug a trench about ten inches wide and roughly as long as McLory himself, Casey tugged on the dead man's boots while Lonnie hunkered low beneath the boulder, hooking an arm around the man's neck, and tugged on his upper body.

After much straining and grunting and groaning, they managed to pry McLory up to the edge of the trench.

Now, he was at least free of the crevice beneath the boulder. But they still had to find a way to get him down off this steep slope and onto the General's back.

Lonnie and Casey discussed it. Then Lonnie scrambled along the shoulder of the slope to where the stallion waited patiently with Miss Abigail. Lonnie removed his lariat from where it hung coiled over his saddle horn, dallied one end around the horn and the other end around Cade McLory's ankles.

As he worked, Casey said, "This is sure some way to treat a dead man."

"I know," Lonnie said, sheepish. "But I figure since he's dead, he doesn't know what's happenin' to him. And me doin' this will help me not end up in his same condition. We sort of got to know each other the other night. I got a feelin' he wouldn't mind helpin' me out."

"He doesn't look very old," Casey remarked, staring pensively down at McLory's waxen, dusty features. "Maybe only a couple of years older than me. Now he's dead when he had a whole long life ahead of him not all that long ago."

"Ain't that the way it goes, though," Lonnie said, straightening. He looked down at Casey kneeling beside McLory. "Will you help guide him around the boulder when I start leadin' the General down the slope?"

Casey nodded.

Lonnie scrambled back over to the General. He turned the buckskin around and started leading him downslope. As he did, the rope drew taut. McLory's body lurched straight out away from the boulder, feet first. It sort of fishtailed around another, smaller boulder around which Lonnie had snaked the rope.

When it got hung up on the boulder and Casey couldn't free the body herself, Lonnie went over and helped her. Once free of the smaller boulder, Casey gave a clipped scream as McLory rolled down the steep slope toward where the General waited, halfway down the incline toward the canyon floor.

McLory rolled on past the General before piling up, belly down, a few yards beyond the startled stallion, who switched his tail edgily, whickering at the smell of a dead man.

Dust roiled in the body's wake.

"Oh, Jesus," Lonnie said.

"Well, that was one way to get him down off this bluff."

Lonnie and Casey glanced at each other, then laughter exploded from them both at the same time. It wasn't that there was anything funny about what they'd done to poor McLory. It was a mutual acknowledgment of the situation's gruesomeness and of their haplessness in effecting the maneuver.

When their brief burst of laughter had died, Lonnie shook his head and started down the slope toward where the General was lowering his head to sniff the dead man. Lonnie rolled the corpse over onto its back. Casey moved down the steep bluff, grabbing large rocks to break her fall. Breathless, she came up to stand beside Lonnie.

"Now, to get him up on the General's back," Lonnie said, joyless at the prospect.

"Yeah, that should be fun."

Lonnie fetched the tarpaulin that he'd strapped beneath his bedroll before he'd left the ranch. He unrolled the tarp and wrapped McLory's body in it, tying the canvas closed with several lengths of rope. It took him and Casey at least ten minutes and several tries to hoist the body up onto the General's back. They dropped poor McLory several times, but Lonnie kept reminding himself that the man was dead and couldn't feel it.

Still, he felt ashamed for the way he and Casey were treating the body. But it wasn't like they intended to be disrespectful. Lonnie soothed his battered conscience by silently assuring McLory that he'd make sure he was respectfully laid to a peaceful rest in a proper grave in Arapaho Creek.

When McLory's wrapped body was lying belly down over the General's back, behind the saddle, Lonnie and Casey took a breather and long drinks from Lonnie's canteen. Using more rope, Lonnie secured the body to the General's back while Casey fetched Miss Abigail. They mounted their horses, splashed across the creek, and headed for the canyon mouth that seemed to beckon warmly to Lonnie though he secretly couldn't keep his mind off the stolen army loot and the possible reward being offered for it.

It was pointless to think about it, however. What he had to concentrate on was convincing Sheriff Halliday not to arrest him for shooting Walleye. Now that he had McLory's body, which proved he hadn't lied about that, anyway, he likely had a good chance of convincing Halliday that he'd only shot Walleye in self-defense *before* he'd known whom he'd been shooting at.

As Lonnie and Casey rode out of the canyon mouth, Lonnie felt his shoulders loosen in relief. Then they tightened again. He reined the General to a sudden stop.

"What is it?" Casey said, stopping her chestnut beside him.

Lonnie stared straight out from the canyon mouth, where he could see three shadows moving in the trees on the far side of Ingrid Creek, about a hundred yards away and moving in Lonnie and Casey's direction.

"Quick!" Lonnie reined the General around and, as much as he didn't want to, he yelled, "Back to the canyon!"

TWENTY-SIX

LONNIE RODE the General back through the canyon mouth, glancing back over his shoulder at Casey, who was galloping after him. "Did you see 'em?" he asked.

Casey nodded. "You suppose they're headed for the canyon?"

"Looked that way."

When they'd ridden around a slight bulge in the eastern ridge wall, Lonnie stopped the General and swung down from his saddle. Casey moved on ahead and then reined the mare in, as well. Lonnie tossed his reins to her.

"Wait here—I'm gonna check it out."

Lonnie stepped back around the bulge in the ridge wall and stopped. He dropped to his haunches as he stared toward the canyon mouth gaping out on a small, grassy meadow through which the creek ran, and the pine forest beyond.

He could see the three riders crossing the creek, coming on slowly, one trailing a packhorse. Lonnie had been afraid that they might have seen him and Casey, but it didn't look that way. They were moving at a leisurely pace, spread out about ten feet apart. They were too far away for Lonnie to make out much about them except that one was riding a big Palomino and was wearing a black opera hat, very much out of place out here.

Lonnie waited, worrying a stone in his hand, as he gazed at the three riders who continued to move toward him. When they did not swerve to either side but rode on into the canyon, Lonnie stepped back behind the bulge in the ridge wall and turned to where Casey sat her mare, gazing toward him with a worried expression.

"They're comin', all right." Lonnie held his hand up for his reins, which Casey tossed to him. "We'd best ride on."

"Deeper into the canyon?"

"Where else we gonna go? Those men might or might not be the fellas who shot those four riders off their horses, but they're likely lookin' for the loot. I for one don't cotton to the idea of hangin' around here to find out if they're friendly. We'd best hole up somewhere out of sight and try to sneak out around them."

Lonnie had just turned out his left stirrup and was about to poke his boot through it, when he heard the thuds of galloping horses growing louder. He frowned and stared back in the direction of the canyon mouth, crickets of apprehension playing hopscotch along his spine.

He glanced at Casey and then walked back to the bulge in the ridge wall. He eased a cautious glance out around it.

The three riders were now galloping toward him.

The man in the top hat snapped a rifle to his shoulder. The carbine belched loudly. The slug screeched toward Lonnie and hammered the ridge wall only a few feet from his face.

Lonnie lurched backward, heart racing.

"Lonnie!" Casey yelled.

"Go!" Lonnie got his boot tangled up as he twisted around and started to run. He dropped hard on his belly, then lifted his head to yell louder, "Go, Casey! *Ride!*"

Casey neck-reined the mare around, and rammed her heels into the horse's flanks, lurching into an instant gallop. Hearing more shooting behind him as well as the smashing of the slugs into the ridge wall only a few feet away, Lonnie scrambled to his feet and up onto the General's back.

The stallion required no urging to flee. Even before Lonnie was set, the stallion broke into a ground-swallowing run, nearly throwing Lonnie. When the boy had recovered, he hunkered low in the saddle and followed Casey and the mare along the gradually rising canyon floor. The ridge walls widened around them, and Ingrid Creek slid away on Lonnie's left. They crossed a clearing and then entered a mix of conifers and aspens.

Lonnie ground his molars as the reports of rifles echoed behind him.

He glanced back and drew a sharp, shallow breath. The three riders were galloping hell-for-leather after him and Casey, the one trailing a packhorse lagging a ways behind the other two.

Their bullets plumed dirt and spanged off rocks wickedly close to the General's scissoring hoofs. That was the encouragement the General needed to run even faster. Lonnie could feel the horse lunging ahead, chewing up the ground and overtaking Casey.

Lonnie glanced back at the girl and said, "Follow me!"

Just then he swerved the General hard left. Casey followed. As they bulled through a stand of aspens, Lonnie glanced back the way they'd come. He couldn't see their pursuers, as they were back behind a bend in the canyon wall. Lonnie steered the General through a corridor between cabin-sized boulders, across Ingrid Creek and up a steep, grassy incline along a belly of shouldering granite.

Lonnie had recognized the gap in the boulders because he'd found a stray calf up this way only a year ago, mired in the creek. Hoping that their pursuers wouldn't see their tracks swerving off the main canyon floor, Lonnie put his head down and pressed his thighs tight to the General's back, to keep from being thrown off as the big buckskin lunged up the steep slope, McClory's body flopping around behind Lonnie.

Lonnie glanced behind, worried that Casey wouldn't make it. But the girl had as much saddle savvy as Lonnie did. She wasn't having any trouble staying seated on the sure-footed Miss Abigail who seemed to almost be racing the General up the steep incline.

When the hill leveled off slightly, Lonnie turned the General to the right and onto the crest of the granite outcropping. He kept climbing into some pines, and then hauled back on the General's reins. As Casey moved through the low-hanging pine boughs behind him, Lonnie dropped out of the saddle, tossed his reins over a cedar sapling, shucked his rifle from its scabbard, and moved back down to the top of the outcropping.

He dropped to his knees and crawled to the edge of the cliff. He lay belly down and removed his hat, making less of him to see from below.

From here he could see the canyon floor from over the tops of the aspens and boulders lining both sides of it. No sign of the riders, but Lonnie could hear the distance-muffled clacking of their galloping horses moving farther up canyon.

Casey crawled up beside Lonnie and lay belly down. Taking his lead, she also removed her hat.

"Did we lose 'em?"

"For now."

"When they realize we're no longer ahead of them, they'll double back and likely see where we left the main trail."

"Maybe." Lonnie sleeved sweat from his brow. "The canyon floor's all rock, though. They'd have to be some mighty good trackers to see where we left it. They'd have to track as good as Injuns."

"What if they can?"

Lonnie pushed himself to his feet. "That's why we have to keep movin'."

"Why don't we head back down and ride on out of the canyon before they double back?"

Lonnie grabbed his reins off the cedar sapling and slid his rifle back into its boot. "And risk meetin' up with 'em again when they double back?" He gave a wry laugh. "No, thanks. Some of that lead they were slingin' was comin' mighty close. Those fellas are used to shootin'... and killin'."

Casey looked around; lines of apprehension cut deep across her forehead. "Where we gonna go?"

"I don't know. I haven't been much deeper in the canyon than where we are now." Lonnie looked up through the pines though he couldn't see much for the trees. "I reckon we go higher, try to put as much distance between us and them curly wolves as we can."

"Yeah, it looks like they're a bit proprietary about that loot." Casey gained her feet and, looking around cautiously, walked up to grab Miss Abigail's reins. "So...this is Skull Canyon."

Lonnie swung up into the saddle and glanced at her. "Yeah." He paused as she toed a stirrup and stepped into her saddle. "You scared?"

She looked at him, incredulous. "It's Skull Canyon. Aren't you?"

Lonnie grumbled a reluctant "I reckon...a little," and then gigged the General on up through the pines.

TWENTY-SEVEN

LONNIE HAD no idea where he was leading Casey. All he knew was that he wanted to get as much separation between himself and the three gun-crazy riders as possible. Following a game path up higher into the forest, he kept swinging cautious looks behind him and occasionally stopping the General to look around and listen.

When he and Casey had crossed a pass and dropped down into what Lonnie assumed was a separate arm of the canyon—separate from the one in which they'd left the shooters—he paused to let the General drink at a small spring gurgling over a bed of polished stones.

Casey rode up beside him and let Miss Abigail lower her head and draw water from a small, dark pool glimmering as the sunlight filtered through breeze-jostled pine boughs. "Lonnie, if we keep riding blind like this, we're going to get lost. This canyon will make slow, painful work of us."

"Better'n goin' out so full of bullets we'll rattle when we walk."

"I say we start back."

Lonnie was looking toward a rocky crag rising straight ahead of him, several thousand feet above the rolling, spruce-green forest. The crag resembled a giant pipe organ jutting its arrow-shaped pipes against the flawless cobalt blue of the sky.

"I heard the canyon has two entrances," he told Casey. "Or exits—however you want to look at it. The other way out is near the base of the crag that's shaped like a skull. I think one of them peaks over yonder is the skull."

"How do you know?"

Lonnie hiked a shoulder. "Workin' with old punchers every spring and fall, you hear stuff."

"How far away do you think those cliffs are?"

"Hard to say. Five, maybe six miles. Once we make it out, we can circle around the canyon and make our way back to Arapaho Creek. It'll take some time, but I don't see as we have much choice."

Casey gave him a skeptical glance. "Lonnie, if you get us hopelessly lost or eaten by a bear...like the one that almost ate us last year around this time...I'll never forgive you."

Lonnie looked off. A pang of jealousy inspired him to mutter with sarcasm, "I suppose the counter jumper in the fancy suit will be expectin' to see you this evenin'. Probably plans to buy you a fried-chicken supper at the Colorado House. Sorry about that."

Casey didn't say anything for a few seconds. Then: "Lonnie, you're not takin' me on a wild-goose chase on purpose, are you? Just to keep me away from that 'counter jumper', as you so indelicately call Niles, who is no shopkeeper but a *bookkeeper*?"

Lonnie turned his head to her, annoyed. "Heck, no! If you done made up your mind about Mister Fancy Dan, I got nothin' more to say to you. Now, let's ride. Maybe we can make them crags before sundown. I for one would not like to spend another night in this canyon...especially with a girl with such poor taste in suitors!"

Lonnie urged the General across the creek and on up the game trail he was following. If he would have looked behind him, which he did not, he would have seen Casey smiling fondly at him as she put her horse across the creek and followed him.

As they rode, the crags grew larger before them. The pines thinned out, the grass grew short and green, and ferns and evergreen shrubs grew shaggy along several creeks that now threaded this leg of the canyon. The air grew cool, and the wind began making that eerie moaning sound as it blew around and over the tall, gray cliffs that stood at the canyon's far end.

Lonnie didn't see that a lake lay at the base of the crags until he was only a hundred or so yards away from it, following the canyon's grassy floor up a steep rise. The lake was pancake flat and the color of iron, with only a few breezy ripples marring its otherwise placid surface. The towering crags were reflected in it.

It was on the surface of the lake that Lonnie first saw the skull grinning up at him. He jerked his gaze toward the cliffs with a slight gasp.

"Hey...see it?" he said to Casey riding up behind him. He pointed. "You see the skull?"

Casey stopped Miss Abigail and lifted her gaze toward the cliffs. "Oh, my...yeah."

The formation indeed looked like a human skull devoid of skin and hair. It sat between two arrow-shaped pinnacles, on its own towering precipice—light gray in color and bearing two roughly circular indentations for the eye sockets, a long, crooked crack for the nose, and a black crevice curved into the shape of a grinning mouth though one corner of the mouth was decidedly higher than the other.

A leering, menacing smile.

The wind whistled through the irregular gaps around the skull, sometimes making a high whistling sound while sometimes making what sounded like an elk's mournful, bugling cry.

Something sat atop the skull. A bird of some kind. Just then, as though to reveal itself to the newcomers, the bird flew up from the skull and vaulted in a long, smooth, downward arc toward Lonnie and Casey. It grew larger and larger. It looked like a large, brown rag with flapping wings. As it grew closer, Lonnie saw the curved talons and the hooked beak.

When the raptor was maybe fifty feet above the lake it swooped upward and gave an eagle's ratcheting, echoing shriek as it sailed off on the southerly wind down canyon, in the direction from which Lonnie and Casey had come.

The skull moaned. The moan echoed over and over only to be followed by another one.

The echoes sounded like an angry giant bellowing through a bullhorn.

Lonnie felt an eerie chill. To distract himself as well as Casey, he swung around, following the bird with his gaze, calling, "Hey, if you see those three tough nuts who tried cleanin' our clocks, drop a load on 'em for me, Lonnie Gentry!"

He grinned, satisfied with himself, at Casey.

Casey had swung down from Miss Abigail's back. She stood beside the mare, arms crossed on her chest, regarding Lonnie dubiously. "What if that bird was tryin' to tell us somethin'?"

"What could that have been?" Lonnie asked, though he thought he knew what Casey was going to say.

"That we shouldn't be here."

Lonnie ignored the cold fingers of apprehension again raking his spine and hiked a shoulder with phony nonchalance. "I reckon it's a little late for that." He glanced at the western ridges. "Sun's gonna set soon. We'd best find a place to camp for the night. We'll get an early start in the mornin'."

As he began leading the General to a stand of shaggy pines to his left, he pointed across the lake. "Looks like there's a break in the cliff wall there. I bet that's the way out of the canyon."

"Why don't we head for it now, Lonnie?"

Lonnie kept walking. "We'd never make it before dark. It's farther away than it looks."

"Is there anythin' you don't know, Lonnie Gentry?"

Lonnie stopped walking and tossed her a meaningful look. "Yeah, there's a few things I don't know about."

His look was direct enough, his tone level enough, that she didn't have to guess what he'd meant.

TWENTY-EIGHT

LONNIE FOUND a place well back from the clearing at the point of the lake in which to camp. He found a dense stand of trees with a well-concealed open area inside them roughly as large around as an Indian tepee.

The first job was to pull McLory down off the General's back, which proved to be far easier than had getting him up there. Lonnie didn't relish the idea of wrestling him back up there again in the morning.

When he and Casey had picketed their horses to a line strung between two trees, they gathered wood and built a small fire. Knowing that when riding into the mountains you had to be prepared for anything, Casey had packed a bedroll, warm clothes, and a couple of ham sandwiches she hadn't yet gotten around to eating.

She and Lonnie arranged their bedrolls and other gear around the snapping flames of their fire. Lonnie hung a pot of coffee on his iron tripod.

He found his food pouch and was happy to discover a bit of deer jerky and two stale biscuits inside. He knew there were likely fish in the lake, but it was getting too dark to make his way back out into the clearing. It no doubt got so dark up here before the moon rose that he wouldn't be able to see his hand in front of his face.

The upside of that was no one else was likely to see him, either.

Still, the canyon gave him the willies. He decided to stay close to the fire as well as to Casey though he was still miffed at the girl, and his heart still ached, knowing she'd set her hat for another. He understood why she'd done it, but he didn't know how he was ever going to stop thinking about it.

He was glad she was with him now, though. At least they had what would probably be their last night together. He hoped it wouldn't be their last night, period, on this side of the sod.

As he gathered and deposited one more load of firewood, the low, windy moaning sounded again from out in the darkness. It sounded louder and more menacing now after night had come down and the last light had bled out of the sky.

"Lonnie, good lord—is that the skull speakin' to us again?" Casey asked, kneeling by the fire, a leather swatch for the coffeepot in her hand. She stared off beyond where the glimmering firelight reached.

"If you look at it that way—or hear it that way," Lonnie said, "you're gonna get the fantods. Just hear it like it is—the wind blowin' around that big rock up there. That's all."

"Are we goin' to have contend with that all night long?"

"I don't know. You want to go on up there and have a chat with the rock, see if you can get it to pipe down a little?" Lonnie chuckled as he sat back against his bedroll and tipped his hat back off his forehead.

"All right, Mister Smarty," Casey said as she handed over a smoking cup to him, "have a cup of coffee. I don't know why I feel so generous, but you can have one of my ham sandwiches, too. Made 'em both last night from the hog my neighbor butchered just last week." She extended a sandwich wrapped in waxed paper.

"You keep it," Lonnie said. "You'll need it for breakfast. You got a long trip back to Arapaho Creek, prob'ly take you half the day. Me—I can set some snares, and I might see if there's any red-throated trout in the lake yonder."

Casey sat back against her own saddle, about four feet to Lonnie's right, and looked at him through the firelit steam of her coffee. "What're you sayin', Lonnie? You're not goin' to stay around here, are you?"

"I might poke around a little."

"Poke around a little for the strongbox?"

"Why not? There's likely a sizeable reward on that much money."

"What about the curse on this place? What about McLory?"

"He'll keep another day. It's cool up here. Then I'll build a travois. I can throw one together right quick. As far as the curse goes..." Lonnie sipped his coffee and looked around, wary. "I reckon if we get through this night there's no reason I won't get through the next night. Besides, I heard there's an old Mexican sheepherder's stone hut around here somewhere. That might be the place where old Crawford Kinch hid the money."

"What about the men who shot at us?"

"I'll lay low. Now that I know they're here, I'll be extra cautious." Lonnie shook his head slowly as he stared pensively out into the darkness. "I could sure use that reward money. What if it's five hundred dollars?" He gave a soft whistle through his bottom teeth. "That's a heckuva stake."

"A stake for what?"

"A stake for gettin' out of here." Lonnie dug a trench in the dirt with his right boot heel. "I think I done let too much grass grow under my feet up here in these mountains. Time to move on."

Casey slowly unwrapped her sandwich, staring at Lonnie and frowning. "Because of me?"

Lonnie glanced at her, hiked a shoulder, and sipped his coffee. "Heck, I don't blame you for takin' up with that counter jumper."

"He's a *bookkeeper*, Lonnie."

"I don't blame you for takin' up with that *bookkeeper*, then. What could I give you? Close quarters with my half-crazy ma and my screamin' half-brother—an outlaw's son."

Lonnie gave a caustic chuff. "We'd struggle every day of our lives, just like ma and I do now. That's no way for you to live. You been through a lot in this life, losin' both parents. You didn't deserve any of that. You're a purty girl, a good person. You deserve to have a happy life without worryin' every day about puttin' food on the table. I'd like to know a little of that myself. Heck, Ma will move to town and find a counter jumper of her own to support her and little Jeremiah. That'd be a better, more fittin' life for her. I'm just in her way."

When Casey didn't say anything, Lonnie glanced at her. He was surprised to see her staring at him through a veil of tears shimmering in her eyes. Then the veil broke. Tears spilled down her cheeks. They were honey-colored in the firelight.

Casey started to scuttle over to him, extending her arms as if to hug him. Lonnie moved back away from her, and rose, tossing the dregs of his coffee into the brush.

"I'm gonna check the horses, gather a little more wood," he said, setting his cup down next to his saddlebags, grabbing his rifle, and walking away from the fire.

There it was, he thought. In his mind he'd broken from her. His words had sealed the deal.

He felt better now. Lighter. Freer. His heart didn't hurt quite so much.

It still hurt. Just not quite so much.

He checked to make sure both horses were well tied to the picket rope. He didn't want either wandering off in the night, frightened by the distant scent of a mountain lion or prowling grizzly. He and Casey had tethered them close to a freshet running through the trees and now winking in the starlight.

Lonnie started to gather more blowdown branches, when he jerked his head up to stare out through the trees toward the lake. He'd heard something. It had to have been the wind because the bullhorn-like roar of the skull was nearly constant now though sometimes louder than at other times.

Now he heard it again—what he'd heard before. It was different, separate from the moaning. It seemed to be coming from not too far away, in the direction of the lake.

Lonnie picked up his rifle from where he'd leaned it against a tree. He took two heavy, faltering steps toward the sound then stopped abruptly, his blood running cold. He heard the sound again.

It was a man's high, mournful voice calling, "Innnngggggg...griiiid-dddddd... Oh, Innnnnggggg...griiiddddd!"

It mixed with the moaning to form a truly horrifying, low wailing sound that stabbed Lonnie deep in his loins.

The boy's heart thudded.

"Ingrid," Lonnie muttered to himself, cold sweat breaking out on his forehead. "Oh...oh, Jesus!"

Then, beneath the wind's moaning rose a man's cackling laugh.

That, too, stabbed Lonnie deep in his loins. Even deeper.

But the assault to his nerves was far from over.

Behind Lonnie, Casey's sudden, ear-rattling scream caused the boy to jump nearly a foot straight up in the air.

TWENTY-NINE

"CASEY!" Lonnie shouted as he ran back toward the fire shimmering straight ahead in the darkness.

He tripped over a deadfall and fell, dropping his rifle. He grabbed his rifle and got up and kept running. Casey's screams had died by the time he reached the outer edge of the firelight. Breathing hard, Lonnie stopped and stared across the fire, where a broad-shouldered man in a battered brown Stetson stood behind Casey, holding a big Bowie knife tight against her throat.

Challenge flashed in his dark-brown eyes as he glared across the fire at Lonnie. He curled one side of his upper lip, showing badly rotted and tobacco-encrusted teeth. "Stand down, boy. Drop the rifle."

Lonnie held the Winchester up high across his chest. He squeezed it in his gloved hands. He looked at Casey. The girl's face was blanched, her eyes wide with fear. Her throat moved as she swallowed. She winced when her throat moved against the Bowie's sharp blade.

Lonnie tossed the rifle away.

"Let her go!" Lonnie shouted, balling his fists at his sides. "Or so help me, I'll—!"

Something hard slammed against the back of Lonnie's head, throwing him forward. He stumbled, hit the ground near the fire, and rolled close to the stones forming a ring around the crackling flames.

"Lonnie!" Casey cried.

The man with the Bowie knife released her. She ran around the fire and dropped to a knee beside Lonnie, who lay groaning and clutching the back of his head with both hands.

In the corner of his left eye, Lonnie saw a man stoop down to pick up his rifle. He was a tall man in a long wool coat with long, grizzled hair curling down behind his ears, and a three- or four-day beard stubble carpeting his craggy cheeks.

He had large, light-blue eyes, which glinted in the firelight as he grinned after inspecting Lonnie's rifle. "Kid comes well-armed. An eighteen sixty-six Winchester repeater. Yellowboy."

"Tough one, huh?"

Lonnie turned his head in the other direction to see the man who'd been holding the Bowie knife on Casey, standing over him, glowering down at him. He wore a quilted deerskin coat and deerskin gloves. He had a round, meaty face and deep-set, cold gray eyes. He, too, had had several days' worth of stubble on his sunburned cheeks.

"Boys got mouths on 'em these days," he grumbled down at Lonnie. "It weren't like that before I went in. Boys talked respectful like to their elders. My, how things change."

"Are you okay, Lonnie?" Casey asked, leaning down to regard the boy worriedly.

Lonnie nodded and looked up at the broad-shouldered gent standing over him. He was about to ask the man who he was but cut himself off when he saw a tattoo peeking out from under his upraised coat collar.

The man grinned and jerked his collar down, revealing the tattoo of a naked lady raising her knees as though she were perched coquettishly on a saloon table, batting her long eyelashes at the men surrounding her.

"You like it, kid? She's some faded—I got her in New Orleans just after the war—but she's still a looker, ain't she?"

"That's disgusting," Casey snarled. "Who are you?"

Lonnie said in a voice hushed with awe, "Crawford Kinch."

Kinch stared at him, vaguely puzzled. Then he smiled, showing his rotten teeth again. "You have me at a disadvantage, boy...even though I'm the one holdin' the Bowie knife, and Engstrom back there has your rifle."

"Lonnie Gentry," Lonnie said, rocking back on his heels. "This is Casey."

"She's some purty," Kinch said, glancing lustily down at Casey. "But I'm an old man who knows his manners."

"Me? I'm an old man but I don't know my manners," said the man whom Kinch had called Engstrom, ogling Casey. "And you're right...she's some purty."

"Stay away from me," Casey said. "Either one of you comes near me, I'll bash your head in!"

Kinch and Engstrom laughed.

"A polecat, that one!" said Engstrom.

Kinch sheathed his Bowie knife and thrust his hand out toward Engstrom, who tossed him Lonnie's Winchester. "Tie 'em up, Dutch," he told his partner. "Good and tight."

"Tie 'em up?" said Engstrom, incredulous. "We're gonna have to kill 'em, Craw. Ain't no two ways about it. The kid knows who you are. Now, they both do. And they're after our gold!"

"We're not after your gold," Lonnie said. His words had fallen on deaf ears.

"Don't make no difference," Kinch said. "I ain't up to killin' kids tonight. I'm old and tired and I got contrary ways about me. You know that, Dutch. Killin' grown men after my gold's one thing." He shook his head as he switched his gaze from Lonnie to Casey and back again. "But two young folk with their lives ahead of 'em is another thing altogether. Saddens me, it does."

He gave a coyote-like, menacing grin at his partner. "We'll do it in the mornin'. Throw 'em both in the lake, see how good they float!"

He laughed at that.

Lonnie and Casey shared a wide-eyed glance of terror.

"You oughta thank us," Kinch told Lonnie. "We got them three curly wolves back there off your trail—didn't we, Dutch?"

Engstrom smiled.

"Huh?" Lonnie said.

"Sure, sure," Kinch said, winking at his partner. "You won't have to run from them no more. And me an' Dutch won't have to worry about 'em, neither."

"This canyon's fillin' up fast with dead men—ain't that right, Craw?"

"Sure is. It's time fer us to pull foot soon," Kinch said. "Before the law starts sniffin' around, finds our blood trail." Kinch cocked Lonnie's Winchester and aimed at the pair straight out from his right hip. "Either of you two move, you're be flappin' your golden wings tonight instead of tomorrow. No use rushin' things. You can live a good long time over the course of a few hours. I spent eighteen years in the territorial pen." His expression turned dark. "I know how long a single hour can be, let alone eighteen years when you're spendin' every minute of it thinkin' about a stash of hidden gold."

"Aren't you the philosopher," Casey said. "You're the convict who stole the payroll money. Lonnie told me all about you. Wicked!"

Staring at the rifle aimed at him, Lonnie said, "Easy, Casey. Pull your horns in—will ya? I for one don't wanna be flappin' golden wings tonight!"

THIRTY

"YEAH, PULL YOUR HORNS IN, GIRL," warned Engstrom, grabbing Lonnie's coiled lariat from where it lay by his saddle. He tossed his head to indicate behind him as he crouched down by Lonnie. "Who's the dead fella laid out back there?"

"One of the men you shot," Lonnie said. "You might not have given him a chance to introduce himself. His name was McLory. Cade McLory."

"Don't know who're talkin' about, kid," Engstrom said, tying Lonnie and Casey's wrists together, behind their backs. "All the men we shot of late we made sure were dead."

"Certain sure," said Kinch. He looked at Lonnie. "Your man was shot by someone else. There's two or three groups of bounty hunters hereabouts. Leastways, they *were* hereabouts," he added with a dark chuckle. "They're after me and my gold. They all want to be the first ones to reach the secret cache, hot on my heels, and they're shootin' each other for the privilege. Don't bother me none. Saves me an' Engstrom from havin' to kill every polecat powderin' our trail!"

He chuckled through his rotten teeth as he sank onto a log a ways away from Lonnie and Casey, holding Lonnie's rifle across his thighs. Engstrom was tying Casey's ankles.

"Fortunately," Kinch added, "there ain't enough lawmen to go around."

Lonnie said, "McLory was a bounty hunter?"

"Most likely. Part of a group huntin' another group. I swear, I never seen the like in this canyon since the War of Northern Aggression. Little battles breakin' out every whichaway! Word spread fast that I busted out of the territorial pen. Dutch an' me thought we wasn't followed, but we led one group right into the canyon, and another group must've been followin' the first group! I reckon eighteen years breakin' big rocks into little rocks made me lose my outlaw savvy," Kinch added, shaking his head in disgust. "I wasn't watchin' my backtrail."

"The old legend don't seem to be keepin' the gold hunters away." Engstrom grinned at Lonnie. "I had you scared—didn't I boy?" He threw his head back and gave a lower, quieter version of his call for Ingrid. "Why, you 'bout jumped out of your boots when you heard that. Not to worry, though. Just a legend prob'ly concocted by some prospector to keep folks out of the canyon and away from his diggin's."

"Don't laugh, Engstrom—it probably helped keep anyone from tryin' overly hard over the past eighteen years to find that strongbox. Just a coincidence I came to bury the loot here. A fortunate one, though. A haunted canyon—yessir. Just what the doctor ordered!"

Lonnie glanced over his shoulder at Engstrom. "Were you one of the gang that robbed the payroll, too?"

"Me? Nah." Engstrom stood and hitched his baggy canvas breeches up higher on his bony hips. "Me an' Craw met up in prison. I was in for murderin' the liveryman I caught...uh...I caught in a *compromising situation*, you might say. With my dear wife, Bertha." He threw his head back and sniffed the night air. "Ahh...sure is nice bein' free, though, ain't it, Craw?"

"Sure 'nough," Kinch said. "Why don't you fetch the horses, Dutch? We'll be beddin' down here at the fire of our new friends. You two don't mind—do you?"

"Would it do any good if we did?" Casey asked in her snooty, haughty way.

Engstrom chuckled as he walked off into the trees. "I don't mind a sassy girl as long as she's purty."

Lonnie looked at Kinch who was helping himself to Lonnie's cup of coffee. "You really gonna kill us tomorrow?"

"Don't have much choice, kid," Kinch said, sipping the coffee and looking at the cup with approval. "That's good. But then, I ain't tasted a good cup of coffee since me an' Engstrom jumped the wall. They don't serve coffee in the pen, you see. Only water. And it ain't much good—the water—neither."

He took another sip of the coffee and shook his head as he looked around. "I'm never goin' back there. Never. I'd die first. That's why we can't leave anyone behind to tell where we been. As soon as we dig up that loot, we're hightailin' it to Mexico."

"No need to tell us that," Lonnie said.

"Why not?" Kinch grinned devilishly over the rim of the cup. "You'll be givin' up the ghost tomorrow. After you done helped us with the gold, that is."

Casey fired another of her raw glares at him. "What're you talkin' about?"

"I buried the strongbox deep—in what I suspect was an exploration hole dug by some prospector long before me and Bentley came along. Bentley was the fella who made it into the canyon with me. All shot up, Bentley was. I put him out of his misery." Kinch aimed Lonnie's rifle at the ground and said, "Pop! Pop! Two shots to the head." Then he grinned his wolfish grin again.

"You probably killed him to keep from havin' to share the loot with him," Casey said with a snort. "Or so he couldn't tell anyone else where it was."

Kinch arched his brows at the girl. "You know, I always heard that brains and beauty didn't mix. After meetin' you, sweetheart, I might have to rethink that old saw."

"You're awful," Casey said. "And you smell bad. How long has it been since you've had a bath?"

Kinch sniffed under his left arm. "Pshaw! I'm sweet as a spring lily." He chuckled. "But to answer your question—oh, say, about eighteen years."

He laughed louder.

"What's so funny?" Engstrom said as he led two horses toward the camp.

The General and Miss Abigail both snorted around and whickered at the smell of the strange mounts.

"The sweet little flower says I smell bad."

"You do smell bad, Craw—that's what I been tryin' to tell ya," Engstrom said, stopping the horses at the edge of the firelight. "You an' me need us a good long bath in a fancy hotel just as soon as we dig up that loot of yours."

"I reckon you're right," Kinch said, grunting as he rose from the log.

"Good to have such a smart fella with such winnin' ideas backin' my play."

"Aren't you two just two peas in a pod?" Casey said. "Why haven't you dug up the gold yet?"

Kinch set his coffee cup down and walked over to tend his horse.

"And lead all the jaspers doggin' our heels straight to it?" said the old outlaw, walking stiffly, hunched a little forward, as though his lower back ached.

As Engstrom tossed his saddle onto the ground near the fire, he said, "We decided to hang low and let 'em all kill each other, or at least cull their own herds, before we dug it up and lit out with it."

"No point in leadin' 'em right to it," Kinch said, "so they could just shoot us and take the strongbox for themselves."

"How did you find us?" Lonnie said. "Way over here at the far end of the canyon."

Engstrom squatted down in front of the boy, his eyes fairly glowing as he said, "Why, because the gold is right nearby, my boy. So close I can smell all that gold blowin' on the southern breeze."

He closed his eyes and drew a long, slow breath, his horsey face fairly blossoming as he took in what he believed to be the smell of gold coins on the eerily moaning wind.

Later, when they'd eaten and had their fill of coffee, the two men rolled up in their blankets and rested their heads against their saddles on either side of the fire. They pulled their hat brims down over their eyes.

Kinch started snoring almost immediately.

Engstrom was looking as though he, too, was drifting off, when Lonnie turned toward Casey to whisper, "These two jaspers are crazier'n a tree full of owls."

"Yep," Casey agreed, nodding. "And we'd best try to work our way out of these ropes before sunrise, or we'll be flyin' off on golden wings before noon."

THIRTY-ONE

"I THINK I'M STARTIN' to work mine loose," Lonnie whispered when he and Casey had been working at the ropes binding their wrists for over an hour. "He tied 'em good, but I'm gettin' some slack."

"Good," Casey said.

Lonnie could feel her shoulders rubbing against his as she worked to loosen her own bindings. Lonnie glanced toward the shadowy lumps of their two captors, one on either side of the fire that had burned down to dully glowing coals. Both men were snoring loudly beneath their hats, bellies rising and falling deeply.

Crawford Kinch whistled faintly with each snoring exhalation.

Lonnie kept working at the ropes, turning his wrists from side to side and clawing at the ropes with his fingertips. He got enough slack in the rope around his right wrist that he thought he could pull his hand through the loop.

Again, he glanced at the two men. They were still asleep, snoring peacefully. They must have been relatively certain that none of the other men hunting the gold had picked up their trail.

Lonnie winced against the pain of the rope scraping his skin as he pulled his hand slowly through the loop. He pulled hard, grinding his molars against the burning pain of badly chafed skin. Feeling the slickness of blood oozing from a cut, he groaned softly, bit down on his lower lip, and pulled his right wrist free.

"Got it!" he said, unable to control his glee despite the skin he'd scraped off.

"*Shhh!*" Casey admonished.

They both looked at Kinch. The old outlaw had stopped snoring.

Lonnie cursed under his breath.

"Stay asleep, you old codger," he said inside himself. "Please, please, please—*keep sleepin'!*"

Kinch grunted, sighed, ran a hand across his mouth then turned onto his side. His hat tumbled off his shoulder. Soon, he resumed snoring.

Casey turned her head toward Lonnie, wide-eyed with anger. So quietly that the boy could barely hear her, she said, "Idiot!"

This time, Lonnie had to agree with her.

Quickly, he used his free hand to free his other hand. As he did, he glanced toward Kinch and then toward Engstrom, who lay as he had before, hat over his eyes, snoring deeply.

When Lonnie was free, he turned to Casey and began untying the ropes binding her wrists. It didn't take him long. Lonnie stood and then helped Casey to her feet. She looked at him as though to say, "What now?"

Lonnie glanced to where his rifle leaned against the log near where Engstrom was lying. The Winchester was on the other side of the man, ten feet from Lonnie.

The boy strode around behind the log, moving nearly silently on the balls of his boots. He looked at his rifle barrel glistening in the moonlight. Slowly, he reached for the jutting barrel, which was about two feet to the right of Engstrom. His hand was a foot away from the barrel when Engstrom rolled over, grabbed the rifle, cocked it, and aimed it from his knees at Lonnie.

"Uh-uh," Engstrom said, grinning winningly, thoroughly satisfied with himself. "I think I'll hang onto it a while longer."

He glanced from Lonnie to Casey, who stood frozen in horror, and laughed.

"What is it? What is it?" Kinch said, grabbing his own rifle and cocking it.

He looked around wildly.

"Oh, nothin'," Engstrom said, holding his rifle on Lonnie, who stood with his hands raised to his shoulders. "Just these two younkers keepin' us two old curly wolves on our toes—that's all."

He gave Lonnie a mocking wink.

Lonnie glanced at Casey, who returned the glance, crestfallen.

Disappointment was a heavy stone inside him. He cursed to himself.

————

KINCH and his friend Dutch Engstrom not only retied Lonnie and Casey, they tied their hands behind their backs and their ankles behind their backs, as well. Their wrist ropes were connected to their ankle ropes by a foot-long length of hemp. They lay on their sides, facing each other on the ground, like two hogs bound for tomorrow's slaughter.

Not long after the two outlaws had rolled back up in their bedrolls, their snoring resumed.

Lonnie looked over at Casey lying three feet away from him. He couldn't see her clearly, as the moon was waning, but he thought she lay with her eyes open, staring hopelessly at the ground.

Lonnie doubted that either of them would get much sleep for the remainder of the night. Their positions were far too uncomfortable for slumber.

"Casey?" Lonnie whispered.

She rolled her sad eyes up to him.

"You all right?"

"Do I look all right?"

Lonnie sighed and winced at the tension that the deep breath added to his strained arms and shoulders. "No, I reckon not. Sorry about all this. I reckon we should have lit out of the canyon back when you said we should."

Casey didn't respond to that. She just went back to staring at the ground.

Keeping his voice low, Lonnie said, "I reckon you were right to throw in with the counter jumper."

"He's a bookkeeper, Lonnie."

"I meant you were right to throw in with that bookkeeper." Lonnie paused. "I reckon Niles or Giles or whatever his name is wouldn't have gotten you in half as much trouble as this."

Casey stared at the ground.

After a few seconds, she made a snorting sound.

Lonnie frowned curiously, staring at her. Then he saw her shoulders jerking, and he realized that she was laughing.

Her shoulders lurched more violently, and she made a strangling sound as she laughed louder, blowing dirt and pine needles into her face. Then Lonnie found himself snorting, as well. His snorts grew into uncontrollable laughter as he, too, saw the dark humor in their situation.

Kinch and Engstrom stopped snoring.

Kinch lifted his head from his saddle. "Good night, children!" he ordered.

Lonnie and Casey pressed their faces to the ground to squelch their laughter, but it took their shoulders a long time to stop jerking.

———

EVEN THOUGH LONNIE knew tomorrow would likely be his last day on earth, morning couldn't come fast enough. The chill mountain air of the long night aggravated the aches and pains in his strained joints. The two old outlaws didn't start rolling and snorting out of their bedrolls until well after dawn, however. They continued snorting and coughing and spitting phlegm for close to a half hour before they came over and cut Casey and Lonnie free so they could limp off into the woods and relieve themselves.

Kinch said, "Either one of you gets the urge to make a run for it, just remember I was a sharpshooter back durin' the War of Northern Greed and Criminal Aggression, and I can shoot the eye out of a June bug at two hundred yards."

Kinch and Engstrom laughed at the exaggeration.

Even if Lonnie had had the urge to run, he doubted he could have run —not after being trussed up like the proverbial fatted calf for half the night. Besides, he wouldn't have left Casey. He doubted she was in any better condition to run than he was.

When he finished his business, he glanced back toward the camp. Kinch was down on one knee, coaxing last night's fire back to life. He had Lonnie's rifle near. Engstrom was off in the trees on the far side of the camp, tending their horses. Kinch glanced up occasionally at Lonnie, making sure the boy didn't run off.

Casey walked up out of the trees behind Lonnie. Her hair was badly mussed. She looked pale and tired out and frightened. Lonnie's heart ached at seeing her so beaten down. He grabbed her arm, glanced toward Kinch who was blowing on the mounded ashes, and leaned in close to the girl.

"As soon as your horse is saddled," Lonnie said, "you climb up on Miss Abigail and hightail it back to town. You understand?"

Casey scowled at him, as though he'd said something ludicrous. "I won't leave you alone with those men, Lonnie."

"There's no point in us both dyin', Casey."

Casey gazed into his eyes for a moment, her eyes soft. "If you're goin' to die, Lonnie, I'm dyin' with you."

"Hey, you two lovebirds," Kinch called, "get over here *now!*"

Lonnie stared back at Casey, shocked by what she'd said. She was a puzzle, this girl.

His throat felt thick and tight. He cleared it and said, "If I don't have to worry about you, I'll find a way out from under them. You know I can do it. That's how I am. So, first chance you get—and you probably won't get one, but *in case you do*—you ride like Miss Abigail's tail's on fire!"

Kinch straightened now and shouted, "What'd I just tell you two? If you ain't back here in three seconds, your end is gonna come sooner rather than later!" He picked up Lonnie's rifle and cocked it loudly.

"We're comin'!" Lonnie called.

He jerked his desperate, beseeching gaze back to Casey. "Got it?"

Dully, turning her mouth corners down, Casey nodded. She strode past him, brushing her hand against his, and headed back to the fire.

"What were you two talkin' about over there?" Kinch wanted to know.

"None of your business," Casey snapped at him.

"If you two try anythin', you're wolf bait—understand?"

Lonnie said, "Wolf bait ain't gonna dig up that gold for you."

Kinch glowered at him, his eyes dark beneath the brim of his battered hat. "Stop your sassin' and gather wood for the fire, but don't you leave my sight, boy. The girl's gonna be here, makin' coffee and corn cakes. If you run, she'll pay. Now, get to work—both of ya. You got you a job of work ahead!"

THIRTY-TWO

WHEN THEY'D ALL padded out their bellies and had their fill of coffee, Kinch and Engstrom led Lonnie and Casey by gunpoint out to where the horses were picketed.

"Saddle up and be quick about it, children," Kinch ordered. "As soon as you're in the saddle, your wrists will be tied to the horn. We're gonna tie her horse to your buckskin's tail, and Dutch will be leadin' your buckskin by the reins. So don't even think you're gonna get a chance to run off —understand?"

He stared pointedly, suspiciously at Lonnie.

Lonnie shook his head as though in grim defeat. "You two got it all figured out, don't you?"

"Let's just say this ain't our first rodeo," Engstrom said. "Is it, Kinch?" he called over the mule's back.

"No, it sure ain't," Kinch said.

Lonnie glanced at Casey, nodding at her to be prepared for a chance to run, then picked up his saddle blanket and tossed it over the General's back. He took his time rigging the General. He wanted Casey to have her mare saddled ahead of him. When the two outlaws had their own mounts saddled and ready to go, Lonnie was taking his time inspecting the General's right rear hoof.

"He's a slow mover, that one," Engstrom said, indicating Lonnie. "You watch him like a hawk, Kinch. He looks like he couldn't toe up a horse apple from a frozen barnyard, but he's sly as a three-legged coyote."

He gave Lonnie a sharp look.

"I'll walk out a ways and make sure we're alone out here. If anyone camped nearby, I'll likely smell their smoke."

"Don't worry," Kinch said. "The kid knows if he tries anythin', the girl's gonna pay."

Kinch narrowed an eye at Casey. Lonnie turned to Casey, and his heart immediately started tattooing a frenzied rhythm against his breastbone.

Casey had her mare saddled and ready to go. She'd seen her chance. With one quick, anxious look at Lonnie, she stepped fleetly up onto Miss Abigail's back, and shot a haughty glance at Kinch, who merely stared up at her dully, slow to comprehend what she was fixing to do.

The outlaw had thought that Lonnie was the one he had to keep the closest watch on. He'd been wrong.

Casey said, "Yeah, but what if the girl hornswoggles you, you cork-headed fool, and tries somethin' herself?"

Cheeks flushed with desperation, the girl neck-reined the mare around on a dime and batted her heels against the chestnut's flanks. With a single lunge off her hindquarters, Miss Abigail was off and running through the trees.

Kinch grabbed his rifle and raised it, cocking it and yelling, "Why that—!"

As the man aimed at Casey, Lonnie threw himself against Kinch, shoving the rifle up as the outlaw triggered it. The rifle thundered as Kinch fell on his back, Lonnie landing on top of him and struggling to wrench the rifle out of the outlaw's hand.

"Lonnie!" Casey yelled in the distance.

Lonnie turned his head and shouted, "I'm all right! Keep goin', Casey! *Ride!*"

He'd just gotten that last shout out before Kinch slammed the butt of his rifle against Lonnie's head. It was a glancing blow, but it threw Lonnie onto his back, where he lay staring up at the sky while little, golden butterflies danced in front of his eyes. Beneath the ringing in his ears, he heard Casey's hoof thuds dwindle quickly into the distance.

"I'll go after her!" Engstrom said, running up to his saddled horse.

"Let her go," Kinch said, pushing up off a knee and heaving himself to his feet, breathing hard, cheeks flushed.

He glared down at Lonnie. "We still got this one here. He'll dig up the gold for us. Then we'll kill the hydrophobic mongrel and be shed of this canyon once and for all. By the time she can bring the law, we'll be halfway to Denver and points south."

———

LONNIE'S HEAD ACHED, and the rough ride around the lake and up a low ridge wasn't doing it any good. He rode with his wrists tied to his saddle horn. Engstrom was leading the General by his bridle reins. Kinch led the way up the steep slope around outcroppings of jagged rock resembling the backbones of dinosaurs.

Tall pines and firs loomed over and around them.

Lonnie had lost his bearings, but he thought they were somewhere near the canyon's far northern end, though he couldn't see the craggy peaks around the skull from this low angle. He could hear the hoarse, raspy breathing of the wind around the giant skull, however.

The two outlaws stopped frequently to study their backtrail, to make sure no one was following. Then Kinch would collapse his spyglass, mount his sorrel, and continue riding.

"You sure you remember where you buried the strongbox?" Engstrom called to Kinch around midday, the blazing sun burning down from straight overhead.

"Well, it's been eighteen years," Kinch said, looking around carefully and also a little anxiously, Lonnie thought. "Excuse me if I don't ride right up to it, Dutch!"

"I'm just askin'," Engstrom said, throwing his hands up in supplication. "Just askin', that's all..."

Kinch started to look around more and more anxiously. By the set of his shoulders, Lonnie thought the old outlaw was beginning to panic, thinking he might not have remembered the route to the gold as well as he'd thought he had. He'd probably gone over the map in his head hundreds if not thousands of times, all those years he'd spent behind bars.

Only to discover, in the end, that the years had fogged the trail...

That was all right with Lonnie. The sooner they got to the gold, the sooner he'd be dead. He was still waiting for a chance to skin out away from these two old bandits. After losing Casey, however, they were being more careful. They'd tied Lonnie's wrists tight to his saddle horn, and

Engstrom looked back often to make sure Lonnie hadn't worked himself loose.

Kinch hauled back suddenly on his sorrel's reins. He sat studying a black granite ridge wall down which a small spring trickled over a glistening path of blue-green moss. At the bottom of the ridge the water had formed a slight pool ringed with deep grass. The water flowed over the lip of the pool and down across the trail in a rivulet that murmured like delicate wind chimes.

"What is it?" Engstrom asked Kinch.

Kinch worked his nose like a dog. "That smell. I know that smell. I remember that smell!"

"I reckon my sniffer's done been fouled by too many full privies and slop pails not to mention that rotten prison food they was always feedin' us. Rotten potatoes and man sweat is about all I can smell anymore."

Lonnie could smell what Kinch was smelling. The smell of green growth and wet rock and mushrooms and the slightly cloying smell of moss and mold. He could tell from the way Kinch was now looking around, sniffing, that those smells were reaching up from the past to tickle his memory.

"There!" Kinch said, pointing on up the slope a ways, toward the base of the granite ridge wall. "That's it right there, or I'll be hanged!"

Kinch galloped the sorrel on up the ridge and stopped near a depression at the base of the stone wall. Wildflowers grew in the high grass over and around the depression. So did honeysuckle shrubs and even a few gnarled cedars and pine saplings.

Kinch swung heavily down from his horse and stood staring at the depression, fists on his hips.

He turned toward Engstrom after a time and grinned. He pointed at the depression. "That's it. We laid up here, makin' sure we were shed of the posse. The old diggin' we found is that low spot right there. We slid the strongbox off our mule and into the hole, and caved it in. That brush has done grown up in the eighteen years since. No one's messed with that hole. I can tell they haven't. The gold is still down there, Engstrom!"

He looked around, and then pointed upslope toward several humps of black granite about the size of large ranch wagons. "Beyond them rocks up there—that's where I buried Bentley, so's no one would ever find him."

He looked again at Engstrom, who'd remained on his horse.

"Come on, come on!" Kinch said, beckoning. "Bring the mongrel." He grinned at Lonnie. "And a shovel!"

THIRTY-THREE

LONNIE RAMMED the folding shovel into the dense, tangled roots at the base of a shrub, and glanced at the two men sitting in the grass about ten feet away from him. Both held their rifles across their thighs, watching him eagerly.

Sweat ran down Lonnie's cheeks. It burned in his eyes.

He'd dug two feet down into the hole and was still coming up against large rocks and shrub roots, which required prying and twisting and heaving away, so that he could continue digging deeper into the hole.

"Come on, come on," Kinch said. "You're young and strong, boy. Keep diggin'!"

"I'm thirsty," Lonnie said, dabbing sweat from his eyes with his neckerchief. "Toss me my canteen, will ya?"

His canteen lay in the grass near where the two old bandits lounged like church deacons at a Sunday afternoon picnic. They were passing a small, flat bottle of whiskey back and forth between them.

"No more water till you're done," Kinch growled.

"The faster you dig down to the strongbox," Engstrom said, "the faster you can have a drink of water—ain't that right, Kinch."

"There you have it, kid. Dig!"

Lonnie started digging again with an angry snort. His head hurt from the braining that Kinch had given him. His shirt and long handle top were sweat-basted to his chest and back.

After another ten minutes of digging, he stopped, breathless, and turned to the two old reprobates still passing the bottle, their eyes growing more and more glassy. "This would go a heckuva lot faster if one of you would take a turn and give me a breather," Lonnie said. "It's hot, and, like I said, I'm thirsty. And who knows how far down that box is?"

Kinch wrinkled his nostrils and narrowed his eyes. "Who raised you to talk down to your elders?"

"I'm just sayin'—"

"What you're doin' is sassin' your elders *and* your betters," Engstrom said, pointing an angry finger at Lonnie. "Now, you get to work or I'm gonna come over there and box your ears."

"Keep it up, kid," Kinch put in, "and I'm gonna drill a bullet into each of your knees. How would you like that?"

"How would that help?" Lonnie said, exasperated.

Kinch merely jutted his jaw at him, glaring.

Lonnie sighed and continued digging.

He pried up another rock and dug a few more shovelfuls of gravel. The shovel met something that had no give to it. Lonnie rammed the shovel down against whatever it was, probing, then turned to the outlaws. "Hey, I think I got it!"

He was relieved that his work might soon be over, even though it meant his life would likely soon be over, as well. He was so hot, tired, and hungry that he no longer cared if he lived or died.

The outlaws scrambled drunkenly to their feet, keeping their rifles on Lonnie, and hurried over to the hole.

"Well, keep diggin'!" Kinch ordered. "Keep diggin'!"

Lonnie kept digging until he'd uncovered the top of the stout wooden, two-feet-by-one-foot strongbox. There was a rusted metal hasp but no lock. The lock had likely been shot away by the outlaws some eighteen years ago.

"Sure as tootin'," Kinch said, running an eager hand across his mouth. "There she is, Dutch!"

Engstrom whistled.

"Come on, kid—put your back into it," he ordered. "Haul it on out there!"

Lonnie went back to work, digging along all sides of the box. When he'd gotten a gap dug all around it, he got down on his hands and knees, grabbed one exposed handle, and tried pulling the box out of the ground.

It was still stuck solid.

"It's not movin' an inch," Lonnie said, sitting back on his heels. "If you two want that box out of there, you're gonna have to help me lift it instead of just standin' there blowin' your horns!"

Engstrom glowered at Lonnie. He started toward him, making a fist. "By God, I'm gonna—!"

"Hold it right there!"

The strange voice stopped both men in their tracks.

They and Lonnie swung around to see Sheriff Frank Halliday hunkered down atop a boulder about fifty feet away, aiming his Winchester, which he now loudly cocked. "I got you covered! Drop those rifles and do it now or I'll blow you out of your boots!"

Lonnie might have been ready to die a few minutes ago, but a wave of relief washed over him like a fragrant spring breeze. Despite the trouble he was in for having shot Walleye, he felt as though a yoke had suddenly been lifted from his shoulders.

Kinch stared, shaking his head in awe. "I can't believe it. I just can't believe it."

Engstrom turned to him, his lower jaw hanging in shock. "How can it be, Kinch? How can this be? We was watchin' our backtrail so close!"

"Drop the rifles!" Halliday repeated.

The old outlaws cursed and tossed their rifles away.

Engstrom took his face in his hands and sobbed. Kinch just stared, bleach-faced. Lonnie sank back onto the edge of the hole and dropped his shovel. He heaved a long, ragged sigh of relief, and sleeved sweat from his forehead.

"Appleyard!" Halliday yelled.

Presently, Deputy US Marshal John Appleyard strode out from behind some shrubs to Lonnie's left, spurs chinging, red neckerchief blowing in the breeze. The federal lawman aimed a Spencer carbine straight out from his right shoulder as he moved toward the two outlaws, squinting down the Spencer's barrel.

"You all right, kid?" Appleyard asked.

"I'll live," Lonnie said.

He stopped seven feet from Kinch and Engstrom, keeping his rifle aimed at them. "On your bellies. *Now!*"

The old outlaws got down on their bellies. While Halliday kept them covered from atop the boulder, Appleyard tossed their rifles away and then handcuffed them each behind their backs.

"All right—it's clear!" the federal lawman called to the sheriff.

Appleyard glanced at Lonnie. "Sure you're all right, boy? That's a nice-sized goose egg you have on your head there."

Lonnie was surprised by the federal lawman's concern. He wasn't accustomed to such concern, especially from a lawman.

"I'm all right—thanks," Lonnie said.

He went over and picked up his canteen. As he did, Halliday walked out from behind the boulder. He moved past Lonnie without so much as glancing at the boy. That was fine with Lonnie. Halliday seemed more concerned about the strongbox, which Appleyard was now kneeling over.

The federal lawman grunted and groaned as he tried to pry up the lid. He'd leaned his rifle against a sapling near the top of the hole. "It's on there tight," Appleyard said, and tried again, wedging his fingers down along the edge of the lid.

The lid slid up out of the box, its ancient hinges squawking. As the lid fell back, Appleyard and Halliday stared down at the burlap pouches mounded inside. The pouches were obviously old. They were threadbare, and the "US ARMY" stamped on their sides in black was badly faded.

Appleyard plucked one of the pouches out of the box. Hefting it in his hand, he grinned up at Halliday standing over him, at the edge of the hole. Halliday held his rifle down low in his right hand. He held out his left.

"Toss one."

Appleyard tossed him a bag, which clinked when Halliday grabbed it.

"There's said to be fifty thousand dollars here," Appleyard said.

Halliday whistled as, cradling his rifle in his arms, he opened the pouch and dipped his hand inside. He pulled out a handful of gold coins. They flashed brightly when the sun caught them. The sheriff dribbled them back into the bag.

They made joyful clinking sounds.

Lonnie felt himself salivating at the sound of all that wealth.

Kinch, who'd risen to his knees, looked up at Halliday. "What do you say we split it four ways?"

Engstrom was rising to his knees now, as well. "That's a helluva lot more money than you'll ever make as a sheriff! You, too, there, Marshal!"

Appleyard shook his head. "That money's goin' back to where it came from—the US Army."

"No, it's not."

Appleyard frowned at Halliday. Lonnie jerked his own startled gaze to the sheriff, too. Halliday was smiling down at Appleyard. Halliday was hefting the money pouch in his left hand. He raised his Winchester in his right hand, aiming the barrel at Appleyard's chest.

"Wait, now," Appleyard said, straightening. "Hold on, now, Halliday!"

As he lunged for his rifle, Halliday fired.

Appleyard grunted as the bullet punched into his chest and blew him backward off his feet. He fell back in the hole and rolled sideways. He lay half over the open strongbox.

Lonnie stared in shock, his ears ringing from the rifle report, as Halliday turned to Kinch. The old outlaws regarded the sheriff with loose-lipped disbelief.

"Wait, now, Sheriff," Kinch said, leaning back on his heels. "Wait now. Hold on!"

Halliday shot him.

Engstrom screamed as Halliday shot him, too.

Lonnie jerked violently with each loud, echoing rifle report.

His heart dropped like a cold stone in his belly when Halliday turned toward him and aimed the rifle at his head.

THIRTY-FOUR

"BURY IT," Halliday ordered Lonnie.

The boy stared at the smoking barrel of the sheriff's rifle aimed at his head. The smoke smelled like rotten eggs in the air around him. Lonnie stood frozen, shocked. He glanced around at the dead men.

"Go ahead, kid—bury the loot."

"Wha...huh...?" Lonnie said. "You want me to...*bury* it?"

"That's right."

Keeping his rifle aimed at Lonnie, the sheriff stepped down into the hole. He picked up one of Appleyard's ankles and dragged the man's body out of the hole. He deposited the dead federal lawman beside Kinch and Engstrom.

Then he took his rifle in both hands again.

"I got no use for the gold. Not now, anyway. If I took it now, folks would get suspicious. Several people in Arapaho Creek know that me an' Appleyard headed to the canyon, to look for Kinch. If I didn't come back, they'd figure I'd found the gold and lit out with it. I'd be hunted."

Lonnie stared at the lawman as Halliday glanced around at the dead men, chewing his bottom lip thoughtfully, anxiously. It was as though the sheriff was speaking to clarify his thoughts on the subject of the gold.

On the subject of his keeping it for himself.

Lonnie didn't like how the man was talking. At least, he didn't like that the man was telling him all this...what he was going to do. It gave Lonnie a bad, bad feeling down deep in his loins. A moment ago, he'd thought he'd been saved. Now, he appeared as doomed as he'd been when Kinch and Engstrom had had him by the short hairs.

"True, folks might think that both me and Appleyard was killed...maybe by Kinch and his old prison buddy," Halliday continued. He stared at Lonnie, but he seemed to be seeing right through the boy and into his own future. "Maybe by the bounty hunters who've been shootin' each other around here of late. But if I rebury the gold and leave it here, on the end of the canyon where no one's likely to look for it, I can wait a month, maybe two. No one else will look for it here. The only reason I knew to look for it at this end of the canyon was because I talked to one of the old posse riders, years ago. He followed Kinch and Bentley up this far, but he didn't tell nobody but me...when he was dyin' of cancer. I knew it was around here somewhere, and, sure enough—good ole Kinch escaped the pen an' led me right to it!

"Yeah, that's it. I'll wait a couple of months. I can give notice to the county that I decided to resign...and ride back out here for the gold and light out with it. That way, no one will hunt me, and I won't have to run to Mexico. Hell, no—I can go east or west. Always did want to live high on the hog in a place like Frisco!"

"What about Kinch?" Lonnie said. "What about...the marshal and Engstrom?" He wanted to ask about himself, too, but he was afraid of the answer.

"Appleyard died in the service of his country—killed by Kinch and his old prison pal. I, of course, killed the outlaws. I'll fetch them all back to town, bury 'em proper. I got no idea where the gold is. Kinch must've forgot where he buried it and was just ridin' in circles around the canyon, lookin' for it. Yeah, that's it. He was just ridin' in circles."

Halliday looked at Lonnie, grinning. "That sounds good, don't it?"

He actually seemed to be waiting for Lonnie's response.

When none came, he said, "With Kinch dead, the other gold hunters will give up the chase. Lookin' for the gold without Kinch to lead them to it would be like lookin' for a single pine needle in all the north-south stretch of the Rockies. Besides, I think most of 'em have done shot each other by now, anyways."

Halliday chuckled, in love with his plan.

"In a few months, the gold will go back to bein' nothin' more than a legend. Except for me." Halliday chuckled again, glancing around again at the dead men. "Except for me. I'll just ride in here, dig it up, and ride away—a very, very rich son of a gun!"

He jerked his rifle at the strongbox. "What're you waitin' for, kid? Get to coverin' up that box!"

Lonnie's mouth was dry. His tongue felt like a parched chunk of ancient leather. He ran it across his lower lip, and said, "What...what about me, Sheriff? What're you gonna do about me?"

"Good question!" Halliday was walking out a ways from the hole, looking carefully back the way he'd come as though making sure that no one had heard the gunfire and come to investigate.

That was doubtful, Lonnie knew. It was a big canyon. Halliday and Appleyard must have cut Kinch's trail up here by a mere twist of improbable fate. Maybe they'd heard the crack of Kinch's rifle earlier, when he'd fired at Casey.

"What do you think I should do with you?" Halliday asked when he returned to the hole, which Lonnie had halfheartedly started to fill in again. "Huh, kid? You think you can keep a secret?"

Halliday hitched up his pinstriped pants and sat on a rock about six feet from the hole. He leaned his rifle against the rock and dug into his coat pocket for his makings sack.

"Yeah, I can keep a secret," Lonnie said with no real enthusiasm. He knew Halliday was just toying with him. The sheriff had killed three men as though it had been nothing more than shooting coyotes off a gut wagon. He'd have no qualm about shooting Lonnie...as soon as Lonnie had finished his chore, that was.

"Let me think on it," Halliday said, dribbling chopped tobacco onto the wheat paper he troughed between two fingers. "In the meantime, you just keep workin'. Come on, come on—put some effort into it, will ya?"

———

LONNIE TOOK his time burying the strongbox. He was in no hurry to die. He'd gotten accustomed to the idea of his death several hours ago. Still, he wasn't going to urge it on any faster than he needed to.

Besides, a vague, deep-down part of him managed to keep hope alive that somehow, he'd come up with a way to save himself. As he worked, he glanced several times over at Halliday sitting on the rock, smoking cigarettes, sipping whiskey from Kinch and Engstrom's bottle, and staring dreamily at the hole Lonnie was filling in, as though he were daydreaming about what he was going to do with all that gold.

While the sheriff daydreamed about his riches, Lonnie considered ways to save himself.

If he could get close enough to Halliday, he might be able to smash him in the head with the shovel, and lay him out cold...

But how was he going to get close enough to the man to do that?

"Sure is hot," Lonnie said, when he had the hole about three quarters filled in. "Would you mind handin' me my canteen, Sheriff? It's that one over there near Appleyard's feet."

"You're almost done. When you're finished coverin' the hole and makin' it look all natural-like, then you can have a drink, though I don't really see much point."

He chuckled darkly.

"I'd be able to work faster if I had a drink, Sheriff."

Halliday gave a disgusted chuff. Leaving the rifle leaning against the rock, holding his quirley in his left hand, he walked over and picked up Lonnie's canteen. The boy's heart quickened as Halliday turned toward him. Lonnie squeezed the shovel, getting ready to lift it quickly for a resolute swing.

But then Lonnie's gut fell with disappointment. Halliday only tossed him the canteen. The canteen hit Lonnie in the chest and fell to the ground.

"Nice catch," Halliday said, chuckling as he walked back over to his rock.

Lonnie felt like crying but held himself in check. He set the shovel down, crouched to retrieve the canteen, unscrewed the cap, and took a drink.

When he'd had his fill, he tossed the canteen aside and resumed covering the hole. As he tossed the last few shovelfuls on the hole, Halliday walked into the brush and dragged back some blowdown branches.

The sheriff had his cigarette in his mouth. He'd left the rifle leaning against the rock. Lonnie stopped shoveling to stare at him, his heart quickening again.

Halliday shouldered Lonnie aside and dropped the branches over the hole, hiding it. Lonnie couldn't believe his luck when Halliday turned away from Lonnie and crouched to pick up a limb that had broken off of the main branch.

His heart galloping like a stallion inside his chest, Lonnie squeezed the shovel. He raised it in a high arc. Halliday straightened and turned toward him, the cigarette smoldering between his lips, his eyes narrowed against the smoke. He tossed the branch down on the hole and widened his eyes as the shovel arced toward his head.

THIRTY-FIVE

HALLIDAY STARTED to raise his hands to deflect the shovel, but he didn't get them halfway to his chest before the shovel smacked his left temple with a resounding *clang!*

"Oh!" Eyes rolling back in his head, Halliday stumbled backward.

He managed to get both feet under him. He shook his head. Blood ran down from the deep gash high on his forehead. As he regained his balance, he dropped his hand to the Colt holstered on his right hip.

Again, Lonnie raised the shovel and swung it down with a grunt.

Clang!

Halliday's hand fell away from the revolver as he twisted around and went stumbling and falling into the brush on the other side of the hole. Lonnie stared at the man. Halliday lay belly down, unmoving. Throwing the shovel aside, Lonnie ran over to where General Sherman stood, ground-tied and nervously twitching his ears.

Lonnie grabbed the General's reins. He was breathing hard, heart racing, shaking with anxiety. He glanced back toward where Halliday lay where Lonnie had left him. He still didn't appear to be moving.

Lonnie turned his stirrup out, but he was so tired and stiff that he had to try three times before he managed to pull himself up by the horn and shove his left boot through the stirrup and swing up into the saddle. He turned the General around and touched spurs to the stallion's flanks.

The buckskin galloped around shrubs and large boulders and pines and then started down the gradual slope toward the canyon floor.

Lonnie hadn't paid much attention to the way they'd ridden up here. He'd been too crestfallen and still dazed by Kinch's assault on his head. There was no trail, only a twisting passage through boulders and pines down the hill that grew steeper until Lonnie had to hold the stallion to a trot or risk the horse stumbling on blowdowns and deadfalls as well as patches of dangerous slide rock.

He'd just gained the base of the slope and had started galloping toward the lake he could see shimmering beyond a stand of firs and pines, when something buzzed in the air behind him. The buzz grew louder. The bullet pinged off a boulder ahead and to Lonnie's right.

Rock dust puffed from the side of the boulder. A quarter second later, what felt like a giant, powerful fist slammed into Lonnie's left temple.

Lonnie heard the echoing crack of the distant rifle as he dropped the reins and was hurled out of his saddle. The ground came up to assault him without mercy. He passed out even before he stopped rolling.

Darkness enveloped him.

The pain was there inside him, radiating out from his head. But it was like a loud knock on a door at the far end of a very large house.

The knocking grew louder. Lonnie opened his eyes to see two familiar faces staring down at him. He had trouble placing them at first, because his brain was like a dark room draped with cobwebs. But then the names of his mother's "guests" came to him—the Pinkerton agents, Brocius and Madsen.

"Looks like he's comin' around," said Brocius, though his voice was muffled by the hammering clang in Lonnie's ears. "He killed Appleyard, you say?"

From even farther away rose another familiar voice: "Hard to believe, ain't it? A kid as young as that." Then Halliday walked into Lonnie's view. The sheriff's eyes were swollen, and dried blood formed a long, red river down over his nose and down his cheek. He held his rifle on his right shoulder.

He gingerly fingered his temple as he said, "Laid me out cold. Don't know why he didn't kill me. Had the drop on me. Maybe he figured he'd done enough killin' for one day."

The bearded Madsen was still crouching over Lonnie, who lay on the ground where he'd landed when he'd been knocked off the General's back by the ricocheting bullet. Madsen shook his head.

"Well, given that he's got no pa and his mother don't seem to know what to do with him—I reckon it all adds up to a bad apple, all right."

"No!" Lonnie wanted to shout at the tops of his lungs. But it was like shouting in a dream. He couldn't seem to get the words out. It was as though a large, wet rag had been shoved into his mouth.

"Gonna take him back to town, Sheriff?" Brocius asked.

"Oh, yeah," Halliday said, scowling down at Lonnie, slowly nodding his head.

Lonnie glanced around. Kinch, Engstrom, and Marshal Appleyard lay belly down over the backs of their horses. The horses stood around Lonnie and the three men now. The General stood nearby, head down, staring at Lonnie skeptically, switching his tail nervously.

"Oh, yeah." Halliday shook his head. "I don't care how young he is. That feral pup is gonna stand trial for murder."

"If he lives," Madsen said, chuckling. "That's a nasty crease on his temple there." He raised his voice as he gazed down at Lonnie. "Hey, kid, you hear me?"

Then all went dark again. When Lonnie awoke, he was riding slumped forward in his saddle. His wrists were tied to his saddle horn. His boots were tied to the stirrups. Halliday was leading the General by his bridle reins. The two Pinkertons rode to either side of the sheriff.

The men were talking and chuckling like old pals as they rode, easing down out of the mountains. Lonnie looked around to get a fix on where they were, but then a big, black hand closed over his face, and when he woke again, he was in a jail cell.

He lifted his head, wincing against the throbbing pain slicing deep into his skull from his temple and setting all his nerves on fire. The cell wobbled around him.

Though his vision was fuzzy, he recognized the sheriff's office in Arapaho Creek. He'd been in this very cell roughly a year ago, when he'd been arrested for the murder of one of the two deputies who'd mistaken him for one of Dupree's gang.

Well, here he was again...

He squinted his eyes to see a man sitting at the rolltop desk against the jailhouse's front stone wall, to the left of a window through which buttery mountain light angled. The man at the desk had his back to Lonnie. It was a broad back clad in a dark-brown wool vest over a pinstriped cream shirt. A white bandage was wrapped around the top of the man's head. Brown hair streaked with gray fell out from beneath it to curl onto his shirt collar.

Smoke curled up from the pipe the man was smoking as he crouched over the desk, writing on a notepad.

Lonnie looked more closely around his cell to see that a hide-bottom chair angled up beside his cot. A light, fawn-colored leather jacket hung from the back of the chair. He could smell a familiar, subtle, flowery fragrance. Casey was standing to his right, staring out the barred window. She was partly silhouetted against the bright sunlight, but her blonde hair sparkled like liquid gold.

She turned her head toward Lonnie and jerked with a little start.

"You're awake." Casey sat in the chair. She crouched forward, gazing at Lonnie, eyes bright with concern. "This is probably a silly question, but how do you feel?"

"Reckon I've felt some better," Lonnie said, pushing himself up a little higher on the cot, which hung out from the cell wall on iron chains.

There was a small, wooden table to his right. A basin sat on the table. Casey reached over to the basin, plucked a cloth out of the water, and wrung it out.

"That's a nasty cut on your head, Lonnie. You're lucky you didn't bleed to death. Doc Hagen said he got you stitched up just in time. He'll be around soon to change your bandage."

Hearing the two of them talking, Halliday turned in his chair. "Well, well," the sheriff said. "You're still kickin', huh, kid?"

Both his eyes were discolored and slightly swollen, the right one more than the left one.

"No thanks to you," Lonnie said. He'd spoken too loudly. The noise clanged inside his head, battering his tender brain plate.

"Lonnie, that's enough," Casey said, stretching the damp cloth across his forehead, which he now realized had a bandage wrapped around it, same as Halliday. "Don't you think you're in enough trouble?"

Halliday chuckled, shaking his head. His chair squawked as he turned back around to face his desk and his paperwork.

Lonnie had a feeling he knew the answer to the question, but he asked, anyway: "What kind of trouble am I in, Casey? What did Halliday say I did, exactly?"

Casey pressed the cloth against his forehead. She stared down at him sadly, lips pursed. "You just rest up, Lonnie. No need to hear about it just yet. Later, when you're stronger."

Lonnie placed his hand on hers. "Tell me."

Casey drew a deep breath. She glanced over her shoulder at Halliday, who had his back to them again. She turned to Lonnie.

"Well, Lonnie Gentry, you're really in the soup this time. You've been charged with the cold-blooded murder of three men, includin' a deputy United States marshal. Your trial is due to take place just as soon as you can walk."

THIRTY-SIX

"CASEY," Lonnie said, squeezing her wrist. "You gotta listen to me. You're the only one I can trust."

He glanced at the sheriff who was still hunkered over his paperwork, filling the office with the aromatic smell of pipe tobacco. The sheriff didn't appear to be listening to the conversation in the cell, but Lonnie knew he was. He was trying to catch every word.

That's why Lonnie kept his voice low.

"Casey, I didn't kill nobody," he whispered, staring at the girl with desperation. "It was him—Halliday. He shot Kinch and his old prison pal, Engstrom *after* he shot the marshal."

Casey glanced over her shoulder at Halliday. "Why would he *do* that, Lonnie?"

"Why do you think? Because he wanted to take the gold for himself. Kinch showed me where it was. I dug it up. But then Halliday and Marshal Appleyard rode up on us. That's when Halliday shot all three of 'em. He had me rebury the money. Now, if we can get someone to ride out to that canyon and..."

Lonnie stared at Casey, who regarded him with a weird expression. "Casey," he said, "you believe me, don't you?"

His head was suddenly aching even more than before.

His stomach felt tight and raw.

"Casey," he urged, squeezing her wrist. "Answer me."

"Sure, Lonnie," she said, regarding him as though he were a strange language she was trying to interpret. She pulled her wrist free of his grip and ran both hands down her face, shaking her hair back from her cheeks. "Of course, I do. It's just..."

"Just what?"

"It's just...that...why would Halliday think he could get away with takin' all that gold? I mean, there are so many men after it. The US Army is after it! How far would he think he could get?"

"That's why he had me rebury it after I dug it up for Kinch," Lonnie said, leaning far toward her.

Keeping his voice low was a hard feat, for he desperately wanted...*needed*...to convince Casey of the truth.

"He wants to let some time pass before he goes after it. So no one gets suspicious. Now, with Kinch dead, everybody...includin' the army...will likely give up on that gold. It'll go back to bein' just one more legend in the Never Summers. Halliday intends to resign his job here in a few months and ride out and dig up the loot and live high on the hog in San Francisco!"

Casey just stared at him, confused.

"Casey, for God's sake—you have to believe me, of all people!"

The girl brushed befuddled fingers across her forehead. "Lonnie, I want to believe you. But you have to admit, that sounds a little far-fetched."

"Sure, it does. But that's the story. Halliday told me what he was goin' to do. Gold will make folks do desperate things."

"Yes, it will."

"What do you mean?"

Casey glanced once more at Halliday and then turned back to Lonnie, gazing at him with renewed gravity. "Lonnie, why did you really want to ride back to that canyon yesterday? Was it really to find the body of Cade McLory?"

Lonnie studied her. He felt the chinking in his own armor begin to grow brittle.

"Yes," he said, finally, after studying his hands for a time. "Yes, it was. But I gotta admit I was sort of wantin' to see about findin' the gold my own self."

Casey pursed her lips, her cheeks dimpling.

"But I had no intention of keepin' it for myself, Casey. I promise. I was only wantin' the reward for turnin' it in!"

Tears began veiling Casey's eyes as she now began to study Lonnie with a vague sort of sadness. She canted her head to one side. And then, with a sharp stab of mental agony, he knew what she was thinking about.

Last year, during their trek over the mountains with Dupree's loot, they were helped by a cynical, old, ex-Confederate soldier, Wilbur Calhoun. Calhoun had lived alone with his dog in the mountains for years, having run away from the nearly destroyed South and his own dark past in the years after the war. For a brief time, Calhoun had half-convinced Lonnie that he and Casey should take the stolen money for themselves.

Casey was remembering that momentary weakening in Lonnie's character. He could see it in the girl's heartbroken gaze.

A single tear dribbled down her cheek.

Staring at Lonnie, she sniffed, brushed the tear from her cheek with the back of her hand, and said, "Sheriff Halliday, I think I'd like to go, now, please."

Halliday rose from his chair. He grabbed a key ring hanging from a ceiling support post and unlocked the door. He regarded Casey with phony sympathy. "I don't blame you a bit, Miss Stoveville. Kind of hard to take, ain't it? Seein' a boy with his whole future ahead of him ruin everythin' out of plum meanness and greed..."

Casey slipped into her jacket. She turned once more to Lonnie, who stared at her in shock. How could she could believe Halliday? But then, he supposed it was understandable, given that he'd actually entertained the notion of running off with the loot from the Golden bank. He had only himself to blame for that.

"Casey, don't believe him," Lonnie urged. "He's a killer. In two, three months, he'll leave town—you can bet the bank on that. He's gonna go dig up the gold and hightail it!"

Halliday opened the door. As Casey stepped out, sniffing, Halliday scowled at Lonnie, shaking his head in phony disappointment. "How he does go on. I'm sorry, Miss Stoveville." He closed the door, turned the key in the lock. "In the boy's defense, he grew up hard. Livin' out in them mountains will drive full-grown men crazy. Here, he's only fourteen. He lost his pa. Now he's livin' with his ma who is, as I reckon you know, less than...well, less than what you'd call a perfect mother. Raisin' that killer Dupree's child..."

"I know," Casey said quietly, closing her upper teeth over her bottom lip as she gazed up at the sheriff. "I did expect more from him, though. After all we'd been through together, I'd thought he'd grown, matured."

She turned her disenchanted gaze at Lonnie. It was like a cold, hard slap across Lonnie's face.

"But, like you said, he's had it tough out there." Casey returned her gaze to the sheriff. "Sheriff Halliday, what...what do you think will happen...if the judge finds him guilty, I mean? He's only fourteen years old. Surely his age must be considered."

"I don't know," Halliday said. "I for one am goin' to ask the judge to go as easy as he can on him. But...you know, there is the problem of his killin' that deputy last year."

"That was in self-defense!" Lonnie yelled, sitting up now on the edge of his cot. He winced at the brutal assault his yell dealt his battered head. "And it was an accident besides!"

Quietly, reasonably, Casey said, "The judge must take into consideration that Lonnie was responsible for returnin' the stolen bank money to Golden."

"Oh, I'll make sure he knows all about that. The problem is, Miss Stoveville, we both probably know that if you, the sheriff's daughter, hadn't been such a good influence on him—well, who knows where he might have taken that money?"

Halliday turned his dark, accusing look at Lonnie. Anyone else would probably have only seen the dark side of that look. The phony side. But Lonnie saw the mockery deep in the man's eyes, as well, and it caused rage to boil up in him.

"You bastard, Halliday," Lonnie said. "You no-good rotten bastard!"

THIRTY-SEVEN

"LONNIE," Casey said, stomping her foot down. "Cursin' the sheriff isn't goin' to help your situation one bit!"

"Please, Miss Stoveville," Halliday said, taking the girl by her shoulders and steering her toward the office's front door. "You'd best go. You don't need to hear any more of what that criminal has to say. You're a fine young lady, and you shouldn't mix with the likes of that... that...kill—!"

Halliday cut himself off when a knock sounded on the door. The door opened and none other than Casey's fancy Dan poked his head into the office.

Seeing Casey, fancy Dan's eyes widened. He smiled and removed his hat. "Ah, Casey, there you are. Mister Hendrickson said I'd find you over here. I just stopped by to see if I could take you to lunch."

He glanced past Casey and the sheriff, and scowled at Lonnie, as though he were scrutinizing dog dung on his boots.

"That's sweet of you, Niles, thank you," Casey said, giving the fancy Dan a weak smile.

She glanced once more at Lonnie, a little sheepishly, and walked over to where her suitor waited by the door.

"You two kids have a good time, now!" Halliday called after them.

The fancy Dan, the banker's son, pinched his hat brim to the sheriff, glanced once more, distastefully, at Lonnie, and followed Casey out of the office. When he'd closed the door behind him, Halliday strode over to

Lonnie, laughing, kicking his boots out happily, planting his fists on his hips.

"Now, see that—you're just a disappointment all the way around! Oh, well—don't worry about Miss Stoveville. Looks like the banker's son will keep her distracted." Halliday whistled. "That girl sure is purty—ain't she? A shame you made her so unhappy. Maybe she'll feel a little better about it all, once the judge decides to play cat's cradle with your head." The sheriff laughed.

A red haze of fury dropped down over Lonnie's eyes. He bounded up off the cot and ran to the cell door, wrapping his hands around the bars and bellowing, "I'm gonna kill you, Halliday! If it's the last thing I do, I'm gonna kill you!"

Just then the office door opened and a pudgy, little man in a slouch hat and cream-colored suit with a red foulard tie walked into the office. He scowled warily at Lonnie, tapping ashes from the dynamite-sized cigar he held in his pale, pudgy fist. He wore a gold ring on his little finger.

"Good lord—is that the little miscreant there?"

Halliday swung around to the man. He switched demeanors as quickly as changing hats. Turning his mouth corners down and wagging his head, he sighed and said, "Judge Peabody, meet Lonnie Gentry. Full of vim an' vinegar even with that notch I carved across his wooden head."

Gritting his teeth against the pain in his temple, Lonnie swung slowly around, more crestfallen than he'd ever been, and dropped back down on the edge of his cot. He leaned forward and took his head in his hands.

"Listen here, young man," Peabody said, striding up to the door of Lonnie's cell and glowering at the boy inside. "It would do you to be on your very best behavior. And I would not consider threatening the county sheriff before you're due to go on trial for murder; very good behavior at all!"

Lonnie merely sighed and shook his head, staring at the floor.

The judge turned to Halliday. "I see he's conscious now, anyway."

"That he is, Judge. That he is. Oh, and, uh...just so you know—that *was* good behavior for him."

The judge shook his head.

"Why don't we go ahead and try him tomorrow, then? I have to be in Denver by the end of the week for a meeting with the governor." Peabody turned to Lonnie and snarled like a bobcat caught in a leg trap. "The governor is making sure that we judges and law enforcement officers are tightening the reins on the criminal element all across this great territory of ours. We've had enough crime. We must bring civilization to the frontier. A peaceful, harmonious future is ours only if we haze the rats into their holes!"

He turned back to Halliday. "I'm having my gallows wheeled up to Arapaho Creek. Should be squawkin' through the mountains right now. They're pulling it up from Benson, where I hung three claim jumpers only yesterday."

Lonnie jerked his head up. "You can't hang me. I'm only fourteen years old!"

"They'll set it up out on Main Street," the judge continued to Halliday. He looked at Lonnie and poked his cigar into his mouth. "Just in case, mind you. Just in case..."

Lonnie was flabbergasted. "I'm only fourteen years old!"

"The kid has a point, Judge. He's only fourteen years old. You can't hang a boy so young!" The sheriff was a darn good actor. He sounded like he really meant it, though the boy also knew that the sheriff was resisting the tremendous urge to cast Lonnie a furtive wink. "Keep in mind his home life has been less than, well, stable. His mother is somewhat of, uh...Jane-about-the-mountains."

"Yes, I've heard about his home life," Peabody said, blowing more smoke. "Too bad, too bad. Of course, I'll take that into consideration."

"Thanks, Judge. There might be a chance of turnin' the little killer around...however slim," Halliday said.

Lonnie glared at the sheriff.

"I can only consider the evidence, Sheriff." Peabody gave a caustic chuff as he turned again to Lonnie. "In the meantime, I suggest you refrain from threatening the sheriff here with bodily harm. That is *not* a good testament to your character!"

The judge poked the cigar back into his little, round, pink mouth, and waddled out of the office.

When Peabody was gone, Halliday turned his wolfish gaze on his prisoner. "You might want to massage your neck muscles, kid. They don't call him Hang-'em-high Hank for nothin'!"

Halliday laughed.

Lonnie sagged back down on the cot. He rolled onto his side and choked back tears of fear, fury, and frustration. It was a hard-fought war, but he would not, could not, let himself break down in front of Halliday. If he allowed himself to succumb, the corrupt sheriff would know he'd broken Lonnie's spirit. Halladay would have won.

Somehow, Lonnie had to keep his emotions on a leash.

And, somehow, he had to figure a way out of this current mess he was in.

As he lay there, calming himself, he drifted off to sleep. He woke once when the doctor came into his cell to replace the bandage on his head. Then his fatigue, as well as the tea that the doctor gave him for the pain, caused him to drift back off into the land of blissful slumber.

He woke later in the afternoon and lay there on his cot, trying to pick his spirits up by thinking positive thoughts. But positive thoughts were few and far between. How could he think positively when he was due to be tried the very next day for three murders he had not committed by a judge known as Hang-'em-high Hank?

Not only that, but he was alone. He did not know if anyone had gotten word to his mother about his current predicament. He hadn't thought to ask Casey about that. Surely, Casey would have sent word out to May Gentry. But even if Lonnie's mother knew about what he was going through, she was tied down with little Jeremiah. She couldn't very well leave the baby to ride through the mountains to visit her jailed son.

Besides, what could she do to help?

She'd probably only become hysterical and cause Lonnie even more frustration, even more worry.

Lonnie rose with a wince, hardening his jaws against the thundering pain that the movement caused his battered head, and moved to the window. There was nothing to see out there but trash and stacked, split firewood and a two-hole privy flanked by pine trees. But it felt good to sniff the warm breeze, to smell the weeds and the creeks that meandered around the edges of the town.

Who knew when he'd be able to enjoy such smells again?

Who knew if, after tomorrow, he'd ever smell *anything* again?

Dead men didn't have much of anything to smell, most likely.

He gave a shiver at the thought of his own demise. Especially his own demise by hanging...

But surely the judge wouldn't hang a fourteen-year-old boy. He might say he would, but when it came right down to it, he'd most likely send Lonnie to some reform school in Denver. The possibility began to seem more and more likely the more Lonnie thought about it, for surely the good, law-abiding citizens of Arapaho Creek wouldn't let the judge and Halliday hang a boy.

No doubt about it. He'd likely be sent to Denver. He should be able to escape such a school for wayward boys fairly easily, given the cunning qualities he was so well known for.

When he managed to make his break, he'd find a way to prove his innocence as well as prove, once and for all, that Sheriff Frank Halliday himself was the one responsible for murdering Marshal Appleyard.

Somewhat relieved by the more optimistic train of his thoughts, Lonnie drifted back to sleep.

THIRTY-EIGHT

LONNIE WAS AWAKENED EARLY that evening by Deputy Bohannon bringing him a bowl of thin stew and a chunk of dry bread from one of the town's lesser eateries. When he was nearly finished with the Spartan meal, Lonnie was paid a visit by the attorney whom the county had assigned to represent Lonnie in court the next day.

Vincent Briggs was a known drunk and whoremonger. His suit was too small for him, and his long handles showed through several places in his threadbare pants. He smelled like a walking spittoon and a beer bucket.

Lonnie dutifully related his version of the tumultuous events to the man with no real passion. His audience seemed to have trouble staying awake and upright. Briggs kept blinking his eyes exaggeratedly, grunting and wetting his pencil's dull point on his tongue.

About all he said was: "Hmm. Uh-huh...hmmm."

Heck, if Lonnie's own girl, Casey Stoveville—at least, she'd once *been* his girl—didn't believe Lonnie's story, why should anyone else including a drunken, old, used-up attorney who couldn't have done Lonnie much good if he'd even believed his tale?

When the attorney left after penciling only a few brief notes in a yellowed pocket notepad, Lonnie lay back down for another badly needed nap.

A raucous clattering assaulted his ears and set his head burning afresh.

He sat up, wide-eyed. Instantly, his guts recoiled.

Randall "Walleye" Miller was raking a tin coffee cup across the bars of Lonnie's cell door. Miller lowered the cup and grinned, his wandering eye roving to the outside edge of its socket. He had a crutch under his left arm. His left thigh was thickly padded beneath his greasy denim trousers.

"Sorry, killer—didn't mean to wake ya!"

Miller chuckled. Judging by how glassy his eyes were, he had a few drinks under his belt.

"Just thought I'd let you know I got office duty tonight. I always got office duty, seein' as how I ain't gettin' around nearly as well as I once did."

The deputy's smile evaporated. He scowled at Lonnie, broad nostrils flaring angrily.

"The doc said I come close to losin' this leg."

"Yeah, well, you only got yourself to blame for that," Lonnie said.

Walleye scowled at him again through the bars. Then he swung around and hobbled over to the ceiling support post from which the iron key ring hung. Walleye removed the ring from the spike in the post and returned to Lonnie's cell.

Lonnie's heart thudded.

"Say, now...," the boy said, staring at the key in Walleye's hand.

Walleye smiled with one half of his mouth as he stuck the key in the lock. There was the metallic rasping, scraping sound of the locking bolt being slid back into the door. The bolt clicked. The door sang as it sagged in its frame.

Walleye pulled the key out of the lock.

"You wanna run, boy?" The deputy paused, eyes narrowed, malicious. "Here's your opportunity."

Walleye hobbled back to the support post. He returned the key ring to the spike then sat down in the swivel chair behind the rolltop desk. He turned the chair toward Lonnie's cell. Walleye removed his sawed-off, double-barrel shotgun from atop the desk, and set it across his lap.

"Go ahead, killer. Make a run for it." Walleye smiled again with challenge, one nostril flaring, a dark flush rising up behind his thick, curly beard. "I want you to."

He caressed the gut-shredder's rabbit-ear hammers with his thumb.

Lonnie looked at the shotgun's wicked double bores. He looked at Walleye's savage features.

Lonnie sagged back down on the cot and rested his arm on his forehead with a ragged sigh of defeat.

———

LONNIE LAY on the cot for a long time, considering his situation.

While the events of the past several days, starting with his being nearly run down by the four horseback riders in the high mountains, galloped across his mind like a herd of wild horses heading for water, he found himself wondering if he really was as bad as everyone said he was.

Was he a wicked, no-account kid who'd been steered in the wrong direction by the early death of his father and his lonely, wayward mother? He supposed he was a headstrong boy. He had things he wanted to get done in this life. And he was bound and determined to make a good life for himself. Before the trouble outside Skull Canyon, he'd wanted to make a good life for himself *and* his mother and brother.

Only after the trouble had not only started but had risen like water in an arroyo during a flash flood, he'd decided to search for the stolen payroll money, collect the reward on it—if a reward was being offered, that was— and light out on his own.

That was probably where he'd gone wrong, he decided. After the trouble with the four riders and then finding Cade McLory on death's doorstep and being nearly drowned in the stock trough by Walleye, not to mention discovering that Casey had set her hat for the fancy Dan, he should have forgotten about the loot. He'd told himself he'd gone back to Skull Canyon to fetch McLory back to town, to help prove his own innocence in shooting Walleye.

But that had been a fib he'd told himself as well as Casey.

He'd really gone back to the canyon because he'd been drawn to the attraction of the buried loot. He'd felt sorry for himself, for the way his life had turned out, for the abuse he'd taken from brutish men, for suffering the indignities of a wayward mother and other folks around him who didn't understand him—who mistook his independence and determination to be taken seriously for recklessness.

He'd intended on abandoning his mother and his baby brother.

Self-pity was what had drawn him back to the cursed canyon and the money. He'd wanted a chance to leave these mountains and start a new life for himself, believing wrongly that you could leave one life cold and start a whole new one without bringing the core of yourself along for the ride.

Self-pity.

That was his mistake.

Self-pity and believing that money could change your life in anything more than superficial ways.

If he got out of this tight spot alive—and that was starting to look more and more unlikely—he'd keep that in mind the next time he considered abandoning his responsibilities to ride off seeking greener pastures. His life was here in these mountains with his mother and his brother. He wished it could be with Casey, too, but that looked as unlikely as his living through tomorrow without having his neck stretched.

Still, he made a mental note to try to be better.

Then he heard Walleye snoring.

Lonnie looked up from his cot.

Sure enough, the big, bearded deputy sat in the chair facing Lonnie, his head dipped to his chest. His hands lay slack on the shotgun. Deep snores rose from his fluttering lips.

Lonnie looked at his unlocked cell door, and his heart gave a hard, anxious thud.

THIRTY-NINE

LONNIE LOOKED AT WALLEYE AGAIN.

Was he pretending, or was he really asleep?

The big deputy's broad, lumpy chest rose and fell heavily as he snored. His lips continued to flutter with each exhalation.

He sure *looked* asleep.

Lonnie dropped one leg over the side of the cot. Then the other leg. He winced when the cot's chains jangled faintly. He rose slowly and moved just as slowly toward the door, walking on the balls of his boots.

He stopped at the door, looked once more at Walleye. If the man wasn't really asleep, if he was only faking it, as soon as Lonnie started to open the door, Walleye would likely lift the shotgun and blow Lonnie to Kingdom Come.

Lonnie's heart skipped a beat.

But, then again, what did it really matter? Tomorrow, there was a good chance he'd be hanged from the judge's famous gallows, which, constructed on a large, wheeled wagon bed, could be moved quite handily from town to town. He knew that hanging was a bad way to die. He'd heard the stories about men strangling slowly and soiling themselves as they danced bizarrely several feet from the ground, a gathered crowd cheering them on while eating popcorn and ham sandwiches.

A far better fate would be a quick death being blown into little pieces by Walleye Miller's barn blaster from a distance of ten feet.

Lonnie placed his right hand on a bar of the door. He gave it a slow, easy shove. The door opened, the hinges groaning very softly but still too loudly for Lonnie's comfort. He pushed the door more slowly, an inch at a time, gritting his teeth at the very low singing sound that the hinges made.

Lonnie's heart raced. The door was open two and a half feet. He could slip through the opening and be across the office to the front door in about three seconds.

Lonnie drew a deep breath. He glanced once more at Walleye. No doubt about it—the man was dead out.

Lonnie sidestepped through the opening. Keeping his eyes on the ugly shotgun resting across Walleye's broad thighs, he made his way across the room on the balls of his boots. He made it to the front door. He placed his hand on the knob and glanced once more at Walleye.

Suddenly, Walleye lifted his chin from his chest.

He threw his head back against the chair and opened his eyes. He stopped snoring.

Lonnie's blood turned to ice. He stared, ready for the hail of buckshot that would end his days.

Walleye's eyes rolled back in his head, showing the whites. His eyes closed and his chin dropped again to his chest without resistance. The deputy wagged his big, bearded head a couple of times, groaning and smacking his lips.

Then he became very still. Lonnie waited, his heart hammering in his ears. Soon, Walleye began snoring again, inhaling slowly, broadening his shoulders and then exhaling through his mouth, making a sawing sound, causing his lips to flutter.

Lonnie's own shoulders sagged with relief. He turned to the door in front of him and started to turn the knob. He stopped when a voice sounded outside the sheriff's office.

"All right, Gandy. I'll be around again in another hour or two. I'll check your back door!"

Deputy Bohannon was heading toward the jail office!

Lonnie jerked another look at Walleye, whose head was still down. But he'd stopped snoring. Outside, footsteps were growing louder. Lonnie swung around and beat a hasty, quiet retreat back to his cell. He drew the door closed behind him but did not latch it.

Footsteps thudded on the stoop fronting the sheriff's office. The front door opened.

His heart beating wildly, Lonnie sat down on his cot and took his head in his hands, rubbing his eyes and yawning, as though he'd just awakened.

Bohannon stopped just inside the open door through which the smells of the night came on a breath of cool mountain air. He looked at Lonnie and then turned to Miller.

"Walleye!"

The walleyed deputy jerked his head up with a start. He rose from his chair, widening his eyes, and aiming his shotgun at Lonnie's cell.

"Hold on! Hold on!" Lonnie yelled, throwing his hands up.

Bohannon scowled at the cell door. He moved forward, stopped just outside the cell, and looked at the gap between the door and the cell. He looked at Lonnie and gave a dry chuckle.

He looked at Walleye, slammed the cell door closed, and said, "Bad luck to cheat the hangman, fool!"

———

LONNIE HAD a miserable night's sleep.

He probably wouldn't have slept at all for anticipating his date with Hang-'em-high Hank the next day, but the head wound kept pulling him under into a harried race of dreams that included images of a shadowy gallows and of hang ropes and a laughing, cheering crowd. Lonnie's own death dreams were confused with images of Cade McLory wandering through a cave and calling for Lonnie to come and bury him.

On the heels of the McLory dream, Lonnie woke in a cold sweat. He'd been so preoccupied with saving his own neck that he'd forgotten about McLory's body, which lay where Kinch and Engstrom had invaded Lonnie and Casey's camp in the mountains. Thoughts of poor McLory being dined upon by mountain lions, coyotes, and wolves added a whole new, grisly dimension of horror to dreams of Lonnie's own demise.

He was almost glad when Walleye woke him by wickedly raking the tin cup across the bars of his cell, even though the sound was like a long, rusty nail being driven into the same place the bullet had cut a nasty furrow across his head. After he'd eaten a breakfast as spartan as his supper, the doctor returned to clean the wound, apply a fresh smearing of arnica, and change Lonnie's bandage.

At ten a.m., both Walleye and Bohannon handcuffed and shackled the boy. They prodded him out of his cell and down the street to the court-house, a two-story log building with a courtroom on the lower floor heated by a large, fieldstone hearth. The dozen or so spectator benches quickly filled with a milling crowd of townsfolk—men as well as women and even a few children—always eager for the spectacle of a trial and a possible hanging.

In fact, trials and hangings were more eagerly anticipated than the revelry that accompanied the Fourth of July.

The two Pinkerton detectives, Brocius and Madsen, were sitting on a bench in the front row. Lonnie wondered if they were still staying out at his ranch. Then he wondered if his mother might have made it to town for the trial—certainly she'd heard about it by now from the two Pinkertons if from no one else—but after sweeping the room with his gaze, he decided she hadn't.

May Gentry had her hands full with little Jeremiah.

As Lonnie's eyes swept the room, he found himself meeting Casey's concerned, worried gaze. The girl sat on a bench in the middle of the room. She wore a small, straw hat trimmed with fake flowers. Lonnie tried to send her a smile, but then he remembered her skepticism regarding his story, and fancy Dan.

Lonnie's cheeks turned to stone. He looked away from the girl.

The trial was delayed when a young collie dog followed its owner into the courtroom and then didn't want to leave when its owner ordered it back outside. Instead, the pup sought refuge behind the judge's bench sitting up high at the front of the room. Enflamed by the crowd and the judge's raucous gaveling, the young dog ran barking around the room while its owner and Sheriff Halliday and Deputies Walleye and Bohannon chased the creature through the laughing crowd and back out the double front doors into the street.

Only after the dog was gone and the doors were closed did someone notice that Lonnie's attorney, Vincent Briggs, was not sitting with his client at the defendant's table before the judge's bench and to the right of where the grim, straight-backed prosecuting attorney, Archibald Fleischman, sat trimming his nails with a clasp knife.

Bohannon was ordered to locate Briggs, who came in ten minutes later smelling as he always did but more so—like a spittoon and a beer bucket. Breadcrumbs no doubt from a free saloon lunch counter clung to his necktie and ratty wool vest.

"Please forgive me, your honor," the attorney said as the crowd settled down. "I was taking notes for the trial while I ate a sandwich, and the time simply got away from me."

Lonnie could tell the man was slurring some of his words as he nervously brushed crumbs and a few chunks of ham that clung to his gold watch chain sagging from his vest.

"The perils of such dedication—eh, Vince?" Judge Peabody said from his bench, giving a caustic snort.

He rapped his gavel down hard on his sound block. The laughing crowd fell silent.

The judge gave Lonnie a grave glance and then swept his businesslike gaze across the small sea of fidgeting onlookers. "Now, let's get down to brass tacks, and maybe we can get out of here by noon!"

FORTY

"THE FIRST AND...UM...THE *only* witness I'd like to call today is none other than Sheriff Frank Halliday himself," announced the tall, gray prosecutor, Archibald Fleischman, gripping the lapels of his claw hammer frock coat as though he were afraid the coat would blow away if he didn't hold it down.

As the sheriff rose and started toward the witness chair beneath the judge's bench, Halliday stopped and turned to Lonnie. He wore a fresh bandage around the top of his head, as did Lonnie himself. Halliday's bandage sported a small bloodstain where Lonnie had beaned the man with the shovel. As he stared at Lonnie, the sheriff turned his mouth corners down, gave a grim wag of his head, then continued walking over to the witness chair.

He took a seat, fingering the bandage gently, making a show of the injury.

Again, he shook his head, as though the tale he was about to tell was a grim one indeed, and not an easy one to relate.

Lonnie snorted at that.

The boy was not shocked to hear the sheriff tell the same story he'd related to Lonnie—about Lonnie throwing in with Kinch and his prison pal for a cut of the gold, and then, getting the drop on both the unwitting and unsuspecting Halliday and Appleyard—"Who'd think a boy so young capable of such savagery!"—opening up with the Winchester he managed to snap up off the ground before laying Halliday out cold with a shovel.

The crowd of onlookers murmured and muttered as the sheriff told his tale. At one point, the judge had to interrupt Halliday and used his gavel to settle the crowd before nodding to the sheriff to continue.

When the sheriff punctuated his tale with another disbelieving wag of his head, Lonnie couldn't help but leaping to his feet and yelling, *"If I'm such a hard-hearted, cold-blooded killer, why didn't I cut you down with the rifle, too, Halliday, you fang-toothed liar?"*

Of course, that had been a grave misstep on Lonnie's part.

Everyone in the courtroom, including the six-man jury seated on the far side of the room, looked at him as though he were a lion on a dangerously long chain.

"You'll get a chance to tell your side of it, young man!" the judge scolded, hammering his gavel down on the sound block. "Till then, you hold your tongue, or I'll have you bound and gagged!"

When the judge asked Briggs if he wanted to cross-examine the sheriff, Lonnie's so-called attorney merely shook his head. The man no doubt wanted to get back to the free lunch counter as quickly as he could, Lonnie thought with another inward chuff.

The prosecutor called Lonnie to the stand. The sheriff refused to remove the shackles on Lonnie's ankles.

"Can't take a chance on him makin' a run for it, your honor," Halliday said, shaking his head darkly.

One of the female onlookers gave a quiet gasp at the prospect of the crazed young killer running wild throughout the town.

The judge nodded his understanding to the sheriff.

Lonnie traversed the space between the defense table and the witness chair awkwardly, chains rattling, boots scuffing on the courthouse's worn puncheon floor. Prompted by the prosecutor, Lonnie told the true story of how Halliday shot Appleyard and then both of his prisoners, Kinch and Engstrom, while they lay handcuffed on the ground.

The crowd gave a collective, incredulous murmur as Lonnie related the grisly events. Halliday sat on a front-row bench, scowling and shaking his head in disgust at the low morals of one so young.

"Why didn't he shoot you, then, too?" the prosecutor wanted to know.

"Because he wanted me to bury the loot for him, so he could come back and dig it up later," Lonnie said. "He would have killed me after I'd gotten the job done, too, if I hadn't laid him out with the shovel!"

Halliday looked around the room, pointing to the bloodstained bandage on his head. Several women gasped and shook their heads at the evidence of such violence in one so young...

"I can prove my story is true, Judge," Lonnie said. "Take me up into them mountains, and I'll show you where the loot is buried, just waitin' for Halliday to come retrieve it after he's let things simmer down for a couple months."

"Why don't you just tell us where it is?" asked the prosecutor, fists on his lapels, a knowing grin tugging at his mouth corners.

"There's no way I can tell it," Lonnie said. "I can't remember that clear. But I can show you, sure enough!"

"Oh, certainly, certainly," the prosecutor said, broadening his knowing smile as he looked around at the riveted crowd. "You'd love to be given a saddled horse, wouldn't you? You'd love to be taken up into those mountains and given the opportunity to escape your grim fate... *wouldn't you, you cunning little devil?*"

The crowd erupted at that.

"Why, I've never seen the like of such a young criminal as that!" bellowed a jowly old woman with small, round steel glasses beneath a gray, lace-edged poke bonnet. She had a thick Southern accent, as did most of the folks in and around the Never Summers.

She'd lurched to her feet and was giving the judge a commanding glare. "We all know who his mother is. Why, she bore an outlaw's child! This critter's father was a no-good *Yankee*. And now he's killed three more men. When will it stop, I ask? *When will it stop?*"

"Sit down, sit down, Mrs. Harmony! If you erupt like that again, I'll have you escorted to the door!" Peabody slammed his gavel down several times, the reports echoing like pistol fire. "Pipe down! Pipe down!" he admonished the loudly milling crowd.

When the din had died, the judge turned to the prosecutor.

"Any more questions, Mister Fleischman?"

"None, sir," the prosecutor said, strolling leisurely back to his table. "None whatsoever. I think we've all heard quite enough!"

"I know I have!" intoned Mrs. Harmony before giving the judge a sheepish glance.

The judge asked Briggs if he wanted to call any other witnesses. Briggs merely opened his hands and shrugged as though to say, "Who is left to call?"

It was Lonnie's word against Halliday's.

The judge asked the jury for a show of hands for guilty or innocent. Lonnie's wasn't surprised when all six hands went up for guilty.

Mrs. Harmony gave a quiet, satisfied chuff.

The crowd murmured its approval.

The judge turned to Lonnie, and said, "Young man, considering your youth and lack of adequate supervision as well as your heroic trek across the mountains last year to deliver stolen bank money to the deputy US marshal in Camp Collins, I'm going to show some mercy. Two years in the Long's House for Wayward Boys in Denver!"

The crowd erupted, shouting its approval.

Lonnie heard Casey cry, "But he's just a boy! You can't hang a boy, Judge! You *can't!*"

Then the girl broke down in tears.

Lonnie looked at her, befuddled. She sat holding a handkerchief to her nose, shoulders jerking as she cried.

"But, Casey," Lonnie said under his breath, "I'm not goin' to hang. Why, the judge said..."

He let his voice trail off when he realized that his mind had played a cruel trick on him. He'd only *imagined* the light sentence. What the judge had *really* said was, "Hang the boy and save havin' to hang the man later!"

And then he'd adjourned the trial and sat back in his chair, crossing his arms on his chest with satisfaction.

FORTY-ONE

BEHIND LONNIE, who remained sitting at the defendant's table, the courthouse crowd was eagerly, loudly filing out into the street to enjoy the festivities over at the judge's specially constructed, portable gallows.

"On your feet, boy," said Walleye Miller, aiming his twelve-gauge at Lonnie one-handed. His other arm was slung over his crutch. "You're about to be the guest of honor at a little necktie party!"

If he'd smiled any more brightly his eyes would have popped out of his head.

"Let's go, kid," said Bohannon, waving his pistol.

Lonnie rose to his shackled feet and looked at Sheriff Halliday, who was the only one in the courtroom still seated. He was staring at Lonnie, grinning around the cigar in his mouth, which he was puffing to life, the match flame flaring as he inhaled the smoke.

Lonnie was too numb to be able to conjure any anger. Last night he'd feared that if he was sentenced to hang, he might make a fool of himself by peeing down his leg, or breaking down bawling, which he knew from reading the occasional copy of *Policeman's Gazette* was what often happened to even the most hardened outlaws in similar circumstances.

But he felt nothing at all. He was numb.

It was as though his body as well as his mind had turned to stone. Around him, everyone seemed to be moving very slowly. All sounds seemed to be emanating from the bottom of a very deep well. He couldn't even work up any sadness or regret that he wouldn't be able to say goodbye to his mother or his little half-brother.

He was going to die.

And it no longer meant anything to him.

"Look at him," said Bohannon as he and Walleye began leading him down the aisle toward the open double doors. "Cold as ice."

"Hang the boy," Halliday said, walking along behind them, "and save havin' to hang the man." He chuckled evilly at that.

But even for the man about to cause him to die for crimes he had not committed, at the hands of the man who *had* committed them, Lonnie could work up no anger. As he shuffled along, his hands cuffed before him, his ankles bound by shackles, he only wished they'd get to it sooner rather than later.

A preacher had materialized, and he was walking up beside Lonnie. Lonnie was not a churchgoer though he'd studied the Good Book some with his mother on long winter evenings when the snowbanks rose to the cabin's windows. He did not know the sky pilot, as men of the cloth were cynically called. He was reading what Lonnie recognized in a vague sort of way, with no actual interest, as the Twenty-Third Psalm.

The gallows lay at a wide spot in the main street of Arapaho Creek, on the far side of the narrow, twisting creek that ran almost directly down the street's center. A cottonwood shaded it from the brassy, high-altitude sun.

A crowd had gathered in a semicircle around the wheeled structure that sat on stout wagon wheels higher than Lonnie was tall. The upright from which the noose dangled, as well as a platform to which a total of eight steps led, was made to collapse into the wagon bed for easy traveling, when a team of two mules was hitched.

Every inch of the combination gallows and wagon was painted red, earning it the nickname Hang-'em-high Hank's Hell Wagon.

Now the red upright stood tall over the red platform, a stout noose dangling from the crossbeam.

The gallows were a frequent sight in mining camps around the mountains. Lonnie had always wondered how many men had died falling straight down through its single trapdoor. When he'd glimpsed the forbidding-looking structure being driven around the mountains by the judge's teamster who doubled as his hangman, Nestor Polk, a chill had rippled along his spine.

Now, he felt nothing. He might have been walking toward a simple, benign lumber dray parked before a mercantile, waiting to be loaded.

Lonnie was prodded up into the wagon by Deputy Bohannon while the other two lawmen and the preacher waited below. Nestor Polk stood waiting atop the platform, beside the noose dangling down over the trapdoor. Lonnie stopped beside the grim, gray-bearded Polk, who wore a long, black, claw hammer coat, a bullet-crowned black hat, and a thick, black four-in-hand tie. His long, curly side-whiskers blew in the wind.

The hangman was legendary in these mountains. He was known to be a strange, silent, humorless man with frosty blue eyes set beneath silky white brows. Lonnie had never been this close to the executioner before. The man smelled like mules, sweat, chewing tobacco, and whiskey.

The corked mouth of a brown bottle poked up out of a pocket of his black coat.

"Want a bag?" Polk asked, holding what appeared to be a black feed sack in his hand. He spoke in a raspy whisper.

Lonnie looked at the bag, puzzled. Then he remembered that men were often executed with bags over their heads.

Lonnie shook his head. He didn't want his last sight to be the darkness of a bag over his head.

"He's a cold one, Polk," Halliday said from the street below.

"Yeah, well, we'll see how cold he is when the trapdoor falls away beneath his boots." Polk looked at Bohannon and said loudly enough to be heard above the crowd's expectant din, "Remove the cuffs and shackles!"

Polk grinned, showing two slightly protruding, fang-like eyeteeth.

"Oh, right." Bohannon chuckled and crouched to remove the shackles binding Lonnie's ankles. "Wanna give 'em their money's worth!"

As Polk tightened the noose around Lonnie's neck, the boy looked out over the crowd gathered before him. Men, women, children, and dogs had gathered for the occasion. Even a few cats rested on the second-story balcony rails of the brightly painted parlor houses. Scantily clad soiled doves milled on the balconies, smoking and staring toward the gallows. They likely appreciated a break in their work, which would likely start booming again in a few minutes.

Two old women were selling sandwiches from a wicker basket, and several of the shopkeepers, Lonnie noticed, had moved their wares outside onto their boardwalks to take advantage of the potential customers gathered in the street.

Lonnie peered around the crowd for Casey. He didn't see her anywhere. That was good. She didn't need to see this.

The fancy Dan—Niles or Giles or whatever his name was—stood beside his father, old Gilpin, the banker, on the boardwalk fronting their bank. The young dandy and his bald-headed, slightly stoop-shouldered old father stared grimly toward Lonnie.

The crowd quieted some as the preacher raised his voice to sermonize to the crowd. It was a long-winded speech and Lonnie was glad when Halliday broke in with: "All right, that's enough, Reverend. Save it for Sunday. We're gathered here for a hangin' not a church service!"

The crowd erupted.

Kids danced around, chasing each other with sticks.

Dogs barked.

"You got anything to say?" Polk asked Lonnie, blowing his sour breath in Lonnie's face.

"Nope."

As calm as he was, Lonnie tensed himself for the drop.

Polk's cheek twitched as he threw the wooden lever. There was a raspy bark as the trapdoor gave beneath Lonnie's boots. The boy fell straight down through the hole in the platform. There was a loud cracking sound, which must have been the breaking of his own neck as he continued to plunge down through the hole.

But wait—the rope hadn't tightened yet.

Now it drew taut. Lonnie's body jerked upward. For a second, he thought the rope was going to rip his head off. His eyes bugged as he strangled, clawing at the rope and kicking.

The crowd was roaring.

Another cracking sound rose faintly beneath the cacophony. Lonnie's belly lurched straight up into his throat as he continued dropping straight down over the side of the wagon. The rope around his neck eased its pressure.

The clay-colored street darted toward Lonnie's boots.

He heard himself give a loud grunt of expelled air as his feet hit the dirt. He fell and rolled onto his side, stunned, automatically clawing at the noose that was pulled up around his jaws, raking his skin.

He looked around. The crowd was screaming, dispersing. Dogs barked wildly.

What the hell?

Someone gave a loud, raking Rebel yell. The sound was strangely familiar to Lonnie's shocked, dull brain. Guns crackled.

Women screamed. Men shouted.

Hooves thundered as two horses bounded toward Lonnie from beyond the crowd. The crowd thinned as it dispersed, women and children screaming, men shouting, Halliday yelling, "What in the hell?"

The horses and one rider came racing through the quickly thinning crowd, the rider triggering a pistol above her blonde, tan-hatted head. One of the horses was the chestnut mare, Miss Abigail. The other was General Sherman.

"Lonnie!" Casey screamed as she ran her horse into the lawmen. "Hop on—let's fog it away from here!"

Miss Abigail pitched, front hooves coming down on Walleye Miller's wounded leg. The deputy screamed. Bohannon was already down, rolling in the dust.

Lonnie looked up at the rope dangling from the gallows. Its end was ragged. Something had sliced it.

The boy ripped the noose up over his head and tossed it away. His neck ached from that first, sudden jerk, but he'd live. As the General came up, dancing in place beside Lonnie and blocking the cursing Halliday, Lonnie threw himself at the horse. The General lunged off and Lonnie ran along beside him, pulling himself up by the saddle horn and hop-skipping as he tried to toe a stirrup.

A pistol cracked behind Lonnie. He didn't have to look back to know the shooter was the enraged Halliday.

Lonnie shoved a toe through the stirrup and swung up into the leather. Casey tossed him his reins, which he caught, frowning at her, not quite believing what had happened.

Maybe he was still strangling beneath the gallows and his oxygen-starved brain was merely hallucinating all this?

He glanced behind as the crowd ran every which way. Halliday ran along the street behind Lonnie, aiming his revolver out in front of him. The dog that had run wild in the courthouse ran up behind the lawman, now, believing the man was playing with it. The dog grabbed the lawman's left pants cuff and shook it.

The lawman's pistol spat smoke and flames, but the bullet sailed wild.

Lonnie turned his head forward. Casey rode just ahead and to his right. When she glanced over her left shoulder and gave him a wide-eyed, anxious smile but also a smile of relief, he realized it was true. He was free.

Somehow, the girl had saved him.

At least, for now.

But who had cut the rope?

He and Casey hit the outskirts of town and galloped into the country beyond, heading for the mountains.

FORTY-TWO

WHEN THEY'D HAD to slow their horses after a quarter mile of hard riding, Casey said, "Let's hold up here."

"Why?" Lonnie said, pulling back on the General's reins.

As if in reply to his question, a wild, raking Rebel yell cut through the air behind them. It was the same yell Lonnie had heard before in town, when the excitement was starting. Now he saw a figure galloping toward them along the trail, silhouetted against the skyline.

The town was a small, dun-colored splotch low on the horizon, behind the horseback rider growing steadily larger.

As the rider approached, Lonnie could make out the gray Confederate campaign hat the rider was wearing. It was battered and weather-stained, the edge of its rim badly frayed. Barreling toward Lonnie on a cream stallion, the rider crouched low in the saddle, glancing quickly behind him then turning his head back forward, the wind pasting the front brim against the man's forehead.

When the man was fifty yards away and closing fast, Lonnie saw a shaggy, black-and-white collie dog running a ways behind the horse and rider, doing its best to keep up.

Wilbur Calhoun drew rein before Lonnie and Casey, the old ex-Confederate's dog loping up behind him, tongue hanging down over its lower jaw, tired. Calhoun poked his hat back off his forehead and grinned at Lonnie. His weathered face was long and angular. It hadn't seen a razor's edge in several days.

Lonnie stared in disbelief at the old soldier turned mysterious mountain rider who'd saved his bacon from the fire more times last year than Lonnie wanted to count.

"Wilbur...*Calhoun?*"

"Helluva party they throwed for you, boy," Calhoun said, breathless. "Sorry I had to be the one to break it up. I was just startin' to have fun, too!" The ex-Confederate glanced behind him once more, squinting against the dust. "Come on, children," he said, turning back around. "A posse'll be after us soon!"

Calhoun galloped on up the trail, the shaggy collie dog loping along behind.

Lonnie gave Casey a curious glance. The girl hiked a shoulder then touched spurs to Miss Abigail's flanks. "I'll tell you later!"

Lonnie booted the General after Casey. They followed Calhoun on a winding course into the mountains. They'd ridden for nearly an hour, pacing their horses, before Calhoun led them up the side of a steep, rocky ridge stippled with firs and white-stemmed aspens.

Five minutes later, the three were lying belly down at the top of the ridge, staring down the other side toward the trail twisting up through the forest.

Soon, hooves thundered. The shadows of oncoming riders darted through the trees down the slope beneath the ridge.

The posse grew closer until Lonnie could make out Sheriff Halliday leading the dozen or so men, including Deputy Bohannon, who rode directly behind him, along the trail, passing their quarry from left to right and quickly disappearing back into the forest.

Lonnie had recognized several of the other men comprising the posse —mostly shopkeepers from town.

"Well, that tears it," Calhoun said. "Kid, they look awful disappointed you didn't get a stretched neck out of that deal back there. I reckon they're gonna keep after us, which means we'd best keep ridin'."

Calhoun climbed to his feet and moved on down the back side of the slope to where their three horses waited near a runout spring, grazing. The collie lay nearby, eyes riveted on its ex-Confederate master. Lonnie and Casey gained their feet. Casey gave Lonnie a brief, reassuring smile. She squeezed his hand, pecked his cheek, and then followed Calhoun down the slope.

Lonnie stared after her, bewildered by her and everything that had happened to him recently, including what had just happened under that gallows in town. He had so many questions that he didn't know where to start asking.

Anyway, this wasn't the time for questions. It was a time for trying to stay ahead of Halliday and the posse.

Lonnie moved on down the slope, mounted up, and rode.

The boy thought he knew every nook and cranny of this side of the Never Summers, but he didn't recognize any of the landmarks around him. Calhoun obviously knew this part of the mountains better than Lonnie did. At least, Lonnie hoped that was so. He hoped the old Confederate wasn't just riding blindly to lose the posse.

That would be a good way to get lost, and no one wanted to get lost out here, in a range so vast. Lonnie himself had been lost, albeit briefly, and it had been a sick, panicked feeling that had filled him from head to toe. That's why he always took care to mind where he was and where he was heading, taking note of landmarks.

Even then, it was easy to get turned around and lose your sense of direction until the panic gripped you and you were assaulted with the belief you would die alone out here, where no one except wolves and mountain lions would ever find you. Of course, Lonnie usually had his horse and his rifle. If he kept his wits about him, he could live for a time off the land.

Still, the terror of finding himself lost and totally alone was a panic akin to being buried alive.

As he and Casey followed Calhoun through valleys and over ridges, Lonnie kept a sharp watch on their backtrail for the posse. There was no sign of them. He didn't hear any distant hoof thuds or shouts, either. The only sounds were the birds, squirrels, burrowing critters, and the endless soughing of the wind.

Late in the day, Lonnie looked ahead, beyond Casey and Calhoun riding ahead of her, to see that they were climbing a steep rise toward what appeared to be the ruins of a stone cabin wedged between two large, pale granite escarpments sheathed in towering pines. Most of the cabin's brush roof was missing, but the half-ruined hovel was shielded by an overhanging lip of rock high above.

Lonnie hadn't seen Calhoun's dog, Cherokee, for a while, but now the shaggy, burr-laden collie came running down a slope on Lonnie's left, through patches of sunlight and shade.

The dog obviously knew this neck of the mountains so well it had even found shortcuts not traversable on horseback.

Calhoun stopped his cream stallion, which Lonnie remembered he called Stonewall after the Confederate general. The old soldier removed his battered gray hat and sleeved sweat from his forehead, floury white where the sun rarely reached it. The white was in stark contrast to the near-Indian red of the man's craggy lower face carpeted in dark-brown stubble threaded liberally with gray.

"Home sweet home," Calhoun said as he stuffed the hat back down on his head and began stripping his saddle from the cream's back.

"Home?" Lonnie said, swinging heavily down from his own saddle. "But your cabin's over to the north, near the base of Storm Peak Pass." Lonnie remembered the cabin from last year, when Lonnie and Casey had spent a night there, after they'd nearly been killed by not only Shannon Dupree but by a rogue grizzly bear, as well.

Lonnie gave an inward shudder as he remembered that time. But then, he was now in circumstances nearly as dire...

"That's *one* of my cabins, all right." With a heavy grunt, Calhoun set his saddle down against the base of a pine. "This one here's another. I figure it was built by some old prospector or maybe a sheepherder or some such. I've seen tufts of old wool caught on branches around here, and patches of ancient sheep dung. Whoever built this place, it hadn't been lived in for many years till I came."

"What brought you here?" Casey asked Calhoun as she stripped her tack from Miss Abigail's back.

Calhoun looked at her, gave a vaguely sheepish grin, then started walking around the stony, needle-carpeted slope, gathering blowdown branches for firewood.

Casey glanced at Lonnie. "So much for indiscreet questions, I guess."

"I reckon," Lonnie said.

Calhoun had confessed last year to Lonnie and Casey that he'd accidentally killed his wife while purposefully trying to kill her lover back in Georgia, after he'd returned home from the war to find them together on Calhoun's own farm. Running from the law, he'd come west to start a new life. But what that new life had entailed, Calhoun hadn't said.

The lack of explanation in and of itself told Lonnie the man had probably gone outlaw. Why else would a man need more than one cabin in the most far-flung reaches of a far-flung mountain range?

Possibly, Calhoun was just a loner who lived off the land. Maybe his secrecy was due to prospecting, as most prospectors held their cards close to their chest. Or, maybe after all he'd been through both during and after the war, he'd gone crazy.

Maybe the true story was a combination of all those things. Or maybe the truth lay elsewhere entirely.

Lonnie didn't know. At the moment, more pressing matters were working over his already-battered brain.

When the General was stripped of his tack and rolling in a patch of soft dirt and pine needles, Lonnie sat down on the stone slope, in a patch of warm sunlight filtering through the pine boughs. His head ached and he was tired, not to mention disoriented as well as puzzled.

He looked at Casey. His expression must have been question enough.

The girl sat down beside him, doffed her hat, set it aside, and ran her hands back through her sweat-damp hair.

"When I rode back from the canyon," she said, "the sheriff was gone. I didn't know what to do, how to help you. Then I saw Mister Calhoun." She cast her gaze down to where the lanky ex-Confederate was gathering firewood. "He'd come out of a saloon with an armload of bottles for his saddlebags. I had no one else to turn to. I asked him if he'd help me find you. But then, when we were fixin' to ride back to Skull Canyon, you rode in...tied to your saddle...with Halliday and the two Pinkertons."

"But the rope. The noose. How...?"

Calhoun, heading back toward them with an armload of firewood, must have overheard their conversation. He chuckled, and said, "I recollect I told you when we first met, I was a sharpshooter back durin' the War of Northern Aggression."

Lonnie remembered the jerk on the taut rope. That must have been one of Calhoun's bullets striking the rope but not severing it entirely. The man must have fired a second, more accurate shot, and that was what had sent Lonnie plunging to the ground.

Calhoun dropped the wood in a gap in the stone floor, near Lonnie and Casey. He looked a little sheepish as he said, "Sorry about that first shot. I used to prize myself on never wastin' a Minie ball." He scratched the back of his neck, glancing around, still sheepish. "I reckon my peepers ain't as good as they was when I was nineteen. But the second shot did the trick, eh, boy?"

Casey leaned toward Lonnie and pried up the bandage on his temple to look beneath it. She made a face and said, "Try as we might, me an' Mister Calhoun couldn't think of a better way."

The girl sighed as she rose and walked over to where her gear was piled near Lonnie's. She glanced back over her shoulder. "But it came down to our hopin' they'd hang you."

"Wait a minute," Lonnie said, staring at the girl in disbelief as he rubbed his sore neck. "You were *hopin'* they'd hang me?"

"Sure," Casey said, scooping her canteen up off her saddle. "After all, there's never been a boy more deservin'."

She winked as she strode back to him.

FORTY-THREE

WITH A TIN COFFEE CUP, Calhoun scooped out a hole in which to build a fire. Casey was hard at work, cleaning out Lonnie's bullet-creased head with a short length of flannel dampened with tepid water from her canteen.

"Figured the only way we were gonna save your hard-luck hide, boy, was to wait until you had a little distance between you and Halliday and them two no-account deputies of his," Calhoun said as he worked.

"Ow!" Lonnie said as Casey rubbed the cut a little too hard.

Casey gave him a dubious look. "You were nearly hanged a couple of hours ago, and *this* bothers you?"

"You don't exactly have a delicate touch, girl!"

"Oh, shut up, or I'll let you clean your own dang wound!" Casey shot back.

Calhoun chuckled, shook his head. "You two have a curious relationship. Anyways, like I was sayin', we needed to get you some space from the lawmen. Figured a crowd would be good, too. Harder for a lawman to shoot into a crowd. And I knew that Nestor Polk always liked to hang his victims without cuffs or shackles on, so they could dance good for the crowd. So, I took my Sharps Big Fifty, holed up in the loft of the Federated Livery Stable, and waited for you to drop through the hole."

As Casey continued to clean Lonnie's wound, the boy gave Calhoun an incredulous look. "If that second shot would have missed, I'd have been doin' quite a dance for that crowd. And that rope would been movin' around way too fast for you to make another shot." Lonnie's heart quickened as he thought through all the grisly possibilities. "And...about now they'd be droppin' me in a pine box, maybe already shovelin' dirt on me."

"Yeah, well," the ex-Confederate chuckled as he shoved some dried pine needles and crushed pinecones into his fire hole, "it's best not to look too close at the more delicate smaller workin's of the past."

"Delicate smaller workin's," Lonnie said, rubbing his throat. He looked at Calhoun. "I'm glad you were there, Mister Calhoun. I reckon if it weren't for you...and Casey...I'd be for sure laid out in that box."

Now that he had time to reflect, the fear came up to wash over him good and hard. His heart was thudding, hiccupping. Fighting back the fear, he turned to Casey, who was pulling some more cloth out of her saddlebags.

"So...you did believe me," Lonnie said, haltingly.

"Oh, of course I believed you, Lonnie. I know you'd never have killed those men in cold blood. I saw right away through Halliday's lie. I didn't want him to think I was sidin' you too hard, though. I didn't want him to get suspicious and keep a close eye on me. If so, I might not have been able to get over to the feed barn and saddle your horse. I had both the General and Miss Abigail tied in an alley near the courthouse, just as Mister Calhoun and I had planned. Fortunately, Mister Hadley was helpin' the hangman with the gallows, so I got in and out of the barn without raisin' suspicion."

Hadley was the manager of the feed barn.

Casey smeared salve into Lonnie's wound. As she did, she looked at him.

"What're you thinkin' about?" the girl asked.

"You two are now as wanted as I am," Lonnie said as it dawned on him just how much these two friends—really, his only two friends in the world —had sacrificed to keep him from hanging.

He shook his head as he slid his gaze from Casey to Calhoun and back to Casey again. "You'll never be able to go back to Arapaho Creek. Not in a million years."

Casey looked back at him. She'd obviously considered that possibility before the dustup in town. But now it was real. She was as much an outlaw as Lonnie. As much as Calhoun, even. That was beginning to sink into her now, just as all that had happened was hitting Lonnie like a runaway lumber dray.

"I reckon you're right," the girl said, a slight tremor in her voice.

"Ah, hell." Calhoun was crouched low over his fire, coaxing some flames to life by blowing on them. "Towns is overrated, anyways. Too many folks. Too much trouble to get into. You two can live out here with me. When our trail gets hot, we'll mosey down Old Mexico way. Good place to spend the winter, down there along the Sea of Cortez. There's a little village down there. *Puerto Peñasco*, they call it."

He made a motion in the air with his hands. "The *señoritas* down there —they come supple as ripe tomatoes, and filled out like..."

Calhoun let his voice trail off as he looked up at Lonnie and Casey staring at him skeptically.

"Well...I'm just sayin' it's nice down there, that's all," the ex-Confederate said, flushing, and continued to blow on his fire.

"No," Lonnie said, staring pensively off through the trees. "There's gotta be another way. Halliday can't win. He's a killer. He's the one who's got to hang."

"In case you didn't notice," Casey said, "we're a little outnumbered, Lonnie. There were a good dozen men in that posse of Halliday's. He's got the whole county convinced you killed the deputy marshal."

Lonnie shook his head, grimacing. "I know, I know. But there's got to be another way. I can't, won't, let that killer...that killer who brained me an' almost hanged me...I can't let him win. He was goin' to let me take the punishment comin' to *him*."

He gritted his teeth with determination. "And I won't let him win."

"Don't see how you can't." Calhoun laid a couple of large branches on the building flames. He looked at Casey and then at Lonnie. "Look at it this way. At least neither one of you is alone in your predicament. At least you got each other."

He pulled a hide-wrapped whiskey bottle out of his canvas war bag and popped the cork. He raised the bottle in salute and took a drink.

Lonnie glanced at Casey. She returned the glance and then looked away.

Lonnie looked away, then, too.

———

WHEN THEY'D EATEN a meager meal of wild berries and jerky washed down with coffee, or, in Calhoun's case, washed down with whiskey, the ex-Confederate hauled his gear into the ruins of the stone cabin, and went to bed. He said that an old man needed even a partial roof over his head, though Lonnie sensed that the real reason he retreated into the cabin was because he wanted to give Lonnie and Casey some privacy.

He probably sensed there were things they needed to discuss. He was right, but Lonnie didn't work up the courage to broach the subject until the fire had died and he and Casey lay in their bedrolls about six feet apart, both staring quietly at the stars.

"Casey?" Lonnie said, keeping his voice low. "You still awake over there?"

"I'm awake."

"I suppose you're thinkin' about fancy Da...er, I mean, Giles Gilpin."

Casey gave a sardonic snort. "It's Niles. But at the moment, I reckon I got more important things to think about but him. Besides, there's probably not much to think about. He is, I am sure, well aware that I was the wild young lady who galloped off like Calamity Jane with Halliday's prisoner, leavin' a bullet-cut hang rope danglin' in the air below the gallows."

"I reckon I pretty much cost you your chance of gettin' hitched to a moneyed fella, and not havin' to worry about supportin' yourself anymore."

"I reckon you did, Lonnie," Casey said with a sigh, raising her arms straight above her, interlocking her fingers, and stretching. "Thank you very much, Lonnie Gentry."

"Sorry."

"You're not sorry."

"No, I reckon I'm not sorry about Giles. But I am sorry about gettin' you into so much trouble."

Lonnie saw her eyes sparkling softly in the umber glow of the coals as she turned her head toward him. "You didn't get me into this trouble, Lonnie. I got into it of my own free will. Because we're friends. You needed my help. And, since we are friends, I had to help you. You would have done the same for me."

"I reckon I would have. But I can't imagine you gettin' into half the trouble I've gotten into."

Casey chuckled softly, half to herself, as though she'd found what he'd said genuinely funny. "No, I can't imagine that, either. But you never know. I am still young." She chuckled again.

"Casey?" Lonnie said after a stretched silence.

"What, Lonnie?"

"You mind if I bring my gear and lay over there beside you?"

She looked at him again, her eyes flashing as though tiny fires burned inside them. He could see the whiteness of her smile in the darkness. "No, Lonnie. I wouldn't mind that at all...as long as you can keep your hands to yourself."

"I will, I will."

When Lonnie had quietly hauled his gear over and was lying beside Casey, only inches away, so that he could feel the warmth of her supple body beside him, he said, "I reckon Calhoun's right."

"About what?"

"At least we got each other."

Casey turned her head to him. "Lonnie, I am not goin' down to Mexico."

Lonnie stretched his gaze to the stars twinkling high overhead, beyond the occasional breeze-jostled pine boughs. "I reckon you won't have to. I'm gonna get us out of this."

"What're you thinkin'?"

"I'm goin' to dig up that money tomorrow. I'll take it over the mountains again, just like last year, and get it into the hands of the deputy US marshal in Camp Collins. Then folks will have to believe I didn't kill that marshal, that Halliday did and that he's the one who was after the money."

Casey stared skyward for a time. Then she shrugged. "I guess it's our only option. It might work...if Halliday doesn't hunt us down first."

"Yeah, there's another problem."

"What's that?"

"Halliday might be figurin' that's what I'd do. He might decide to dig that money up now himself and hightail it. We have to get to it before he can."

Lonnie jerked with a start as Calhoun's quiet, anxious voice sounded from the direction of the ruined stone cabin. "Will you chil'uns pipe down over there? We got company!"

Lonnie heard the man click a gun hammer back.

FORTY-FOUR

"COMPANY?" Lonnie reached for his Winchester and pumped a round into the chamber. He aimed the rifle into the darkness.

Casey lay beside him, keeping her head down, blankets drawn up to her chin.

Lonnie peered into the trees around the camp, caressing his Winchester's trigger with his finger, the blood rushing through his veins as he waited for the gun flashes and the bullets screeching toward him.

Calhoun ran down the slope, both his old Confederate Griswold & Gunnison revolvers in his hands. Cherokee came running out of the woods, barking, hackles raised.

"I don't see anything," Lonnie said, keeping his voice low.

"I don't, either," Casey whispered.

"I do!" Calhoun said, his voice echoing loudly in the quiet night.

Cherokee had followed its master and was barking furiously now.

Lonnie could no longer see the man's silhouette in the darkness. He jerked with a start when Calhoun fired one of his pistols. The report was a hard crack. The gun flashed redly, silhouetting the tall, lanky man against it.

Calhoun fired his other pistol. Again, Lonnie jerked, his heart hammering in his ears now as he waited for return fire.

Footsteps sounded as Calhoun continued running down the slope.

"I know you're out there!" he bellowed, triggering both his pistols again.

"Wait here!" Lonnie told Casey. "Stay low!"

Lonnie scrambled to his feet. He pulled his boots on and then ran with his rifle down the slope toward where Calhoun had fallen silent. The dog had stopped barking. The night as quiet as the bottom of a well now on the lee side of the man's pistol shots and Cherokee's barking.

Lonnie wasn't sure where Calhoun was. The moon had not yet risen, and not much starlight penetrated to the forest floor around him.

Calhoun's pistols barked loudly and flashed brightly to Lonnie's right and down the slope a ways. "I see you, you sumbitches!" the ex-Confederate shouted. "Come on out here and face me like men 'stead of possums 'fraid of their own shadows!"

He fired again...and again.

Lonnie couldn't help flinching at each loud report that vaulted around the forest, chasing its own echoes.

Lonnie pricked his ears as the echoes died. For the life of him, he couldn't hear anything more than the soft sighing of the breeze and the occasional, soft thud of a pinecone falling to the ground. No night birds hooted. No coyotes called.

There were no sounds of men moving in the forest around him.

The horses were milling back where they were picketed near the camp, but that had only started after Calhoun had started shooting. Cherokee was sort of mewling curiously deep in his chest, but he was no longer barking.

Lonnie said quietly, "Mister Calhoun, I'm to your left and behind you a little. Don't shoot me."

"I know where you are, boy," Calhoun said in his gravelly voice. "I got the ears of a bat and the eyes of a prairie falcon. Been that way since the war."

"I don't hear anythin'," Lonnie said. "Are you sure they're out here?"

"I'm sure." Calhoun fired again. "Right there—you see him? Runnin' around like coyote scopin' out a fresh trash heap! Cherokee, get after him!"

The dog barked once but remained sitting to the ex-Confederate's right, staring into the darkness.

Lonnie dropped to a knee to avoid possible return fire. He looked in the direction that Calhoun had fired, the flashes of the ex-Confederate's pistol still flashing dully on his retinas.

"I didn't see nothin'," Lonnie said. "Didn't hear nothin'. I don't think Cherokee did, either."

"They're here, all right. Boatwrights. Sneaky sons of Satan!"

Lonnie frowned toward where he could make out the tall Southerner's vague shadow. "Who?"

Calhoun fired again. "Come on out here, Danny! Come out here, Collie! Who you got with ya? You got ole Cousin Earl Sapp here, too?" Calhoun chuckled and fired two more times.

Lonnie licked his lips and scowled skeptically. "Who're you talkin' about, Mister Calhoun?"

"Boatwrights," Calhoun said after a brief silence. "Virgil Allen Boatwright's mountain folk from Tennessee. Mangiest bunch of curs you'll find in any hollow in Appalachia. I shot Virgil when I found him with my dear sweet June, after the war. Shot the sumbitch in my own cabin, though shootin' was too good for him. He deserved slow Apache torture, Virgil did. I shot ole Virgil, and Virgil shot June as he fell. Shot her with a bullet meant for me. Killed her, the polecat. They both died. The Boatwrights been shadowin' my trail for the past twenty years. Followed me west to avenge their kin. They been shadowin' me ever since, bidin' their time. I even seen 'em a time or two when I was huntin' Injuns with the frontier army."

Calhoun raised his voice. "You hear that, Danny? You hear that Collie? Yeah, I know you're foggin' my trail! I've knowed it for a long time. Been waitin' for you to work up enough sand to face me like *men!*"

He fired again.

"That's probably been plum foolish of me, though, ain't it?" Calhoun said. "There ain't nary a Boatwright that's ever done anythin' a *man* would do. Not a real man. All the Boatwrights do is steal other men's women! While said men are off fightin' the war that the Boatwrights cowered from!"

Soft footfalls sounded behind Lonnie. Before he could turn around, Casey said quietly, "It's me."

Cherokee was whining now as he sank to his belly on the forest floor, ears pricked and looking around incredulously.

"Come on out here, Boatwrights!" Calhoun shouted into the darkness. He extended his left pistol. The hammer clicked benignly down onto the firing pin, empty.

Casey moved up to stand beside Lonnie. She held up a whiskey bottle.

There was no cork in it. She turned it upside down to show that it was empty. She looked at Lonnie, pursing her lips.

Lonnie looked at Calhoun who had holstered one pistol and was now busily reloading the other one.

"Mister Calhoun."

Lonnie moved on down the slope. He stopped beside the tall ex-Confederate and looked at the revolver he was expertly reloading from the leather pouch on his shell belt. Lonnie could smell the sour stench of alcohol.

"I don't think there's anyone out there, Mister Calhoun," Lonnie said. "I haven't heard anything. Haven't seen anything, either. I don't think your dog has, either. I think you must've dreamed it."

He glanced over his shoulder at Casey moving on down the slope to stand beside him.

Calhoun looked at Lonnie, frowning deeply. He looked at his dog.

He swung a look into the darkness again. He turned his head this way and that. Then he just stood there for a time, staring, listening.

"If that don't beat a hen aflyin'," Calhoun said at last, his shoulders relaxing. "I believe you're right, boy. I must have dreamed the whole thing."

"I think that's what must have happened," Lonnie said. "You'd best go on back to bed. Still a few hours before sunup."

"Yeah," Calhoun said, slowly easing the pistol into its holster. "Yeah...I reckon I'd best do that." He chuckled incredulously. "Imagine me...dreamin' the whole thing. I reckon I'm gettin' spookier'n a tree full of owls."

"It's all right, Mister Calhoun." Despite the brouhaha, Lonnie felt sorry for the man. Calhoun had left a trail of trouble behind him. And a trail of ghosts.

But then, who hadn't?

Calhoun turned to start back up the slope toward the ruined cabin. Cherokee followed him.

He stopped and glanced back at Lonnie and Casey. "Them Boatwrights are right sneaky. That's why I dreamed it. They're out there somewhere. Maybe not close. Not tonight. But they been trailin' me a long time. They won't rest until they've settled up for me killin' ole Virgil. They'll be huntin' me till Gabriel blows his horn."

Again, he started walking away. "Virgil. Can't understand what my dear sweet Junie ever saw in that spineless scalawag..."

He gave a sardonic shake of his head as he climbed the slope in the darkness, his dog behind him.

"Whiskey and that man don't mix," Casey said when Calhoun was out of earshot. "We should've remembered that from last year."

"No, they don't mix. Not with all the demons poor ole Calhoun's got lurkin' around between his ears." Lonnie glanced at her. "You go on back to camp. I'll stay out here a bit and keep watch. If Halliday heard them gunshots, he'll be comin'."

Casey sidled up to him, pressed her hand against his. "I wish the other men in this world were half the man you are, Lonnie Gentry."

She kissed him and walked away.

Lonnie stood there, staring into the darkness, his cheek on fire.

FORTY-FIVE

LONNIE SAT up the rest of the night, occasionally wandering around the perimeters of the camp, looking but mostly listening. He knew that the General would likely alert him to trouble, but he wanted to be on his toes when and if trouble came, though he had no idea how he'd fend off a dozen men.

Fortunately, he didn't have to.

The rest of the night was peaceful, with only a night bird hooting now and then and the breeze scratching around in the branches. He wondered where Halliday was. Had he lost his quarry's trail? Apparently, he hadn't been close enough to hear Calhoun's wild, drunken gunfire.

As soon as dawn brushed a pale blush across the eastern sky, the ridges standing black against it, Lonnie quietly gathered his gear and saddled his horse. Casey slept curled on her side. She did not stir as Lonnie walked back into the camp, stepped around her, and strode over to the ruined shack. He moved on through the low doorframe and dropped to a knee beside Calhoun.

He hesitated, wary of waking the man out of a dead sleep. Calhoun had proven himself to be one jumpy old soldier. One who slept with both his holstered pistols close.

Cherokee growled softly from a corner but flapped his tail when he scented Lonnie.

Lonnie silently slid Calhoun's holstered guns out of reach and placed his hand on the snoring ex-Confederate's left shoulder.

Calhoun was instantly awake, reaching for his pistols.

Whispering, the boy said, "Easy, Mister Calhoun—it's only me, Lonnie!"

"Wha...where...wha...?" Calhoun sat abruptly up, blinking and looking around, maybe imagining Union soldiers or Sioux warriors overtaking his camp. "What is it? Where's my pistols?"

"Shhh!"

Lonnie glanced through an empty window frame toward where Casey lay asleep by the fire ring.

"Please, keep your voice down, Mister Calhoun. I don't wanna wake Casey."

"Why? What's goin' on, boy? Trouble?"

"No, no trouble," Lonnie said, shaking his head. "I'm headin' back to Skull Canyon. I gotta find that money, get it back to a bona fide lawman so I can clear my name. *Our* names, I should say," he added, glancing at Casey again.

He doubted that anything would be able to clear Calhoun's name, as there was a good possibility the old soldier had a long list of old warrants on his head. His most recent transgression, freeing Lonnie from the hang rope, was likely the least of his transgressions.

"Wait—what?" Calhoun scowled at Lonnie, blinking sleep from his eyes. "What are you talkin' about? Skull Canyon?"

"That's where the money is buried. Didn't Casey tell you?"

"No, sir. She never told me nothin' about Skull Canyon." Calhoun placed a big, strong hand on Lonnie's shoulder and leaned close. Lonnie could still smell the whiskey on his breath. "That canyon's a bad, bad place boy. You don't wanna have nothin' to do with it."

"You believe the old legend? You believe it's cursed?"

"Hell, yes, it's cursed. Listen, son, I come from the old South. The Appalachians. Back there, folks is taught to respect them old legends. Some places is haunted, and that's a fact. Restless souls, sometimes demons, lurk in places where bad things happened. I was raised near a hollow where a man killed and ate his whole family. Any man, woman, or child who visited that hollow turned into a bag of bones. I know that to be true, because one of my uncles wandered in there without knowin' it, huntin' coons. Guess what happened to him?"

Lonnie felt chicken flesh rising across the back of his neck. "He turned into a bag of bones?"

"That what my mother told me, and that woman wouldn't have lied to save her own son's soul!"

"The damage is already done," Lonnie said, darkly, feeling a deep chill. "I've already spent a night in the canyon."

Calhoun shook his head. "That ain't one bit good, boy. If so, you're likely wearin' the curse on your shoulders. What you need to do now is not go back to that infernal place but find you a witch to get the curse lifted. Until then, draw a circle around yourself, wherever you're gonna be for any length of time, and try to stand in it as much as possible. And when you get home, hang a horseshoe on your door!"

"I spent a whole night in that canyon several nights ago, and I ain't dead yet, Mister Calhoun. And I ain't been drawin' no circles or hangin' horseshoes!"

"You ain't dead yet—no. But not because folks ain't been tryin'!"

Lonnie considered that. Calhoun had a point. "What about the money?"

"Forget the money!" Calhoun squeezed Lonnie's arm tighter. "Listen, I know an old Ute medicine woman. She lives over in—"

"Forget it!" Lonnie straightened. "I don't have time for none of that hokum. I have to get that money back and turn it over to the law. The *right* law. Standin' around here lettin' you scare my bones to putty ain't gettin' it done. The reason I woke you in the first place is I want you to take care of Casey for me. When she wakes, tell her to wait here with you. I'll try to be back before sundown. Whatever you do, don't let her come after me. It's too dangerous."

Calhoun stared in disbelief. He wagged his head slowly. "Well, if I can't talk you out of returnin' to that infernal place, you don't have far to ride."

"Huh?"

"Step outside and look to the northeast."

Lonnie did as the ex-Confederate had told him to. His blood quickened in his veins as he stared at the crags, including the giant stone skull, towering above the first near ridge. The first copper rays of the rising sun were touching it. Oddly, those rays touched none of the other formations around it.

Just the skull.

As if pointing it out to Lonnie staring at it now, mouth agape.

Calhoun stepped up beside him. "Ride on down this hill here. When you come to a big spruce tree, swing left. You'll run into an ancient horse trail. The Spanish or ancient Injuns likely carved it. Follow it out of this valley, and after a couple of hours, it will take you to a notch in the wall of Skull Canyon."

"How do you know?" Lonnie asked the man, skeptically. "You've never been to Skull Canyon."

"No, but I know what that demon sounds like when you get close. You'll hear him, too. If you're smart, you'll take heed and ride right on past!"

"You're talkin' about the way the wind sounds when it blows around the skull. Am I right?"

"You call it what you want, you mulish little polecat. The least you can do is turn your hat around." Calhoun grinned with cunning. "They say evil spirits have a tougher time recognizin' you if you wear your hat backwards."

"Ah, balderdash," Lonnie grumbled, and started walking toward where the General waited, still tied to his picket line.

"Boy?" Calhoun whispered, glancing toward the sleeping Casey.

Lonnie glanced back at him.

"Don't you tarry now. Don't let another night catch you in that canyon, and once you're out, you boil you up some dandelion tea then count the leaves at the bottom of your cup!"

Lonnie gave a caustic grunt. "Just keep an eye on Casey, Mister Calhoun."

He walked away, mounted up, and quietly booted the General out of the camp. He tried to tell himself that what he'd heard was all hokum, but he couldn't ignore that gooseflesh had now risen over nearly every inch of his body.

It only got worse when he started to hear the Skull Canyon demon blowing its infernal horn.

FORTY-SIX

LONNIE HEARD the tooth-gnashingly eerie bellowing as he followed the ancient horse trail east of the camp in which he'd left Casey asleep and Calhoun staring after him, shaking his head.

The moaning had started about an hour later. He looked up to see that he'd entered a narrow valley over which the skull-like formation jutted with its accompanying crags ahead on his left. The wind was blowing from the north. It was being caressed, plucked at, and ripped by the giant skull, creating those bizarre moaning sounds that changed pitch from time to time so that occasionally it sounded like a throaty wail.

The sound would die for a time and then start again, softly at first but gradually growing in volume before dying and starting all over again.

Lonnie followed the trail through a copse of aspens and across a narrow creek, heading for the red, crenelated cliff jutting ahead of him, the sun caressing it gently, burnishing it, stretching dark-purple shadows out from lumps and knobs and boulders that had likely tumbled from the crest but had gotten held up on their way to the valley floor.

The sun was as clear as a lens. Everything appeared close. Lonnie could see every dimple and piece of shale along the side of that towering cliff.

Somewhere in that cliff, a notch opened, offering a way into Skull Canyon beyond.

Lonnie followed the trail over the shoulder of a gravelly spur. On the other side of the spur, he could see the base of the sandstone cliff littered with stone rubble, twisted cedars, and pinyon pines. Another creek ran along the base of the ridge. Little wider than a freshet, the brown water glistened like copper in the intensifying sunlight as it rippled over rocks and gravel and sluiced around slab-sided boulders.

The General whinnied and shook his head so hard he almost threw his bridle.

Lonnie looked down at the horse. "What is it, General?"

As he continued riding along the trail now paralleling the ridge, Lonnie looked around cautiously. His belly had drawn itself into a tight knot. The horse had heard or smelled something that Lonnie hadn't detected.

He rode several more yards, following a slight curve in the face of the ridge, when he drew back on the buckskin's reins. A notch opened before him. It was like a half-open door sheathed in willows and tufts of green grass nourished by the freshet. Lonnie looked at the mud around the narrow creek, and the knot in his belly tightened.

Someone had been through here before him. The clear print of a horse's hoof marked the mud of the spring, to the left of a leafy willow, the indentation filled with water that was very slowly wearing it away.

Apprehension throbbed like a war drum in Lonnie's head.

He stared at the notch. He didn't want to ride through that ominously beckoning doorway and enter the canyon. But he had to. There was a chance that whoever had ridden through here before him was merely a line rider looking for cows. Maybe a prospector. Maybe a drifter. Lord knew there were all three breeds of men in these mountains, and more.

That hoofprint didn't necessarily have to belong to Frank Halliday.

Something, however, told Lonnie it did belong to Halliday. He'd probably been scouring the canyon for the gold for a long time, after talking to the old posse rider, and had come upon this hidden entrance, which Lonnie hadn't known about until Calhoun had told him.

Lonnie reached forward with his right hand and slid his rifle from its scabbard. Quietly, he racked a cartridge into the action, depressed the hammer, and set the Winchester across his saddlebow. He clucked to the General. As though sensing his rider's apprehension, the big buckskin moved slowly, haltingly forward.

The stallion's hooves made wet sucking sounds as it crossed the freshet. The willows brushed Lonnie's calves as he and the General pushed through the entrance. The skull blew its whining breath down from the ridge above Lonnie as though in warning. A warning that went unheeded as the boy and his horse followed a twisting path between steep walls of pink, eroded rock before coming out onto a ridge overlooking the main canyon, which swept wide before Lonnie, a good hundred feet below.

The skull moaned shrilly, and then the wailing died with the wind.

Lonnie halted the General and looked around, trying to get his bearings. He looked at the broad skull looming whitely high above on his left. Staring straight out before him and down, he saw a stretch of flat water beyond a fringe of pines. That must be the lake near the side ravine in which Crawford Kinch had buried the payroll loot.

Lonnie gigged the General forward. The buckskin took one step then stopped. The horse blew hoarsely, twitching his ears, staring off to the right and ahead.

"What is it, Gen—?"

Lonnie let his voice trail off.

The skull's ominous call was rising again, gradually.

Something moved among the rocks strewn along the base of the ridge wall, several yards above Lonnie on his right. A man was coming through a narrow corridor of rock that hugged the side of the steep ridge, heading toward Lonnie, whose heart was beating almost painfully now.

"Help," the man said. "Please...help me!"

At first, Lonnie thought the call was a trick of the rising wind. But no. It was a man's voice. A familiar voice. The man's tall, black-clad figure disappeared behind bends in the narrow corridor, but now Lonnie could hear the man's footfalls, the ringing of his spurs as he continued moving down the crooked corridor toward Lonnie.

The moaning wind rose, kicking up dust around Lonnie and further obscuring the halting figure up the rise before him.

Lonnie aimed his Winchester toward the staggering figure and clicked the hammer back.

The figure came out of the gap in the rocks. He stood there on a mound of slide rock, staring down at Lonnie. His shoulders sagged. His chest rose and fell heavily as he breathed. He wore a black frock coat. His hat was gone. A bandage shown whitely around the top of his head.

Halliday's eyes were still swollen from Lonnie's assault.

What looked like cherry jam stained the sheriff's coat, high up on his right side, just below his shoulder. But Lonnie knew it wasn't jam.

The sheriff clamped his left, gloved hand over the bloody wound.

Blood oozed between the fingers of that hand. He held a pistol straight down along his right leg.

"Help me," Halliday said, breathless. He staggered forward. "Please, you gotta...help me!"

He stopped. He stared at Lonnie, frowning. Then he glowered.

"Ah, hell...it's *you!*"

He triggered his pistol into the rocks at his boots and then fell forward. Dropping the gun, Halliday rolled down the slope toward Lonnie, causing the General to fidget and sidestep, whickering nervously.

Dust rose around Halliday's violently rolling figure. The sheriff rolled up hard against a boulder with a sharp smacking sound, just ahead and right of Lonnie. Halliday grunted, wheezed.

"Ah, *Christ!*" he said, miserably. "You killed me, kid!"

The voice of the canyon's demon fairly bellowed as though in response to the sheriff's yell.

FORTY-SEVEN

LONNIE LOOKED around for the man or men who'd shot Halliday.

Seeing no one, he stepped down from his saddle and walked over to where the sheriff lay on his back beside the rock that had so unceremoniously stopped his roll. The man was writhing in pain, wincing, stretching his lips back from tobacco-stained teeth.

"What do you mean I killed you?" Lonnie stared coldly down at the man. "Not that I wouldn't mind the honors, but I just got here."

"You as good as done it...when you...cheated the hangman!"

Lonnie stared at the man, incredulous.

"I had to come out here...try to dig up the money...before you got to it." Halliday grimaced and shook his head. "I swear, kid—you're a pile o' of unfettered trouble. Now I'm lyin' here dyin' on account of you!"

"You got that wrong, you bottom-feedin' dung beetle. You're lyin' here dyin' because of *you*. What I want to know is: who shot you?"

Lonnie looked around again, cautiously.

"Why, the Pinkertons, that's who!" Halliday laughed without humor. "They must have figured it all out, after the other day. They must've followed me an' the posse out from town. When I cut the posse loose, I rode up to where I had you rebury the money, and the sons o' Satan shot me after I'd dug up the money. I managed to scramble away before they could finish the job."

"Where was the posse?"

"I sent 'em back last night, when we lost your trail. Kid, help me up. I gotta get back to town. I gotta get to the sawbones."

Lonnie took a step back. "Where are the Pinkertons?"

"Hell, I don't know. They gave up on me and rode on out of the canyon, I reckon. They'll probably climb up over Storm Peak Pass, head on over to the railroad line by Camp Collins. After that"—Halliday laughed in caustic frustration—"who knows? Likely, Mexico. That'd be the only place for a couple of crooked Pinkertons packin' a mother lode of army gold!"

Halliday extended his hand to Lonnie. "Come on, kid—help me up. I gotta get back to town, see that old pill roller!"

Lonnie looked off toward where the lake shone in the distance beyond the trees, glimmering in the sunlight. His heartbeat quickened. Mostly to himself, he said, "If they're headin' over the pass, they'll need supplies and fresh horses. The closest place to find fresh horses around here is the Circle G—my own ranch!"

His mother was there alone with little Jeremiah...

Lonnie swung around and started back to the General.

"Kid, you gotta help me!" Halliday begged.

Lonnie turned to look at the man. He remembered how the rope around his neck had felt. He'd likely remember that feeling on his deathbed.

Fury welled up in the boy. He spat to one side, and said, "You die slow. Right here, all alone, listenin' to that demon breathin' over you."

He glanced toward the pale, skull-like mass of rock looming in the north as the wind wheezed and moaned around him, lifting chalky dust.

He looked at Halliday once more. "Then you burn in hell!"

Lonnie started once more toward the General. He stopped dead in his tracks when he heard the unmistakable click of a gun hammer being cocked.

He turned around slowly. Halliday must have been packing a hideout pistol. He held the small, pearl-gripped derringer in his right hand. He grinned as he aimed the little popper at Lonnie.

Automatically, Lonnie swung his rifle up, aimed hastily, and fired.

Halliday triggered the derringer wide. The bullet plunked off a rock behind Lonnie. Halliday dropped the pistol and stared down in shock at the blood oozing from the hole in his chest.

He looked at Lonnie through the gun smoke billowing in the air between them. He frowned as though hurt that the boy would be so cold as to kill him.

Then his eyes rolled back into his head. He fell onto his back and lay still.

Lonnie looked at the rifle in his hands.

It was shaking.

Lonnie drew a deep breath, fighting the urge to be sick. He didn't have time for that. He had to get back to the ranch. He had to get his hands on the loot. Besides, who knew what the Pinkertons might do to his mother when they tried to steal the horses from the Circle G corral?

Lonnie glanced once more at Halliday. Then he swung around and ran over to the waiting buckskin, who thrashed his tail testily. Lonnie mounted up and galloped away from the dead sheriff.

Was it just a trick of the wind, or was the canyon demon laughing at him?

As he rode, heading for the canyon's southern entrance, where all the trouble had started, Lonnie turned his hat around backwards.

———

LONNIE WAS glad to ride out of the canyon.

But it took him another two hours to reach the outskirts of the Circle G. The pines and aspens at the edge of the yard glittered softly in the late-afternoon sunlight. Lonnie slowed the General down to a walk as he rode under the portal's crossbeam and into the yard.

He looked around cautiously, wondering if the two Pinkertons had already been here and left, or if they were still here. He got his answer when he spied the Pinkertons' two horses in the main corral off the barn's side shed. Lonnie's other four horses were there, as well.

The Pinkertons were still here. Maybe they intended to spend the night, enjoying the ministrations of Lonnie's mother, including her cooking, before getting a fresh start in the morning.

The cabin was quiet, vaguely ominous-looking. The front door was closed. The sunlight reflected off the dark windows.

Lonnie swung the General around and rode back out through the portal and into the trees west of the yard. He dropped the General's reins then slid his Winchester from its scabbard.

"You stay here, boy," Lonnie said softly, patting the horse's neck. "Hopefully, this whole nightmare will be over soon." He racked a shell into the Winchester's breech. "And I won't have a bullet in my hide for my trouble."

Lonnie removed his spurs and dropped them into a saddlebag pouch. He gave the horse another pat then strode up along a small creek to the north. He worked his way around the yard and behind the cabin then dropped to a knee to survey his surroundings.

The long, low cabin lay hunched before him, beyond the privy. The keeper shed, where meat was stored, lay to the far right of the privy. A small, roofed, open-sided woodshed sat between the privy and the cabin. More split firewood lay against the cabin's rear wall, peppered with pine needles. A rain barrel stood back there, as well. The pine needles as well as dead leaves left over from last fall blew in the wind gusting down over the western ridges.

Lonnie thought he could hear the skull's moaning in that wind, but it had to be his imagination.

He was a long way from Skull Canyon.

The cabin was ominously silent, but he could smell smoke from the range issuing from the chimney pipe. Lonnie licked his lips, squeezed the rifle in his hands, and then started to push off his knee. A sound stopped him. He let his knee drop back to the ground.

A man's muffled laughter rose from the other side of the cabin.

Anxiety flared in Lonnie's veins.

The laughter grew louder and then Bill Brocius came around the front corner of the cabin, following the well-worn path around to the back. Lonnie jerked with a start and retreated a few feet into the trees.

Brocius's laughter died as he moved toward Lonnie, following the path that led to the privy. The rogue Pinkerton drew on the cigarette smoldering between his lips then flipped the quirley into the brush, blowing smoke into the wind.

"Good way to cause a wildfire, fool," Lonnie muttered under his breath, hunkered behind an aspen bole, watching Brocius follow the path to the privy. The Pinkerton walked a little unsteadily, as though he was half drunk.

The privy door opened with a squawk. Brocius's boots thudded hollowly as he entered the privy and then closed the door and dropped the nail through the hasp, locking it.

Another wave of anxiety washed over Lonnie. He drew a deep calming breath and stared at the privy. "There you go, you snake," Lonnie said, nodding slowly, pulling the Winchester up taut against his chest. "Now, I got you."

He stepped out around the tree and began walking toward the privy.

FORTY-EIGHT

LONNIE WALKED UP to within five yards of the privy and then dropped behind a tree stump, waiting. Inside the privy, Brocius grunted. The man's boots thudded and scraped.

Done with business.

Lonnie lurched up off his knee and strode quickly up along the side of the privy. He stopped, pressed his left shoulder against the privy wall.

The door opened with a squawk. Lonnie glanced around the corner to see Brocius standing in front of the door, crouched slightly, buttoning the fly of his wool trousers.

When the Pinkerton had finished the maneuver, he lifted his hat, ran his hand through his hair with a sigh, then set his hat back on his head, giving it a rakish angle, and started following the trail toward the cabin.

Lonnie fell into step behind the man, quickly caught up to him. He kept his voice low as he said, "Stop right there!"

Brocius stopped, shoulders tensed. Lonnie pressed his rifle barrel taut against the man's back. "If you call out, I'll shoot you. Now, nice and slow, ease those pistols out of their holsters and drop 'em on the ground."

Brocius glanced over his right shoulder. "Well, well, if it ain't the young fugitive."

"Drop your guns."

"What're you gonna do, kid?"

"You'll know soon enough...after you've dropped those guns."

"What're you gonna do if I don't?" Brocius asked, a defiant smile quirking his mouth corners. "Kill me?"

Lonnie kept his gaze level, hard. He'd shot Halliday, he told himself. He could shoot this man, too, if it came to that. "That's right."

Brocius studied Lonnie from over his shoulder. Lonnie glared at him. Gradually, the smile faded from the Pinkerton's lips. "All right." He lifted his two revolvers from their holsters. He held them up and then tossed them underhand. They landed in the yard several feet to his right.

"You got a hideout?" Lonnie asked.

"Nope." Brocius shook his head, grinning. "Two's enough for me."

Lonnie nudged him forward. "Get movin', then. Inside. Like I said, you call out, I'll shoot you."

"Okay, kid, okay. Take it easy. We wouldn't want that long gun to go off by accident—now, would we?"

"You wouldn't, that's right," Lonnie said.

Brocius started walking slowly forward. Too slowly. Lonnie nudged him again with the rifle. Brocius stopped, swung around in a blur of quick motion, slamming the back of his right hand against the rifle.

The move had caught Lonnie off guard. The rifle bounced off the cabin's stout wall and landed in the brush growing up along the stone foundation. Brocius continued to wheel toward Lonnie. Lonnie saw the savage glint in the man's eyes. And then he saw the man's left fist smash toward him.

It smacked Lonnie's right cheek, sending the boy flying backwards and sideways. Lonnie's head slammed against the cabin. Feeling like a rag doll given a thrashing by an enraged child, he dropped in the brush, his face on fire. The blow had kicked up the pain in his bullet-notched head, as well. It was a searing, blinding fury, momentarily paralyzing him.

"Thought you were gonna take the money from us—eh, boy?" Lonnie felt the man's hands on his back, pulling him up off the ground and lifting him several inches off his feet before slamming him back down on his feet and giving him a shove.

Lonnie lunged forward, hit the ground with a groan, and rolled. When he looked up, Brocius was on him again, the man's cheeks flushed with fury, his eyes small and round and filled with hate.

"I don't think so!" the Pinkerton said through clenched teeth, lifting Lonnie to his feet once more.

The man grabbed Lonnie by the back of his shirt collar, swung him around, and threw him toward the cabin's front corner. Helpless against this big, powerful man, his head on fire, his vision blurry, Lonnie bounced off the cabin. Brocius retrieved his pistols then grabbed Lonnie again and gave him another shove, sending Lonnie lunging along the front of the cabin to the front stoop.

At the steps, Lonnie swung around to confront Brocius, balling his hands into tight fists, but Brocius smashed the back of his left hand against Lonnie's right cheek.

Lonnie went down hard on the porch steps. His ears rang. He could already feel his right eye beginning to swell.

Brocius pulled Lonnie up by his shirt collar again and shoved him up onto the porch. The Pinkerton came up behind him, gave him another shove. Lonnie kept his feet moving so he wouldn't fall. He raised his hands as he flew to the door, but then the door opened.

Madsen looked incredulous as he said, "What the hell's—?"

He stepped back out of the doorway, and Lonnie went stumbling inside and falling across the eating table, scattering plates and glasses. A pan tumbled to the floor with a *bang!*

"Lonnie!" his mother cried, her back to the range.

Lonnie pressed his right cheek to the table, sliding his boots beneath him.

"What's going on?" May Gentry yelled.

"Got us a little problem here," Brocius said to Madsen, as he pulled Lonnie up off the table and hurled the boy into the parlor.

Lonnie hit the braided rug on the parlor floor and rolled up against the stone hearth in which no fire burned. From back inside the lodge, little Jeremiah began squealing loudly.

"My god!" May Gentry screamed, running toward Lonnie.

Lonnie looked up at her. She wore her hair in a neat chignon. It was shiny from a recent brushing. Her nicest house dress—pink with white lace—was drawn taut across her hips and bosom. Her cheeks, lightly rouged, were flushed with shock as she glanced behind her at the two suited Pinkertons standing just inside the parlor, staring darkly down at Lonnie.

Their Pinkerton badges were pinned to their wool vests. What a joke, Lonnie thought.

"Like I said," Brocius said grimly to Madsen, "we got us a little problem. Found him out back. Or...he found me, I should say. Stuck a rifle barrel against my spine."

"Lonnie?" May said, a vague tone of accusing mixing with the befuddlement in her face. "What are you up to? Where have you been these past several days?"

She looked genuinely bewildered by his absence. Obviously, neither Brocius nor Madsen had told her about the necktie party. She couldn't have come looking for him because she couldn't leave Jeremiah. She hadn't looked overly worried when Lonnie had first entered the cabin, however. It looked as though she'd been preparing a hearty meal for her guests, after she'd prettied herself up a bit.

No, she hadn't been too heartbroken about her missing boy to enjoy the company of a couple of crooked Pinkerton agents, who were every bit as much outlaw as Shannon Dupree had been.

"Suppose you didn't know about that, May," Brocius said, mildly sheepish. "Your boy here was tried for murder. The judge was about to hang him when someone with a rifle and a keen shootin' eye saved his bacon."

"*Murder!*"

"He killed a lawman."

"*Another* one?"

"I didn't kill him, Ma. Halliday just *said* I done it..."

"*Halliday?* You mean *Sheriff* Halliday?"

"...because he done it himself—shot Marshal Appleyard, I mean."

Lonnie's mother stared down at her son, bereft. "Oh, Lonnie—what kind of trouble have you gotten yourself into *this* time?"

FORTY-NINE

LONNIE WAS BEGINNING to think that Skull Canyon's curse was riding him hard. He'd had a perfectly good year until he'd ridden past that forbidden ground up in those high and rocky reaches.

Then it was as though demons loosed from hell had started chasing him, and even after the four who'd nearly run him down a week ago were moldering on the floor of Skull Canyon, demons of their same ilk were still dogging Lonnie's heels.

Eventually, one of those demons was going to catch up to him and turn him toe down. Or maybe it would be two demons, like the two staring down at him now from over his weeping mother's shoulders—Bill Brocius and George Madsen.

Lonnie looked around. A pair of bulging saddlebags lay against the wall to his right, near the old bullhorn rocking chair in which his father had once sat, studying the Good Book on cold winter nights while sipping hot tea, his feet stuffed into elk hide slippers that May had sewn for him, from an elk that Calvin Gentry had shot himself up near Skull Canyon.

Lonnie pushed up onto his elbows and glared at the two Pinkertons. "Is that the loot?"

The two men glanced at the pouches.

"So what if it is?" Madsen said. "We're takin' it back to the army."

"If that's so, why'd you shoot Halliday and leave him for dead in Skull Canyon?"

The two men glanced at each other. They cast Lonnie a dark, menacing gaze.

"What's going on here?" May wanted to know. "Someone, please tell me!"

"Nothin', Mama. You don't wanna know." Lonnie looked at Brocius and Madsen. "You two got the loot. Your horses are probably rested by now. There's feed out in the barn—I'm sure you done already helped yourself to that. Why don't you just leave?"

May studied each man in turn, bewildered, as though they were all speaking a foreign language.

"And waste all that good food your mother's cookin'?" Brocius sniffed the air teeming with the smell of roasting elk, drawing a deep breath. "Wild game and onions and fresh bread? No man in his right mind could leave a meal like that!"

"Besides, we kinda like the company," Brocius added, glancing lasciviously down at Lonnie's mother.

"*Besides,*" Madsen said, "we want our horses to be good and fresh when we leave in the mornin'. Got us a long ride ahead. We'll be takin' two of yours, as well."

"With two horses apiece," Madsen said, "we'll be able to ride harder and longer...until we get all the way to Mexico!"

Cold dread pooled in Lonnie's belly. He didn't like the look in these two rogue Pinkertons' eyes. And the fact that they'd just told Lonnie and his mother where they were heading didn't bode well at all.

Not at all.

"I don't understand," May said, straightening and turning her full attention to the Pinkertons. "What's this about loot? And...Mexico?"

Madsen walked over and picked up the bulging saddlebags. They looked heavy, both pouches deeply sagging. He slung them onto the table with a grunt. There was a dull clinking sound.

Madsen gave Lonnie a sly glance and then opened the flap on one of the pouches. He dipped his hand in and pulled out one of the canvas pouches stamped "US ARMY".

"Oh, my Lord," May said, staring darkly at the bulging sack.

Madsen untied the rope from around the lip of the pouch. He turned the bag over. The gold coins clanked and clattered onto the table, glistening in the waning rays of sunlight angling through the cabin's windows.

May gasped, covering her mouth with her hand.

"You ever seen the like, May?" Brocius asked her.

May stared at the gold, but she didn't look at all happy to see it. She looked scared, horrified. She sensed the trouble it had come wrapped in.

"Where did that come from?" she asked Lonnie, as though he would know even better than the Pinkertons.

"Skull Canyon," Brocius told her.

Jeremiah had been squealing since Lonnie had been thrown into the cabin. Now he was screaming even louder. May turned toward her bedroom as though she were hearing the infant's cries for the first time, and, rubbing her hands nervously up and down her thighs, she strode toward the bedroom door. "I...I have to see about the baby."

She went into the room, glanced worriedly back at Lonnie, and then closed the door, muffling the baby's cries.

Lonnie started to heave himself to his feet.

"Stay down there," Brocius ordered, aiming his cocked Colt at Lonnie.

"What're you gonna do with us?" Lonnie asked, sitting back down on the floor.

His eye was really swelling now but the pain in his head was fading. It had been replaced with the cold fear that these two rogue Pinkertons would kill not only Lonnie but his mother and baby brother, as well.

Maybe he shouldn't have come here, Lonnie thought. Maybe the Pinkertons would have just taken the horses and left in the morning with the loot, sparing his mother and baby brother.

By coming here and confronting the two men about the loot, Lonnie might have just made the biggest mistake of his and his mother's lives.

There was nothing to do about that now. He had to keep his wits about him and try to figure a way out of one more mess he'd gotten himself into.

If the curse would let him, that was...

When neither Pinkerton answered his question, Lonnie repeated it, "I asked you what you're gonna do with us?"

Brocius glanced at Madsen and jerked his head at Lonnie. The men's faces were hard and blank. "Tie him," Brocius said. "Tie him good and tight. He has a way of gettin' out of tight spots, this one."

"Well, he ain't gonna get out of this one." Madsen grabbed a rope dangling from a peg in the front door. "We can't afford to let him get out of this one."

Brocius kept his eyes on Lonnie as he said, "What're you thinkin', George?"

"What do you think I'm thinkin', Bill? Make him promise to keep a secret for the rest of his life?"

"He's just a kid," Brocius said. He appeared genuinely reluctant to kill a boy. He was probably also thinking about killing the boy's mother and baby brother, as well. His lean, clean-shaven face was splotched white. He was thinking it all through, and he was feeling grim about it.

As Madsen tied Lonnie's hands behind a ceiling support post delineating where the kitchen ended and the parlor began, the bearded Pinkerton said, "If you know another way, let's hear it. I'm open to suggestions."

"I won't tell," Lonnie said, shaking his head, not knowing if he was speaking truthfully or not. But he was desperate to keep his mother and little brother alive. "I promise, I won't. If it means you not harmin' Ma and little Jeremiah, I'll take the secret to my grave. Heck, no one would believe me, anyway. I'm wanted for killin' a deputy US marshal! I'll tell 'em I killed Halliday, too! *That* they'll believe!"

FIFTY

BROCIUS CROUCHED DOWN in front of Lonnie. "You really expect us to believe that you'd hold to that story—long after we were gone from here and livin' high on the hog in Mexico?" He looked at Madsen. "Besides, old Pinkerton himself would figure it all out when we didn't show up at the home office."

"Nah, we can't risk it." Madsen turned to Lonnie. "No way you'd hold to that story, and there's a chance someone would believe the truth when you told it. You need to disappear. Folks need to think you killed Halliday and absconded with the loot. No one'll figure out our part in it for days, maybe weeks, and we need to buy as much time as we can. Sorry, kid."

As though he'd heard and understood what his older brother's fate was going to be, little Jeremiah began crying louder in May's bedroom. Brocius cursed and whipped an angry look toward the closed door on the far side of the cabin. "Dammit, May—will you quiet that child? I'm sick to death of hearin' that infernal squealin'!"

Lonnie heard his mother cooing to the baby. A few minutes later, when Madsen and Brocius had sat down at the table and poured themselves glasses of whiskey and started building cigarettes, the bedroom door opened. Lonnie's mother stepped out, holding the screaming, red-faced infant in her arms. May, too, was flushed with anxiety.

"Lonnie's the only one who can soothe him when he's like this."

May looked with beseeching eyes at the two rogue Pinkertons. Little

Jeremiah continued bawling, raising his two, tiny, red fists in the air as though trying to squirm out of his mother's arms.

Both men stared at the woman, incredulous, wincing at every tearing scream issuing from the baby's mouth.

"Can't you please untie him, so he can rock little Jeremiah? He'll get him back to sleep in fifteen minutes. He always does!"

The two men looked at Lonnie then at each other.

"I'm all for it!" Brocius rose from his chair and walked a little unsteadily over to Lonnie. He pulled a big Bowie knife from a sheath belted against his back. He held the wide-bladed, savage-looking blade up in front of Lonnie's face. "One false move, boy...one false move. Understand?"

He glanced at the blade then looked again at Lonnie, eyes filled with threat. "You'd best consider your ma and that screamin' little crib rat, too."

"I'm no fool," Lonnie said. "I won't try nothin'. Untie me, and I'll settle him down."

Brocius cut through the rope tying Lonnie's wrists together behind the ceiling support post. When the ropes were off, Lonnie climbed heavily to his feet and walked around the table. He took the baby out of his mother's hands then, rocking him gently in his arms and cooing to him, he slacked down into his father's old rocker, the same rocker in which his father had once rocked Lonnie to sleep when he was Jeremiah's age.

As soon as he started rocking, little Jeremiah's cries grew less shrill.

"Say, there," Madsen said as he shuffled a deck of cards, a quirley smoldering between his lips. "Sounds better already."

"Good to know the kid's good for somethin'."

"I'm going to go out and get some firewood," May said. "I have to keep the range stoked, so the food will cook. We'll be able to eat soon."

Brocius grabbed the woman's hand and pulled her toward him. He stared at her hard, then gave a stiff smile. "No tricks—okay, sweetheart?" He glanced with menace toward where Lonnie was rocking the baby.

"Tricks?" May said, staring at the man as though she didn't understand the word. "Bill, I swear...you have me fit to be tied!" Her lips quivered. Tears dribbled down her cheeks.

"All right, all right," Brocius said, releasing her hand. "Don't cloud up and rain on us, now. Go out and fetch your wood. Hurry back, or I'll miss you, honey!"

He gave a wooden laugh as May turned around, rubbed tears from her cheeks with the backs of her hands, and left the cabin, leaving the door half open behind her. She returned a minute later with an armload of wood, which she dropped into the box beside the range. By now, Jeremiah had entirely stopped crying and was fidgeting contentedly inside his tightly wrapped blanket.

"Why, look there," Madsen said while he and Brocius played two-handed poker. "The kid really does have a hand with babies!"

He chuckled and shook his head.

"Keep him quiet, kid," Brocius said. "If there's anythin' I can't stand it's a squealin' crib rat." He dropped a card onto the table, looked at his partner, and said, "You're tryin' to fill a straight, aren't ya? By God, I know you are!"

Madsen chuckled as he refilled both their whiskey glasses.

May was making gravy at the range, stirring flour and water into the grease. As she did, she glanced over her shoulder at Lonnie. She appeared sick with worry. Her expression was a vaguely beseeching one, as well. The plaintive cast to his mother's gaze made Lonnie feel even worse than he had before.

She apparently wanted him to do something. To save them, somehow.

But, how?

When supper was ready, May began setting the pots and pans on the table. The men cleared away their cards and money. "Time to tie Junior back up," Brocius said.

"Oh, can't he please eat at the table with us?" May implored, wringing her hands. "I can't stand to see him tied down there against that post!"

Lonnie looked down at little Jeremiah. The boy was dead asleep, his little, pinched-up face turned toward Lonnie.

"Besides," May added, "I'll probably need him to quiet little Jeremiah when he wakes up for another feeding in an hour or so."

"Oh, I reckon," Brocius said, his voice thick with drink. "Can't hurt nothin'. He knows what's at stake, if'n he tries anythin'."

When all the food was steaming on the table, Lonnie handed little Jeremiah over to his mother. He took his father's old place at the head of the table, since Brocius was sitting in Lonnie's usual place. May returned from the bedroom, closed the door quietly until she heard the soft snick of the latch, then removed her apron and sat down beside Brocius, who had already started filling his plate.

Again, May glanced at Lonnie. When the boy met her gaze, she gave him a faintly crooked smile then looked away. Lonnie frowned.

She was trying to tell him something.

What?

Lonnie looked at her again, but now she wouldn't look at him as she passed the potatoes to him. She followed with the gravy bowl, still not looking at him. She was telling him something, all right, but for the life of him, Lonnie couldn't decipher what it was.

The Pinkertons wolfed their meals and then slid their plates away to continue their poker game. As May began to clear plates from the table, she glanced at Lonnie, giving that crooked smile, that same obscure look as before, and said, "Lonnie, honey, would you please fetch me a pail of water from the rain barrel, so I can wash these dishes?"

She held his gaze for about one second with her own. It was as though her eyes were burrowing into his. And then she smiled and turned toward the dry sink.

"Hey, wait a second," Brocius said, scowling at Lonnie. "Where's the rain barrel?"

"Out back," May said offhandedly as she scraped food scraps into a wooden bucket. "Lonnie knows where it is. While you're out there, honey, please grab a few more chunks of wood off the stack, too, will you?"

"I'll go," Brocius said, starting to heave himself out of his chair. "That kid ain't leavin' the cabin." He stumbled backward a little, drunkenly, before getting his boots set beneath him.

"Yeah, you go," Lonnie said, glaring at the man. "Just because you're rich don't mean you're above a few supper chores. I think I'll sit in Pa's rocker."

Madsen chuckled as he tossed out another poker hand. "The kid sure has sass. I for one ain't gonna be at all sorry to, uh..." He glanced at Lonnie pointedly then gave a fleeting devilish grin.

Brocius pulled his pistol and aimed at Lonnie. "You're gonna fetch the water and the wood. I'm just gonna tag along to make sure you don't get no ideas."

"What ideas?" Lonnie scoffed.

"*Any* ideas," Brocius said, clicking his Colt's hammer back. He wagged the gun toward the door. "Move."

"I so hate guns," May intoned, looking at Lonnie. There was something strange in her eyes again. "Lonnie, you know how much I hate guns. Please be careful!"

"I will, Momma, I will," Lonnie said, heading for the door.

FIFTY-ONE

BROCIUS OPENED the door and backed outside onto the stoop, holding his cocked revolver on Lonnie.

Lonnie walked out onto the stoop, down the steps, and around the cabin's west front corner, heading for the rear. Brocius followed, his pistol aimed at Lonnie's back.

Halfway to the cabin's rear, Lonnie stopped suddenly. A thought occurred to him. Behind him, Brocius's foot thuds stopped. "What's the matter?"

"Nothin'," Lonnie said, his heart lurching, hands tingling.

His mother always kept one of her husband's old Confederate pistols in the drawer of a table near her bed. Lonnie had given her the pistol when he'd started staying away from the cabin overnight. He'd wanted her to have a way to protect herself if she ever needed to. He'd tried to teach her how to shoot the old Navy Colt, but she'd refused, regarding the old, brass-cased pistol as though it were a coiled diamondback.

Had she hidden the Colt out here somewhere? Is that what she'd been trying to tell Lonnie?

Probably not. He couldn't imagine her touching the gun much less finding the nerve to steal out of the cabin with it.

Still, Lonnie turned to the woodpile with his heart thudding in his ears. He stopped dead in his tracks again. His heart lurched violently into his throat. The brass of the pistol's case glistened in the late-afternoon light angling down from the western ridges. She'd partly covered the gun under a couple of split logs. Lonnie could see the small screw at the base of the brass trigger guard.

He glanced behind him. Brocius stood off the cabin's rear corner, staring at Lonnie, head canted to one side.

"Will you stop your gallblasted fidgetin' around, kid? I know what you're tryin' to do. You're wonderin' if you're fast enough to take me. You're wonderin' if you can get this pistol out of my hand." Brocius grinned darkly. "Go ahead. Try. Save me havin' to tie you up for the night just to shoot you in the mornin'."

"I'll get the water first," Lonnie said, grabbing the wooden bucket that hung from a nail in the side of the steel-banded rain barrel.

"Just to save time, I'll grab some wood."

Anxiety ripped through Lonnie like lightning. If Brocius grabbed the nearest top logs off the woodpile, he'd find the gun . . .

Lonnie's mind scrambled. He didn't know how he did it, but he found himself turning and giving the man an angry scowl and saying, "Yeah, make yourself useful. Here, I'll load you up."

Lonnie grabbed a couple of split logs off the top of the woodpile, to the right of the gun partly hidden on the pile's second tier.

"Hold on, hold on!" Brocius snapped, holstering his pistol. "Just remember, I'm faster'n greased lightnin', so don't you try a damn thing— understand? Less'n you want your ma and little brother joinin' you in the same ravine."

When Brocius had holstered the pistol, he held out his arms. Lonnie grabbed several split logs off the pile and laid them across the man's chest. Next, Lonnie plucked up the log over the old Navy Colt. Lonnie grabbed the Colt, clicked the hammer back, and aimed the revolver at Brocius's chest.

The Pinkerton's eyes snapped wide, and he took one step back, dropping the wood at his feet.

"Call out or go for your pistol, and I'll gut shoot you," Lonnie said, narrowing one eye and curling his upper lip, grinning with challenge. "Go ahead. Save me a lot of trouble."

Brocius stared at him, mouth half open. Shock glazed his eyes. He held his hands just above his hips, half open, palms down.

"You with me, now? Or do you want to make a play?" Lonnie took two steps back, so the Pinkerton couldn't easily lunge at him and wrestle the Colt out of his grip, like he'd done before. Lonnie didn't know if the old cap-and-ball would still fire. He'd fired it about a year ago, and it had worked fine. Still, he wasn't sure.

Lonnie grinned, fury surging in him on tidal waves of hot blood. This man had been going to kill him. He'd probably been going to kill Lonnie's mother and little brother, as well.

But now, Lonnie had him dead to rights. He was amazed at how light-headed and powerful that made him feel. This time, he would not squander his opportunity of removing this scum from his ranch cabin.

What he'd do with the two Pinkertons, he had no idea.

First things first...

"Easy, kid," Brocius said, nervously licking his lower lip, staring at the revolver in Lonnie's hand. "Just take it easy, now. You don't wanna do this. You might have me...for the time bein'...but you'll never take down Madsen, too. You're gonna end up gettin' your ma and little brother killed."

"Nah," Lonnie said, his mild expression belying the anxiety churning in his gut. "I'm gonna end up gettin' you killed if you don't slip those pistols from their holsters and toss 'em back behind you. Real slow! Use just your thumbs and first fingers."

Lonnie aimed his Colt at the man's head, narrowing one eye as he aimed down the barrel.

"Easy, now—easy, easy, easy!" Brocius slid the guns from their holsters and tossed them out behind him.

Lonnie wagged his own Colt toward the front of the cabin. "Nice and slow. If you call out, try to warn your partner, I'll shoot you in the back. If you don't think I will, you're dead wrong."

"Tough guy, huh?" Brocius said as he started to walk toward the front of the cabin. "We'll see about that."

Having learned his lesson from before, Lonnie followed the man from seven feet behind, so Brocius couldn't turn and grab the gun before Lonnie could shoot him. They walked around the cabin's front corner. Brocius glanced over his left shoulder as he headed for the porch.

"Just keep movin'," Lonnie said softly, so Madsen wouldn't hear him from inside.

Brocius climbed the porch steps.

"Stop at the door," Lonnie said behind him.

"Whatever you want, kid. Whatever you want."

When he'd stopped before the door, Lonnie walked up behind him. He pressed the pistol against the small of the man's back and tightened his finger on the trigger. He was ready to shoot if Brocius began to make any quick move. Any quick move at all.

It would be easy. It was almost frightening how easy it would be to kill this man, Lonnie thought. His life and his mother and little brother were at stake.

"All right—open it," Lonnie said.

FIFTY-TWO

BROCIUS TRIPPED THE LATCH, shoved the door open.

Lonnie pushed Brocius inside. Madsen was sitting at the table, rolling a quirley. He frowned up at Brocius, looked at Lonnie. He lowered his gaze to the gun in the boy's hand.

"Stand up—slow-like," Lonnie said, keeping his pistol aimed at Brocius. "If you stand too quick or reach for your gun, I'll shoot your partner."

Madsen's face turned brick red. "What in the *hell?*"

The sudden outburst gave Lonnie a start. He took his eyes off Brocius for half a second.

A half a second too long.

Brocius whipped toward him and nudged the Colt wide just as Lonnie fired. The bullet sliced through the air along Brocius's right cheek and clanked off an iron kettle hanging from a ceiling beam.

Brocius reached for the Colt, grabbed it, but Lonnie didn't let go. As he tried to pull it back away from Brocius, in the corner of his right eye he saw Madsen lurch to his feet.

As he did, Lonnie's mother screamed, "No!" and swung a cast-iron kettle around hard. It slammed against the back of the man's head with a loud, crunching thud. As Madsen fell forward, grabbing his head with both hands, Lonnie stumbled backward, tripped over a table leg, and fell to the floor.

He still had the pistol in his hand.

As Brocius came toward him, eyes wide and filled with fury, Lonnie started to click the hammer back.

"Oh, no you don't!" the rogue Pinkerton snarled, and kicked the pistol out of Lonnie's hand.

The old Colt flew back over Lonnie's head. He saw it bounce off an arm of his father's rocking chair and fly to the floor on the chair's other side.

He heard his mother screaming and Madsen yelling, but there was nothing he could do for his mother now. Brocius kicked Lonnie in the side and then strode past him, reaching for the pistol.

Ignoring the ache in his ribs from the man's savage kick, Lonnie lunged for him. He grabbed him around the waist. Brocius cursed as he twisted around and flew backward. His head hit the side of the hearth with a dull smack.

"Oh!" Brocius said, wincing.

Lonnie saw the Colt lying on the floor.

"No, you don't you little devil!" Brocius kicked at Lonnie, who avoided the man's scissoring feet as he dove for the Colt. He hit the floor on his belly and chest. He grabbed the Colt, clicked the hammer back, and swung around just as Brocius gained his feet and lunged for him.

Lonnie gritted his teeth and fired.

Brocius stopped with a jerk.

Lonnie shot him again. He saw the two holes in the man's wool vest. Blood oozed from them. Brocius looked down at the blood. He staggered backward, flaring his nostrils at Lonnie.

His tone pitched with surprise, the rogue Pinkerton said, "Why...why...you killed me, you little..."

He let his voice trail off as he dropped to his knees, looked at Lonnie again then fell forward to hit the floor on his face. He shook, as he died, spurs rattling.

Lonnie heard violent scuffling sounds. Madsen cursed tightly.

There was the muffled pop of a pistol. Lonnie's mother screamed.

"Momma!" Lonnie shouted.

He gained his feet and ran to where Madsen lay atop May Gentry, facing her. Lonnie's mother lay taut against the floor, her head tipped back. She was wincing, her eyes squeezed shut.

Little Jeremiah's squeals issued from the bedroom.

"Momma!" Lonnie yelled again, staring down in horror at his mother, who lay shockingly still beneath Madsen.

"Get off her, you bastard!" Lonnie screamed, cocking the Colt again and aiming at the back of the man's neck.

But then Madsen turned and looked up at Lonnie. He had a faraway look in his eyes. As he continued rolling backward off May, Lonnie saw the blood on Madsen's chest. Flames from the close gunshot licked at the man's shirt and vest. Acrid smoke filled the air.

Lonnie also saw the gun as the man drew his hands away from it. Now only May Gentry's hands were on the gun—Madsen's own Smith & Wesson. Her right index finger was curled through the trigger guard.

Lonnie's mother opened her eyes and stared up at Lonnie. Her eyes were glazed with shock. She looked down at Madsen and then up at Lonnie again. Her dress was bloody, but it didn't appear to be her own blood.

Madsen sighed. His eyes rolled back in his head, and he lay still.

"Momma!" Lonnie cried as he dropped to the floor and threw his arms around May Gentry's shoulders, holding her tight. She tossed the gun away and returned the boy's hug, sobbing quietly against his shoulder.

Lonnie held her like that for a long time.

Finally, May drew her head away from his, and tried a little smile though her eyes were still bright with the awe of what they'd both been through.

"Lonnie," she said in a thin, faraway voice, "would you mind...looking in on...your brother?"

Lonnie laughed at that. It was as though a dam had burst inside him. Relief washed through him like a warm soothing wave.

"Sure, Momma," he said, rising. "I'd be happy to."

He went into the bedroom, plucked the screaming infant out of his bassinet and carried him outside, away from the smell of wafting gun smoke and spilled blood. He walked out into the yard, jostling his little brother in his arms.

The thuds of an approaching rider grew louder. The sun was down but there was still enough light left in the valley for Lonnie to see the blonde rider gallop under the ranch portal and into the yard.

Casey stopped Miss Abigail just beyond Lonnie. She stared at him, wide-eyed.

"I heard the shootin'," Casey said, her voice trembling. "I thought..."

She swung down from the saddle and walked over to where Lonnie stood holding his baby brother.

"Everythin's fine," Lonnie said. He couldn't quite believe those words himself, so he said them again. "Everythin's...fine." He frowned at her. "I told Calhoun not to let you come after me."

"What was he goin' to do—hog-tie me? Thanks to the skills you taught me, I tracked you here."

"Did you find Halliday?"

Casey drew her mouth corners down and nodded.

"Where's Calhoun?"

"I don't know. He wanted nothin' to do with Skull Canyon. I'd venture to say that after I left him, he headed in the opposite direction—rather quickly." Casey heaved a sigh of relief. "Oh, Lonnie."

She threw her arms around him and Jeremiah, who had quieted considerably. The baby poked his tiny index fingers up at Casey and gurgled contentedly. She squeezed one of the little fingers and gave Lonnie and the baby another hug.

"You know, you're gonna make a good father someday, Lonnie Gentry." She kissed him straight on the mouth, then brushed her nose against his.

Lonnie was not so stunned by all that had happened that he couldn't appreciate the rich suppleness of the girl's lips on his. Every taut muscle in his body turned to warm mud.

"If the curse of Skull Canyon don't get me first," he said.

"You forget that old legend," Casey said. "If there's really a curse, it's a curse on bad men. Good men ride out alive. And you're one of the best men I've ever known, Lonnie Gentry."

Lonnie arched a skeptical brow at her. "What about...fancy Dan?"

"You forget about him," Casey said, pressing her cheek to his. "I know I have."

IF YOU LIKED THIS, YOU MIGHT LIKE:
THE ABILENE KID: DEAD MAN'S HAND BY JOHN V. MADORMO

AN EPIC YA WESTERN TIME-TRAVEL ADVENTURE BEGINS...

Twelve-year-old Dominick Dalesandro is obsessed with the Old West—outlaws, lawmen, and dusty frontier towns. But when a mysterious library book transports him back to 1888 Abilene, Kansas, history is no longer just a subject he studies... it's a world he must survive.

Sheriff Amos "Lone Wolf" Malone has chosen Dominick as his apprentice, giving him the chance to live out his Wild West dreams under a new name: Pete Moss. But adventure quickly turns to danger when Pete learns that the sheriff is doomed to die in just one month. Determined to change history, Pete must navigate gunfights, town secrets, and a daring rescue mission—all while trying to stop a fate that the sheriff refuses to outrun.

As the stakes rise, Pete faces an impossible choice: save the kidnapped children he's sworn to find or prevent the sheriff's tragic end. One decision could change the past forever—but at what cost?

Perfect for fans of time-travel adventures and YA Westerns, The Abilene Kid: Dead Man's Hand delivers heart-pounding action, historical intrigue, and an unforgettable hero. Ride into the past and join the adventure today! Grab your copy now and step into the Wild West!

AVAILABLE NOW

ABOUT THE AUTHOR

Peter Brandvold grew up in the great state of North Dakota in the 1960's and '70s, when television Westerns were as popular as shows about hoarders and shark tanks are now, and Western paperbacks were as popular as *Game of Thrones*.

Brandvold watched every Western series on television at the time. He grew up riding horses and herding cows on the farms of his grandfather and many friends who owned livestock.

Brandvold's imagination has always lived and will always live in the West. He is the author of over one hundred lightning-fast action Westerns under his own name and his pen name, Frank Leslie.

www.peterbrandvold.com